*Extraordinary praise for*

# END OF DAYS

"A whirlwind of high adventure and
edge-of-your-seat plot twists. . . . *End of Days* is
**an incredible tapestry of real world implications
mixed with stellar story telling.**
Brad Taylor still has the touch."
—*Mystery & Suspense Magazine*

"**Pike Logan returns with a thundering force. . . .**
Taylor's own military experience and insights
bleed onto the page, but in an honest and
informative way that makes his story seem
a little too real for comfort. . . .
**Taylor [is] one of today's finest storytellers.**"
—The Real Book Spy

"**All action from start to finish. . . .**
Another solid novel in the series."
—RedCarpetCrash.com

**"A blistering, explosive read. . . .**
*Hunter Killer* is one of the best in the series to date. . . .
An intriguing tale, full of twists, turns, explosions
and fisticuffs. By the book's conclusion, you will be
wondering why all thrillers can't be this good."
—Bookreporter.com

"Brad Taylor knows his stuff. . . .
*Hunter Killer* has the gun metal ring of authenticity
and the crisp writing of a military communique. . . .
It makes you pause and think while you're being
thoroughly and rapidly entertained.
**It's an excellent read, and I greatly enjoyed it."**
—Nelson DeMille

**"Taylor continues to tell flawless stories with
his stellar cast of characters. . . .**
It's amazing that after so many novels
Taylor can still maintain the high-level quality and
breathless action readers expect, while also
getting better with each tale."
—*Booklist* (starred review) on *Hunter Killer*

"Taylor brings an unquestionable level of
authenticity to his Pike Logan series. . . . Throw in
some former Israeli Mossad agents and the cast of
elite operators along with the level of bone-crushing
violence is almost overflowing.
**A surefire hit for those who like contemporary foreign
affairs spiced heavily with page-turning action."**
—*Kirkus Reviews* on *Hunter Killer*

## Also by Brad Taylor

# BRAD TAYLOR

# END OF DAYS

## A PIKE LOGAN NOVEL

WM
WILLIAM MORROW
*An Imprint of HarperCollinsPublishers*

END OF DAYS. Copyright © 2022 by Brad Taylor. All rights reserved. Printed in the United States of America. No part of this book may be used or reproduced in any manner whatsoever without written permission except in the case of brief quotations embodied in critical articles and reviews. For information, address HarperCollins Publishers, 195 Broadway, New York, NY 10007.

First William Morrow premium printing: August 2022
First William Morrow hardcover printing: January 2022

*Cover design by Lisa Amoroso*
*Cover images © Alamy Stock Photo; © Shutterstock*

Print Edition ISBN: 978-0-06-288611-8
Digital Edition ISBN: 978-0-06-288612-5

William Morrow and HarperCollins are registered trademarks of HarperCollins Publishers in the United States of America and other countries.

22 23 24 25 26   CWR   10 9 8 7 6 5 4 3 2 1

And when he had opened the fourth seal, I heard the voice of the fourth beast say, Come and see. And I looked, and behold a pale horse: and his name that sat on him was Death, and Hell followed with him.

—*Book of Revelation*

## CHAPTER 1

Long haired, olive skinned, and with a scraggly beard, Mustafa stood out from the other paragliders laying out their kit for the first flight of the morning. He was most definitely not of the Nordic stock who usually took tourists over the landscape of Interlaken, Switzerland. The men around him glanced curiously, but didn't broach any questions, because Interlaken itself had become a hub of tourism for rich Arabs around the world. He was just a sign of the times as far as they were concerned, like the Halal menus and prayer mats offered at the hotels. The other pilots belonged to individual tour companies, and as such, knew each other well. Mustafa belonged to no company, but he'd taken the place of an individual operator who did.

High on a hill in Beatenberg, about twenty minutes from the town of Interlaken, it was one of the most popular places from which to launch. Overlooking the twin lakes of Thun and Brienz, plenty of tour groups used it, with the excited patrons driven by bus from the town. Mustafa knew his customer wasn't coming on a bus. His fare was special, with unique requirements.

Content with the layout of his equipment, he took a sign not unlike a realtor's, with the name of the company for which he'd supposedly worked, and jammed it in the ground uphill of the canopy, where it could be seen from the road. He turned to go back to the harness when he noticed a splotch of red on the corner, like someone had flung a strip of paint on it. He glanced around to see if anyone else had noticed, but the other operators were too busy with their own rigs. He hurriedly wiped it off with his glove, finding it had congealed enough for him to have to use force.

For the life of him, Mustafa couldn't fathom how a splotch of blood had ended up on the sign. When he'd shot the man who owned this canopy, he was across the room from where it had been leaning against a wall. It was a head shot, and messy, but how could the blood have splattered that far?

The mess he'd left behind was of no consequence now. No matter what they found of his passing—DNA, footprints, fingerprints, whatever—it didn't matter, as he wouldn't be alive to be caught. He was going to die in the next hour, along with the man strapped to him.

An expat from Iraq, Mustafa was ostensibly in Switzerland as a political refugee, but in reality he had another agenda. He was a sleeper, sent out into the world to wait until activated for a strategic attack. He'd lived in Switzerland for six years without a whisper from his higher command, until three months ago, with a plan that was so audacious it gave him chills.

Unknown by the intelligence infrastructure in Switzerland that had granted him asylum, he was a member of Keta'ib Hezbollah, a Shia militia in Iraq. Funded by Iran, they'd fought the United States early on in the Iraq War, killing soldiers with explosively formed penetrators provided by that theocratic state. Later, ISIS began to rampage throughout the country and the militia had been given sanction by the Iraqi government as a "Popular Mobilization Unit," as anyone who could fight was needed to stop the slaughter.

They'd actually fought remarkably well against ISIS, even after the United States returned. While ISIS had given both a common foe, the militia had never forgotten the real enemy. Once ISIS was driven back underground, they'd returned to attacking the Great Satan, rocketing bases with impunity and killing with roadside bombs. They'd felt they were invincible—and had been told so by the very commander of the Iranian Qods Force, General Soleimani, who provided them with training, equipment, and expertise. They were the vanguard of a new Iraq, driving out the infidels of the Great Satan, the goal being a Shia-dominated country under the watchful eye of Iran.

And then the Great Satan had slaughtered the leader of Keta'ib Hezbollah with an air strike inside Iraq. Even worse, along with him they'd blown apart the Qods Force commander, General Soleimani. The strike came out of nowhere, the Americans killing with impunity.

The spasm of rage had been intense, but the revenge had been slow in coming. Iran had sworn vengeance, but other than a pathetic show of force involving rockets against Al Asad Air Base—where the Americans were stationed—nothing else had been done.

Until now.

Mustafa saw a minibus approach the turn-around point at the top of the hill, then disgorge eight people, four passengers and four pilots. Even though it was early June, all were dressed for the weather, as it was crisp at eight in the morning, and would be even colder on the flight.

They spread out on the hill, giving each room to take off. Within minutes, the passengers were in the harnesses and the first pilot was screaming, "Run, run, run!"

Down the hill they went, the canopy lifting gracefully behind them. It caught the wind and their feet left the ground, the paraglider soaring out over the valley below, the passenger shriek-ing with delight. As soon as the first one went airborne, the next was running down the slope, then the third, and finally the fourth. Mustafa watched intently, ensuring he could get air-borne.

Like the pilots on 9/11 who'd learned to fly but not take off or land, he'd had *some* instruction on paragliding, but he was by no means an expert, and the worst thing that could happen was face-planting his target on the slope without getting airborne.

Another bus pulled in, and this time it was only passengers. They went out to meet their designated pilots already positioned on the hill, and within a few ticks of the clock, he was alone again.

He waited another seven minutes, then saw a two-car caravan headed toward his location. The cars stopped and a swarm of men exited, taking positions of security. An older man, looking to be about eighty, exited the car and stood, waiting.

The target. One Gideon Cohen. A former head of the Mossad—otherwise known as the *Ramsad*—he was the man who had killed many, many of Mustafa's clan, from patriots in the Gaza Strip to nuclear scientists in Iran. He had nothing to do with the killing of Soleimani, but he was a symbol. A powerful one.

It had been known that he summered in Switzerland, and apparently a plan had been developed the year before to assassinate him, but then COVID had struck, and made any such attack impossible. There was no way to conduct surveillance for an operation or develop any type of infrastructure necessary because of the shutdown. A year later, COVID was still rampaging about, but the vaccine was available, and various parts of the world were slowly coming back to life.

The biggest obstacle to targeting Gideon had been his security detail. They were very thorough, and very skilled. The only way to kill him was to separate him from them without a fight—and that had proven impossible, right up until they'd learned that Gideon had taken an affinity to paragliding.

Once every two weeks, he used the same

company to take flight. A pastime he enjoyed, but also something that gave the security detail fits. And perhaps that was part of the enjoyment. Being free from the chains of his past.

But those chains would follow him into the air on this day.

## CHAPTER 2

After Mustafa had been activated, he'd spent three months learning the skills required to paraglide. He had no idea where the funding had come from to take the courses, believing it was from his masters in Iran. He was wrong on that point, but the death would come all the same.

The security man who'd talked to Gideon marched down the hill to him, his tie flapping over his shoulder in the breeze, a distinct bulge on his hip. A large man wearing sunglasses and a black mask, he had no humor in him whatsoever.

The man reached him and said, "Where's Ulrich?"

Mustafa pulled his own mask up and said, "He might have COVID. He's not sure. He came into contact with someone who's come up hot and asked me to take this trip. To protect the client."

"We don't fly without Ulrich."

Mustafa knew they'd conducted a background check on the man he'd killed, and understood this was the endgame, because he had no such check. He said, "Okay by me, but you still have to pay. Whether I fly or not, I'm getting my charter for this trip."

The man fiddled with his mask for a moment, muttered, then went back up the hill. Mustafa held his breath.

And he saw Gideon shaking his head, wagging a finger, and then coming down the hill, the security man following. Mustafa exhaled, now feeling the adrenaline of what he was about to do. They both marched up to him and Gideon said, "Are you competent?"

"Yes, yes. I've done this as much as Ulrich. He's my friend. We both work for the same company."

The security man said, "Do you have the same safety equipment? Reserve parachute?"

Mustafa pointed at a bag on the ground and said, "Of course. I would never leave earth without it."

What he didn't say was the reserve bag had nothing but cloth in it. And a note.

The security man grunted, and Gideon started putting on the harness. Mustafa jumped forward saying, "Let me help you."

Gideon waved him off with a laugh, saying, "I think I know how to do this now."

Mustafa put on his own harness, then waited under the watchful eye of the security man. Gideon turned around to him and held his arms out. Mustafa pretended to check the harness, but honestly, didn't know what anomalies or mistakes he was supposed to find. His limit of experience was flying solo, and he was beginning to panic about flying someone else.

The security man looked at him with some bit of concern, and Mustafa put his sunglasses over his eyes, shielding them. With the mask in place, he was now unreadable.

He stood up and said, "Looks good. You ready to go for a ride?"

Gideon said, "Yes, yes. Are we landing in the same place? In the field in the center of town?"

Mustafa really wanted to say, "Yes, but a lot harder than you're used to." But did not.

He said, "Yes, same place as all the others."

He snapped the carabiners designed to hold Gideon to himself, tugged on them once to make sure they were secure, and glanced at the security man, seeing him staring at him like he wanted to use a knife. He turned forward and said, "Run, run, run!"

The old man started trotting down the hill, and Mustafa overtook him, almost falling on top of him. He staggered forward, the old man now dragging his legs on the ground, held up by the harness attached to Mustafa. In a panic, Mustafa leaned back, getting the man's legs back underneath him, and then he began to fall forward. His worst fears realized.

He pumped his legs as hard as he could, dragging Gideon along, and then the canopy caught the air, lifting them off the ground. For a split second, Mustafa couldn't believe it, dangling in the harness like a child in a bouncy chair. As the land fell farther away, he realized they were flying, and reached up for the toggles to gain control.

He swerved out over the valley, and his target

said, "This is so beautiful. I never get tired of looking at it."

Completely embroiled in controlling the canopy, Mustafa said nothing. Eventually, he calmed down, realizing that flying with a passenger wasn't that different than flying alone. It just took a little longer for the controls to react. He began soaring over the valley, looking for his landing spot.

High over Lake Thun, he could see Interlaken to his left, but found the winds more than he expected. Try as he might, he couldn't get back over the town. He realized that he should have started turning as soon as he was off the mountain, but didn't have the experience to know better.

He completed a circle in the air, finding a thermal, and went higher. The target thought it was for his benefit, saying, "Yes, yes. Ulrich never does this."

Consumed with his task and fearing failure, Mustafa thought about bringing out the hook knife right then, but that wouldn't accomplish what his masters wanted. For one, they might actually remain alive after hitting the water. With the canopy still above them after the riser was cut, they would fall rapidly, but it would still slow the descent. For another, the letter in his reserve parachute pouch would be destroyed. The entire point of the mission gone.

He began to panic.

And then the wind died, falling away as if it had grown tired of the fight, allowing him to drive the canopy forward, over Interlaken itself. He saw the field smack in the center of town where he'd landed on his many individual training flights and steered toward it.

Gideon said, "So soon. So soon. I'd like to stay up here forever."

Mustafa didn't even hear him, entering another plane of existence. Knowing what was coming. He gritted his teeth and steeled himself, turning on the final leg of what would be the last controlled flight pattern he would ever do. His eyes closed, he withdrew a hook knife from his vest, similar to ones first responders use to cut seat belts. He opened his eyes and said, "Alluha Akbar."

Gideon whipped his head around at the words, saw the knife, and began to rotate in his harness, trying to fight. Mustafa knocked his hands away, reached up, and sliced the nylon strap running from his harness to the carabiner of the left riser.

Gideon screamed, and they slipped to the left, the right riser still having some lift, the fall much slower than Mustafa expected. It wasn't like jumping off a roof. The canopy lost air in slow motion, but eventually, they picked up speed, reaching terminal velocity at five hundred feet, both barreling straight to earth with the disabled sheet of nylon fluttering over them like a macabre flag celebrating the fall.

Mustafa screamed, "Alluha Akbar!"

And they hit the ground right where they were supposed to, only a lot harder than Gideon was used to, both bodies splattering open like watermelons tossed off a building.

## CHAPTER 3

Aaron Bergman picked up the Guinness beers at the bar, paid the tab, and turned back to the table, ignoring the fact that the bartender recoiled at his mere presence. He'd seen that before. He did his best to hide it, but short of wearing a burka, there was no way to camouflage what he was. People just instinctively recognized him as a threat, like a pit bull growling at a visitor.

He saw his partner staring intently at the door, waiting on someone to enter. He unconsciously shook his head, hoping the man who came in didn't have a problem for them to solve.

Anytime the Mossad asked for their help, it was because they didn't want to risk actual assets. It was painful to admit, but they were expendable. But that *did* give them options. If they weren't officially Mossad, they could solve the problem like they wanted, without the oversight.

Small blessings.

He went back to the table, set a beer in front of his partner, and said, "Irish bar. Irish beer."

She scrunched up her nose and said, "Seriously? They don't have any rum?"

He smiled at the inside joke. A good friend

of theirs only drank rum and Cokes, and she'd taken to the drink to prove she had something to hold on to as a human being. Using his normalcy to prove she was normal. Which she was decidedly not.

"They have it, but the beer is the near side signal."

She took the drink and said, "What's taking so long? The meet time has come and gone."

Aaron took a sip and said, "Calm down, dark angel. He'll be here."

They were in a place called the Temple Bar, an Irish watering hole that was one of several such franchises in Tel Aviv, Israel. This one was unique, in that it was within spitting distance of the headquarters of the Mossad. If one looked on Google Maps, one would see a hundred different stores or restaurants surrounding a large field of grass with nothing. Roads going in and out, but nothing to say why. Go to satellite, and one would find a large building in that field, with once again no representation of why that building was there.

Because that's the way the Mossad wanted it.

His partner took a sip of the beer, winced, then said, "You think they have a mission for us? Is that why the call came in?"

Aaron grinned at her eagerness and said, "If it is a mission, when it comes to us, it's guaranteed to be a shit storm. I'll listen, but I'm not jumping in just because they want us to. We've both been here before."

She said, "Yeah, but this is the Caesarea. They wouldn't have called unless it was urgent."

Caesarea was the section in the Mossad that dealt with targeted killing. The sharp end of the spear. In a previous life, Aaron and his partner had belonged to the unit, eliminating terrorists all over the world. Now they were private contractors, sometimes working for the Mossad, sometimes for others.

Aaron said, "We have the wedding. That's more important. We leave in two days."

"Yeah, but that's just the rehearsal. We could probably do this mission and make it in time for the real thing."

Aaron looked at her and said, "Seriously? After what they did to attend *our* wedding? You're really going there? This was our vacation. We haven't been anywhere for over a year because of the damn pandemic. And you love Charleston."

Chastened, she said, "Nephilim would understand. If it's important. But you're right. Some things are worth more than others. I won't miss the wedding, no matter what this guy says."

She took another sip of the beer, winced again, and said, "Why on earth did you buy this mud?"

"Because that's the near signal. If we had a rum and Coke, he'd wave off the meeting."

She muttered, "Well, that's one strike against this asshole."

She turned to the door again, her urgency causing him to smile. He took her hand and said, "You look like a dog waiting on someone to throw a ball. Do you mean what you say? Because when he comes inside, he's going to ask us to commit."

She turned from staring at the door to him,

took his hand in both of hers, and said, "Yes. I will not let Nephilim down. Or Jennifer. No matter what he says."

Aaron nodded, and the door opened, the commander of Caesarea walking through it. He looked around the room casually, saw them, then the beers in front of them, and came over.

The bartender watched the scene intently. He didn't have any ulterior motive, but he knew where his bar was located and was curious. He saw the man lean across the table and kiss the woman on the cheek.

The visitor turned to the seated man, and the size difference was palpable. The new man looked like a bureaucrat. The one seated looked like a killer. He stood and was a head taller than the visitor, his frame overshadowing the other. The pairing with the woman was confusing to the bartender. She was lithe, like a teenage boy, without any womanly curves, but her face was like a porcelain doll. Model pristine, but hiding something sinister. When she'd talked to him, it had been disconcerting. She did some kind of weird stare, reaching into his soul. It scared the hell out of him.

Both of them were people he didn't want to meet ever again. He didn't even want to serve them again. If they left right now, he'd be happy. He knew something was happening in his small bar a stone's throw from one of the deadliest intelligence agencies on earth, but he knew better than to pry.

The men shook hands, then glanced his way. He ducked his head and moved to the back of the bar. They went deeper into the establishment, getting out of his earshot.

The new man gestured to seats at a corner table, saying, "Shoshana, it's been a while. Still in the game, I see."

She gave him a stare that caused him to recoil, saying, "Jeremy, I don't play games."

She took a seat, setting her beer on a windowsill to grow warm. He looked at Aaron, who smiled and said, "I don't, either. Why the call?"

They both sat down and Jeremy said, "We have a delicate situation in Europe. We want you to investigate. We'll pay the way, of course."

"But?"

"No but. This time we aren't looking for a cutout for operational reasons. Well, we are, but not why you think. We believe we've been compromised over there, and we need someone completely clean. A team that hasn't been used in a while, with no contact to Mossad."

"What happened?"

"You know Gideon Cohen, correct?"

At the name, Shoshana stiffened, a little of her dark angel leaking out. Aaron said, "Yes, of course. Way back when he was the man who placed Shoshana on my team."

Shoshana said, "He was the only one in the Mossad who believed in me."

Jeremy nodded and, without any preamble, said, "Well, he's been killed."

Shoshana took the words like a physical slap, her eyes going wide. Aaron put his hand on her arm, then said, "What do you mean, 'killed'?"

"He summers in Switzerland, and he'd taken

to paragliding. The man who took him up into the air killed him."

"How on earth did that happen? He's a former *Ramsad*, for God's sake."

Jeremy raised his hands and said, "I know, I know. Trust me, the security team is going through their own hell. The bottom line is that the man that usually takes him up—who had a background check—was found murdered. And the new man who took his place killed him."

Shoshana hissed out, "Who did it?"

"We don't know. That's why we want you. It's like 1972 all over again. If they're starting to target us, they certainly knew enough to penetrate. We can't trust our infrastructure there. In fact, we're spending all our time protecting others in the continent now. We need someone clean. Which is where you come in. All we want you to do is find out the connections to the paraglider, track them down, and then give us the intel. No wet work. Just tell us who it is."

Shoshana said, "That's not going to happen. If I find them, I'm going to kill them."

Jeremy drew back and said, "No, you won't. You operate under our parameters. We don't want to start an international war here. That's the mission. Can you do that?"

Shoshana started to spit something out and Aaron touched her hand again, saying, "We can do that. What do you have?"

Jeremy went from Shoshana to Aaron, then said, "The riser to the paraglider was cut intentionally. The rescue parachute on the pilot's back was nothing but dirty laundry. Inside of it was a note. It was intentional, no doubt, and the note says it's going to get worse."

He reached into his pocket and pulled out a single sheet of paper. On it was a facsimile of what had been found on the bodies.

Aaron took it, seeing,

You attack us with impunity in Syria and Iraq from the air, like cowards. And now we attack you man to man. Our reach is long, and our patience is infinite. This man is not the first to die, and it will not be the last, Little Satan. Tell the Great Satan they are next.

Aaron looked up and said, "Who is it? The Iranians?"

"We honestly don't know. The pilot is an Iraqi expat who earned refugee status in Switzerland. After digging into his past we've found some contacts with Keta'ib Hezbollah, but the money train isn't there. We have tracers on all of their accounts. Keta'ib Hezbollah paying for a man to learn to paraglide and then killing a *Ramsad* is something we would have found. At least we think we would have. Something else is going on here. And we want you to find out what that is. Which is why there is no lethal authority."

He turned to Shoshana and said, "You want to find the man who killed your mentor, and I get that, but he is dead. He blasted into the earth just like Gideon. We want to know what's happening. Some in the Knesset and the military are already demanding action against Iran, but we want to make sure it really *is* Iran before we end up in a war we didn't want. And we can't use anyone in Europe to do it, because they penetrated us somehow. Whoever it is sure as shit isn't a militia in Iraq. It's something else. That's what we want to know."

Shoshana nodded, but he could see her mind spinning. He said, "Can you do that?"

She said, "Yes. But we'll need some support."

"Can't happen. You guys are on your own. We'll give you a complete data dump on what we have, front any costs, and you'll report back to us, but there will be no contact with any other Caesarea personnel. Sorry. We don't know where the leak happened or how they planned this attack. We're not sure who has been penetrated. If we use Caesarea personnel there now, it might automatically be a compromise, just because they've identified them as such."

Shoshana smiled at that and said, "I'd expect nothing less. So we're on our own?"

"Yes."

"Can we get our own support, or is that something that's too big of a shit storm, too?"

"What do you mean? What support?"

"Well, we have to go to America in two days for a wedding. Is that okay?"

Jeremy looked at Aaron, then back at her, saying, "The wedding can wait. Your country is calling."

Aaron knew where Shoshana was going. He said, "You've given us a mission with no support. We're going to the wedding."

Perplexed, Jeremy said, "What's a damn wedding got to do with this?"

Shoshana leaned into him, getting face-to-face. She tried to be calm, but the anger leaking out was a visceral thing. She said, "I'll find the killer of Gideon. Not for you or Israel, but for me. And the wedding is how I will do it. I need passports for four individuals."

I stared at Jennifer in her white dress, slowly walking up the path to my position next to the minister. She reached it, smiled at me, and then took my hand. The minister smiled as well, happy to be here on a warm June day for the wedding. I glanced at the gate to the Ashley Hall grounds and saw it shaking, like someone was trying to barge in. The gate broke, and three terrorists entered, screaming and firing weapons.

Jennifer ripped off the lace of her dress, exposing three hand grenades held in place by their pins.

*Wait, what? Who would attach a grenade to themselves by the damn pin?*

She pulled two, threw them at the gate, and then . . .

And then . . .

A voice entered my head. "Pike!"

I felt a slap to my belly and was brought out of my Walter Mitty daydream.

Jennifer glared at me and said, "What in the world are you doing?"

Sheepishly, I said, "Nothing. Sorry. Where were we?"

She glared at me and said, "We're *rehearsing our wedding*!"

I saw Amena with the rings, going from foot to foot, embarrassed for me, and my best man Knuckles looking at me like I'd had a stroke.

I said, "Uh huh . . . Got it. Let's keep going."

Jennifer looked like she wanted to gut me, but turned with all sweetness and light to the minister. Amena snuck up behind me, pulled my pant leg, and said, "You're really terrible at this."

I said, "You wouldn't be any better."

She laughed and said, "Oh yeah I would."

Jennifer glared at her as well, and she scampered away, going back to her position for the rehearsal.

Twenty minutes later it was over, and I was in the alcove of the McBee House on the campus of Ashley Hall, getting an earful from Jennifer for not taking this seriously. She really, *really* wanted a legitimate wedding to match our justice of the peace certificate, and I suppose I wasn't helping, but it was getting a little ridiculous.

I said, "Jenn, come on. We're not even allowed to have a crowd here because of the damn pandemic. We've got like ten people. How much rehearsal does this take? I've seen less rehearsals on an assault in the Al Anbar Province against a terrorist force hell-bent on killing me."

Even with the vaccine rollout, things had been slow to return to normal. Now, with all the new, exotic mutations running amok, the projection from the powers-that-be was next fall, which aggravated me to no end.

She glared at me, made sure we were out of

earshot, then said, "I only asked for one thing: a wedding ceremony. You can at least do that."

"But we can't even *have* a real ceremony because of the damn pandemic. Why don't we wait six months? The vaccine is out, and this will all be a bad dream then."

"I don't want to wait. The only people I care about are here. Except for Shoshana and Aaron."

She said that last part without any rancor, but while she didn't show it, I knew she was upset. Shoshana was her maid of honor, and had promised to be here for the rehearsal. She was also an Israeli assassin who was about two beers shy of a six-pack, but for some reason she and Jennifer had bonded.

I said, "They'll be here. They promised. They've probably just had a plane delay or something."

She looked a little wistful and said, "I can't believe they didn't come. After what we did for their wedding."

I thought of my daydream and said, "Well, it might be for the best. If they'd shown up, you might have been throwing grenades attached to your skirt."

She said, "What?"

"Nothing. Here comes Wolffe."

George Wolffe was the commander of our little extralegal unit and while he was officially my boss, he was also a friend. In official top-secret traffic the command was called Project Prometheus, but since that was classified, we couldn't run around saying the code name like we were the 82nd Airborne, so we just called it the Taskforce. He was invited to the wedding, but wasn't actually *in* it like my team, so he didn't really need to be at the rehearsal, but since things were quiet in DC, he'd decided to come down for a little rest and relaxation.

He kissed Jennifer on the cheek, saying, "You're going to wear a dress for the ceremony, right, Koko?"

Jennifer was in jeans and a T-shirt for the rehearsal, her blond hair askew, looking like a surfer ready to go to hit the breakers on Folly Beach. She grimaced at his use of her callsign. She hated the name, and he knew it, using it solely to poke her a little bit.

She smiled and said, "That depends. You going to show up dressed for a wedding instead of like some billboard for 5-11 commando clothes? And why is your callsign the Wolf? Why do I get to be a gorilla?"

He smiled back and said, "A mystery for another time. I'll never tell." He glanced around the setting, seeing majestic live oaks, a fountain, and an expanse of lawn surrounded by stately brick buildings. He said, "Pretty nice place for a wedding, though. How'd you get it?"

"It's the school Amena goes to now. The place that convinced the Oversight Council to let her stay. They're giving us a break on the rental cost because of COVID, but they're still enforcing the crowd mandate."

The Oversight Council was the board that controlled all Taskforce activity, and I'd pushed the limits of their approval to the breaking point with Amena, our little Syrian refugee project. They'd wanted to ship her ass back to Syria when they'd found out I'd smuggled her into the country using Taskforce assets, but had eventually agreed to let us sponsor her, provided we became a legitimate family.

Jennifer and I had hastily married with a justice of the peace, then enrolled Amena into Ashley Hall as a boarding student. Which brought us to the wedding ceremony being planned now. Jennifer couldn't stand the justice of the peace thing. She wanted a *ceremony*, and wasn't willing to wait for the pandemic to subside to get it.

Wolffe said, "Well, I'm glad I made the cut line for the trip. I feel honored. I was hoping to see that crazy Israeli, though. Where's she?"

Aaron and Shoshana had conducted more than one operation in support of the Taskforce, all off the books of even the Taskforce, and Wolffe respected her skill—even as he also knew she was a little . . . off.

Jennifer said, "I don't know. She said she'd be here. I suppose I can switch out Amena for my maid of honor."

That was probably a good trade in my mind. Amena was only fourteen, but she had seen enough of the world to give her the maturity of someone twice her age. And she wasn't liable to strangle the priest because she "saw something."

But I knew that wasn't what Jennifer wanted. I said, "The wedding isn't for a week. We can always talk her through it on our own. She'll be here."

Jennifer was looking away from us, toward the back gate on Smith Street. Two people were talking to the security guard, trying to get in.

She broke into a radiant smile and said, "Speak of the devil."

## CHAPTER 5

Garrett shook himself awake like a dog wringing water off its body, the blackouts becoming something he was getting more comfortable with. After the killing, after the trauma, his brain would literally shut down, and he would collapse, catatonic. The first time it was scary. Now, with the third death, it was becoming routine.

He looked to his left and saw the dead prostitute. One more woman who didn't want to connect, but he'd learned from the first one. Don't use a blade. Too messy. It was just as easy to strangle the life out of them.

The first killing had been a disaster—the woman running around the small room with her hand clamped to her neck, the blood flowing like a water balloon squeezed by a child.

Make no mistake, it wasn't the death that shocked him. He'd killed people before in the heat of combat, but never with a knife. Most had been with a bullet at a distance of eighty or a hundred meters. That killing had been another level of intensity entirely.

He looked at her dead eyes and thought, *Why*

*did you laugh? Why couldn't you just give me what I paid for?*

Like the other two women, all he'd wanted was what she had offered. A chance to connect with her. Someone who wouldn't care about his deficiencies.

Everything had gone well, right up until she'd pulled his pants down. He couldn't get an erection. She'd worked furiously, and he'd encouraged her on and on, and then she'd tried to cup his testicles. Located his shame.

"You got no balls? What is this?" she said.

And then the rage had struck. A red level of violence he had lived with for four years, which cost the woman her life.

He knelt down and recited the Lord's Prayer, then glanced at the body, a niggling bit of his subconscious realizing that he was growing used to the killing. Scarier still, he was growing to like it, wanting to inflict pain in an attempt to release his own.

This time he was in a decrepit Airstream trailer on the outskirts of a greenspace in the center of the same neighborhood he'd killed the other two. Called Esposizione Universale Roma, or EUR, it was south of the city center of Rome, Italy.

Built by Benito Mussolini in preparation for the world's fair in 1942, it was designed as a new urban hub celebrating fascism and his rule. World War II put a stop to that fantasy, and now it had the ignominy of being known as the red-light district of Rome. While the city looked away from the streetwalkers in the area, it still didn't allow actual brothels, which meant the men and women had to get creative to ply their trade. In this case, a trailer on the edge of a park.

He rose from his knees and leaned over the soiled mattress where the woman lay. Ignoring her open eyes, he kissed her cheek, whispering, "I'm sorry."

He glanced at his watch, seeing it was almost seven A.M. He'd been unconscious for nearly six hours, making him late for the meeting with his men at the Priory. Even worse, making him late for the command of the next attack.

He hurriedly searched the room for any traces he'd left, using his cell phone to call his men, not worried about anyone tracking him through the cell towers because he was calling through the Wi-Fi in the woman's trailer. She'd paid for the service with a portable Mi-Fi device to show porn videos to prospective clients. But it hadn't helped his mood. In fact, it did nothing but elevate the rage when he saw the virile men.

Using an app called Zello, he connected and said, "Hey, I'm running a little late, but I'll be there soon. Are we good for today?"

"Yes. He's headed south just like he's done every single weekend."

"We can't make a mistake here. The PMU in Iraq needs to be blamed. Keta'ib Hezbollah."

"They will be. We have the note ready to go."

"What's the timeline?"

"Probably an hour. Maybe more."

"And Paris? What's happening there?"

"I'm waiting on the news now. Nothing yet."

He said, "Okay, I'm headed to the Priory. See you soon."

He opened the trailer door, peering out the grimy window first to make sure he wasn't seen, then jogged to his vehicle.

Driving north out of the neighborhood, he knew it would take him a good thirty minutes to get to the Priory in Rome's city center, and every second was precious. He traveled as fast as he dared without drawing attention, eventually circling around the Colosseum, the crowds much sparser than they would ordinarily be on a June morning before the pandemic, but coming back to life. Reaching Via Sistina, he miraculously found a parking spot adjacent to the top of the famed Spanish Steps—a luxury even considering the lack of traffic due to COVID.

He leapt out of the car, not even bothering to lock it. He bounded down the wide steps like he was running from the police, ignoring the small smattering of tourists taking selfies on the ledges. Still wearing masks, they reminded him of sprouts of flowers after a horrendous winter—the first beginnings of new life in Rome.

He hit the lower level, reaching the Piazza di Spagna and the fountain there, then raced to the narrow alley of Via dei Condotti. Full of expensive stores, it was the high-end shopping district of Rome. Most were closed still because of the pandemic, but a few were open, and the slowly recuperating tourist industry was helping that along, with more and more people coming to shop. He ignored them. While many were drawn here to buy the latest in fashion, he was going to a building that had been bequeathed to his organization almost two hundred years before.

He reached a stone archway leading to a courtyard, sandwiched between a store selling Hermès on the left and Jimmy Choo on the right. He went forward to a small security checkpoint and presented his credentials. A man checked his identification and let him through without issue, but he could tell the attendant wondered about the sweat cloaking his body from his jog in the cloying June heat.

He speed-walked across the courtyard to the main door of the Magisterial Palace of the Knights of Malta. Known formally as the Sovereign Military Hospitaller Order of St. John of Jerusalem, of Rhodes, and of Malta, it was an organization that had been around since the First Crusade in the eleventh century, and was one of the last papal sovereign orders of chivalry.

Formed initially by a Benedictine monk to help the faithful on their path to the promised land, it had morphed much in its history. First, a hospital to help the pious on their quest to Jerusalem, then, when the faithful were attacked, as an army to defend them, and finally, when they were defeated in the defense of the Holy Land, they became a sea power protecting the Catholic empire, first on the island of Rhodes, and finally in Malta.

As with most of the papal benedictions of the day, the order eventually lost favor as it grew in power—perceived as a threat to the Holy See. But the Knights of Malta were cunning. They'd learned early on who the true authority was. When the famed Knights Templar were burned at the stake as heretics, even as they did the bidding of the Holy Roman Empire, the Knights of Malta knew it was because they had become too powerful. The Grand Master of the Knights of Malta had learned a valuable lesson: It doesn't pay to be the king. Better to be the court jester.

When the Templars were destroyed, the benefactor had been the Knights of Malta. They were bequeathed the lands and treasures of that order. Having been kicked out of Jerusalem, then Rhodes, and finally Malta—from no less than Emperor Napoleon in the late eighteenth century, which was a legitimate black eye, as the Knights had literally saved the European continent from the Ottoman hordes in the sixteenth century—they had been given a plot of land in Rome. They had existed there ever since.

Now returning back to its roots of charity, the Knights of Malta worked worldwide to help the downtrodden. They were a weird anachronism of history. They had their own passports, produced their own currency and postal stamps, had observer status in the United Nations, but owned no terrain. In effect, they were a state entity without a state. Given its nonprofit work around the world, and the support of the Holy See, it still had its pedigree, but no longer had a martial bent. At least that's what they said on official documents.

Garrett was the martial side of the house. A devout Catholic, he had been contacted by the Knights when they went into Syria the first time, during the barrel bombings of the Assad regime in early 2013.

The Knights wanted to help the refugees there like they had been doing for hundreds of years the world over, but realized that they couldn't do so without at least some protection. And they'd approached Garrett, a lowly Knight of Magisterial Grace from the United States Order of Malta. A former soldier of the United States Army's Special Forces, he had contacts they wanted access to, both in Syria and from his past.

Having spent his formative years in Croatia, his life had been one war after another, first the hell of the Bosnian conflict, then the hell after 9/11. He'd fought in countries he couldn't have even found on a map as a student. But after his life in the army, he *did* have contacts.

Garrett went through the large front door of the mansion, ignored the anteroom with the secretary, and took a left down a hallway, to a stairwell leading to the basement.

The Knights didn't want to advertise his services—being a humanitarian organization—so he was relegated to the basement section of the mansion, to a group of hastily renovated closets that were once used solely for the cleaning crew.

Now the little rat warren was his office space.

He reached the bottom of the stairs, the faint odor of mildew creeping out, the ceiling at just seven feet causing him to duck his head even if he wasn't going to hit it.

He walked down to his office and opened the door, finding Leonardo inside waiting.

In his late twenties, Leonardo had hard eyes,

having seen much more of the hatred that man-
kind can bring than the locals in Rome would
ever understand. He lived in a so-called civilized world, but at the edges, where the monsters
roamed, it was still a vicious, brutal existence,
which is why Garrett had recruited him.

All four of his team were former members of
the Croatian Special Forces Command, a unit
that had been formed after the horrific violence
of the Bosnian war. They had been too young to
understand the incredible trauma that war per-
sonified, but became old enough to see it inflicted
elsewhere. They'd served their time, learning
invaluable skills, and then had returned to civilian life only to find it wanting.

They'd lost the camaraderie and focus of the
military, and all four were floundering, working
dead-end jobs when Garrett had sought them
out, one by one.

Born in Croatia, he was now a United States
citizen, with one foot in both camps, and he had
the same zeal that they had. He'd recruited them
for a single mission in Syria, and they'd signed
on. A good mission—protecting the Knights of
Malta as they helped the victims from all sides
of the conflict. At least it was a good mission on
paper.

That mission had turned into a cauldron of
violence, with all of them scarred—none more
than Garrett—and because of it, they would now
follow him into hell, convinced his new mission
was the way to cleanse the world of the scourge
they'd witnessed.

When he'd opened the door, Leonardo was

sitting behind Garrett's desk staring at a small flat-screen TV mounted on the wall. He'd leapt up, embarrassed to be taking Garrett's seat. Garrett waved a hand, telling him it was nothing, and then pointed at the television.

"What's happening?"

"It's Paris."

## CHAPTER 6

G arrett turned up the sound, hearing a BBC report about an Israeli diplomat named Etyan Malka having been murdered in a street mugging. The report detailed that the perpetrators were Muslim refugees and still on the loose, with the focus on the "refugee" slant. What it didn't say was that the man killed was no diplomat. He was the head of the European Protective Services division of Shin Bet, the Israeli security service responsible for shielding the homeland from threats.

Originally focused solely within the borders of Israel, after the killings of the Israeli athletes in 1972 its sphere went worldwide, with a mandate to protect Israeli interests all over the globe, to include El Al airlines and Israeli embassies on foreign soil.

He was a perfect target for the signal Garrett wanted to send. It showed that the man responsible for protecting Israeli assets in Europe couldn't even protect himself.

The report also failed to mention the letter he knew his assets had left at the scene, but he had no doubt Israel had it. One more bit of gunpowder loaded in the shell he wanted to fire.

Garrett smiled and said, "I was beginning to worry those savages didn't have it in them, but after Interlaken I suppose I should have had more confidence."

His eyes still glued to the television, Leonardo barked a laugh, almost as if he was embarrassed by what was on the screen. By what he had facilitated.

Garrett sat down behind his desk and used the remote to cut off the TV, saying, "What about our own operation today?"

Glad for the reprieve, Leonardo put a map on the desk, pointing out a position near the coast and saying, "Donatello, Michelangelo, and Raphael are set. We expect the hit in the next hour." He looked at his watch and corrected himself, "Actually within the next twenty minutes now. Raph is the trigger. Donnie and Mikey are the hit team."

Garrett insisted that they never use their true names, no matter what they did, as a protection of the reputation of the Knights if anything went wrong. He wanted to make it as hard as possible to put a link to his martial skill and the Knights' charitable contribution. Which is why he was hired.

After recruiting them, he'd buried their names to the point that even he couldn't remember what was on their birth certificates. They'd used false passports created by the Knights for years, but he had to keep them straight, so he'd devised nicknames, no matter the name on the passport.

He had anointed them with the names of the Teenage Mutant Ninja Turtles. They had all thought it funny originally, but the monikers had taken on a life of their own, with each man liking the tag he'd been given. He, of course, was Splinter. At least to his face. When he was out of earshot, they called him the Eunuch.

Because of his insistence on cloaking their names, they were known derisively as the Turtles to the hierarchy of the Knights of Malta, but the officials using the term had no idea of the violence they were capable of inflicting. They would learn that soon.

Garrett rubbed his face, the blackout sleep not giving him the rest he needed. He said, "Can they do it and project the hit on our partners?"

Leonardo said, "Yes. We have his route, and we're going to use the same method that Israel does. It will send a signal, and when the car is disabled, we'll execute him and his wife with a bullet to the head, then throw the letter in the front seat. It will work."

"How sure are we he's going to use that route?"

"He's done it every weekend since Italy opened back up. He takes his wife on a day drive down the Amalfi coast. He eats at a different restaurant, but he takes the same route to get there. He'll do it again."

Garrett nodded and said, "Okay. Okay. Good."

Leonardo nodded, then shuffled from foot to foot. Garrett said, "What?"

"Our contact says he needs more money. We have it, and he needs it for the next hit. The one in Bahrain."

"We've already paid him. He knows that. Is he trying a play here? I know it's not because he's a true believer. If he was, he wouldn't have taken our money to begin with."

In Syria, before it had all gone bad, the majority of the Turtles' actions had been paying off various rebel groups—in effect, buying the ability of the Knights to help the very people the groups were harming. To be sure, that in itself had involved significant danger, and when they had to go to the guns, they did, but money was something the Knights had, and it was much easier to pay with cash as opposed to blood. In so doing, they'd found a man who could interface with the various rebel groups, and that was the man they were using now.

Leonardo said, "I don't think so. He's scared. He says they're going to kill him if he doesn't deliver. I think he's telling the truth. I think he needs the money to make it happen."

"Why? We set the parameters before we paid him. If he's playing us, I'll cut his heart out."

"He says Bahrain is more than they expected. More effort, more men, more everything. And we need that hit before we do the big one. We need to build the death count before we trip the final wire. If we don't, we won't get the reaction we want."

Garrett rolled his head back onto his chair, staring at the ceiling and thinking. He didn't like the choice of paying off a man who had already been a weasel in Syria, skimming off their money to enrich himself. But he *had* done what he'd said he'd do, protecting the Knights.

He said, "Okay. Pay him what he wants. But this is bullshit. If there's one place Keta'ib Hezbollah can operate, it's Bahrain. I mean, they can kill an old chief of Mossad in Switzerland, a Shin Bet head in Paris, but they need more money in Bahrain, a Shia state?"

"It's because of the level of the target and the Sunni security apparatus. They say it makes it harder to operate than in a European country. And they might be right."

Garrett rolled his eyes and said, "Fine. Use the cutout account, but this is the last time. We aren't made of money, and we aren't in Syria anymore. I can't steal the money here in Rome like we did there, but I agree. We need that hit."

Leonardo nodded and Garrett changed the subject. "What's the status on Raphael? Do we have contact?"

Leonardo raised a cell phone and said, "He's on Zello. We'll hear as soon as he has the target."

Zello was an application that basically turned the cell phone into a multiplex walkie-talkie, with everyone who was tuned to the channel able to listen instead of the usual point-to-point communications of a cell phone.

No sooner did he say that than the phone chirped, "Donnie, Donnie, this is Raph. Target just passed my location."

Donatello came back, the sound crystal clear, "Roger that. We're set. What's the traffic status?"

"You're clear. He's a singleton. Light traffic, and they're running slow."

In the office, Leonardo smiled and said, "Told you."

* * *

At the same time Garrett was hearing the radio traffic, the small trailer next to the park in the EUR neighborhood was being surrounded with crime scene tape, the body having been found, a small crowd forming outside.

Inspector Lia Vairo parked her car next to the perimeter and exited. She pushed past the tape outside the trailer, saying to the carabinieri at the entrance checkpoint, "Another one?"

"Looks that way."

She entered the crime scene, thinking she was solving a murder. She had no idea of the threat the death represented.

Most of the people living in the neighborhood didn't care about the murders happening. In fact, if asked, almost all would say they brought it upon themselves by littering the neighborhood with their trade. Just one more whore killed doing her job. But Lia *did* care. She was someone who didn't look at the life of the victim, only the death.

And because of it, Lia held the fate of many more in her hands.

## CHAPTER 7

I pulled into the parking garage on Wentworth Street, right next to the Restoration Hotel in the historic district of Charleston, saying, "I still can't believe you guys got a room here." I parked, turned around, and said, "You trying to poke me in the eye?"

Aaron laughed and said, "No, when we did that operation for you here Shoshana really liked it. And truthfully, it was the only hotel I knew about on the peninsula."

A couple of years ago we'd tracked some Russian assassins to this hotel after they'd killed my boss and former commander of the Taskforce, Colonel Kurt Hale. Since they were gunning for me and hit him by mistake, and thus knew me on sight, I'd asked Shoshana and Aaron for a little bit of help and together we'd returned the favor.

I nodded and said, "You could have asked us for some recommendations. This place isn't cheap, but it *is* nice. See you guys tomorrow for breakfast?"

Shoshana floated her weird glow over me, reading me, and it was disconcerting, not the least because I knew she only did that when she was trying to determine my mindset. She was one complicated woman—which is a polite way of saying a little bit off—but she had this ability to see inside a person's soul. I don't know how she did it, but I'd become a believer—although I'd never tell her that.

One thing was for sure; she didn't do it without reason. Something was coming.

She said, "Pike, come up to the room for a nightcap."

I looked at my watch and said, "It's after one A.M. Didn't you get enough of me tonight?"

After they'd appeared at Ashley Hall, and after the reunion kisses and handshakes, we'd restarted the rehearsal, getting everything right in Jennifer's mind, and then had broken up to allow Shoshana and Aaron to check into their hotel and everyone else to do whatever sightseeing they had planned—which is why they were here a week early for a wedding.

I didn't want to impose on their time, so we'd agreed to meet at my Grolier Recovery Services office on Shem Creek at seven P.M., just across the Ravenel Bridge from Charleston.

The company, of course, was a front for the Taskforce. Jennifer and I were civilian partners, ostensibly traveling the world assisting archeological projects by cutting through government red tape and security on-site, but in truth, the business allowed us to penetrate just about anywhere, because there were few spots on earth that didn't have some sort of archeological work going on. Until COVID-19, that is. Then it all shut down.

My entire team had shown up for the rehearsal, but I couldn't possibly put them all up in my small row house. When school had let out in May, Amena's boarding room privileges had ended, so I only had one spare bedroom. I'd offered it to my best man, Knuckles—who was also the second in command of my team—and he'd declined, which I thought was strange. Why pay for a hotel when you can rack out for free? Lord knows he'd spent enough time sleeping on my couch in the past. Instead, I'd given it to Veep and Kylie.

Veep was the junior member of my team, and he was dating the niece of Kurt Hale, the commander of the Taskforce who had been killed. In the past, before he had died, I'd paid her to act as Amena's nanny after she'd first arrived from Syria, so it was a good fit. Giving the two of them the room solved my Amena problem for the week. She could definitely take care of herself, but she loved Kylie and would think twice about pushing my buttons with her in the house.

The first to arrive at my office was Knuckles, and when he'd walked through the door I'd realized why he'd wanted his own hotel room. Behind him was a woman named Willow Radcliffe, someone we'd saved in Brazil from a horrendous death. Jennifer's mouth had dropped open, and Willow had seemed a little bit self-conscious. I'd said, "Willow! I didn't know you were here."

She'd glared at Knuckles, saying, "Knuckles said this was just a vacation to Charleston. He didn't mention the wedding. I'm sorry if I'm intruding."

Sensing her hesitance, Jennifer jumped up and said, "Not at all. Pike, get them some drinks."

I said, "Beers on the back deck. Knuckles, want to give me a hand?"

He nodded and we left the office to a small balcony that fronted Shem Creek. I went to a mini fridge I'd built into the wall for the sole purpose of sitting and watching the sun set, pulled out four beers, handed him two, and said, "What the hell is that about?"

He shrugged and said, "What? She's a hammer, and she seemed to like me after Brazil, so I gave her a call."

Knuckles was a man whore of the first order. He stood a little over six feet, with ropy muscles like a swimmer, which stood to reason, because he was a Navy SEAL, but somewhere he'd lost any semblance of being in the military. His hair was long and shaggy, and he perpetually dressed in tight T-shirts with some eclectic saying that was bound to offend someone, like some hippie from the seventies.

Women swooned over him, and he obliged more times than not, which made me a little sick. Not that he did it, but because he could.

I said, "What happened to the SECSTATE?"

Last I'd heard, Knuckles had been dating the secretary of state, another woman who had fallen for his charms, which had caused no small amount of consternation with me due to her position.

He opened his beer and said, "She's good, but that shit is just too complicated. Too much hiding and political bullshit. I broke it off."

Which concerned me, because she was also an Oversight Council member. I didn't want them making any decisions about my team based on some lovers' quarrel. He saw my face and raised his hands, each holding a beer, looking like he was directing a Delta flight to a gate.

"Hey, I see where this is going. Don't worry about it. We're good. It was a mutual decision. She saw the problems just like I did."

I'd nodded and said, "Okay. If you say so."

We'd reentered the office only to find that everyone else from the team had shown up. After a round of beers, I'd taken them to a place across Coleman Boulevard called Saltwater Cowboys. Also on Shem Creek, it was a great location to watch the dolphins and the sunset.

We'd ended up staying there for hours telling war stories and just reconnecting, and then, while everyone else Uber'd to their hotel, I'd offered to take Aaron and Shoshana back in my vehicle. It was the least I could do since they'd come from Israel.

Something I was now regretting with Shoshana staring at me.

## CHAPTER 8

Shoshana said, "Come on up. It's just one drink. You'll still be able to drive."

My internal radar starting to fire, I said, "Can't we do this tomorrow? It's really late and we're having breakfast together."

I saw her scowl and said, "Usually, you're trying to kill me, and now you can't get enough of me?"

Which was true. When we'd first collided, we'd both tried mightily to slaughter each other. Luckily, we'd both failed. Since then, she'd threatened to kill me on a number of occasions, but she'd also saved my life just as many times.

Jennifer misread the situation, thinking that Shoshana was just trying to be a normal person, trying to fit in and show how she had an ordinary relationship with Aaron, which, given the person, was impossible. Jennifer thought of herself as a mentor, and honestly probably was.

She touched my arm and said, "One drink. I'll drive home."

I shook my head and said, "Okay, okay. Let's get this over with."

Shoshana said, "That's how you feel? This is something to get over with?"

"No. I mean whatever it is you're about to tell me."

She gave me her weird glow, her face splitting into a smile that looked like a wolf, full of teeth without any joy. She said, "You *are* like me. You can see into someone's heart."

I rolled my eyes, opened the door, and said, "Okay, Carrie, let's go."

She scowled at that, exiting on the far side. Carrie was the callsign Knuckles had given her on an operation, because she really did act a lot like the Stephen King character. Aaron exited on my side and said, "Careful. She doesn't like being toyed with."

I closed the door, watched Jennifer and Shoshana walk out to the street, and said, "I thought she liked that callsign?"

"She does, when you use it for real. Not as a joke."

We followed behind the women and I said, "So what's this about?"

"Upstairs. Let's get to the room."

I shook my head, now knowing my radar was right. We went into the small alcove for the boutique hotel, up the elevator, and down the hall to their room. We stopped outside the door and I said, "Are you shitting me? You have the same room the Russians were in? Was that on purpose?"

Shoshana smiled and said, "Complete coincidence, but I thought it appropriate."

She unlocked the door, turned on the lights,

then the television, raising the sound. The last thing she did was unplug the Alexa on the desk, grinning at me as she did so.

We'd hacked that very Alexa to determine our kill box for the Russians.

Aaron opened the minibar and said, "Rum and Coke, right?"

I said, "Let's forget the drinks and get to the point here."

Jennifer heard my tone and said, "Pike, what's that mean?"

I turned to Shoshana and said, "You want to tell her?"

Aaron opened his suitcase and pulled out a piece of paper, placing it in front of me. I read:

You attack us with impunity in Syria and Iraq from the air, like cowards. And now we attack you man to man. Our reach is long, and our patience is infinite. This man is not the first to die, and it will not be the last, Little Satan. Tell the Great Satan they are next.

I passed it to Jennifer and said, "No idea what that is. Did you think I did? I can't help with that."

Shoshana said, "No. We already know what it is. It was on the body of Gideon Cohen, but the police have kept it quiet."

*Gideon Cohen? Why do I know that name?* And it clicked. He was the guy who had bailed Jennifer and me out of an Israeli jail after we'd stopped a terrorist attack. And was also . . .

Like fog dissipating under the sun, it became

clear. Gideon Cohen was the only person on earth who had believed in Shoshana. The one man who'd ignored her past and put her on Aaron's team. And Aaron had nurtured her back to the world of the living, until she'd become a ferocious force of nature.

I said, "He's dead?"

Shoshana's eyes flashed. "Yes. He's dead, and this letter on his body proves it wasn't an accident."

I shook my head, saying, "I have no idea what you're talking about. Accident?"

Aaron gave me the background on the killing, then said, "There will be more. We want to stop it."

At a loss, I said, "Okay . . . I'm not sure why I'm here. You want me to leverage Taskforce assets to do some digging?"

Shoshana said, "No. I want you to help us. I want you to come with me to solve this problem. Before they kill again."

I looked at Jennifer, then said, "I'm getting married in a week. Are you serious? I have no idea about any of this. Use some Mossad assets."

Shoshana scoffed and said, "They won't help. They think they've been penetrated—and they probably have been. They gave this to us because if we fail they can burn us at the stake, but I will *not* fail."

She got into my face and I saw the full fury of her pain. "I *will* find who killed Gideon, but this fight is more than that. It's biblical. The man who did it wants a prophecy. I can feel it."

I looked at her like she was crazy, which, of

course, she was, and said, "What the hell are you talking about?"

Aaron glanced at Shoshana and she backed off, taking a seat. He spoke, breaking the tension. "Pike, we were given this mission, and the note is clear, Americans are going to be killed as well. What we don't know is why, or who's doing the killing. We would like your help."

I stood up, doing a circle, then walking to the window. I said, "What the hell do you want from me? How can *I* help? You've got the whole Mossad to help. What can I do?"

I turned back around and said, "I'm getting married in a week."

I saw Shoshana holding Jennifer's hand. The two connecting yet again. Jennifer hadn't said a word, but apparently, she was all in.

I said, "Are you serious? You're good with this?"

Jennifer said, "It's more than the death. It's like Kurt Hale all over again. She came when we called. We should do the same. He was her Kurt Hale."

"Jennifer, we're basically shut down because of the damn pandemic. We can't fly anywhere because we're Americans. Shit, you guys have had the best vaccine rollout on earth. You can go anywhere. We're still catching up."

Aaron said, "But you've had the vaccine. Both doses."

Which was true, although I had no idea how he knew it. As Taskforce members, we were at the front of the line, which is sort of shitty, given that teachers and grocery clerks should have gotten it before us, but it was true.

I said, "Yeah, we have, but we still can't fly. America is still the COVID center of the universe. Nobody will let us into the country without official government diplomatic business, or some other official thing. Since we're the Taskforce, everything we do is precisely *not* to show a government footprint. Grolier Recovery Services cannot travel."

Shoshana went to her suitcase and said, "You are right. Israel has done a good job with the vaccine. And because of it, we're allowed to fly anywhere."

She rummaged around for a moment, then pulled out a package. She opened it and laid it in front of me.

Passports. From Israel.

She said, "I need help here, and when I was given the mission, I didn't hesitate on who I wanted. I want you, Nephilim. And your team."

I ignored her use of my given name and opened one, seeing my face. I was astounded at the level of work that had already been done. And was also a little flattered. "You're going to have me help you as an Israeli citizen?"

She said, "Yes, if that will get you in. If you will commit."

I smiled and said, "Who else? Did Jennifer get one?"

"Of course she did. Along with Knuckles and Brett."

Knuckles I understood, but Brett was a little strange. I said, "How did you get a passport for a black man? There aren't any black men in Israel. At least not citizens."

Aaron laughed and said, "You're wrong. We rescued thousands of Ethiopian Jews in Operation Brothers in the eighties. You're just like everyone else, full of misconceptions about Israel."

Chagrined, I said, "Okay, but if I have those misconceptions, so will anyone else who looks at this passport. And one crack, we're done."

Shoshana said, "I want Brett. I know him. He is a killer, but also a man who doesn't kill. He comes. He is necessary."

I was surprised at her vehemence, but absolutely couldn't argue with that. Brett was one of the finest operators I'd ever served with, and if they thought he'd work, I wasn't going to bitch.

I realized I was actually beginning to think about doing this crazy thing. I stopped myself and said, "Look, this has obviously taken some work, but what are we going to do? I mean really? All you have is a letter, and the guy that killed Gideon is splattered on the pavement. What's the mission?"

Shoshana said, "The mission is to find out who's behind this. It isn't Keta'ib Hezbollah. It's someone else, and they're going to start killing Americans, too. I think they want to initiate a prophecy. They want war."

I fell into a chair, saying, "You keep saying that. What do you mean? What prophecy? This is just a murder."

She said, "Right up until the murder causes a war."

Aaron saw she was losing me and stepped in,

saying, "Look, forget about Shoshana's talk of prophecies." She glared at him, but he continued, saying, "The bottom line is we want to find out who's doing the killings. That's all. Everyone in Israel thinks it's Iran. Some in the Mossad don't. Will you help?"

I rubbed my head, thinking, then said, "You know I'm going to have to tell Wolffe, right? I can't just jet out of here with Israeli passports and start ripping scabs on the European continent. Right?"

"We would prefer it if you didn't do that until the first American is killed. Which will happen soon."

"So you want me—us—to fly out of here without a word, then say something after the fact? *If* an American is killed?"

"Yes. It's going to happen, and, as you've told me before, it's better to ask for forgiveness than permission. The Taskforce can't even move between countries right now because of COVID. We can. Use that now."

My head spinning at the implications, I said, "Why? Why should I do that?"

Shoshana bent down in front of my chair and said, "Because I'm asking, Nephilim. Nothing more. Because I'm asking."

She knew that was the chink in my armor. The way to my soul. I couldn't turn down my family, and she was a part of it.

The television blared a news story about some death in Paris and Shoshana whipped her head to the screen. I followed, seeing that an Israeli diplomat had been killed. The name appeared on the screen and Shoshana hissed. She turned to Aaron, saying, "It's coming. This is it."

I said, "What?"

He ignored me, leaning forward and listening. When the story was over, he said, "That man wasn't a diplomat. He was Shin Bet. That killing wasn't random."

He turned back to me and said, "This is real, and it's happening right now. Your country is next. I promise. Help us."

I looked at Jennifer, wanting some advice. Shoshana followed my gaze.

Jennifer ignored her, looking at me. She nodded her head and said, "I don't know if what they're saying is true or not, but we go. Because she's asking. We asked her once before and she came without any conditions. She saved both my life and yours. Only because we asked. We should do the same."

I sagged in my seat and said, "Damn it. Now I've got to talk everyone else into this bullshit."

Shoshana sat down next to me. She said, "No you don't. They'll follow you because you ask, Nephilim. Just as I do. All you need to do is ask."

I sputtered for a moment, floundering at the words but knowing what she said was true. I said, "This had better be worth it."

She said, "Saving lives is always worth it."

## CHAPTER 9

Sitting on a Vespa scooter, Raphael saw the convertible coupe pass his position, winding now at slow speed on the Amalfi coast road. He raised the phone and said, "Donnie, Donnie, this is Raph. Target just passed my location."

Sitting on a larger motorcycle around a curve of a switchback, Donatello's voice reflected the adrenaline he was feeling, "Roger that. We're set. What's the traffic status?"

"You're clear. He's a singleton. Light traffic, and they're running slow."

Donatello turned to Michelangelo sitting behind him on the motorcycle and said, "You ready? We got about a minute."

Michelangelo rummaged in a backpack, pulled out what looked like a section of metal pipe with two magnets attached, and flicked a rocker switch on the side, saying, "Yeah. I'm ready. Just get me close to the rear axle."

Donatello nodded, then returned to scanning the road. Stationed on a small cutout off of Via Esterna Chiunzi, the two-lane blacktop snaking through the mountains to the Amalfi coast, they'd picked a specific bit of terrain for the hit.

For the most part, the road from Rome to the Amalfi coast was a straight shot, but once it began to wind out of the mountains, it was a spaghetti mess of switchbacks, the lane a sheer cliff on one side and a wall of granite on the other, the turns causing all traffic to slow down to safely navigate the terrain. And also giving his hit team the ability to kill the target before another car appeared.

This would be the first attack executed by the Turtles, but it needed to be blamed on others. Namely, Keta'ib Hezbollah. To that end, they'd decided to use the same method that the Mossad employed in Iran, where they'd hunted the nuclear scientists one by one.

Over the last decade, Iran had endured a spate of their scientists being assassinated, the last killing happening in 2020 against the head of the entire nuclear program. Most were done with a magnetic mine slapped on the scientist's vehicle on the way to work. In the congested traffic of Tehran or other cities, it was a way to attack that allowed an instant getaway. Slap on the bomb, and immediately ride away.

The Turtles had decided to do the same for this hit. Not because they had no other way to get the man, but precisely to send a signal. A magnetic mine attached to the vehicle to disable it, then a couple of well-placed rounds to seal the deal. Once that was accomplished, they'd throw a note into the car, letting the world know that Keta'ib Hezbollah was on the hunt even here.

Their target was Geoffrey Combine, the United States ambassador to the Holy See.

A political appointee, he posed no real threat

to anyone, but his position was a valuable signal that the Turtles wanted to send out to the world: Keta'ib Hezbollah's reach was global, and they were on a killing spree as revenge against Christendom's sanctions and targeted attacks. Obviously controlled and funded by Iran, the West needed to harshly confront the theocratic state. In so doing, confront Islam writ large.

When Garrett had come up with the idea nearly a year ago it was much grander in scope, involving not only Iran but actors from the Sunni states in the Persian Gulf. Since that time, Israel had signed peace deals with multiple Sunni states, to include Bahrain, the UAE, and Sudan. Saudi Arabia was probably not too far behind, restricting his plan to Iran itself, but he still thought it would work.

The United States was constantly rattling sabers against the mullahs, and Israel certainly had no love for the state. All he had to do was get a big enough spark going that they would retaliate. Garrett hoped to show that the attacks were in retaliation for the killing of the Qods Force commander General Qasem Soleimani, and the murders would continue unabated unless action was taken. Only by confronting Iran—with Islam in the crosshairs—would the killings stop. And in so doing fulfill the prophecy of the Bible for the second coming of Christ.

In his heart, Michelangelo wondered if Garrett understood the levers he was pulling, but fully believed in the mission he was executing. In his own country, he had seen the cleavage of religion unleash a spasm of violence unseen since World War II. In Syria, he had seen the cleavage turn medieval, and because of it, he'd become convinced—like the other Turtles— that the only way to achieve true peace on earth was to eradicate Muslim influence on the world stage. And that would only come by fulfilling the prophecies of the Bible.

In his mind, Christianity alone had shown a level tolerance that facilitated goodwill the world over, unlike Islam. They had done nothing but slaughter, even against their own people. Their false god had brought only pain and misery to the world, and the way to combat it was the return of the one true God's son.

After what he'd seen in Syria, he believed that to the core of his being. If he'd been forced to face the truth of Catholic Croats and Orthodox Christian Serbs who had horrifically massacred the Muslims in his homeland, he would have come up with a reason why that was just. The facts no longer mattered. Only his faith did.

He didn't hate Muslims per se, but he fully believed they were bringing about the collapse of civilized society. One only had to look at the atrocities in Syria to see that. Burning a Jordanian pilot alive? Who does that? In his mind, not a Christian, that's for sure. He was too young to have lived through the atrocities of the battery factory in Srebrenica, where upwards of eight thousand Muslims were slaughtered solely because of their religion, running through the woods like rabbits as the Christians hunted them down one by one, burying them in mass graves. Even if he had known, he would have found a way to justify it. There was only one right way, and it was to be found in the Bible.

He, and the rest of the Turtles, believed whole-heartedly in the end-of-days prophecy that the Bible dictated. In order to end the suffering around the world, the second coming of Christ needed to happen, and he believed the only way that would occur was by building the third temple on the Dome of the Rock in the heart of Jerusalem. But that couldn't happen because the Islamic Waqf of Jordan controlled the terri-tory. After Israel seized Jerusalem in the Six-Day War, many in Christendom thought the final Bible prophecies were coming true, but the gov-ernment of Israel allowed the Islamic Waqf to maintain control of the most sacred sites, refusing to allow the building of the temple on what was now a religious icon for the Muslim faith.

That needed to change. If a temple was to be built, Israel needed to assume control of the area, and the only way to do that was to force a confrontation that both religions clearly wanted, but heretofore had been afraid to wage. A push was needed to force the issue.

And so he was stationed on a small cutout for a highway that looked like a spaghetti noodle draped on the earth, waiting on the arrival of a poor political appointee from North Carolina, solely to kill him.

Raph said, "I'm behind him, and he's driving slow. Taking his time."

"Roger all. We're ready. Give us a time hack at thirty seconds."

The spit of gravel they were on was still in the mountains, right before the highway began dropping to the valley and coast below. Full of switchbacks, it held incredible views, and as such was frequently traveled for them alone, but it was also the perfect place for the magnetic mine. They could cut him off from all other traffic simply because of the winding nature of the road.

Michelangelo saw three cars pass by his position, all driving slowly because of the serpentine nature of the blacktop. He heard, "Thirty seconds," and started the motorcycle.

He saw an Alfa Romeo Spider convertible pass his location, a man driving with a woman in the passenger seat. Right behind it was a Vespa scooter trying mightily to keep up. The scooter pulled into the cutout, and Mikey saw Raph flipping up the visor on his helmet. Mikey nodded and pulled out into the lane. The scooter followed, now driving much slower to clog any traffic that appeared behind them.

Mikey caught up to the convertible around a blind curve, now right behind it. He waited until they crested another switchback, then goosed the engine, pulling abreast of the car.

The man behind the wheel looked at him in confusion, wondering why he was trying to pass on a section of road that was potentially suicidal. But Michelangelo wasn't trying to pass. He slowed next to the rear axle and behind him, Donnie pulled a strip of paper off from the top of his pipe like he was loading a new toner cartridge in a laser printer, flicked the rocker switch one more level, then slapped the magnetic mine right above the rear tire. Mikey laid off the gas and let the car continue forward.

Mikey saw the next hairpin turn growing closer, the four-foot rock wall along the side the only protection from falling into the valley below. The mine should go off before the turn, forcing the target to the side of the road.

Inexplicably, the Alfa Romeo sped up, racing wildly into the turn too fast by far. Mikey saw the driver's eyes in the rearview mirror, staring at him with fear on his face.

*Not good. Not good.*

The driver powered into the turn like he was auditioning for a movie, the car skidding through the curve with the rear end breaking contact with the pavement. And then the mine went off, shattering the rear axle just as the vehicle began to straighten out. The rear end of the vehicle bounced against the sheer rock wall of the mountain, then the vehicle ricocheted to the small barrier protecting the drivers from the drop below. Mikey saw the driver's face, a look of terror, his mouth screaming, just as it hit the wall sideways. It flipped over the stone and turned upside down, the woman flung out of the vehicle in midair, the man held in place by his seat belt and the steering wheel.

Mikey went through the curve and pulled over next to the shattered brick of the wall. He ripped off his helmet, looking at the burning wreckage far below, seeing the woman's body broken open on a ledge halfway down.

He shook his head and said, "What the fuck. What do we do now?"

Donnie said, "Get the hell out of here."

"What about the letter. We can't leave the letter. It'll look like he was just a drunk. They won't even find the explosive damage in that mess."

"Nothing we can do about that now. Keep going. Get out of the blast radius. This mission is done."

## CHAPTER 10

L ia Vairo showed her badge at the door to the trailer and said, "Is it messy?"

The carabinieri at the entrance said, "Not like the other one. It's pretty clean. Although the place is a mess. Pretty sure COVID would get its ass kicked in here fighting the other diseases. Might want to wear some gloves."

She smiled and raised her hands, encased in thin latex. "Always."

She entered to find a photographer she knew snapping pictures of the scene, along with an investigator already there and a coroner's assistant she didn't know examining the body. She said, "Hey, Jonathan. What do we have?"

Jonathan was nothing more than a recorder of events. He had no official stance as an investigator, but because of his job, Lia had found that he noticed things. Saw connections through his lens.

"My opinion? It's the same guy."

The investigator scoffed, aggravated at her appearance. He was much more experienced than Lia at murder scenes, and he clearly didn't like her presence. Especially since she was in charge of the investigation. She was an impediment to his work. Nothing more than a social experiment to prove that Italy was diverse.

She ignored him, looking at the dead body on the mattress, lying flat with her panties still on but her half shirt raised to expose a single breast.

She said, "Why do you say that? The first had her throat cut, spraying blood all over the place. The second died from blunt force trauma. And this one?"

The coroner looked up and said, "Strangulation. Whoever it was choked her to death with his hands."

He went back to work and Lia said, "So, why, Jonathan? What do you see?"

The investigator said, "Why are you asking him? All he does is take pictures."

Jonathan snapped a photo, then let the camera fall to his waist on its sling. He glanced at the investigator, not wanting to pretend what he was not, then said, "I don't know. They just look the same, despite the manner of death. No penetration, no sex assault. Just a dead body. Who kills a prostitute *without* raping her? If that's what they want to do, they go through with it. This one still has her underwear on. We have three dead prostitutes, and none of them have been penetrated."

Lia looked at the coroner's assistant and he said, "I can't confirm until I get her back to the lab, but from what I can see, he's right. No penetration. Just a dead body, like the guy came in to kill her."

*What the hell.*

Lia said, "So we have a man or woman killing

prostitutes for a purpose. He finds them and then kills them outright. Sex isn't the issue. The occupation is. He or she doesn't like the chosen profession, and is now sending a signal?"

The investigator scoffed, saying, "That's obvious."

The coroner's assistant said, "I don't think so. The first death was incredibly violent. It was done in a rage. He didn't go in there to kill her, he *ended* up killing her. This one is the same. Whoever is doing the killing starts out wanting the woman, and then erupts. This woman was strangled to death with bare hands. The other one was beaten to death with a lamp. Nobody plans to do that. That's a reaction."

"Why?"

"I have no idea. But I don't think this guy is out killing prostitutes because he hates prostitutes. He hates something within himself. And then he kills to relieve the pain."

He raised the woman's head, the eyes half lidded, rigor mortis not set. He pointed at her neck, where the purple bruises were evident. He said, "Nobody plans to kill someone and then does it with their bare hands. If he hated prostitutes, why not show up with a knife?"

The investigator said, "He did on the first one."

"No, he didn't. He used her own X-Acto knife to kill her. He didn't show up to kill. He just snapped. The second one was done with a lamp."

Lia heard the words and thought, *So I have my own Zodiac Killer. Great.* She said, "Is there anything we can use here? Right now? Or is it like the other ones, devoid of evidence?"

The coroner smiled and said, "Yes. He kissed her after she was dead. Right on the cheek."

Now interested, she said, "How do you know?"

"I have saliva on the cheek. I can't see how it would have gotten there before she died. It's pronounced, and against her nose. It's an awkward location. Nobody would have done that if the person was alive. I could be wrong, but I think he kissed her after he killed her."

"Can you get DNA off of it?"

"I think so. It's not a guarantee, but I think I can."

"Do it. This asshole thinks he's smarter than us, but he's not."

The coroner said, "This guy is twisted. Something is wrong in his head. He's not hiding. And he's not going to stop."

Lia went around the room, cataloging everything in her mind, trying to find connections with the previous deaths.

The investigator said, "You going to do anything besides stand and look?"

She turned to him and said, "Do you have a problem with me?"

He shook his head and said, "No. I have a problem with you being in charge. You don't have the experience for this work."

She ignored him, seeing a Mi-Fi device taped to the window.

She said, "What's that?"

The investigator said, "Internet connection

through the cell network. They don't have Wi-Fi here, so she paid for her own."

Intrigued, she said, "Is it still on?"

Dismissive, he said, "Yeah, but it's just a Wi-Fi connection. It doesn't show anything. It's just a pass-through for her to show porn. They all do it. You'd know that if you worked this area."

"Does it show who's connected to it? Did she have to give him permission to access it?"

The investigator, examining the carpet next to the mattress, realized where she was headed and stood up, looked at her, and said, "Yeah, she would have to do that."

"Does it have a memory of people she's given access to?"

Now animated, he pulled it off the window and said, "Yeah, it would have that."

He scrolled through the last attachments to the Wi-Fi and saw a MAC address. He said, "This is the guy. It was registered last night. He was on this Wi-Fi."

He laid it on the table, his face showing a new appreciation, writing down the MAC in a notebook. When he was done, he stuck out his hand and said, "I'm Franco Rossi. Sorry if I was rude."

When she'd entered the room, she'd felt his disdain, as she had from the other men investigators in the past. She really didn't want to get into a shoving match over who was in charge—because *she* was in charge. As before, she'd let her abilities do the persuading. She'd found out early on that she had a knack for this, and all she had to do was show it.

Sometimes it created a situation where someone else felt threatened, but most of the time—like now—it caused the men to realize she was special. She was in charge because she was better at this than they were, regardless of her time in service.

She smiled and accepted his latent apology, shaking his hand. She said, "Is it a cell number?"

He began scrolling through the history of the device, saying, "No. It's the MAC address for the phone, tablet, or computer he used. A unique identifier for the device. It's a number that registers every time you attach to a Wi-Fi node."

She said, "Can we get a cell number from the MAC? Or trace that by itself?"

"No, it's not like a cell number that interfaces with the network. Its trace ends here at the sign-on to the Mi-Fi. But that number is a unique address to whoever killed her. If we get his phone—or whatever he used—we can prove he was here."

She liked the "we" part of that. Franco was now on board. And like many endeavors involving teamwork, the sum of the parts was greater than the whole. They would find this man. All they had to do was keep digging.

She only prayed that they'd locate him before he killed again.

Franco said, "Whoa. Whoever has that MAC just signed on again. He's live."

Lia came over and saw the device registered one active user. "It's the same MAC?"

"Yeah. My bet is the guy lives near here and his phone automatically connected when he went to a window or something, like when you enter a

Starbucks you've been in before. He doesn't realize it's connected."

Lia thought for a moment, then said, "No. We're in a trailer next to a park. The closest living spaces are blocks away. There's no way it's someone staying nearby. That thing doesn't have the power."

Franco said, "So the device is in here somewhere. Left behind."

"But you just said you saw it appear. If it was left behind, it would have been connected when we entered." She turned in a circle, going through the problem set, then said, "I think you're right. He's here, close by, but doesn't know it's connected."

"Why?"

"He's come back to see the murder. To watch us work."

Sitting in his car across the street, Garrett watched Lia exit the trailer, seeing a lanyard with a badge on her neck. The same woman at the last murder scene. He assumed he had made mistakes and that the woman was going to find connections between the killings—something he needed to short-circuit. Not for the long term, because his plan was in motion, and if he died after it succeeded, it wouldn't matter. He would be in heaven with the Holy Father, but he couldn't afford to have her interfere with the plan.

Maybe he'd disrupt whatever theory she'd created. Kill her like he had the others. That would really cause a reassessment on their part. Make it look like the others, only it wouldn't be a prostitute.

Something to think about.

He studied her, going through the problem, then realized she was looking at the line of cars on the street where he'd parked. As if she knew he was close and was searching.

*How could she know?*

Unnerved, he put the car in reverse, did a three-point turn, and drove away without passing her.

## CHAPTER 11

The flight to Switzerland was about nine hours, which meant almost a full workday of Shoshana sniping at me about telling George Wolffe what we were doing. I saw her glowering after takeoff, and I'd opted to go to sleep, telling Jennifer to keep an eye out because I wasn't sure of Shoshana's intentions.

Jennifer punched my arm and said, "Come on. Don't be mean. You *did* say you wouldn't tell Wolffe."

"That was before the U.S. ambassador to the Holy See was killed."

She ignored my request to act as my guardian angel and snuggled into my shoulder to fall asleep herself. I closed my eyes, waited a bit, then cracked them open.

Sitting across from me in the plush leather chair of the Gulfstream aircraft was Shoshana, the dark angel, still scowling at me.

I pretended not to notice and tried to go to sleep, wondering if she was going to do something while I was out. I didn't *really* think that . . . but a part of me did. She'd come close to killing me a few times already, and I hadn't realized how my interactions with George Wolffe would set her off. I still wasn't sure if it was what I'd discussed, or just the fact that I *had* discussed it after telling her I wouldn't.

Eventually, I'd fallen asleep, and seven hours later had awakened, groggily rubbing my eyes. When I opened them, she was still awake. And still glowering.

I looked to her left, seeing Aaron racked out next to the window, then shifted in my seat slightly, not wanting to wake up Jennifer. I'd learned early in my military career that you never knew when you'd get sleep, so you had better take it while you could.

Seeing no help around the aircraft, I said, "You're still mad at me."

She said, "I told you not to say anything— *especially* about the Israeli passports."

"Shoshana, I *had* to tell him. If it was just me and Jennifer, I could make it up, but you wanted Knuckles and Brett. I can't take my team on a mission using Israeli passports without letting him know. Come on. We're acting like spies now, and the Taskforce has some level of risk involved just by our presence."

She scoffed and said, "There is no risk. This isn't an 'Omega Operation' as you Americans like to talk about. It's Alpha."

Aaron and Shoshana had conducted a few different operations with us in the past, as unofficial help, and she'd learned our lingo. The Taskforce teams had levels of operational permission based on the Greek alphabet, with "Alpha" being the introduction of forces to explore a potential problem, running down to "Omega," when we were given execute authority to eliminate the threat.

I said, "I hear you, but you have to admit that the ambassador's death was strange—right after you told me they'd attack us as well as you."

"He ran off a road on the Amalfi coast. No claim of responsibility."

"You don't think that's part of this? The car had signs of an explosive device on the rear axle."

"The car had signs of explosives because it exploded."

"You believe that?"

She sagged back in her seat and said, "No, I don't. It's strange, but it fits with what we were told to find. Something else is going on here. Whoever it is wants Keta'ib Hezbollah to get blamed, but they didn't have the chance to blame them."

"But the guy who killed the *Ramsad was* Keta'ib Hezbollah, right? That's why we're in the air to Switzerland."

"Yes. Yes and no."

"What's that mean?"

"I don't know. That's why we're flying to Switzerland. But you still shouldn't have told the United States government that we've given you the ability to help us by using Israeli passports."

"I didn't tell the government. I told George Wolffe. We're good. Look, if I hadn't disclosed what was going on, we'd be flying in coach on a commercial flight. Now we're riding in style on the Rock Star bird to a small airport an hour and a half away from Zurich. You'd rather be crammed next to a toilet on a commercial flight?"

The aircraft we were flying was a Gulfstream 650, something that rock stars take when traveling on a tour. In Nickelback's version, it was a "big black jet with a bedroom in it, gonna join the mile high club at 37,000 feet."

I still hadn't done that, but mainly because our aircraft was a little bit different. Paid through about a hundred different cutouts and shell companies, it was ostensibly leased to Grolier Recovery Services, but I still had to get George Wolffe's permission to use it. Instead of a bedroom, it had a complete arsenal built into the frame in hidden compartments, everything from surveillance systems to weapons. Something we might need soon, no matter what Shoshana thought of the mission.

I waited, and she finally said, "Okay, this is a good thing, but you still shouldn't have done it. You promised."

I knew at that point the argument was over and she was going to let it go, although she had no idea how hard it had been to get this ball moving. After breakfast, I'd had Jennifer take Aaron and Shoshana on a touristy Charleston carriage ride and had pulled aside George, Brett, and Knuckles.

During the night, the death of the ambassador had made the news, which gave me some leverage. I'd explained everything to Wolffe, saying I wanted to take Knuckles and Brett with me to explore it because there was a threat working— and it was going to be against American as well as Israeli interests. He'd asked if it was Iran, and if so, why hadn't Israel said anything to the U.S. intelligence community, especially since there had been no reporting on a Keta'ib Hezbollah connection to any of the deaths.

At that point, I was treading on dangerous ground with Shoshana's information. Because they weren't sure of the provenance of the Keta'ib Hezbollah linkages, a select few power brokers in the Mossad wanted to keep the linkages secret until they were sure—which I could tell was grating on Wolffe's good nature.

"How am I hearing about this at a wedding rehearsal from a subordinate team leader? They actually gave you a cover without even asking about the help with the Taskforce? What the hell happened to coordination between the intelligence agencies?"

Wolffe was an old-school paramilitary officer from the CIA who had done more clandestine operations than Hollywood could ever produce. And he didn't like being the last to know. He especially didn't like the subterfuge the Israeli team had used.

I held up my hands and said, "That coordination is coming, I'm sure. You saw the 'diplomat' killed in a mugging in Paris?"

"Yeah. What about it?"

"He was Shin Bet, and Keta'ib Hezbollah claimed credit for it, but Israel has kept that under wraps. From what Aaron and Shoshana have told me, the Knesset is split right now, but the forces for attacking Iran are growing. Trust me, they'll come to the U.S. for help soon. You'll be hearing all about it. Right now, they're trying to figure out what to do."

"So why you? Why are *you* going with Aaron and Shoshana?"

"There are some power brokers in the Mossad that think this is a false flag. That someone else is driving the killings and they aren't Keta'ib Hezbollah. They think someone wants a war and has somehow co-opted that militia for the killings. That's why Aaron and Shoshana were chosen. Off the books, away from Mossad headquarters. They don't have to report to any politicians. They want us to see what we can find before this leaks, which it eventually will. Once it blows up in the news, the war drums will start beating."

"That 'off the books' thing works both ways. They'll cut you free in a heartbeat. You get found out, and you're now not an American spy, but an Israeli one—while being disavowed by both states."

"Well, Lord knows I've been in the 'if you get caught, you're on your own' territory before. That's not an issue. It's just Alpha. We're only going to do surveillance work, and I think it's worth exploring."

"It sounds like an Israeli problem."

"Until it becomes an American one. They continue killing diplomats with an Iranian fingerprint and it will become overwhelming for both of us. I'm talking biblical times overwhelming. If Israel goes to war with Iran, Iran will launch whatever they have to protect their regime—especially if

Tehran had nothing to do with it—and Israel will retaliate."

Left unsaid was that Israel had a nuclear arsenal.

I could see him thinking about it, and drove home the last bit I had. "The note said that the Great Satan would also reap the whirlwind, and now we've lost the American ambassador to the Holy See."

"He died in a car crash."

"Did he? I mean, did he crash all by himself?"

"Nobody's claimed credit for killing him."

"Maybe because he wasn't supposed to go over a cliff. Maybe he was supposed to be killed on the road and his hit got screwed up."

"They'd still claim credit."

"Maybe. I get it's screwy. That's why we're going."

He thought about it for a few seconds, then looked at Knuckles and Brett, saying, "You guys are good with this?"

Brett said, "Hell yeah, sir. We've been sitting on our ass for close to a year because of the pandemic. At this point, I'd be okay going if you told me I was going to get arrested upon landing."

Wolffe turned to me and said, "What about Amena?"

"Veep and Kylie are already at my house. They can stay with her."

Wolffe sighed and said, "So you've got it all figured out. I was wondering why there was a week gap between a wedding rehearsal and the real wedding. Tell me you didn't set all this up in advance and ambush me."

I'd laughed and said, "No, sir, not at all. That

week thing was Jennifer's idea to get you guys some vacation time. That's all. I swear I was as surprised as you when Shoshana broached it."

He'd said, "You'll be back for the wedding? One week?"

I grinned. "Yes, sir. Promise."

"You'll get no Taskforce help on this. Don't be calling my office for reach-back hacking support or analytical help. You're on your own here."

"I get it. Right up until they start killing Americans, right?"

He nodded and said, "Yeah, that would change the equation. Which is why I'm allowing this buffoonery to go."

"Understood . . . but I was thinking about the Rock Star bird . . . since it's leased to Grolier Recovery Services anyway and sitting here in Charleston . . . you know, so I can get home rapidly for the wedding."

He shook his head, but had agreed, a tacit admission that he thought I could potentially do some good.

## CHAPTER 12

Garrett tossed another newspaper on the desk and said, "What the fuck? Why isn't anyone talking about Iran? Every report is that each death is some individual event. It's barely making the front page. The damn killing of the ambassador to the Holy See is already off the news cycle. And unless you're in Paris, nobody's talking about the death of the Shin Bet agent. Even in Paris it's a back-and-forth about getting rid of refugees, not an assassination by Keta'ib Hezbollah."

Michelangelo said, "I know. Nobody's talking about the evidence. It's like it's been hidden."

"That's not going to work for us," said Garrett. "We need the press on this building up the tension so when we do the final hit in Israel, it's a tripwire. We need all the hawks to be actively talking about attacking Iran, making their case. All we have right now is the usual blustering because of rocket attacks in Iraq and the smuggling of weapons into Syria."

Leonardo said, "Surely someone's talking about it. I mean, in the CIA and Mossad. They have to know and have to be discussing it."

"They might be, but that's not going to cut it."

Raphael said, "It'll leak. It always does. Sooner or later, someone's going to leak the connection."

Garrett glared and said, "There *is* no connection to the ambassador. He's categorized as an accidental death."

Raphael shifted in his seat, saying nothing. Michelangelo said, "That wasn't our fault. We couldn't predict he would go full-speed into the wall."

Garrett waved his hand, saying, "I know, but it's frustrating. How are we looking in Bahrain? Did we transfer the funds to Qassim?"

"Not yet. He hasn't passed the new account information. I think he's laying low after the *Ramsad* hit."

"I thought they had to have that money for the target in Bahrain?"

"That's what he said."

"That hit is supposed to be in two days. Either they need the money or they don't."

Leonardo said, "I'll contact him again. Ask what the situation is, but honestly, without the money I don't think that target will be hit in two days."

Garrett thought for a moment, then said, "I agree. We're not sending him any more money. We'll take it to Bahrain ourselves." He turned to Donatello and said, "You'll go. I want our eyes on this to make sure that hit happens like we want. This has to make the news."

Taken aback, Donatello said, "How am I going to do that? I'm a Croatian Catholic."

"You speak Bosnian, right? Spent some time in Tuzla?"

"Yeah, but that doesn't mean anything."

"Sure it does. Tell them you're a Bosniak. A Muslim wanting to help with the cause. They won't know the difference."

"Except I don't know the religion."

"You know it well enough, and Iran has been funding the Bosniaks for years. It fits. They'll believe you if you tell them the Qods Force trained you. Any discrepancies between 'your' version of Islam and theirs, just blame on how it works in Bosnia. They won't know any better. Hell, when I was there with the Special Forces they all drank alcohol."

Donatello slowly nodded, then said, "How on earth will I meet them? I have nothing."

Garrett turned to Leonardo and said, "Contact Qassim and tell him we're taking the money directly to the team in Bahrain. Get the contact information from him and have him set up the meeting."

Leonardo said, "I don't think he has any operational knowledge of the plan. He's just the money conduit."

"Well, he had to pass the money to them somehow, so they have contact. Just have him establish the linkup."

He nodded and Garrett continued, turning back to Donatello: "That hit *has* to make the news with an Iran link. Take a look at their plan and help them where you can. Don't let them do anything stupid. Use your skill."

Nodding, liking the fact that he had been chosen and now getting into the mission, Donatello said, "No issues. I can do that."

Garrett tapped his finger on the desk, then said, "Michelangelo, I want you to go to Zurich immediately. Wait until Qassim has given us the linkup information, then take him out."

Michelangelo said, "Kill him?"

Garrett laughed and said, "No. I meant take him out to dinner. Yes, kill him. They're going to find those Keta'ib Hezbollah cells eventually, and that will lead them to him. He's the only link between the militia and us."

"He's been good to us. Are you sure?"

"Yes, I'm sure. That bastard caused me to get captured in Syria. He's been good on *this* mission, but he deserves some retribution. Once Bahrain is in motion we no longer need him."

All of the Turtles knew the torture Garrett had suffered in Syria, and the rage that had come out of it. In truth, they felt a little survivor's guilt that they hadn't been captured as well.

Michelangelo said, "Can I get a visa that quickly? I'm from Croatia."

"Use the Knights of Malta passport. It's valid for travel to Switzerland without a visa. In fact, use one of the diplomatic passports. It'll allow you to take a weapon without going through customs. Just make sure you only contact us through Zello. No cell calls whatsoever. If you can, put the phone on airplane mode and only use Wi-Fi. And be sure your geolocation feature is on. I want to be able to keep track."

Scribbling furiously in a notebook, Michelangelo finally looked up and nodded, but said nothing, like the rest of the Turtles.

With a rubber band around both index fingers,

Garrett rotated his hands around each other, his eyes looking at the ceiling, lost in thought. Finally, he said, "I'm not sure the Bahrain hit will be enough. We need more press reporting. More splash. The hit in Israel is in five days, and that *has* to trigger the war."

Michelangelo said, "What are you thinking?"

"I'm thinking we need another killing."

"We haven't contracted for that. We don't have a Keta'ib team anywhere that we can leverage, and if we kill the contact we most certainly won't."

"That's fine, I'm talking about one *we* can execute. One we can make sure makes the news with a link to Keta'ib Hezbollah."

"Who are you thinking of?"

"I don't know. You guys figure it out. Do some research. Who can we kill that will make a splash? Maybe someone that we can link to the dead ambassador, get them talking about both killings."

He stood, letting them know the meeting was over. He said, "You two find a target while Michelangelo is in Zurich, but whatever you do, make it spectacular. Something the press can't ignore."

## CHAPTER 13

We began our final approach to a business airport called Payerne, a little under two hours outside of Zurich, and I continued to calm Shoshana about the leaking of the mission to Wolffe.

"I had to at least tell him I was traveling overseas. I mean, really, what was I going to say when he showed up to my house for dinner tonight and I wasn't there?"

Still miffed, she said, "This aircraft is great, and I appreciate it, but you really shouldn't have told him about the passports. You should have just come with me. He will be mad that he wasn't informed by Israeli intelligence of the information I passed to you."

Which, of course, is exactly what had happened, but I wasn't going to tell her that. I said, "He was okay with it. Not good, but okay. But I do have to ask why you guys haven't engaged our intelligence systems."

"I don't know, but if I were to guess, it's because they're fighting about it right now, and my side of the equation wants evidence before we go off with our knives out."

"Good. Because that's exactly what I told him to make him feel better."

She finally smiled and said, "So you play games like we do."

"Not a game. I just wanted to defuse the situation, and it seemed logical. Unlike you guys. You have two dead and no mention on the news that some Iraqi militia is claiming credit. One is a tragic paragliding accident, the other is a random mugging. And yet nobody in official circles in Paris and Switzerland seems to know that. Don't tell me about games."

She said, "We're doing that for a reason. It's the people who hired me. Some in my country are always spoiling for a fight. Trust me, after the death of the Shin Bet head of European Protective Services, they're building up steam. They want to send a message to Iran, and not like the Wrath of God teams. They want to eliminate Iran completely. The only thing holding them back is the fact that we kept the claims of the killings secret. If that hit the news, there would be overwhelming pressure to respond. And that response would require an escalation, when we don't know if what's happening is what it appears."

I said, "You're not worried they'll just leak it?"

"Somewhat, but if they did, it would be treasonous. Right now, that will hold them in check."

I nodded and said, "What do we have to work with in Zurich? Why didn't we go to Paris? Seems like that would be more logical, given the active-duty nature of the target."

"Paris is being handled by Shin Bet. It's a

firestorm. We can't get anything done there. They control everything. The man that was murdered is responsible for the protection of all Israeli assets on the European continent. Trust me, we won't get anywhere with them."

"So they were responsible for the security of the *Ramsad* as well?"

She heard the question, thought about it, then said, "Yes, actually, that's correct, but because the head of the European service was killed, we'll have an easier time in Interlaken. They are getting their just due for allowing him to be killed, but the Shin Bet is consumed with the killing in Paris. We will have no interface with them."

I saw her face draw inward, thinking, then she said, "Nobody cares about a retired person. Only the active ones."

I said, "Well, maybe we can change that. Get some justice for him."

She leaned forward and took my hand. "That's why I wanted you, Nephilim. You and the team. You don't care about politics. Only the truth. And I think this truth is going to be something people don't want to see."

As always, her gaze was disconcerting. I pulled my hand away and said, "Turn that shit off."

She laughed and I said, "I'll help you with the truth, but only if it's the *truth*. Don't pull me into some Mossad political fight."

She said, "I don't do politics. You should know that by now."

And I did. In her earlier days, she'd been

what's called a "honey trap," where she'd entice a Palestinian terrorist into bed so her hit team could kill him. She'd used her weird ability to read people and realized that the men she was setting up for the kill were innocent. And the man doing the killing wasn't working for Israeli security, but because of profit. Black market profit. She'd turned him in and he had been cut free, but she had still been cast aside as a some-one who couldn't be trusted within the Mossad. She'd eventually landed on Aaron's team as an outcast. Aaron had recognized her talents and her frailty because of the way she'd been used. She definitely didn't do politics, but I knew how she felt about the dead *Ramsad*, and vengeance was a different story.

We'd crossed paths on a separate mission with her original team leader—the one who forced her to sleep with innocent men so he could mur-der them. She'd pretty much stopped Europe from going into World War III, and as a return favor, I'd help set up the team leader because he had been involved in the plot.

And she'd slaughtered him.

I leaned back and said, "So, where do we go from here? What are we doing when we land?"

"This fight is biblical. I can feel it. We're going to find the man who killed the *Ramsad*, but that's just a first step. He killed him for a reason, and it's prophecy."

I said, "Please, stop that. Let's work with what we know, not some crazy theory about biblical prophecies. Is that okay?"

She squinted at me, then said, "Okay. If you want me to start questioning your judgment, what are we going to do with the American pilots flying this plane? They don't have Schengen passports, and I don't understand why we didn't just fly straight to Zurich. It won't matter where we land, they'll still have problems."

The Schengen Area in Europe was a no-border zone encompassing multiple countries where anyone living within it could travel freely. Even in the time of COVID. Since the vaccine rollout, and Israel's incredible response, they'd been included as free travelers as if they were on the Schengen list, and didn't require a visa. Americans, unfortunately, while also not needing a visa, were required to quarantine for fourteen days.

I said, "No, you're wrong. Zurich would have raised a fuss because it's a central hub. The airport we've chosen won't. And beyond that, I don't want this aircraft anywhere near where we might operate. That's why we aren't flying into Zurich. The place we're going to has overnight accommodations, and it's pretty close to the target area. It's a clean break from us and the aircraft."

"That still doesn't solve the problem of the pilots."

"We all have negative PCR tests, and they'll have to quarantine at the airport, but that's not our problem, since we're 'Israeli.' They'll let them in, and then let them stay. They just won't get to do the usual flyboy stuff. They sit until we call."

She nodded and said, "So we have Taskforce help here?"

I laughed and said, "No, we most definitely don't, at least until there is an American threat. What do you have? What are we going to do here?"

"We have the location of the refugee sponsor of the paraglider. He's an older guy, an expat Syrian who fled the fighting. The killer stayed with him. The police have cleared him of any involvement, but they don't have the information we do. Because of it, they've determined the whole paragliding thing was an accident."

"Even with the other guy being shot in the head? The paraglider who was originally supposed to take him up?"

"His case is being treated separately, as a stand-alone murder. They don't want to hurt the recovering tourism industry. Israel didn't push, and they were happy to let it go."

"So this graybeard is connected to the attack? Or just a guy that's now involved in something he has no idea about?"

"That's what we need to figure out, but he's connected. He's the conduit for the money, I'm sure. He'll have information."

The pilot rang the intercom, then said, "We're coming into final. Everyone needs to put on their seat belts. Thank you."

Jennifer woke up, then leaned back into her seat, stretching like a cat. She saw me looking at Shoshana and said, "You guys make up?"

Shoshana gave her little wolf grin and said,

"We were never in a fight. Pike knows better than that."

Jennifer leaned into me and said, "Told you this would work out."

I said, "Let's wait until we get on the ground before we say that. Anytime we do anything with Carrie, bodies seem to follow."

## CHAPTER 14

Qassim Khaled woke up to his phone bleating out a tone. One that he recognized was from his sugar daddy. The man paying the bills.

It was a Zello call, meaning the voice message would be saved to his history like a chat message. He thought about just letting it sit, but knew he couldn't.

He groggily rolled over, picked up the phone, went to the saved history, and hit play. He heard, "Are you there? It's the Turtles. Answer the phone because the money is in jeopardy."

That woke him up. He slid over his bed in his grimy undershirt, put his feet on the floor, and initiated the Zello push-to-talk feature. End-to-end encrypted and running over the internet, he knew that nobody hunting him could hear what he was about to say.

He clicked on a channel called Ninja Turtles and pressed the push-to-talk button, saying, "I'm here. I'm here."

"This is Leonardo. The one you met in Palmyra. You remember me?"

He closed his eyes, trying to recall the time he'd brokered the penetration of Jabhat al Nusra's area of Palmyra for the Knights of Malta. And he remembered. The man on the phone was the one that looked like Matt Damon. Blue eyes and lots of muscles.

He said, "Of course. Yes. Are you sending the money?"

"No. We're not sending any more money. We're going to take it to the men directly."

Valiantly trying to clear the cobwebs in his head, Qassim said, "That's not how this works. I have the conduit for transfer. You give it to me, and I give it to them. That's what we agreed."

"That's not happening this time. I need to meet them. I need contact information."

"That's not what I do."

Qassim heard the heat through the phone. "It's *exactly* what you do. You did it in Syria and were good at it. You'll do it again now. Or we'll cut off our arrangement."

Qassim sagged on the bed and said, "I'm thinking we should do that anyway. There was a death here, and I've been roped into the investigation. An Israeli was killed by a man I let stay in my house. I want no part of that. I'll transfer money, but I don't want to be involved with what that money does."

Qassim heard a chuckle over the phone, then, "Are you serious here? We've paid you an enormous sum to help us, and we appreciate what you've done, but you can't just turn off the spigot because you feel the water is too hot. I need the connection in Bahrain."

"How am I supposed to do that? All I do is

transfer the money you give me. I've done every-thing you've wanted."

"No, you haven't. In Syria, you took our cash and then had my boss captured. You owe more than money here. And if you want me to extract that payment, I will."

Qassim rubbed his face, saying nothing. He heard, "You still there?"

"Yes, yes, I'm still here. But I don't want to be involved in this. It's not my fault that things went bad in Syria."

"You *are* involved, whether you like it or not. Just set up a meeting."

Qassim said, "I can try. But I can't promise. All I can do is pass the information; whether they want to hear it or not is another story."

"That's all I'm asking. You tell them I'm com-ing with the money, and then tell me where to meet them. That's all."

Qassim closed out the chat, stumbled to a chair, and sat down, thinking. This wasn't where he wanted to be. A dentist by trade, he'd built a lucrative business in Aleppo, catering to the high-class clients of the regime. Then the Arab Spring had exploded. He'd spent seven months living hand to mouth, but was lucky that he was single, without having to worry about a family. Everyone else he knew was hunkered down eating the leftovers from dogs to survive.

His first break happened when a client of the regime needed his teeth fixed, right in the mid-dle of a war zone. He'd done so, and had been granted access to other clientele. The next thing he knew, he was treating patrons from all sides of the fight, from Al Qaida to ISIS, each patient an important figure in the war. Because of his connections and absolute neutrality, he began helping all sides with something other than dental work. The selling of fuel oil, the brokering of ransom demands, the slipping of gold out of the country . . . until he became a middleman for everyone.

It reached the point where he'd become indispensable to all sides, a broker who could deal with any faction, which is when Garrett had met him.

All the Knights of Malta wanted to do was provide medical services to the downtrodden in the mess of misery inside Syria, and Garrett knew they could do that with bullets, or with dollars. He'd chosen dollars, and Qassim had paved the way, allowing the medical personnel to operate without fear of attack, brokering truces among the warring factions.

It had worked out well, right up until Garrett had been captured.

Six years after that awful spell, Garrett had contacted him again, this time wanting to contact the leadership of Keta'ib Hezbollah, the militia from Iraq that was now growing its tentacles worldwide. He wasn't sure he could do it, because he no longer worked in that world. After Syria had devolved into a prehistoric mess of survival of the fittest, Qassim had taken his money and fled to Switzerland as a refugee, leaving behind all of the death and destruction.

When Garrett had called, Qassim had first thought he was being set up to be killed, because he'd basically brokered the truce between the warring factions that had ultimately captured Garrett, leading to his horrendous torture. In effect, he'd taken Garrett's money, then not come through on his promises, leaving Garrett in the hands of the very men he was supposed to pay off. But it turned out that the money was real, and all Garrett really wanted was exactly what he said—contacts into the hierarchy of Keta'ib Hezbollah.

He still had his black book, and while a lot of the numbers no longer existed, either because the owner had a new phone or had been obliterated in a drone strike, he'd managed to work his way up the ladder until he was speaking with the leadership. And Garrett's money had done the talking.

The men he'd contacted thought he was representing the Iranian regime, and had taken the money as if he were a colonel in the Qods Force directing attacks against the Great Satan. He remembered when they'd actually come back to ask him for clearance to kill the man in Interlaken, and he'd been frozen in fear.

All he did was pass the money. He knew Garrett was up to no good, using the funds to assassinate others, but Qassim was just a conduit. A middleman. That was all. He was just making a living. He wished he'd never answered the phone when Garrett had called, but he felt a level of guilt because of what had happened to him.

Leonardo was correct in one respect—he *did* know how to contact the men in Bahrain. It just wouldn't be easy or fast.

He opened his laptop and double-clicked on an application called SSuite Picsel Security, a steganography program designed to hide data inside an otherwise innocuous file. In this case, a JPEG digital photo. It asked him for a carrier file and he pulled one up, a JPEG of him in Switzerland posing down by the river. He loaded the file, then typed out a message in the chat window beneath it. When he was done, he hit "encrypt" and the text message was buried in the ones and zeroes of the picture. He looked at the picture, seeing himself happy on the banks of the flowing water. The promise of a life he believed he was earning when he fled Syria. A life he now realized he would never have.

He downloaded the encrypted file to a thumb drive, and then, for the first time ever, he downloaded the original picture onto the same thumb drive. That was a tradecraft mistake, but not one he thought was catastrophic.

The program he used wasn't complex, and wouldn't hide Word documents, Excel spreadsheets, or maps. It only allowed him to camouflage simple text messages that were typed into the program itself, but that was good enough. It wasn't like he was trying to coordinate operations using GPS data, and this program had a valuable simplicity: the only way to decrypt it was to have the original JPEG file, doing a reverse of what he'd just done. In effect, the picture itself was the password. Without it, the text was lost forever.

Usually, he'd send the unencrypted JPEG first, then send the encrypted file later to break up the signature, but he didn't have the time for that now. He needed an answer without waiting a day between transmissions. It was a risk, but without the program, nobody would be able to decrypt the file. The only strange thing would be an email with two copies of the same picture— one slightly larger than the other.

He palmed the thumb drive and then began his walk to the hotel across the river. In no way did he want his own computer to transmit the pictures over the shaky Wi-Fi of the apartment he rented. No telling who was watching that. Better to do it in an environment where anyone at all could access the computer.

He put on his jacket, skipped down the stairs, and exited out onto the cloistered streets of old-town Zurich. Full of college students who refused to wear a mask and tourists who wouldn't go to the bathroom without one, it was the perfect place to blend in. An eclectic mix that allowed him to swim among the population without being seen.

Except for the fact that he had a name. And that name was tied into the death of a member of the Mossad.

## CHAPTER 15

Sitting at an outdoor café on the Rathause-brucke promenade in the old-town section of Zurich, I was enjoying the June breeze coming off the Limmat River, patiently waiting on some activity from the target building while I licked my ice cream cone. Truthfully, I was just enjoying the ability to travel again, and didn't really think anything was going to happen here. At least for Jennifer and me. We'd left the hard work to Aaron and Shoshana—if they even had the correct intelligence.

After landing at the Payerne airport, we cleared customs relatively easily—while I sweated the whole Israeli passport thing. We'd had no issues, including our American pilots, the negative PCR COVID test the one big thing authorities wanted to see. The pilots had been happy to learn that the quarantine was now only a five-day wait instead of fourteen, and we'd remained at the airport until they officially had rooms at the on-site hotel. I didn't have the heart to tell them that the whole mission might be over before they were allowed to leave their room.

We'd rented a couple of Range Rovers and set

out for Zurich, two hours away, planning as we went. Through a Mossad dossier, Shoshana and Aaron had the location of a man called Qassim Khaled, and they were convinced he was a conduit for the money flow for the killing of the retired *Ramsad*. They knew the suicide pilot had stayed in his apartment, and also knew that Qassim had fled Syria as a refugee years before meeting the pilot. Meaning they thought the two were connected on the battlefield. They had a photo of the guy and an address.

Other than that, they had nothing. Just a guy with a past who might have been connected to a killing in Interlaken.

I'll admit the suicide pilot's stay was a little strange, but it was easily explained by other events. The pilot was fleeing persecution just like Qassim had done, and he had to have a place to stay once he arrived. Qassim might be Doctor Evil, but then again, he could just be collateral damage because of a shared hardship. I had a Syrian refugee who could be blamed for just such a connection. I'd seen the mighty United States make linkages the same way—seeing a forest fire when there was only a whiff of smoke—but I was willing to help, if only to sit by a river in Zurich and eat ice cream.

Jennifer licked her cone and a bit ran down her hand. She raised it to her mouth, cleaned it off, and said, "You think this is all BS, don't you?"

I took a bite of my ice cream and said, "Yep. I think it's bullshit."

She said, "I've never seen Shoshana be wrong. When she has an intuition, it's right. There's something here."

I said, "Really? She tried to kill me in Istanbul when her intuition told her I was the bad guy."

Jennifer smiled and said, "You *were* the bad guy. You ripped her off of a moving motorcycle. And if memory serves, she quickly learned otherwise."

I said, "Okay, I agree. There is something here, but it's not the big conspiracy they think it is. This guy is probably running some coyote scam to get refugees into Switzerland, and now he's going to get burned because one of them ended up being a terrorist."

She nodded, going back to her cone. I said, "Hey, at the end of the day, we're in Zurich, paid for by Israel, eating ice cream in the old town. Can't beat that."

She said, "Aaron and Shoshana are outside his door right now. They believe, and we should, too. At least until this is over one way or the other."

I turned to her and said, "Seriously? You're giving *me* advice on staying alert here? You think I'm slacking because I don't think this will go anywhere?"

Chagrined, she said, "Well, you seem to be enjoying the ice cream more than the mission."

I laughed and said, "Don't take my skepticism of the strategic mission as slacking on the tactical side. Getting into his apartment is *not* bullshit. It's volatile, and we need to protect them, so I'll do that without regard to what I think."

Qassim lived in a rat warren of a seventeenth-century building above a consignment clothing shop called Blenda Vintage, the surroundings a maze of stairs and apartments right in the middle of the old town on the east bank of the Limmat River. The mission was fairly simple: Aaron and Shoshana would trigger when the target left, wait for the roadblock teams to pick him up, then they'd break into the apartment to search for evidence that he's a bad guy.

The way the apartment was situated, he'd have only two ways to go to get to the city—south, toward us, or north, toward where Knuckles and Brett were sitting on the only other bridge within walking distance over the Limmat River, where the city center was located. We knew he didn't have a car, and we surmised that when he left his place, he would travel west, toward the city center.

In a perfect world, we'd have the forces to cover all avenues of approach, but we were a little light, so we did some analytical work and decided where to position. If we were wrong, and he went east, away from the city center, we'd just re-cock and try again, this time positioning ourselves to box him going that way.

Surveillance in and of itself is a shadow game. You don't want to force the issue with aggressive actions to find the target, because he or she will invariably find you from those same actions. Patience is the name of the game, and missed opportunities help to build the pattern of life we needed to know.

Our job, outside of eating ice cream, was to keep Qassim in sight while Aaron and Shoshana penetrated his apartment. Basically, we were to be the early warning to let them know if they had to abort. An easy assignment—especially since I got to sit in Zurich's old town with my wife, licking a frozen treat.

Jennifer wrapped another napkin around her cone in a losing battle to keep it from melting before she could finish. She said, "What if she's right? What if there's something going on here? Do you think we can get the Taskforce to engage?"

I chuckled and said, "You mean beyond letting us take the Rock Star bird? No. They'd better find the diabolical plan to start World War Three before Wolffe will engage. He's got enough political bullshit to deal with besides telling them he let us freelance using Israeli passports. It would have to be pretty big."

Jennifer glanced at me, and I could see she wanted to say something. I said, "What? Can't we just sit here and enjoy this?"

She said, "You're always asking for a fight, and now you're just wanting to eat ice cream."

That sort of ticked me off. I said, "I didn't ask to come here. They interrupted our wedding, for God's sake. We were supposed to spend a week in Charleston with our friends."

She grinned and took my hand, letting the ice cream run down her other arm. She said, "You are *so* full of crap. You *wanted* this to happen. I saw you at the rehearsal."

I reached up and wiped her arm with a napkin, saying, "I didn't want this to happen, but you have to admit it's pretty cool."

She laughed and said, "I *knew* it. I knew it."

I grinned and said, "Come on. This is nothing.

No shots fired, no danger. We get to spend a weekend in Zurich and we don't even have to pay for it. Tell me you don't think this is cool, too."

She said, "Yeah, right up until it's not."

And then my phone buzzed with a text.

*He's on the move. Headed south.*

Which meant toward our location. I looked up from the phone to see her reading the same text. I said, "Looks like vacation time is over."

## CHAPTER 16

We went across the promenade so we'd be facing in the direction of his approach, both of us pulling up the target's picture on our phones for a final memorization of what he looked like.

He was an older guy, about sixty-five, with salt-and-pepper hair. Truthfully, he looked a lot like the Iranian general Qasem Soleimani—the guy we'd eliminated in a drone strike. Bushy black eyebrows and a neatly trimmed gray beard. He could have been a university professor. Or Doctor Evil.

Time would tell.

We finished our cones sitting right next to the river, waiting on him to appear.

He did not.

On my earpiece I heard someone whisper, "We're breaching. We're breaching. Status."

I said, "I don't have him. No breach. No breach."

Jennifer slid her hand down my arm and I looked at her. She flicked her eyes, and there he was, walking down the promenade like he was just another tourist.

Shoshana said, "Pike, find him. He's there."

I said, "I have him. I say again, I have him. Clear to breach."

We stood up after he passed, falling in behind him as he crossed the river.

His pace was a little bit less than someone with a place to be and a little bit more than a person just enjoying a stroll, but with the small crowd on the promenade, it didn't really matter. We could stay behind him with little difficulty and keep him in sight.

I called Knuckles, gave him our location, and told him to close in on the far side of the river to give us some options to keep an eye on him.

The target wound around, eventually walking by the famed Saint Peter's Church, the large clock in the bell tower shadowing his moves, before heading again toward the river, back the way he had come.

Which was strange.

He threaded through the streets until he hit an avenue called Schipfe, right along the water, passing by the promenade we'd just crossed over.

Stranger still.

He picked up his pace along the river's edge and then took a left in a narrow alley. Before he turned, he did a brief glance behind, surveying the river walk, which gave me some concern. I pulled Jennifer next to me on the water's edge, pretending to watch the spectacular view. I gave him thirty seconds, then went to the entrance of the alley, seeing a cascade of stairs, the buildings so close it wasn't even an alley. It looked more like an indoor fire escape in a New York apartment.

It was a choke point that would advertise anyone who entered behind him, the ancient stairwell so narrow any target above would see who was behind. I saw his back rising up the stairs at a trot and immediately retreated before he turned around and saw me.

I waited a bit, and then started to go again, the mission of keeping him in sight for Shoshana the foremost in my mind. Jennifer pulled my arm saying, "You want to follow him up that? We'll be burned for anything else. Call Knuckles and have him interdict."

Her words broke through my mission focus. It dawned on me. *That son of a bitch is conducting a surveillance detection route.*

I clicked my earpiece, saying, "Knuckles, Blood, what's your status?"

I heard, "On the west side, moving your way. About thirty seconds out."

"This guy is running an SDR. I can't follow. Get on him."

I sent them my location through the phone and waited. I saw the realization blossom in Jennifer's eyes. She said, "Shoshana's right. This guy *is* bad."

I smiled and said, "Maybe. Maybe you're just paranoid."

Standing there with her now-melted ice cream cone, looking out over the Limmat River, she hip-bumped me and said, "I guess being paranoid was worth it."

I laughed and said, "Still got to prove it."

I contacted Aaron and said, "Target is still on the move. Temporarily unsighted due to terrain.

Got the other team about to lock on, but they haven't yet. What's your status?"

He came back and said, "We're in. Not a lot here. We have control of his computer and the only thing suspicious is a steganography program."

"Okay, keep working it. I'll let you know if we lose control. If they don't find him in five minutes, get out."

"Roger all."

I then contacted Knuckles, saying, "Do you have him?"

He said, "No. Unsighted."

I turned to Jennifer and said, "Get up there. As fast as you can." I knew if he was conducting a surveillance detection route, he'd have pinged on me instead of Jennifer. And I was sick of waiting around.

She nodded at me and took off like a gazelle, her long legs pumping up the stairs like she was trying to power a generator. She reached the top, and said, "Unsighted."

I went to the stairs myself, and started jogging up them saying, "Find him. He's close."

Brett came on, saying, "I got five-five. I have the target. He's on a street called Rollengasse. Still moving, but looking around. I'm ahead of him, so no threat. But he's definitely running an SDR."

I said, "Can we come up?"

"Yeah, bring it. Knuckles is down the street so he's boxed."

I contacted Aaron and said, "Target acquired. Continue the mission."

As I reached Jennifer I heard, "Roger. Still working the room. Let us know when he's coming back."

Jennifer said, "I told you. This guy is up to no good."

I said, "Yeah, probably so, but let's make sure it's not just some coyote refugee bullshit before we go crazy and say he's the next bin Laden. Keep working the problem."

We went up the stairs, faced a split, and I glanced at the location of Brett's phone on our moving map. I said, "Right."

Jennifer went that way and Brett said, "He's on the move again. No longer looking at the staircase. I'm on him."

Knuckles said, "I see you. I see you. I have backup."

We followed the blue icons on our phone without seeing the target again, winding through the narrow alleys of the old town, until both of the icons ended up together, outside of a building.

I said, "What's happening?"

"He went inside a hotel called Kindli. Knuckles is inside keeping eyes on."

We raced to the location, found Brett, and I said, "What's he doing?"

He said, "No idea. Why's it matter? All we have to do is keep him in sight to let the Israelis do their thing."

I glanced at Jennifer, thinking about what she'd said earlier, then at the door, and said, "Because I think he's bad. We need to get on him." I went to the net and said, "Knuckles, Knuckles, where are you?"

"In the lobby. Target went deeper. He can't leave without passing me. What's up?"

I said, "Did he go to a room?"

"No. The elevators are in my sight. He went down a hallway. No idea what's there, but he didn't go to a room."

I said, "He's doing something here. This is no longer tag and trace. It's penetration."

"You want me to approach?"

"No. I'm clean. You're not. Stay where you are to pick him up again. I'm doing an intrusion. I'll go by you and stay until he's gone."

I turned to Jennifer and Brett and said, "I don't know what that guy's doing, but it's not good. You guys have the box out here. Knuckles is the trigger. You follow when he leaves."

Brett nodded, glanced at the street, and said, "I'll take north; Koko, you've got south."

It was happening so fast that I didn't even get a chance to address Jennifer directly. She looked at me and said, "Yeah, I got south. I *told* you."

I grinned and said, "Yeah, you did." I pecked her lips and said, "Don't screw up the follow. Aaron and Carrie are still inside."

Brett rolled his eyes, saying, "When do I get a kiss on the lips?"

I rotated to him, leaning into his face, and he batted me away, saying, "Get that shit out of here."

Jennifer laughed and I turned to the hotel entrance, saying over my shoulder, "You had your chance."

I entered a long hallway leading to a lobby. I reached the front desk and saw Knuckles sitting on a small chair eating peanuts out of a bowl. The area was regal, in a shabby sort of way, meaning it was probably the heat in 1980, but was now living on borrowed time. It was much smaller than I'd envisioned, the lobby no larger than a kitchen. I'd expected to be able to find Knuckles, do a quick data dump away from everyone else, then continue, but that was impossible in the small space.

I stopped at the front desk, saw the elevators, but didn't know where to go.

The receptionist said, "Can I help you?"

Caught off guard at the cloistered size of the lobby, I said, "Bathroom?"

She smiled and pointed, saying, "Right down that hallway."

In my earpiece I heard, "Did you not think to ask me where to go before you entered? Seriously?"

I started walking, knowing Knuckles was absolutely correct. Out of earshot of the receptionist I said, "Okay, big surveillance detective, where do I go?"

"Go to the bathroom just like you asked. He went that way."

I walked down the hallway lined with pictures and artifacts from when the hotel was a player and saw our target standing next to an ancient computer. And I mean standing. They had a computer fastened to a wall at chest level on a shelf with a cheap inkjet printer to the right, which I guess was their version of a business center, and he was typing something. I went behind him and saw that he had a thumb drive loaded into a USB port. He was pounding on the keys furiously, but stopped when I approached, hunching over the screen to block it.

I continued on to the bathroom, seeing only that he was using ProtonMail, an end-to-end encrypted email system with servers located here, in Switzerland. Nobody used that as an individual contact method, because it required everyone you emailed to have the same application. It was analogous to everyone you wanted to call being required to have a special phone that would only work with the one you had. The people who used Proton were journalists transmitting the next blockbuster investigation, dissidents trying to coordinate activities against an authoritarian state, paranoids afraid of the black helicopter coming to get them—or terrorists.

I found the men's room and entered. I clicked on the net, saying, "I'm stuck in the bathroom. Let me know when he leaves."

Jennifer said, "What's he doing?"

I said, "He's Doctor Evil. Shoshana is right."

## CHAPTER 17

S itting on a wicker chair that had seen better days, Salim Kalibani waited for the Proton encryption to load, then downloaded the two pictures that had been sent, watching the computer bar take forever due to the spotty Wi-Fi.

Unlike the upper end of Manama, Bahrain, which had excellent broadband Wi-Fi like any other developed nation, the close-packed concrete jungle of the slum he was in, called Sanabis, had to rely on a derelict system the cinder-block apartment provided. While other sections of Bahrain had generous government infrastructure, there was no such thing for this section of the city. As the location for repeated uprisings against the monarchy, the punishment was an oxymoron: you'll continue living in the slums for your transgressions, which only increased the outrage for the very people that lived there. A perfect hiding spot for Salim and his men.

A slight man with a whisp of a beard that made him look vaguely Asian, he smiled when the small clock finally showed the pictures had downloaded to his laptop. He booted up the steganography application, loaded the picture from Qassim into the program, and like magic, the application extracted the text message, displaying it below the picture. He didn't like what it revealed. He needed *money*, not a new compatriot for the cause.

Three other men in the room were waiting on him to finish the task, two sprawled on a dilapidated couch and one sitting in an overstuffed La-Z-Boy, the stuffing starting to seep out through the cracked vinyl. The ones on the couch were playing a *Call of Duty* video game, acting like they were interested in what Salim was diligently working on while continuing to slay on the small HDTV Salim owned. The one on the La-Z-Boy waited with more interest. When Salim remained silent, staring at the screen, he said, "What's up? Did we get the money?"

"Yes and no."

"What's that mean?"

"The contact says a man is going to deliver the money personally. A specialist. A killer. He wants to make sure our attack is solid. They don't trust us."

Bahrain was an island nation just off the coast of Saudi Arabia, with a single causeway leading from one country to the other. Its biggest claim to fame was as the host of the United States Fifth Fleet, the naval behemoth that was responsible for patrolling the Hormuz Strait, where the majority of oil exports passed—a headquarters that guaranteed Bahrain's survival whenever any dissident organization raised its ugly head. Because of the strategic nature of the location,

Bahrain could count on the United States to turn a blind eye to any transgressions from the ruling monarchy.

Not unlike a few countries in the Arab world, Bahrain had a disparity between the rulers and the ruled. In this case, the majority of the population was Shia, but the monarchy of the island was Sunni—a fact that caused friction on a daily basis. In 2011, when the Arab Spring was running amok in the Arab world, the Shia rose up, demanding a greater voice in the government. It grew to a point where the monarchy was on the ragged edge of being overthrown, until Saudi Arabia invaded across the causeway, clamping down on the protests in a brutal way. It wouldn't do to have a Shia majority running a country right next to Saudi Arabia. The monarchy would need to be propped up at all costs. And was.

Iran saw the unrest, and like that theocracy does all over the world, it began to invest in it. The governing body was Sunni, but the majority of the population was Shia, just like Iran, and the Shia majority under the boot of a Sunni minority took that help from Iran wholesale. All of the men in Salim's room had been sent to train in Iraq, under the tutelage of the Qods Force of Iran and the militia known as Keta'ib Hezbollah. They'd learned how to build bombs, how to communicate securely, who to assassinate to promote the cause, and other things. In short, how to instill fear in the ruling class, and to begin banging on the levers of power to cause the monarchy to fall. So far they'd failed in that task, but now they had a target that would take it to the next level.

Salim said, "They're sending us someone from Bosnia. Some guy who apparently knows more than we do."

The man on the La-Z-Boy leaned forward. Named Khan, he was a squat, burly hulk, looking more like a bear than a human, right down to the coarse hair on his arms and face. He said, "Why is that a bad thing? Maybe we could use his expertise."

Khalid, one of the video game players, punched a couple of buttons, rotating his arms with the controller in the air, fighting an invisible army and saying, "Why do we need him?"

Salim said, "I don't know. But I guess Iran does."

Barely out of his teenage years, Khalid was the youngest man on the team. Wearing a flat-brimmed baseball cap and a Wu-Tang Clan T-shirt, he didn't instill confidence in others with his affection for Western culture, but he had proven himself in training and in real-world operations. He was respected in the room, despite his affinity for video games and other sins of the Great Satan. He said, "We've followed the Fifth Fleet commander for a month. We can kill him without their help."

Salim wanted to agree, because the text from the steganography program was an insult, but he also knew they couldn't do it on their own. They were at the end of their rope, both fiscally and tactically.

He said, "We ran out of money a month ago. We have no idea what he's doing now. The last time we paid that clerk in the office was five weeks ago. The last schedule we have is two months old. Yeah, we could have killed him then, but we didn't get the word to do so. Now we have that order, and we have the man bringing the money to make it happen."

Khalid set the controller on the couch and said, "Why didn't we just kill him then? When we had the chance? Why did we wait until we have to start all over? Do they not care about retribution for the general?"

Salim said, "I don't know, but I'm sure it was for a good reason. When they assassinated him it set everything back. But now it's going forward again."

Jamal, the other video game player, said, "Who are they sending?"

"Someone who has a specialty for assassinations. Someone from Bosnia. A killer."

"What are we supposed to do?"

"Meet him. The contact is asking for linkup information. He'll have the money, which we need. We can decide whether we want his expertise or not. Where should we do it?"

Khalid said, "Near the causeway. As far away from Manama as possible. Don't have him fly in. Have him fly to Khobar in Saudi Arabia. If he gets rolled up there, it won't taint us. If he doesn't, and he makes it across the border, we'll meet him in a vehicle here."

Salim nodded and said, "That makes sense. I'll

use that petrol station right across the causeway. The one with the restaurant just past the toll-booth. If he makes it past that, he'll be clean."

He typed up a short message, giving specific instructions, then said, "What picture do I use this time? You guys want to be famous?"

CHAPTER 18

Inside the basement headquarters of the
Knights of Malta, Garrett read his response
to the phone text, satisfied it held nothing in-
criminating. Well, nothing that he couldn't clean
up afterward by taking her phone. He hit send
and said, "We're on for tonight. At her place."

Raphael smiled and said, "So you liked the
idea?"

"Yeah. Yeah I did. This is the statement we
need, and we have the connections to make it
happen without a lot of work."

Meaning *he* had the connections.

He turned to look at his computer screen, the
image of a thirty-something woman with a bi-
ography from the U.S. State Department. Her
name was Gabrielle Hernandez, and she was
the chargé d'affaires of the U.S. mission to the
United Nations agencies in Rome.

Known as the world headquarters for food
and agriculture, the United Nations agencies
in Rome were involved with every single humanitarian disaster on the globe, from Yemen
to Myanmar, and the Knights of Malta had
dealt with them extensively in Syria, helping

them wade through the myriad militias fighting each other to deliver life-giving sustenance to the people just trying to survive the war. It was a goal that both the United Nations and the Knights of Malta wanted to see happen. Which is where he'd met Gabrielle.

He felt bad about the target, but couldn't fault Raphael for the choice. She was someone they'd both dealt with in Syria, which meant they could design a meeting, and she was also of such importance that her death would not be overlooked by the press. Especially the way they intended to do it.

Garrett turned from the computer, held up his phone, and said, "It's at her residence in the Eurosky Tower. Thank God she still had the same cell number. I've been there before, on Knights' business. She's on the twenty-seventh floor."

"Why did she agree to the meeting? What did you tell her?"

"Only that we need some new help with the UN. Just paperwork stuff. She asked if we could come to her office at the U.S. embassy and I told her I wouldn't be free until after business hours. She agreed to meet in her residence."

Donatello said, "Good. Makes it easier."

"Where do we stand with Bahrain?" said Garrett. "Are we in play there or what?"

Leonardo said, "The message has been sent. Just waiting on the response."

Garrett looked at Donatello and said, "Are you good to go? When they send the linkup, can you fake it? Being Muslim, I mean?"

"Yeah, I can fake it. I read a book on Islam. I can fake the prayers and other things, but not for long."

"It won't take long. Just remember, you're not from Saudi Arabia or Iraq. Any quirks are because you're from Bosnia."

Donatello nodded. Garrett looked at his watch and said, "We need to go. It's a forty-minute drive."

An hour later, they were winding through the very same EUR neighborhood where Garrett had left the slain bodies, headed to the one skyscraper in all of Rome, the Eurosky Tower.

Completed in 2013, it wasn't without controversy, as every building in Rome by law must remain lower than the basilica of the Holy See. It didn't matter that the building in question was almost an hour away from the Vatican. Rome had its prestige to keep in mind, but that didn't stop the real estate mavens trying to make a buck. Built as a "live-work-play" concept in an area named the "Europark" business park, it was a supposedly green building, with giant solar panels on the roof of the tower and multiple amenities to entice a potential resident to travel south from the city center to live.

Looping through the EUR neighborhood on Via Cristoforo Colombo, they crossed a lake that spread across a park, then by the Airstream trailer, still surrounded by police tape.

Raphael said, "Did you see that? Apparently, there's some sicko out here killing women because he can." He paused, then said, "I'd like to meet that man one day. Show him some justice."

Garrett watched the Airstream trailer disappear behind them, then said, "How is that different from what we're about to do?"

Taken aback, Raphael said, "We aren't taking life for the pleasure of it. We're doing it for a greater purpose. We're bringing about the second coming and ridding the world of heretics and unbelievers. Those dead women helped no one and the man who did it was not working with God. We're creating paradise, not murdering unsuspecting innocents."

Garrett smiled, his lips curling with little joy. He said, "We're doing both. In order to create paradise, some unsuspecting innocents will be martyred, but don't think for a minute that He will forgive us for our sins. We'll surely suffer just as the martyrs we have taken."

The three Turtles remained silent at his words, the tension growing thick, all of them unsure how to answer. Garrett saw them glancing at each other and realized he might have overstepped his leadership role by explaining the truth to them. Sometimes it was better to keep the troops about to fight in the dark on the odds of survival. Something he'd learned early on in Iraq.

He broke the silence, getting them back into the mission. "The letter is ready to go?"

"Yes. But I'm not sure why we didn't just use the one we had planned for the ambassador. What's up with all the homosexual stuff? Is that necessary?"

"Gabrielle is a lesbian. Islam hates that. It will

factor in, especially by the means of death. Trust me, it's necessary."

Raphael nodded, and Garrett said, "And the *Misbaha*? We have that ready to drop?"

Donatello said, "The what?"

Exasperated, Garrett said, "The Muslim prayer beads. The ones you were given in Syria as a gift. I want to leave them as well. Leave no doubt about who did this."

Donatello said, "Oh, yeah. I've got them."

Garrett turned to him and said, "You're about to fly to the cell in Bahrain. I would expect you to know the Islamic term for them just like you do the rosary. You said you studied."

Donatello ducked his head, saying, "I did study. I'm ready. If it had come up, I would have done what you said and simply told them we didn't use them in Bosnia."

They exited the expansive tree-lined park in the EUR, passing by the PalaLottomatica sports and music arena, the Eurosky Tower stabbing the sky on their right about a mile away. Raphael changed the subject, saying, "Are we going to leave the letter in the apartment?"

"No. I want a statement. We'll meet her, she'll offer drinks, and then we'll go out onto the balcony."

He continued, telling them his plan and dividing up tasks. They nodded, asking questions about escape and other details. By the time they pulled into the circle drive of the Eurosky, they were ready.

## CHAPTER 19

They parked out front, giving the valet a story of why they were here and that they had permission to leave the vehicle where it was. He didn't question them, and they left the car where it stood. They went into the lobby of the residential tower, seeing an architecture of a modern bent, all glass, understated wood, and gleaming chrome, but far removed from the Italian historic flair.

Garrett approached the security desk, gave his name and the person whom he was meeting, but not the one that he was actually seeing. In order to reach Gabrielle's apartment clean, he had to get past the guard, who would log them in like everyone else, and then past the security cameras, which would record them for posterity, and he couldn't do it using her name for the police to find, so he'd called up an American friend who had an apartment in the building.

The man was in the United States, but had told Garrett that if he ever needed a place to stay, his apartment was always open. Earlier today, he'd taken the man up on the offer, and now he was hoping the friend had sent in the security clearance for them to enter.

The security guard scrolled through the computer, causing sweat to break out on Garrett's head. He prayed that Gabrielle hadn't done the same thing. She'd told him to call when he arrived, using the phone from this very desk, and she'd talk to the guard. If she'd put in a pass and he was on it, they were done.

After what seemed like an eternity, the guard found the visitor's pass in the name of the friend. He printed out a piece of paper with a bar code for the elevator. Garrett thanked him and they entered the building proper, moving to the elevators in full view of the cameras.

Exiting on the twenty-fifth floor, they went past the apartment printed on the visitor's pass and entered the stairwell, walking up the two flights to the twenty-seventh floor. Stopping just outside the exit, Garrett pulled open a backpack and withdrew a ski mask, pulling it over his head. The other three Turtles did the same. When they were ready, he opened the door to the stairwell, facing the one camera near them.

They went past it at a trot, traveling to the end of the hallway, out of its view. Once there, Garrett paused outside the door, looking at his men. He saw saucers for eyes. He removed his ski mask and they did the same.

He said, "Calm down, Turtles. This is easy. Just follow the plan."

They nodded and he knocked on the door.

He felt someone on the other side, and then it

was opened by a plain-looking woman in a non-descript pantsuit. Short hair and bare minimum of makeup, just like he remembered in Syria.

Smiling, she said, "Garrett, it's been too long."

He said, "Hey, Gabrielle. Thanks for seeing us."

She hesitated for a moment, then said, "How'd you get up here? I didn't get a call?"

He sheepishly held his arms out and said, "All we did was say we were here to see you. He gave us a pass and sent us on our way."

She swung the door wide with a scowl, saying, "I'll have to talk to them about that. This place is supposed to be secure."

He walked through it, saying, "It's not a big deal. It's not like we're terrorists or something. Not like we dealt with in Syria."

She smiled and said, "Are you still working Syria?"

"Not after the Americans left, but my organization is still trying to help. We wanted to talk to you about coordinating again with the United Nations. We've lost our contact with the UN World Food Organization here and hope you can help."

She watched the remainder of the Turtles enter and said, "Who are your friends?"

Garrett said, "You remember Raphael, right? He was with me in Palmyra."

"Oh yes. I remember. From Croatia, right?"

"Yes, ma'am."

Garrett walked into the center of the apartment and said, "These other rogues are also from Croatia. Donatello and Leonardo."

She scrunched her eyes a little and said, "Why

do they have Italian names? Is their heritage here?"

Garrett laughed and walked to the balcony, saying, "They're just nicknames. They help with the Knights of Malta. Being Catholic only gets one so far."

She grinned and said, "Can I get you guys something to drink? A beer maybe?"

Garrett said, "Yes, please. Can I show them the view from here? Is that okay?"

She disappeared into the kitchen, saying, "By all means."

Garrett went outside on the balcony, seeing a field hockey arena almost thirty floors below, two teams battling it out. Just one floor above, he heard the clink of glasses and vague conversation from the rooftop garden deck. He looked at Donatello and said, "You have the door. Watch our back."

He nodded and went back into the living room. Garrett said, "You guys ready?"

Raphael and Leonardo both nodded. He said, "Hand me the note."

Raphael did and they waited.

Gabrielle exited onto the balcony holding three bottles of beer. She passed them out and said, "I love this view. I should live closer to the embassy, but I just like it here too much."

Garrett said, "Now. Do it now."

She looked at him in confusion, and a small part of her brain went into overdrive when the beer bottles shattered on her balcony from their dropped hands, the broken glass telling her to run. But it was too late. Leonardo and Raph ripped her off of her feet, one holding her arms and the other holding her legs. In shock, she tried to scream, but Garrett slapped his hand over her mouth. She began to writhe like a snake, almost getting out of their hands. Garrett hammered her in the temple and she sagged back, all fight gone.

He grabbed her jaw, opened her mouth, and crammed in the letter, balling it up until it was stuffed in her cheeks. Her eyes opened again and she began to fight once more.

Garrett said, "Over! Get her over!"

Leonardo and Raph swung their arms like they were tossing a sack of concrete, back and forth then back again, releasing her over the railing. The letter stuffed in her mouth muffled the screams as she plummeted down.

Garrett looked over the railing and saw her broken body on the pavement right outside the gate to the hockey park. Families watching the practice through the fence heard her impact, and in seconds there was a crowd, some looking up toward him.

He ducked back and said, "Let's go, let's go."

They raced out of the apartment, hit the hallway, and before the door closed Garrett remembered the prayer beads, sticking his hand in the jamb to stop it from locking. He said, "Did you drop the *Misbaha*?"

Donatello said, "Shit. No, I forgot."

He raced back in while Raphael said, "Why is that critical? We need to leave."

Garrett held the door and said, "She was a lesbian. ISIS used to toss gay people off of roofs as punishment. It will prove the devout nature of the perpetrators. It's a small thing that will pay big dividends."

Donatello came back out saying, "I threw them under the couch. It'll be found, but it looks like it was lost accidentally."

Garrett let the door close, saying, "Perfect. If this doesn't get some press, nothing will."

## CHAPTER 20

George Wolffe fidgeted in a chair just inside the portico for the West Wing of the White House, the badge around his neck having a prominent red *V* for visitor. Meaning he was forced to wait on an escort because he was "uncleared" like other White House staff or officials from departments like State or Defense. It was a pain, but he knew it was necessary.

Every official badge to the White House went through extensive background checks and clearances, which was something he couldn't do as the commander of Project Prometheus. Nobody in the established architecture of the United States government could know who he was, so every time he showed up, he had to act as if he were simply a visitor—like every other scum-sucking lobbyist who appeared in the building more than he did.

He saw the national security advisor, Alexander Palmer, coming down the hallway, glasses down his nose and a widow's peak for hair. Wolffe stood up. There was no love lost between the two, even as they both held a grudging mutual respect.

Palmer thought Wolffe was a loose cannon whose unit could potentially cause catastrophic damage to the administration, and Wolffe thought he was a political beast who cared more about the optics and poll numbers than any perceived good from Taskforce actions.

Luckily for Wolffe, the president of the United States believed in the Taskforce mission—even as he inexplicably kept Palmer on in the national security position. Charitably, Wolffe hoped it was just to keep a balance of viewpoints within the Oversight Council for Taskforce operations.

The two had come close to literal blows before. The only thing stopping the scuffle was Palmer knowing Wolffe would send him to the hospital, and Wolffe knowing such a thing was counter-productive to his unit's mission—as much as he would like to have done so. Wolffe had grown up in the paramilitary branch of the CIA and understood knife-point politics like few others, and because of it, had resisted shoving his boot up Palmer's ass on a number of occasions.

Palmer reached him and said, "You got any surprises up your sleeve?"

Wolffe was required to brief the Oversight Council about Taskforce operations on a quarterly basis. Since the advent of the pandemic, he'd still held to that schedule, even as operations were basically shut down, only it hadn't been to the full council of thirteen over in the SCIF in the Eisenhower Executive Office Building next door, but to what was known as the "principals" of the council here in the Oval Office. Every time he came to brief, Palmer wanted to know what he was going to say before he said it, purely for political reasons.

They began walking toward the Oval Office without a handshake, both barely tolerating each other. Wolffe said, "No surprises today. Same ol' same ol'. Nothing going on but servicing cover platforms and keeping the wheels greased. COVID has stopped us short like every other thing on the planet."

They reached the door and Palmer said, "Good. Best thing that's come out of this damn disease."

Wolffe stopped short and said, "Seriously? You think our inability to operate is a good thing?"

Rebuffed, Palmer said, "No, no, that's not what I meant. What I meant was that the pandemic has stopped the terrorists from doing things. Small blessings. Silver linings. That's all I meant."

Wolffe opened the door and said, "You are naïve. *We* can't operate because of our cover relationships and inability to travel, and because of it, the terrorists have breathing space. Only one side has been stymied. And it's not the bad guys."

Wolffe entered, seeing the principals of the council seated on two couches in front of the Resolute Desk. The director of the CIA, the secretary of state, the secretary of defense, and the president of the United States. The ones who really mattered when discussing the intricacies of Project Prometheus.

Looking like a bespectacled accountant—which

he had been in a previous life—President Hannister was sitting in an unassuming office chair to the right, reading an iPad. The others on the couches glanced at Wolffe expectantly when he entered.

Hannister laid the iPad on the corner of his desk and said, "Okay, let's get this over with. I have a meeting in twenty minutes with a farm bureau from Nebraska. I'm assuming nothing is going on? Same brief as last quarter? No Taskforce activity?"

"Sir, no targeting activity. We have one team in motion in the UAE, but only doing signature work designed to support their cover. No teams moving on the continent due to travel restrictions targeting nongovernmental United States citizens—which, of course, is how we operate—but we're still busting at the seams here in the United States doing cyber tracking and other threat analysis."

He passed out a folder to each member, saying, "We have several potential threat streams right now, specifically with ISIS variants in Africa, but nothing that our other intelligence or special operations forces can't handle. If something pops that can't be contained by conventional assets, I'll come back to you, but right now the threats are nascent, and we have a handle on them. My only concern is the people they're talking to. The ones they're radicalizing right now. They're going to metastasize while we wait for travel authority."

Hannister nodded and said, "Not a whole lot

we can do about that right now." He held up the folder and said, "You're talking with SOCOM and CIA on this?"

Kerry Bostwick, the director of the CIA, said, "Yeah, we're working closely together." The secretary of defense nodded, saying, "Same here. We have what they have. We're wired tight."

President Hannister looked at his watch and said, "Okay, shortest Oversight update in history. Anything else?"

Wolffe knew he was about to detonate a grenade, but couldn't *not* say anything. "Yes, sir. Something just to keep you up to date. It's not Taskforce, but it involves Taskforce personnel."

Wolffe saw Palmer sag back, then heard him say, "Oh, Christ. Tell me someone didn't get a DUI or something."

Wolffe flicked his eyes to Palmer, then ignored him, returning to the president, who gave a short chuckle. Wolffe said, "Sir, you remember the Israelis Aaron and Shoshana?"

The smile left Hannister's face. "Yes, of course. Why?"

Wolffe swallowed, knowing Hannister understood what they represented. "Well, they asked Pike and Jennifer to help them out on something in Europe, in turn Pike asked me for permission, and I told them they could do it, since we're on basically a stand-down due to the pandemic. Sort of like what happened in Poland a few years ago. You remember that?"

"Of course I do. It's how I got this job."

Wolffe internally cringed. That mission was

the same one where *Vice* President Hannister had become *President* Hannister when the current president had been blown out of the sky on Air Force One. The goodwill seed he wanted to plant was how Aaron and Shoshana had helped prevent World War III, not that the same mission involved the assassination of the president of the United States.

"Yes, yes. Of course. I just wanted to let you know they were doing some contract work with an ally. That's all."

Palmer said, "Wait, what? He's operating in Europe with Grolier Recovery Services? That *is* Taskforce."

"No, no. He's there purely as a civilian. No connection to GRS or the Taskforce. Period. And it's not some sort of hit mission. It's just some investigative work for Israel. Aaron and Shoshana are doing any hard work. Pike's just helping out with the effort."

Amanda Croft, the secretary of state, said, "How's he in Europe as an American? You just said you guys can't travel, and now you've got Pike traveling as a civilian?"

Wolffe had hoped this discussion would be brief, saying Pike was in Europe and that would be the end. He didn't expect the questioning. He cleared his throat and said, "Well, he's not there as an American."

Amanda said, "What's that mean? Is he going as a Martian?"

Wolffe heard the sarcasm and realized this was going south quickly. He decided to rip off the Band-Aid. He said, "No, ma'am. He went as an Israeli. They have no restrictions on travel like we do."

Palmer snapped upright and said, "What? He's doing *what*?"

## CHAPTER 21

The door to the Oval Office opened and a State Department aide appeared, looking hesitant. Hannister said, "Not now."

The man said, "Sir, I really need to pull Secretary Croft from this meeting. It won't take a second."

Hannister waved his hand forward and the man scurried to Amanda, whispering in her ear. Wolffe saw her eyes go wide, then look at a tablet the man held. She turned to the president and said, "Sir, we need to end this meeting right now."

Palmer said, "What's going on?"

Amanda turned to the president and said, "One of my diplomats was murdered in Italy. Literally thrown off of a roof."

That caused a change of focus in the room. Wolffe inwardly sighed, feeling dirty for the reason, but grateful for the reprieve. He said, "Sir, thank you for your time. I'll be on my way."

He started packing his briefcase, putting in charts and folders, and glanced at the scrum now around the Resolute Desk, the president behind it, firing questions. He heard the aide say, "There was a note from some Islamic group. It looks like a targeted killing."

And Wolffe stopped what he was doing. He stood up and Palmer said, "You're excused, but I'll want a briefing on what Pike's doing to brief the president at a later date."

He advanced to the desk, seeing a gruesome picture on the aide's tablet. A woman splattered on the pavement, her head split open in an enormous pool of blood. He saw Hannister's face grow cold, then his palms close into fists.

Palmer said, "Wolffe, I said you were excused. This isn't your concern."

Wolffe said, "Was it Keta'ib Hezbollah?"

Amanda turned and said, "What did you say?"

"Was the killing from Keta'ib Hezbollah? Is that who claimed it?"

The aide said, "Yes, yes it was."

President Hannister said, "How did you know that?"

"Because that's what Pike's helping the Israelis with. They had two government officials killed with the same group claiming credit. Or apparently the same group. Pike is helping them sort that out."

Palmer said, "Pike's doing *what*? Have you lost your mind? You have no sanction for that."

Wolffe said, "I told you, it's an Israeli mission. Not Taskforce. I don't need sanction for that."

"Damn it, you can't just freelance the Taskforce like a bunch of mercenaries from Russia! I want to know what—"

President Hannister cut him off with a hand, saying, "Be quiet, Alexander."

He turned to Wolffe and said, "Pike's on this same thread? Right now?"

"Yes, sir. The Israelis aren't sure if it's truly Keta'ib Hezbollah. That's what they're trying to sort out. Did this one come with a note?"

The aide said, "Yes. It was shoved in her mouth."

He flipped the screen and they saw a picture of a bloody piece of paper that had been crumpled at one time, now spread out.

The "mighty" Great Satan hires the abomination against Allah to serve their corrupt regime even as they assassinate the pure from cowardly drone strikes. Little Satan tries the same, killing the pure from the air. Now we kill you. The first was the Ambassador to the Crusaders. Who's next? Only time will tell, but the punishment will continue until you leave our lands.

Hannister said, "What the hell does that mean? 'Abomination of Allah'?"

Amanda said, "She was gay. She was a lesbian."

The SECDEF nodded and said, "In Mosul, ISIS did a 'cleansing' of the city, throwing anyone who was suspected of homosexuality off of roofs."

Incredulous, Hannister said, "She was killed because she's gay?"

Nobody responded, causing Hannister to pound his fist on the desk, saying, "Damn *animals*. I'm sick of this shit." He immediately regretted his outburst and said, "I apologize. That was uncalled for."

Wolffe said, "No it wasn't."

Hannister shook his head and said, "What about the 'ambassador to the crusader' statement?"

Croft put her hand to her mouth, realization hitting. She said, "They're claiming credit for Geoffrey Combine. The ambassador to the Holy See."

"That was an accident. Wasn't it?"

Palmer said, "Yes. According to the Italians." Hannister tapped his pen on the desk, now back in control, saying, "So a militia run by Iran is assassinating American diplomats. And openly admitting it."

Palmer said, "That's what it looks like."

Hannister turned to the SECDEF and said, "Start looking at options. We're going to have to respond, but I'll be damned if I know how. The last thing I want to do is be drawn into another quagmire in Iraq by blowing up a bunch of militia members."

Wolffe said, "Before we go off bombing targets in Syria and Iraq, we should make sure it's true."

That brought everyone up short. Hannister said, "What's that mean?"

"Pike's mission is precisely to see if Keta'ib Hezbollah—meaning Iran—is really behind this. The Israelis aren't sure, which is why they've kept that connection quiet. They've covered it up until they can get proof. There are components within the Mossad who think someone's trying to gin up a war with Iran."

Kerry, the D/CIA, said, "How do you know all of this and I don't? What the hell are the Israelis doing? What happened to coordination among allies?"

Wolffe spread his hands and said, "Hey, man, I'm sorry. I was just as pissed as you are when I was told. In fact, I said the exact same thing. According to Pike, there's a ferocious fight going on in Israel right now. The majority want to start hammering Iran immediately, but a section thinks it's a false flag. That section sent Aaron and Shoshana on their mission. They aren't even sanctioned by the Mossad, but a powerful segment is afraid of going to war for the wrong reasons, and they've managed to convince the others to keep it secret until they're sure."

Hannister looked at the aide and said, "Can we do the same?"

"Unfortunately, no, sir. This is all over the news in Italy, and will be all over our news right now, within minutes, if it isn't already."

Hannister sagged back in his chair, rubbed his eyes, and said, "I see where this is going. We're about to get foot stomping and screaming from the hawks in Congress to attack Iran. Performance art."

He pulled his hand away, a thought coalescing. He said, "Do you have contact with Pike?"

"Yes, of course. He has his Taskforce phone."

"And he's on this thread? The Keta'ib Hezbollah one?"

"Well, he's in Switzerland, but yes, it's the same thread."

"Does he have assets there he can use and still be Israeli?"

"Yes, sir. He does. He can operate."

Growing apoplectic, Palmer said, "*What* assets?"

Hannister raised his hand again, shutting Palmer down.

He said, "Call him. Find out what he knows. I need answers before we go to war."

Wolffe nodded, then said, "They're talking about another assassination here. I can get what he knows, but I can't stop the next one without authority. Can I put him in play? Officially?"

Amanda Croft said, "How can you do that officially if they're operating under the cover of Israelis? We can't protect them like we could if it was a Taskforce mission."

Wolffe smiled and said, "Pike will figure that out. The hardest part might be getting the Israelis to agree—because they have their own restrictions—but he'll figure it out. If I get permission."

President Hannister glanced at the faces around the desk, and then didn't even put it to a vote, as was required by the Project Prometheus charter.

He said, "Yeah. I want him hunting, before I'm forced to use a sledgehammer."

## CHAPTER 22

I was once again enjoying the old town of Zurich, this time at sunset, and I had to admit this mission continued to get better and better. Instead of ice cream, Jennifer and I were drinking coffee at an outdoor café at one of those ridiculously small tables they like in Europe. You know, the ones that are about the size of a half dollar, so small they have trouble putting two glasses on it.

The café was located in a cobblestone square, our table facing a tunnel that went past the consignment store Blenda Vintage and up into the apartments overhead, where Qassim lived. Now it was our turn for the breaking and entering, giving Aaron and Shoshana a chance at protecting our backs.

After Qassim left the hotel across the river, he'd continued his meandering walk through a park and back to his apartment, only stopping once for some take-out lunch to bring home with him. We'd left him after he returned and had regrouped at our own hotel, trying to sort out what we had. Which was very little.

He most definitely had had some type of

training, having run a surveillance detection route into and out of the hotel—most notably using a series of narrow walled alleys and stairs that channelized and highlighted anyone behind him—and the very fact that he was transmitting via ProtonMail from a public computer anyone could utilize indicated he was attempting to disconnect his actions from his own persona, but the search of his apartment had turned up nothing. The only thing Aaron and Shoshana had found was the stego program, which in and of itself gave us no clue of what was going on. We felt the guy was bad, but we weren't sure why.

The one thing we needed was the thumb drive he'd used. Given his use of the hotel to break himself from his own systems, I figured he probably compartmentalized everything on removable media, so we'd decided to do another break-in when he went to dinner tonight, only this time it would be Jennifer and me, hoping to find the mysterious thumb drive when he left.

Honestly, we didn't know if he lived on ramen boiled with a hot plate in his apartment, but Aaron and Shoshana hadn't seen a lot of cookware, his refrigerator and pantry held only staples like fruit and water, and he'd brought home takeout for lunch, so we were betting he usually went out for dinner. If he didn't, we'd just re-cock and think of something else. Patience, patience, patience.

Jennifer took a sip of her latte and said, "Not sure how we ended up being the break-in crew. Shoshana said we'd just be security for the work."

I said, "Yeah, well, why should she get all the

fun? We followed the guy all day today and they're clean for the next follow. We're clean for the break-in. Should be fun."

She smirked, snaked her hand across the table, and put it on top of mine, saying, "I thought you wanted to spend some time with your wife in Zurich?"

I chuckled and said, "I do. What better way to spend it than breaking into a potential terrorist hideout?"

She grew serious, saying, "Do you think we should have contacted Wolffe before going active like this? We promised him we'd just be doing surveillance work. It's why he allowed us to leave."

I said, "Honestly? Yeah, we probably should, but we don't know what turns this is going to take, and Wolffe knows me. Knows how I think. He wouldn't have let us go if he didn't think it was worth it."

"He didn't know we'd be doing this."

Jennifer was still a little black-and-white when it came to authority for something. Still wanting to ask permission, when I was more likely to ask for forgiveness after the fact. I knew she didn't give a damn about breaking into this guy's house, but instead was more worried about breaking her trust with George Wolffe. But I also knew that Wolffe understood that I wouldn't do something crazy without calling first.

This little B&E wasn't crazy. At least in my mind.

I squeezed her hand, saying, "What's the use of walking on the edge if you don't lean over every once in a while?"

She grinned and said, "I'm pretty sure I've heard you say that in the past. Right before we fall off. I'm not sure why I ever listen to you."

"Because you'd never get any high adventure if you didn't, that's why."

She pulled her hand away and I said, "What? I was making a joke—"

She cut me off, saying, "He's on the move."

I glanced at the front of the tunnel and saw Qassim exiting at a leisurely pace. He stopped and watched a street performer in front of a fountain, then continued on.

I got on the net and said, "The Professor is loose, going north."

I always liked giving a target a nickname. That way, on the off chance someone heard me speaking or our radio calls were intercepted, they still wouldn't know who I was talking about. This time, I'd anointed Qassim "the Professor" because that's what he looked like.

He took a right and disappeared from view. I said, "Knuckles, he just entered your alley, Nerd-duffus-strasse or whatever it's called."

The surveillance box was much tighter this time, as there were plenty of places to eat threaded throughout the maze of alleys, forcing us to use singleton positions to stake out each potential egress.

I heard laughter coming through the net, then, "You mean, Niederdorfstrasse?"

I said, "Whatever," and watched Jennifer begin working a knapsack at her feet, getting our tools ready.

When she was done we still didn't move, patiently waiting for Knuckles to get lock-on, because an unseen target is an unknown threat. The last thing we wanted was for him to meet us at his door as I was picking the lock.

I heard him say, "Got eyes on. Clear to breach," then heard him starting to coordinate the surveillance effort against Qassim with Brett and the Israelis.

Jennifer swung her arms through the straps of the small backpack, a grin on her face, her eyes lighting up from the adrenaline. I stood up and threw some euros on the table, saying, "Showtime."

## CHAPTER 23

We left the café and walked to the tunnel holding hands, just another couple of tourists out enjoying Zurich. The good part of this op was that the Israelis had already done the hard work for us, having given us a complete data dump of exactly what to expect. We only had two barriers to penetrate, and we'd come prepared for both.

Harshly lit by overhead fluorescent lamps, the tunnel had the air of a cheap carnival house of horrors, some of the lights flickering like a Saw movie. We passed by several smaller shops, then reached a set of stairs. The building had five floors, with the ground floor reserved for the shops, and each subsequent floor owned by different companies that rented out apartments, with the final floor having office spaces. We went up three flights, took a right down a hallway, and reached a set of double-glass doors with a keypad on the wall, a small lobby behind it. The first barrier.

I checked the doors on the off chance the magnetic lock was turned off, but no luck. Jennifer took a knee, rotating her back with the knapsack toward me, and I bent down, ripping open the zippers. I pulled out what looked like a thick coat hanger covered in rubber with a T-handle on one end and a square hook on the other. Called a double-door tool, it was designed to defeat exactly what we were facing.

Everyone entering the apartment lobby had to punch in a code on the keypad, which meant we either had to sneak in behind someone using the keypad—a definite nonstarter—or figure out the code, which we didn't have time to accomplish. Fortunately for us, because of fire codes and general convenience, everyone that *left* the complex only had to hit a push bar to exit. And that was what we were going to bypass.

I tapped Jennifer on the shoulder and she rotated around for early warning from anyone else coming up the stairs. I slid the tool through the small gap between the doors, rotated it around, seated the box end against the push bar, and pulled. The door opened like magic. I held it and snapped my fingers. Jennifer scuttled inside, racing through the lobby, then cutting left down a hallway. I walked through the door, let it close, then did a survey of the other two hallways leading to the lobby. Both were empty.

On the net, I said, "You're clear," then took a seat on a bench, protecting her work on the apartment door.

I heard "Roger," and started the chronograph on my watch. Fourteen seconds later, I heard, "I'm in."

That caused my eyebrows to rise. I stood up

and started jogging down the hallway thinking, *No way was she that fast.*

I reached the door, saw it cracked, and entered, finding Jennifer going through a credenza. I looked at the lock set, seeing an Abloy cylinder bolt-lock just like Aaron had said. A brand that wasn't cheap crap. I closed the door and engaged the bolt saying, "How'd you get in so quick? Was it unlocked?"

She closed a drawer and said, "Really? No, it wasn't unlocked. The pins just worked out. Sorry about that."

I grinned and went to the other side of the credenza, opening a drawer and saying, "That might be a Taskforce record. We should have recorded it. Knuckles will never believe you."

She gave me the side-eye and I winked, saying, "Remember to put everything back exactly like you found it."

She nodded and we continued going through the drawers. They gave us nothing. The apartment was small, with a kitchenette adjacent to a tiny den, and a closet-sized bedroom in the rear. It took us no time to go through the major places for hiding a thumb drive, to include the refrigerator, stove, wall vents, bottoms of drawers, and other secret spots.

We'd both had instruction from DEA and ICE on the various ways criminals hid stuff—you'd be amazed at the ingenuity—but all of our tricks came up empty. We found nothing. I was beginning to suspect he had it on him, or he'd hidden it in a place that would take wall-penetrating radar to find.

I got on the net and said, "Knuckles, what's the status?"

"You're good. He's at an outdoor café eating steak. About a ten-minute walk from you. I'll give you warning. What do you have?"

"Nothing. He's either got the drive on him, or he's created some hiding spot that will take peeling back the floorboards to find. My bet is he has it on him. Probably sleeps with it."

Shoshana came on and said, "Keep looking. Check his computer again."

I rubbed my face, knowing it was a waste of time. Jennifer said, "Can't hurt to look."

"Yeah, you're right."

We went to his small desk, opened a late-model Apple MacBook Pro, and were confronted with a password screen. Which wasn't a problem, because the Israelis had already cracked it with their Mossad magic earlier. I typed in the password they'd given me—Jennys#, believe it or not—and the screen magically cleared. I began going through the files, but knew it was a waste of time. I pulled up the steganography program only to find just the program itself. It had no saved files or other history to exploit.

I looked at Jennifer and said, "Let's go. We're getting nothing from this and increasing our risk every second we're here."

She was staring at the screen, her eyes scrunched up. I said, "What?"

She leaned over me and said, "He's using Apple's Time Machine backup."

"So?"

"So let's go back in time."

I'd spent enough effort with our own hacking crew to have a healthy appreciation of computer network exploits, and I saw exactly where she was headed.

I got on the net and said, "When did we engage Professor today? What time was that? When did he exit?"

Shoshana said, "He left the building right around 1240. Why?"

"Stand by."

Jennifer got behind the keyboard and pulled up Time Machine, saying, "This thing keeps a backup every hour for twenty-four hours, but it also takes a snapshot every fifteen minutes when the computer is being used."

I said, "Damn good thing you have a Mac."

The time machine opened up, a sprout of windows retreating back into the screen like a bad Pink Floyd video, starting with "right now," then scrolling backward at specific intervals that seemed random. She pulled up 1248 and loaded it, then the steganography program. It looked the same—empty. She repeated the procedure for the next available time, 1232. The stego program came on the screen, only this time it had two pictures in the load spots and a box of text below it.

I said, "Holy shit. You are a genius."

She smiled and said, "No, we're just incredibly lucky. Time Machine took a snapshot at the exact moment he was working the program, saving everything just like it was when he was using it."

My earpiece came alive. "Pike, Pike, Professor is done with dinner. You have about ten minutes."

I said, "Roger that." I took a picture of the screen, then said, "Load back to today. Don't let him know we were here."

She began to do so when we heard the front door lock being manipulated.

*What the hell?*

On the net I said, "You have Professor? I got someone coming in."

"We have him in sight. I say again, we have lock-on."

*Damn it.*

I looked at Jennifer and motioned to the computer, telling her to keep working. I went to the door and put my eye to the peephole, seeing a maintenance guy in a uniform. He was working one key after another into the lock, trying to find the right master for this apartment. He was probably the maintenance man for every different apartment company in the building and had masters for them all.

*Decision time.* Take him out and flee? Bluff our way out? If I took him out, it would most definitely alert Qassim that something was up when the police arrived. But bluffing our way out would also leave a gaping compromise. But it was probably our best bet. We'd simply have to pray that the maintenance guy never talked to Qassim.

I hissed to Jennifer, "Are we good? Is it back like it was?"

Her eyes wide, knowing we were about to be compromised, she said, "Yeah, we're back like when we entered."

I moved to the right of the door and said, "If

he enters, I'm going to try to bullshit him. Give him a story. You check the back. See if there's another way out. Now."

She sprinted into the bedroom and I heard her opening a window. There was a pause, and then she hissed, "Pike, on me. We can get out here."

I heard one more key enter the lock and sprinted to her, finding her outside the small window holding on to the sill, a back alley three floors below her. I glanced up and down, then said, "Are you nuts? What are you going to do? Climb down the bricks?"

Jennifer was a little bit of a freak when it came to climbing. I was pretty sure if she spit on her hands she could, in fact, climb down the bricks, but there was no way I was going to try to do that.

She said, "Follow me," and swung out to the left, letting go of the sill, and clamping on to an old-fashioned iron gutter pipe about four feet away. She began scampering down it like a monkey, and I cursed, thinking I'd just clock the maintenance guy in the head. I'd rather have the police find him instead of me splattered on the pavement.

I heard the bolt-lock turn, raced to the bedroom door and closed it, then crammed my frame out of the window going feetfirst. I slithered down until I was hanging by my hands, then glanced at the pipe a mere four feet away. It looked to me more like four hundred, and if I missed, I was going to have a serious impact with the pavement. I swung a little bit right, then violently left, pushing off the wall with my feet and releasing my hold in a dynamic move.

I gave it way too much energy.

I slammed into the iron pipe hard enough to clock my skull, clamping my hands around it like it was life itself. Which it was.

I cleared my head, then began scampering down to the earth, landing between a row of trash cans, Jennifer waiting on me.

She touched my forehead, a bruise starting to form, concern on her face. I let her take a look and said, "Do you do that shit just to make me look bad?"

Confused, she said, "What?"

I grinned and said, "Nothing. Let's get out of here, spider monkey. You just saved the day, in more ways than one."

## CHAPTER 24

Back in our Israeli-paid-for Hyatt Regency high-end hotel room, we discussed what the next steps would be. We now knew beyond a shadow of a doubt this guy was somehow involved in the killing of the *Ramsad*, but we still had no proof of who his masters were—Iran or otherwise—which was the mission.

The text box—which was presumably embedded within the photo on the thumb drive that Qassim had used to send via ProtonMail—was asking about a linkup in Bahrain, and mentioned that the money would be coming with the man to pay for the next "operation." He was apparently some sort of badass from Bosnia, and had impeccable credentials for unspecified skills. It didn't say what, but I assumed it was for killing. Included, of course, were the usual bowing down to Allah and proclaiming the world would be free of the infidels, *In'shallah*. Meaning if God willed it.

The strange thing was the text seemed to be begging the far site to accept the parameters. It wasn't like Qassim was just stating facts. He was asking for permission, which was weird, given that they were supposedly all working together. He made a hard sell that Iran was demanding this—which also didn't sound right. If Iran was demanding it, it would just happen. No questions asked. He wouldn't need to flaunt it in a text.

Given that, there was no doubt in my mind now that this asshole was in the kill chain. The only thing missing was proving it. Right now, we really only had a lot of smoke. A text message that said nothing other than a meeting about money with everything else cloaked in innocuous wording. Nothing illegal, in and of itself, and nothing pointing the smoking gun at Keta'ib Hezbollah.

By the text, he was going to return to get the linkup specifics at noon tomorrow, so we had a time frame. What we didn't have was a new lead. Or any idea of what we should do about it.

Shoshana said, "So what do we do now? I can't take this back to Mossad. We have nothing to prove that Keta'ib Hezbollah killed the *Ramsad*, or anything to prove they didn't. All we have is evidence that he was involved."

Knuckles said, "Let him do his little dance again tomorrow, then we just repeat what you guys did. Brett and I will do the B&E, clock back the Time Machine, and see what the message says."

Jennifer said, "That's a long shot. There's only one in a hundred chance it will work. We were lucky that his Time Machine backup took a snapshot at that precise time he was using the program. He could do the entire message thing and more than likely it will be in between snapshots."

I nodded, thinking. Then said, "There's only one way to get that message."

Shoshana said, "How?"

"We need to roll up Qassim after the drop tomorrow. We need that thumb drive."

Nobody said anything for a moment, still processing my words. Finally, Brett said, "Did I hear that right? Are you talking about conducting an Omega operation on foreign soil when we're not even operating as Taskforce? Seriously?"

I considered his words, nodded my head, and said, "Yeah, I guess that's what I'm saying. We need to interdict him after he gets the instructions tomorrow, but before he transmits them. Make it look like a mugging. Rough him up a bit, steal his watch and wallet, and get the thumb drive. We get that lead, and we continue on."

I looked at Aaron and said, "The point of this is to prove or disprove Iranian involvement, right? This guy that's doing the linkup isn't Iranian. He's sketchy, and he's sounding like what your Mossad skeptics think—somebody else pulling the strings. We need to sort that out. He's the guy we ultimately want."

Aaron said, "So how does our interdicting the Professor before he has the ability to transmit the plan help us? The guy won't get the instructions."

"No, he will, but *we'll* be controlling the information. I say we roll up Professor, get the message, and then craft our own linkup plan— make him think we're the cell. We go to Bahrain, roll up his ass, and squeeze him. That's where the answers will come. And we'll short-circuit anything they had planned as well. It's a win/win."

Aaron nodded, saying, "Yeah, that sounds good to me. Shoshana?"

She said, "I agree. We have a hit time tomorrow for him to retrieve the message, and we know his route. We'll actually get two shots at it, since he'll have to retrieve the message, come home to use the stego program to decode, then shack up his own message to the Bosnian guy, and finally return to the hotel to send it. We can hit him after he leaves the hotel, and if that fails, after he leaves his apartment again. We could do it."

Knuckles tugged his ear, then glanced at me. I said, "What?"

"You're forgetting we have no sanction over here. We can't just go ripping people off the street because Israel thinks it's a good thing. We can't do it. Or more specifically, Brett and I *won't* do it. You guys are civilians, so go ahead and get your jihad on, but we're standing down."

Knuckles was still an active-duty Navy SEAL, and Brett was officially part of the CIA's Ground Branch paramilitary division, unlike Jennifer and me, who were civilian owners of an archeological research company. I understood where they were coming from.

I said, "Come on. This is what you do. We're derailing their ability to assassinate our allies—or maybe our own guys. You know what's in Bahrain? The Fifth Fleet. You don't think that's a juicy target? They're going to kill *someone* in

Bahrain. We can stop it. And maybe stop a war with Iran if the hits are truly a false flag."

He said, "That may be the case, but I'm not conducting an Omega operation without sanction. This 'being an Israeli' thing only goes so far, and you're stretching it."

I glanced at Jennifer. She pursed her lips and shook her head, telling me Knuckles was right. I turned to Brett and he said, "You know where I stand. Need some authorization for this."

Shoshana said, "Pike, we can do this on our own. Just you and us. I don't need authorization. I already have it."

I looked at Aaron, and saw he was torn. He wanted my help, but understood my restrictions.

I took a deep breath and then let it out. I said, "I'm sorry, Shoshana, but my team's right. I'd love to tag this guy, but we're going to need authorization. Let's take a look at what we can do without ripping the Professor off the street."

Knuckles exhaled at my words, the act letting me know he didn't want to go against me, but was going to do what he thought was right. It made me smile, because the worst thing a team leader could ever become was convinced he alone was correct.

I glanced at Jennifer, and she winked, letting me know she thought it was the right decision as well. Shoshana became incensed, springing up and saying, "We'll do this on our own, then."

I said, "Calm down, Carrie. We're still going to help, but just within the charter we have. Which is surveillance only."

She hissed, saying, "*Your* side is next. *Your*

people are going to get killed next. And we could prevent that right now."

I said, "I'm sorry, but until Wolffe gives me sanction to conduct offensive operations, I can't do it."

And then my phone came alive, with the distinctive Taskforce ringtone telling me to go encrypted.

CHAPTER 25

After finishing the establishment of his kill zone during daylight, Garrett sat in his car in the fading twilight, waiting on the darkness to fall, a precursor required before the streetwalkers began plying their trade like nocturnal animals digging through a trash can. Parked in the EUR neighborhood next to a small man-made body of water called Lago dell'Eur, waiting on darkness to fall, his mind drifted unbidden to the ramifications of what he was about to do, kill an innocent solely to protect the mission.

Leonardo was going to get the linkup information for Bahrain tomorrow, but that still left about three days for the female police inspector to hunt him down, and he had no idea how close she was. For all he knew, they were within twenty-four hours of knocking on his door and asking for his DNA or fingerprints. He knew he'd left both at every crime scene.

The murder of Gabrielle Hernandez, the United States diplomat, had certainly generated the news he wanted, with the U.S. press's endless cycle of cable talking heads demanding the obliteration of Iran. But the female inspector had nothing to do with that, and he was sure the investigation was going full speed ahead. He'd tried mightily to find out her identity or where she lived, but had so far failed. The police had held several news conferences discussing a "ripper" type character on the loose in the EUR neighborhood, but that story had now been overshadowed by the spectacular death of the American—but even before, the woman detective never took the microphone, was never introduced, and nobody ever referred to her by name. She apparently preferred to operate in the shadows, which concerned Garrett a great deal.

He needed to remove her from the equation to short-circuit the investigation, which necessitated him first discovering her identity. After he'd repeatedly come up empty using every investigative technique he could think of, wasting hours on the web trying to find her and calling various people he knew from his past, he'd decided on a different tack—instead of him searching for her, bring her to him.

The quickest way to do that would be another killing, but unlike the other three, this one would be premeditated. No rage, no sexual frustration, just a goat staked to a tree for the tiger to come find. When that happened, he'd learn who she was because he'd ensured that he would control the space where the body would be found.

At night, the streetwalkers were all over the EUR neighborhood, the majority clinging to the alleys that surrounded the park around the lake, but, as he'd learned, most had no place to go, with some wanting to offer their services in the darkness of the park itself, and others simply using the patron's car. Earlier, when he was genuinely searching for sexual gratification, he hadn't liked either choice, forcing him to solicit multiple women before he'd found one who had a place to stay. He wasn't going to do that tonight. He couldn't take a chance on another trailer encounter. He needed to prepare the location prior to arrival, and so he'd rented a VRBO apartment on the east side of the neighborhood, away from the lake.

That in itself had been a chore, because he had very specific requirements. The biggest hurdle was finding a host who didn't require verified identification to rent. That cut his choices in half, as Airbnb not only required an official government ID, they also did a background check on the identification submitted before giving the renter "verified" status.

VRBO recommended verification, as some hosts wouldn't rent without it, but didn't actually require it, allowing him to use a fake driver's license from the United States. The license had been bought off the internet just like any underage college student had the capability of doing, but he figured unlike a bouncer in a college town bar in the United States, nobody in Italy would know what to look for to prove it false. That, coupled with the complete collapse of rentals from COVID, made Garrett sure the host wouldn't even attempt to verify. He or she would just want the money.

Beyond the identification problem, he had other needs. The rental couldn't require him to meet the owner or agent of the apartment to gain access. That eliminated "apartments" that were really just makeshift rooms at the back of a house where the owner still lived or apartments that insisted on an in-person meeting with a rental agent to receive the key.

Finally, the location was key. He needed a place that allowed him to get within a hundred meters of the apartment without being seen, and not just by driving up like he had before. He wasn't going to risk being discovered in his car again, and he would need to remain for possibly hours, which required a site that would allow such a stay.

It seemed to be an exhaustive list, and he'd actually considered renting a trailer himself, parking it somewhere in a dark alley to use, but assumed there was no way a whore would follow him into a sketchy back-alley trailer that she didn't own.

After six hours of research, he'd stumbled upon a perfect location. It was a VRBO in a four-story apartment complex right next to a park called Parco Mattia Preti, on the east side of the EUR neighborhood. With a school across the road—which would be closed at night, ensuring no coincidental eyewitnesses—a myriad of alleys surrounding it, and keypad entry that didn't require him to meet anyone, he submitted his application. Four hours later, it was approved, and he paid for four days.

He'd driven to the location, carefully looking for surveillance cameras and seeing two mounted on the walls to the front entrance, one focused on the parking lot, the other focused on all who entered. He'd avoided them, entering through a side door and walking up two flights of stairs. He checked numbers, reached his door, and held his breath. He punched in the code he'd been given, and the lock clicked open. He exhaled and entered, taking stock of the surroundings.

It was small, a one-bedroom with a kitchenette and a bathroom, the tiny den barely big enough to hold the two chairs and a coffee table the host had provided, which was perfect for him. He opened his backpack and went to work.

He began installing Wi-Fi cameras and small, covert microphones throughout the apartment, using the cheap artwork on the walls, smoke alarms in each room, lamps on tables, and air vents along the baseboards. When he was done, he connected the system to the apartment Wi-Fi and checked the feed on a tablet. It appeared to work inside the apartment, but the real test would be outside.

He turned on the television, raising the volume to conversation level, then went back to his vehicle and drove to the park entrance a scant hundred meters away. He entered it, walking with a backpack until he reached a bench, ignoring the people out enjoying the sunshine. He opened the pack, pulled out the tablet, and attempted to connect to the apartment complex Wi-Fi. The signal was too weak. He stood up and began walking back toward the complex, looking at his tablet. He entered a wooded section, the fence to the park only twenty meters away, and feared his plan wouldn't work. He found another bench and sat down again, waiting.

The tablet found the signal and connected. He dialed up his network of surveillance devices and smiled. The system worked perfectly. He had a clear view of both the bedroom and the den and could hear the television even inside the bedroom. He tapped the tablet, shifting cameras, pleased. Sometimes it paid to have specialized training and equipment.

He'd started to put away his tablet when a dog ran up to him with a ball, a young boy of about thirteen scampering behind. The boy approached and said, "What's that?"

Before Garrett could answer, the boy saw the camera feeds and said, "Are you flying a drone? Can I see?"

Flustered, Garrett stood and said, "No, no. It's pictures of my apartment."

He walked rapidly away, regretting the contact and his reaction to it. The boy would remember Garrett. If he lived around here, he might be contacted in a canvas of the neighborhood.

Maybe he should kill the boy, too. Right now, before he could return to his parents. The thought made him physically ill.

He returned to his car, slammed his fist into the dash, and then began praying for his soul. He was on the verge of creating the return of Christ, but he was burning his afterlife to do so. He couldn't believe he'd actually considered killing a thirteen-year-old child simply because he'd seen the tablet.

Three hours later, he was waiting for the sun to set next to the lake, trying to return to the promise of the mission. He feared he was losing focus of what constituted the work of Satan and what was for the greater good of humanity. The woman would be the greater good. The boy was not.

He thought it no different than Rahab in the Bible, a harlot who had protected Israelite spies in Jericho. She'd hidden them, and when the Israelites came to sack the city using the spies' information, she had been spared by hanging a crimson rope outside her window.

This whore would be doing the same thing. Protecting a spy for the promised land. With that thought, he closed his eyes, waiting on the sun to set.

Two hours later, someone bumped his hood, startling him awake. Under the harsh glare of a streetlight, he saw a couple headed into the park. It was full night now, and the usual hookers were stalking around the greenspace next to the lake.

He left his vehicle and entered the park, surveying the various prostitutes walking about. He saw a black woman with a tube top, tight shorts, and sandals sitting on a bench, her hair in cornrows. She caught him looking her way and smiled. He went to her.

He knew how the game was played. Prostitution wasn't technically illegal, but solicitation was, meaning the women couldn't come to you and ask if you "wanted a good time." You had to go to them.

She was small, about five foot four, which was

in his favor. She was also a different race, which would help throw off the investigation. His other victims had been someone he was sexually attracted to, but he had none of that here, and any confusion he could interject on the case would only help.

In his broken Italian, he said, "You out here by yourself?"

She looked him up and down, saw no threat, and said, "Yes."

He nodded and said, "You want some company?"

Hearing the magic words, she smiled. She hadn't solicited him, so it was okay. "Sure. What would you like to do?"

He said, "My Italian isn't that good. Do you speak English?"

She smiled again and, in English, said, "Yes. My Italian is better, but I speak English. You are American?"

He sat down next to her and said, "Yes, I am. Here on business. I have a rental apartment about a mile away. You want to go get some drinks?"

She stood, threw her purse over her shoulder, and said, "Sure. I can do that. What's your name?"

"You can call me Splinter."

She said, "My name is—" and he cut her off, saying, "I don't want to know."

He walked her to the car, making small talk. She was from Senegal and had been in Italy for close to two years. She lived with a group of women, but had no pimp. She was here illegally, but wanted to get a work permit to let her quit this life. Endless chitchat, making Garrett sad.

He was convinced he was doing her a favor. She would never leave this purgatory, and he was giving her a second chance for the afterlife. She would be a brick in the wall of the second coming. Like Rahab, it was probably the greatest thing she could ever aspire to.

He drove east, winding through the neighborhoods, eventually passing the park next to his rental complex. He stopped his car in the shadows of the west end of the building, leading her through the darkness to a side door away from the security cameras and streetlamps from the primary entrance. When they continued in the darkness instead of moving to the light of the main entrance, she became suspicious, saying, "Why aren't we going in the front?"

He said, "My apartment is right above us. It's just quicker."

She nodded and he opened the door to a stairwell with a flourish of his hand. She entered and they went up two floors, then exited into a hallway. He led her forward, reaching the apartment door.

He punched in the code to the door, heard it unlock, then swung it wide for her. She smiled again and entered.

He followed behind, pulling a red cord out of his jacket pocket, each end having a piece of wood threaded through to make it easier to use.

## CHAPTER 26

I checked my watch for probably the fortieth time, seeing it was now 11:30 A.M. Almost showtime. I was sitting on a bench in Lidenhof Park, right smack-dab in the center of Zurich's old town, this time all by myself. I got on the radio and conducted a comms check with all of my bumper positions, making sure they were prepared to execute, and each one acknowledged they were set and ready to go. That was small comfort, because this operation was running the ragged edge of my team's capability.

The mission had changed, and we were no-where near the size needed for the new scope, but after the Taskforce call last night, everything had ratcheted up.

It had been George Wolffe on the phone, and the situation had morphed drastically from me being on a boondoggle with the Israelis, out in the wind on my own. A U.S. diplomat had been executed in Italy, with the same type of note the Israelis had found on their dead *Ramsad* crammed in her mouth. Keta'ib Hezbollah had claimed credit, and the president of the United

States was now out for blood. Which was good for me, but bad given the size of my team.

I'd told Wolffe my plan about the mugging to get the thumb drive, then the follow-on hit in Bahrain, and, for the first time in my Taskforce career, he had stunned me. Instead of the usual mealy-mouthed Oversight Council pushback whenever I wanted to do something, he took it to the next level, telling me to drop the mugging idea and go with a full-on takedown. He wanted me to extract the target from the middle of Zurich—a metropolitan city—in broad daylight, then get him on the Rock Star bird and evacuate him to Aviano Air Base in Italy, a U.S.-controlled facility where Taskforce interrogators would be standing by.

The idea held merit, because clearly this guy knew a lot of what was going on, so when he'd asked me if I could accomplish the mission, of course I'd said yes. After all of my bitching on other missions about being held back because the Oversight Council were a bunch of cowards, there was no way I was going to say no. But it *was* going to be a little tight.

I had Shoshana as the trigger at the apartment, but we were going to rely on his habitual pattern from there. Knuckles would pick him up at the hotel, leaving Brett, Aaron, and me to take him down. Jennifer would be up the street with a Land Rover for exfil. Once the action had occurred, and we'd loaded him up, Shoshana would use the other Land Rover to evacuate the team. Easy day, except it left nothing for contingencies. If it went the way we planned, there would be no problem, but like Mike Tyson said, everyone has a plan until they get punched in the mouth.

At 11:43, Shoshana came on the net, "Professor is on the move. Same direction as yesterday."

I said, "Roger. Knuckles, that means about fifteen minutes until he breaks the door of the Kindli hotel."

He said, "Roger all. Standing by."

Shoshana came back on and said, "He's got his laptop with him this time."

*Shit.* While we intended to take this guy off the board, the original plan was still in play. We'd get the thumb drive information and still have the option of executing my original mission, if that's what the Oversight Council thought was best. That plan required us to take the Professor before he had a chance to transmit the linkup information to the mysterious Bosniak, allowing the Taskforce to set up their own trap. If he had the laptop, he had the ability to extract the message and resend in one trip. But maybe he had it just to surf porn after he had the message.

One could hope.

I fidgeted on the bench, watching some elderly gentlemen playing chess on permanent tables set in the park for that purpose. Still wearing masks, they refused to let a pandemic alter their routine. I envied them in a way, wondering about each of their life stories. As usual when seeing someone that age, I wondered if maybe they'd been dropped behind enemy lines in France or were Swiss spies in the Reichstag, but given the march of time, probably not. Those gems were leaving this earth every single day.

My radio came alive: "All elements, all elements, this is Knuckles. I have eyes on. He's at the computer."

I said, "Roger," and waited, feeling the adrenaline rise. If he followed his pattern of life, he would leave the hotel and travel up a ramp to the hill in the park, the ramp itself cut into the side of the hill and lined with cinder-block walls until it reached the top. It was a perfect surveillance detection route because it would highlight anyone behind him.

If he kept true to form, he would exit the park on a similar ramp, dropping down off the hill to the streets below with walls on his left and right growing as he sank back down. As before, it was a perfect use for an SDR, but unfortunately for him, it was also perfect for a hit.

Once he started down that ramp, he would be lost to sight from anyone who wasn't actually using the same walkway, and that's where we were going to take him. Brett was at the bottom, prepared to walk up. I was at the top, coming from that end. Knuckles would provide rear security, locking down the back door, while Aaron would do the same from the bottom, both prepared to react. But I really didn't think that would be necessary. He was an old dude, and I was sure the sight of a suppressed pistol would gain us compliance.

The streets around here were pedestrian only, so Jennifer was parked about a block away on an avenue called Kuttlegasse. All we had to do was walk him there, and we were done. I didn't have any real qualms about the mission, because we weren't dealing with a hardened terrorist who had seen combat and would rather die than be caught. We were interdicting a money guy, who would probably soil himself when he saw my pistol.

But there was always Mike Tyson.

Knuckles said, "Bad news. He's got the message, and he's plugging it into his computer."

Which was something I didn't want to hear. I said, "Is he going to transmit the message out?"

"Yeah, I'm sure. No other reason to bring the laptop."

I said, "Can you interdict? Force him to leave before?"

"You want me to make a scene here? Pull out my pistol and start ranting about Muslims or something?"

I realized I was grasping at straws. I said, "What about cutting the hotel computer? Can you do something to interdict it? Maybe walk to it while he's on his laptop and make it crash?"

"Too late. He's done. He's put the thumb drive back into the computer, and he's typing."

*Damn it.*

I said, "Okay, okay, we got a Mike Tyson punch. Continue the mission. We get the next punch."

Two minutes later, Knuckles said, "He's on the move. I have five-five. Same path."

I clicked on the net and said, "Koko, Blood, you ready?"

Jennifer said, "Car is staged. Engine running."

Brett said, "Yeah. You call him on the ramp, and I'm on the move."

"Roger all. Carrie, what's your status?"

"In the Rover and on the way. Don't wait on me. I'll be there."

"Good to go."

Two minutes later, Knuckles said, "He's in the park. Headed your way."

I glanced left and saw the Professor, moving at a leisurely pace and glancing around. Looking for the bad man. He passed right in front of me and began the long walk down the far side ramp out of the park. I said, "All elements, all elements, I have control. Stand by."

And rose to follow.

When he reached the point where his head was below the walls around him I said, "Execute," and saw Brett coming up the other way. We closed on him rapidly, meeting at the bottom of the ramp, with about twenty feet to the street. I tapped the target on the shoulder and he turned. I put my pistol into his gut and said, "Don't move."

Brett came up behind him and trapped his arms behind his back. His eyes went wide and he sagged into the stone wall.

*Perfect.*

He was the bad guy, and he knew it. But he wasn't willing to fight.

I said, "Hand me the laptop."

He did so. I continued, "We're going to walk out of this park and one block up. If you try to fight us or flee, you'll be dead. Do you understand?"

He nodded dumbly and I said, "Let's go."

From the top of the ramp, Knuckles said, "Hold what you got. Biker on the way."

I pushed Professor into the wall and said, "Just remain quiet. Any noise, and you're dead."

I glanced up and saw a guy on a mountain bike coming down the path, decked out in cycling gear. Brett let go of the target's arms, but I kept the pistol in his gut, hidden by my body. The biker slowed down due to the slope of the ramp and the stairs at the bottom, coming almost to a standstill right next to us. I heard Brett hiss, "Gun!" and then heard a suppressed pop.

The Professor's head exploded right in front of me, the stone wall coated with brain matter. He collapsed like someone had turned off the power to his body, rolling on the ground, his left eye open, unseeing, his right a gout of blood.

*What the fuck?*

For a split second, I couldn't assimilate what had happened, but my reflexes took over. I rotated my pistol to the biker and saw him racing away, Brett chasing him with his own pistol out. The biker jumped down the small set of stairs at the bottom and disappeared.

Aaron came on, saying, "Couple coming up about to enter. What's the status?"

I said, "Stall them."

Brett came racing back to me and said, "What the hell just happened?"

I said, "I don't know. Find the drive. Get the drive."

We ripped through his clothes, Brett finding a thumb drive in his jacket pocket. He held it up and I said, "Let's get the hell out of here."

We speed-walked down the ramp and stairs, passed Aaron asking a couple for directions, and then began sprinting up the street, me on the net saying, "All elements, all elements, abort, abort, abort. Meet back at the hotel."

## CHAPTER 27

George Wolffe finished his overview of Pike's actions in Switzerland and paused, waiting on the inevitable questions from the Oversight Council. Unfortunately for him, the lead-off batter was President Hannister himself.

He leaned back in his chair and said, "So we gave you authority to capture this guy in Switzerland, and you killed him instead. That's not something I would expect with Taskforce operations. You are the scalpel I use when absolutely necessary, not a killing force like Putin employs. This guy was in no way DOA. I never said that, and from your briefing, I'm unsure if that's exactly what Pike executed."

DOA was a Taskforce designation rarely employed, meaning the threat was so great to United States interests that the target could be neutralized dead or alive. It was the closest designation in the United States government sanctioning an assassination, but only if capture was not feasible, and only if the threat was so great it posed an existential threat.

It was one more example of the illegality of the unit, because it directly went against EO 12333, an executive order that prohibited assassination signed by President Hannister, like every president before him since Gerald Ford had created it. Wolffe knew the delicate nature of the designation, not the least because he knew how Taskforce operators treated it when assigned.

When it was given, the Taskforce operators colloquially called it "Dead on Arrival," because it was much easier to kill a man than capture him. If DOA was given, nine times out of ten, the target was going home in a body bag. But that wasn't what had happened here.

Wolffe said, "Sir, as I said, Pike didn't kill him. Someone else did, and we think it was precisely to keep Pike from knowing what was in his head. In my opinion, the Israelis may be right on this. There's something more at play than Keta'ib Hezbollah. This isn't Iran pulling strings because we killed General Soleimani."

"The Israelis? They're breaking down my door through back channels to attack Iran using nothing more than letters as proof. They're pushing me to a place I don't want to go. And they're not the only ones. I have bipartisan commendation of Iran building exponentially. The death of Gabrielle in Italy is going to force my hand, regardless of the truth."

Wolffe knew the pressure he was under. One only needed to turn on the television to see the massive number of "experts" preening about regime change in Iran.

He said, "I meant the small section of Mossad that gave Aaron and Shoshana the mission. There are some who think this is deeper than just Iran projecting power through proxy forces."

Alexander Palmer chuckled and said, "Well, that would be good news, if it's true. Please tell us you have something to prove it."

Wolffe flipped a slide on the screen, showing the two messages from the courier. He said, "Unfortunately, no, I don't. All Pike was able to glean was a lead. There's a linkup planned for the transfer of money to a Keta'ib Hezbollah cell in Bahrain. They're apparently targeting someone in that country. We don't know who the target might be, but we *do* know where they're going to meet for the transfer of the funds."

Palmer said, "*Another* Keta'ib cell? How is this not proof in and of itself? We aren't talking about a letter here supposedly created by an imposter."

President Hannister said, "Where's the money coming from? Who's the paymaster?"

Wolffe used a laser pointer and went through the two messages. "The cell thinks it's Iran, but Pike doesn't. The guy coming is from Bosnia—apparently some sort of trained killer—and the entire linkup plan is strange. If it were Iran, they'd just order the guys to meet. In this case, the first message is asking, not telling, and it's not some Qods Force trainer like Iran would ordinarily send. It's a Bosniak assassin."

The secretary of defense said, "Iran was neck-deep in Bosnia during the war there. A Bosniak involved doesn't seem that strange to me. Sounds more like plausible deniability."

Amanda Croft said, "Can't we track the money backwards? From the guy who was killed?"

"We have his laptop, and the network operations guys are going through it remotely right now, but from what Pike's seen, the contact had pretty good operational security. He doesn't think anything's going to be on it."

Palmer started to ask another question and President Hannister interrupted, saying, "We're not going to get anywhere from inside the Oval Office. What are you asking here? What's the next step?"

Wolffe said, "Sir, let Pike take the team to the linkup in Bahrain. He's convinced the Bosnian is the key here. Pike wants Omega to roll him up. He's bringing the money, and he'll obviously know where it came from. If it's Iran, at least you'll have solid evidence instead of shooting in the dark. If it's not, we'll have the thread to pull it apart—and Pike's starting to think it's not."

Palmer said, "Based on what?"

Wolffe said, "Based on his intuition. He's the man on the ground."

Hannister looked around the room and said, "Put it to a vote."

Before they did, Palmer said, "Wait, sir, how are they going? What's the cover status?"

Wolffe said, "They're going as Israelis."

"Seriously? Does Israel know?"

Wolffe shut down his laptop, then turned to President Hannister, ignoring Palmer. He said, "Sir, I don't know who in Israel is read on to this, but Aaron and Shoshana are providing the support, and Bahrain recently signed a peace deal with Israel. They're sure it's not an issue, and Pike is game. Trust the man on the ground."

Palmer said, "That's asking for compromise not only from the operation, but from Israel. Before, this was just a reconnaissance operation. Now you're asking for Omega when the last one ended up with a dead target. Given the target was provided by the Israelis, they've got to be looking into that, and if they don't know, and find out an American team was operating as Israelis, they'll lose their minds. Israel will throw us under the bus as soon as they can."

Wolffe said, "The Israeli passports Pike's team is using came from the Mossad. Someone there already knows they're operational."

Palmer threw his hands in the air and said, "Someone with power? Or some Mossad lunatic who's operating outside of its own charter? There's a big difference between one lone operative going off the reservation to provide passports and the sanctioning of an operation with the blessing of Israel's version of the national command authority."

Wolffe said, "It is what it is. You're afraid of the compromise, but not the impending casualty. If we do nothing, and another American diplomat is killed, what then? We're out of threads to chase, and looking at war. Even if this *is* Iran, stopping the assassination in and of itself should be enough to launch."

Hannister said, "I agree. The benefits outweigh the risks. Anyone else have an issue with this?"

Palmer held his tongue, and the room remained quiet. Hannister gave it a moment, then said, "Okay. Tell Pike it's a go." He turned to Kerry Bostwick, the director of the CIA, and said, "Keep your ear to the ground with Mossad. Any hint of them exposing this, I want to know."

Kerry grumbled, "Fat lot of good that'll do. So far, they haven't told me squat."

President Hannister ignored him, returning to Wolffe. "Tell Pike to get me something. The pressure is growing exponentially. I'll have to respond to the death of our diplomat in Italy regardless. I can't let that go even if it's *not* Iran. No way can I allow the murder of one of my people. It will show nothing but appeasement that Iran will use even if they didn't execute the mission. Worst case, Iran sees it as a signal that they can attack with impunity. Right now, I can get away with some air strikes against Keta'ib targets in Syria, but eventually it's going to get worse."

Wolffe nodded and said, "I'll get it done."

Hannister flicked his head to the SECDEF and said, "I've already got the Fifth Fleet on alert. Tell Pike to keep me from using it, because that's where this is headed."

CHAPTER 28

Donatello took the Coke that Salim offered him, raised it for a sip, then surveyed the men around him. Jamal and Khalid were both barely in their twenties and looked like they hadn't been fed in a week. Wearing ratty T-shirts, jeans, and Adidas shower shoes, they didn't give him much confidence. Especially since they seemed to be more enamored with the video games in Salim's apartment than the mission itself.

The man known as Khan seemed more competent, if not a little savage. Donatello wasn't sure of his skill, but was convinced of his propensity for violence.

The leader, Salim, also appeared solid, if a bit effeminate. He was definitely intelligent, and constantly surveying his surroundings, like a wolf afraid something was going to take its meal. Not necessarily jumpy, but wary of anything that entered his domain. Donatello thought that a plus and something he could leverage, even as it had caused the linkup to become overly complicated.

He'd flown into Saudi Arabia's King Fahd

International Airport and had immediately encountered problems. It turned out that the Kingdom didn't recognize the diplomatic passport of the Knights of Malta. They'd almost turned him away until he'd brought out his actual Croatian passport. He'd already used his cover story about working with a charitable organization in Khobar—a story that the Knights of Malta passport was supposed to backstop.

He knew that if the shifting of passports had raised their suspicions, and they'd done any checking at all on his cover story, he was dead in the water. They did not, more concerned with him purchasing a visa than why he was visiting. They'd taken his picture and fingerprints, then allowed him to go on his way, but he knew he was flagged within the Kingdom now.

Luckily, he wasn't doing any work inside the country. He'd rented a car and driven to Khobar, then ran into more trouble trying to exit Saudi Arabia via the causeway to Bahrain. The immigration officer ran his passport through the scanner, saw he'd arrived on the same day, and demanded to know why he'd landed in Saudi Arabia if he intended to travel to Bahrain. Donatello told him that the flight was cheaper. The man seemed satisfied until he saw that Donatello had no visa for Bahrain, causing more questions.

Falling back on his Special Forces interrogation training and years of experience in hostile places, Donatello fended off each one expertly, until he was presented with the final hurdle—a negative COVID test. He had one just in case something like this happened, but hadn't been asked to present it upon arrival in the airport and knew from research that, due to vaccines, a quarantine was no longer in place in either KSA or Bahrain. Apparently, either this man hadn't been apprised of the updates or he was simply busting Donatello's balls, but after presenting the negative PCR test he was grudgingly allowed to leave.

He drove across the causeway, reaching what looked like a tollbooth on a turnpike, the overhang spanning all the lanes of the causeway with a sign proclaiming "Immigration." He waited in a line of cars, inching forward, then finally reached a booth with an immigration officer.

He didn't even bother to try his Knights passport, instead presenting his Croatian one, telling the officer he was working in Khobar and simply visiting for a few days as a tourist, a common occurrence. He'd been forced to purchase another visa to allow him entry, and was on his way.

As instructed, he'd driven to the first interchange and exited, heading south until he saw a modern gas station called Oil King. He parked and went inside to a counter serving soft-serve ice cream, being careful not to glance around. He knew he was now under surveillance. He ordered a chocolate cone and was told they only had vanilla. Saying he didn't like vanilla, he thanked the vendor, exited the store, and went to an ATM station that looked like a phone booth on steroids. He entered, closed the door, and pretended to use the machine, killing time.

Eventually, a man approached and stood outside, waiting on him to finish. He feigned frustration, then exited the booth. In English, the man said, "Is it not working?"

Donatello said, "Not for me."

The elaborate bona fides dance over, the man stuck out his hand and said, "I'm Salim. Come. Leave your rental here. We'll pick it up after we're done."

He'd let Donatello retrieve his overnight bag, then led him to a beat-up white Hyundai, opening the passenger door.

They returned to the expressway and Salim said, "What's your name?"

"You can call me Donnie."

Salim nodded, then said, "Did you bring the money, Donnie?"

"Yes. Five prepaid Visa cards with five hundred U.S. dollars each."

"And why did you need to come to deliver it? Why not just do what we used to?"

Donnie looked at him and said, "Okay, I'm not here to take over the operation, but I have some unique skills that may help."

They drove in silence for the next twenty minutes, Salim exiting the freeway into a concrete jungle of alleys and apartments, the outsides dotted with clotheslines and TV dishes. He pulled to a stop, exited, and said, "Follow me."

Salim led him to the second story of a building in need of repairs and entered an apartment. He introduced Donnie to the rest of the men, and then handed him a cold Coke.

Donnie took a sip and Salim said, "The money?"

At that, the two other men took off their headsets and put down their game controllers. Khan leaned forward in his chair.

"I told you, I have it, but first, I need to know the plan."

"The money *is* the plan. Khan's supposed to purchase weapons today, Khalid is paying off a patrol man to avoid an area, Jamal is getting explosives, and I have to pay the secretary in the target's office for his itinerary."

"So you don't have a plan? Is that it?"

"No. We do. I have the itinerary; I just need to pay the woman for it."

And Salim laid it out, piece by piece, ending with, "This will make a bigger statement, just like that CIA chief in Lebanon who was tortured to death while America could do nothing about it."

In spite of himself, Donatello was impressed. He saw a few flaws, but nothing that couldn't be fixed. The main problem was the end state. Capture was always harder than killing, and keeping this guy alive for days while sending out videos of his torture—while perfect for the Turtles' needs—was exceedingly risky.

He said, "I like it, but you're not going to be dealing with the United States coming to his rescue. It'll be the Sunni intelligence apparatus of Bahrain. You won't last more than a day with him, I promise. Especially if you're paying off police beforehand. It's a dead giveaway with a trail right back here."

"We understand their capabilities, trust me. The policeman is Shia—one of the few. He won't talk. He hates the monarchy just like we do. And we're not bringing the target back here."

"Okay, but still, may I suggest just putting out a single message with him, on the same night, and then killing him? You'll get nearly the same impact without the enormous risks."

Khan said, "We're prepared to die for the cause. Aren't you?"

"Yes, but not when I don't have to, any more than I'd jump out that window right now for the cause."

Salim said, "We'll consider it. Now, time is short. The money, please."

Donnie dug in his pack, then handed over an envelope. Salim passed out the cards to the men. After the three had left, Donnie said, "If they don't get what they need today, do you have a backup plan for the following day?"

"No. He's not leaving the base the following day. But the third day he's out again."

Donnie nodded and said, "What's the Wi-Fi password here?"

"Why?"

"I need to call my imam, and I'm not using the cell network to do that."

Salim gave it to him, Donnie hooked up to the internet, then turned on his Zello app, dialing Garrett. When he answered, Donnie began speaking in Croatian. "It looks like it's a go here. They have a pretty good plan, and it's set for tomorrow night. I'll need to smooth over some rough edges, but I think it'll work."

"And do they suspect you in any way?"

"No. As a matter of fact, nobody's questioned

me about my religion or anything about my past. They just assumed I've been sent by Iran."

"Good. Get this done and come home immediately. I now have the final target's itinerary. Things are speeding up. We need to leave for Lebanon soon, before the Grand Master goes to Israel."

Donnie glanced at Salim, saying, "Trust me, I'm out of here as soon as the capture is done. These guys are true believers, and I'm pretty sure they'll all be dead within forty-eight hours. I don't intend to be in the blast radius."

## CHAPTER 29

Sitting in a rental car on Shabab Avenue—
otherwise known as "American Alley" here in
Manama—I was parked right under the smiling
face of good ol' Colonel Sanders, and thinking
about getting some fried chicken just to see if it
was the same as in the United States. Surely the
Colonel's secret recipe of eleven herbs and spices
hadn't made it over to Bahrain. Unfortunately, it
was a mystery that would have to wait. Instead, I
clicked on the net and said, "Shoshana, how's it
looking?"

She came back, "I'm walking by now. Pentest
is operational in the backpack. Getting some
looks, but nothing sharp. I'm good."

I said, "Roger. Blood, Aaron, you copy?"

Brett came back. "Roger all. We're staged two
minutes out. No issues."

"Roger. Shoshana, just get the penetration
test done. No crazy stuff here."

She didn't reply, which meant she didn't like
me telling her what to do. Jennifer said, "You
know she speaks fluent Arabic. With her black
hair and dark skin, she'll blend right in."

I said, "She'd blend in with a bunch of Arabs

who are strangers, like in an airport, but that neighborhood is tight. They won't do anything because they suspect she's an Israeli—but they might just because she doesn't live there."

I'd gotten Omega authority for the Bosnian guy not more than four hours after sending it, which surprised me. Actually, it made me a little bit squeamish, which was unusual, because I was wondering what was behind the blanket approvals. Usually, I had to fight my ass off to get the Oversight Council to approve anything, but now they were doing it every time I asked. It made me wonder if they knew something I did not.

We'd flown out of Switzerland to Bahrain, getting clearance to land and taxi away from the commercial aviation section to the private, rich man's land of flying. Once again I was happy to be in a Rock Star bird, but I was sure immigration would be a different story, since we were apparently all *Sabra* Israelis.

Aaron had made a few calls while we were taxiing, then said, "We're good."

I'd said, "How? We're about to be questioned why we're here—in a Sunni-dominated country while holding Israeli passports."

We parked and waited for the interrogation, and then I was surprised. The man who had entered wasn't Arab. He was Israeli. He asked what we needed in the way of help, and Aaron said, "A couple of rental cars. One sedan and one SUV."

The man nodded, and I said, "Can we just walk out of here with our luggage? No interference?"

He said, "Yes. The monarchy wants to improve relations with Israel. There will be no repercussions because of your heritage. Let me bring in the immigration officials and get your passports stamped."

He exited, and I looked at Aaron, saying, "What's going on?"

"We've had a secret embassy in Bahrain for years. A front company supposedly doing commercial work. It's been full of Israeli dual-citizens for over a decade, giving us plausible deniability. When Bahrain signed the peace accords, they meant it, but they understand the pressure that's going to be brought to bear from the Shiite majority. Because of that, when we arrive, we get special treatment, away from the usual immigration and customs lines."

I said, "I wonder what Saudi Arabia thinks of that shit."

He laughed and said, "Everything Bahrain does is with KSA's approval. They don't use the bathroom without clearing it through KSA. It was the Kingdom that flooded forces in here to stabilize the Sunni monarchy after the latest uprisings. Trust me, Saudi Arabia knows and approves. We're hoping to get the Kingdom to come on board soon."

The Israeli returned with an Arab man in an ill-fitting immigration uniform—like they swapped them out at shift change. He took our passports and gave them the requisite stamps and visas. They both left, and I said, "Mossad?"

Aaron said, "Honestly, I don't know. Could

be. Or could just be a guy working at our secret embassy. Not sure."

"What about the pilots?"

"As Americans, they're on their own, but *as* Americans, they'll have no trouble."

I went up to the cockpit and told the pilots the situation, which made them happy. No quarantine, and I promised we weren't flying for at least two days, so they could get their own jihad on at the Bahrain nightlife.

I returned to Aaron and said, "So we can just unload a bunch of weapons and get out of here?"

"Pretty much. First, we need to get some vehicles."

He'd sent Jennifer and Shoshana to find them, and then Aaron, Brett, and I had started taking the plane apart, pulling out surveillance gear and weapons we might need, packing them in ordinary suitcases. By the time we were done, Jennifer and Shoshana had returned with a nondescript sedan and another Land Rover.

We'd loaded them up and driven to a hotel, realizing we had little time. The meet was supposed to occur in the next two hours. That, in itself, wasn't a problem, because the entire island nation could be crossed in forty minutes, but we wanted time to assess the linkup location.

We'd spent about twenty minutes planning an assault, and then traveled out to the linkup point. When we'd arrived, I saw that the man who'd sent the message had been very, very careful. It would be very hard to take down the Bosnian here. The final point was an ATM right out front, in full view of anyone coming into the gas station.

We knew the entire bona fides for the linkup from the messages, and inside the gas station Jennifer had triggered the first—the fake ask for chocolate ice cream. At that point, we knew we were in play, but there was nothing we could do beyond taking pictures. The target walked out, went to the ATM booth, and then was met by a second man. We recorded it all, impotent. I'd seriously thought about just running up and thumping him in the head, but knew that was a nonstarter.

We settled for following them, which had been easy on the expressway. Eventually, they left it and began driving through the concrete jungle of the Sanabis neighborhood of Manama. A hotbed of Shiite folks who didn't take kindly to strangers.

In the eyes-on position, I saw the vehicle leave the highway and start threading through the narrow streets of the neighborhood. I followed for about three turns, and then pulled off. From studying the driver of the vehicle at the gas station, I knew he was looking for the bad man. He had that wolf scent in everything he did. I'd called Aaron and Shoshana and told them my position, and they picked up the follow, eventually finding the apartment, but there was no way we could maintain surveillance in this place.

With the sun going down, we'd pulled off and made a plan for the next day, which, for me, was an almost impossible task. We had no idea what these guys had planned and no way to find out.

I'd put my boss's ass on the line for this—not to mention the entire Taskforce—and now had no way to solve the problem. Failure was not an option here, and I was really regretting that I didn't take down the Bosnian in the parking lot. We would have had to run like no tomorrow, possibly taking his contact as well, but we probably could have made it to the plane. Probably could have prevented the hit that was coming.

The glaring truth was that there was no way to penetrate that neighborhood for an assault. It was like every small neighborhood in Boston or Houston—or Fallujah for that matter. The folks there knew who belonged and who did not. Because the terrorists were involved in subversive activities, there was no doubt that they had an early warning net established. They'd been hunted by the surveillance state of Bahrain for years, and had managed to survive. Which meant they were skilled.

And yet, a hit was coming. Something I'd promised to stop.

Inside the hotel room, we'd bantered about various courses of action, and all of them were a no-go. From using a small drone to acting like homeless folks, there was no way we could maintain surveillance on the place. Given the atmospherics, it was impossible.

At that point, we'd shifted to just slamming the place, taking it down with all inside. We knew the location of the hornet's nest, and we knew they were planning a hit, so it wasn't out of the scope of our authority, but doing such a thing had so many different points of failure that it was a last resort. The odds of us being in a Bahrain jail after such an action were very, very good. And our defense that they were planning a killing wouldn't amount to much if the opposition denied it.

I'd finally canceled the planning, saying it wasn't a course of action that was feasible. Shoshana had bristled, saying, "It's not your decision. It's ours. That Bosnian knows who killed the *Ramsad*, and I'm going to peel him like a grape."

And that laid bare the operational framework we were in, finally ripping open the confusing command chain. I'd been waiting on it. The Taskforce had given us Omega authority, meaning it was a Taskforce operation, but we were here under Israeli passports gleaned by Aaron and Shoshana, meaning she thought they still had primacy.

I looked at Aaron, and saw he was a little pissed as well, but I could tell he understood my position. He wasn't going to fight me, but it would be up to me to convince Shoshana. He would be no help.

The truth is I had been more than willing to play the follower for their operation in Switzerland, but we'd entered a new world. *I* was the team leader here. That sounds arrogant, but I had given my word to Wolffe. If this mission failed, it would be because of me, not because I'd followed the Israelis.

I looked at Shoshana and said, "The mission is to find out who's doing the killing, not revenge.

I get you want the Bosnian, but peeling him like a grape isn't going to solve our problem. The way we'll do that is through my assets. The Mossad has given you nothing but passports. My team has given us the ability to penetrate. Don't make this a fight here. *I'm* in charge."

She surprised me, like she did every single time we operated together. She walked up to me, gave her little disconcerting deep stare into my eyes, and said, "Okay, Nephilim. You can be in charge. I'm not here to fight you, but you won't allow me to solve the problem."

Taken aback, I said, "What's that mean?"

"We can't put surveillance on the outside, but we *can* on the inside. I promise. They're kids. They have Wi-Fi, and they're bound to be using all sorts of applications. Let me penetrate that. We'll get what they're doing from the inside instead of watching from the outside."

I looked at Jennifer and she raised her eyebrows. I glanced at Brett and he said, "It is the twenty-first century. We have the best hackers in the world."

I turned to Aaron and he gave me what I wanted, saying, "You're in charge here. Up to you."

He knew what I was going to do, but it was the final nail in the coffin of who was running this circus. Now it really *was* up to me. I returned to Shoshana, seeing her grinning.

"What do you say, Nephilim? Want to turn me loose?"

I shook my head, then said, "Not really, but

apparently we don't have a lot of choices. So letting Carrie roam free is probably the best of the bad ideas."

She laughed and said, "I can penetrate the neighborhood. I can move like a fish in water. You know that. What I need is the ability to penetrate the Wi-Fi in that apartment. And you can provide that. Call that guy Cream. He'll figure it out."

Jennifer was already digging through a backpack, looking for a device that did nothing but sniff out Wi-Fi nodes, then search for a weakness to penetrate. She said, "His name is Creed, not Cream. And he's pretty good at his job."

## CHAPTER 30

Garrett parked his car and went into the greenspace next to the apartment complex with the dead woman, booting up his tablet. He walked to the near end for his signal, just like he had done before, and then took a seat on a bench, keeping an eye out for the small child who had seen him before. He wasn't in the park, letting Garrett focus solely on his feeds.

Like he had done the last two days, he waited on someone to find the body and initiate a response. Yet again, nobody had shown up. On his feeds, he could see the body in the living room, sprawled on the hardwood floor with her eyes open. She hadn't started to bloat with internal gases, but that was coming.

In retrospect, he realized he'd made a mistake renting the VRBO for four days without checking the scheduled cleaning for his unit. He'd shown up the next day, expecting at least a maid service to empty the trash or change the sheets, but nobody came. After that, he'd checked his rental agreement and saw there was no maid service. At that point, he'd simply waited each day, hoping someone would find the body.

So far, they had not, and he was growing aggravated. He needed to learn the police inspector's name and address, or this entire trap was worthless. He considered "finding" the body himself, and calling in an anonymous report, but believed that was a risk. From his time hunting terrorists, he knew that such a contact could be peeled back, even if he was careful.

He decided to return to the apartment and initiate an alarm that would tell him when someone opened the door. He had the tools to do so, and could slave it to his laptop. Then he wouldn't have to keep coming here in person hoping the body was found.

As he was musing about the problem, his phone rang, surprising him.

He pulled it out, saw the Zello app as the culprit, and answered, speaking Croatian. "Donnie, so how's it going?"

"Good, sir. The hit is tonight, and I think it's going to be exactly what we want. They're still hell-bent on a capture, which is fine by me, but once the mission is over, I'm out of here. These fucks are crazy, and they won't last a day."

"You have to make sure it works. Get out of the blast radius later, but don't let them screw it up."

"I got it, sir. I'm on it. The target is taking a small delegation out to dinner at 1900 tonight, at a restaurant called Rodeo Bahrain. Apparently, it's an American-themed restaurant, and his guests are foreign. The contact that gave us the itinerary said it was a little bit of a tradition since he took command. As for me, I already have my ticket out for tomorrow morning. I'll make sure it works, and then bug out."

Garrett saw a van park with a cleaning emblem, then saw three women exit and go inside the building. He leaned forward, hoping they were going to his apartment.

They did not.

Donatello said, "Did you hear me? Hello?"

Garrett realized he had zoned out. He said, "Yes, I hear you. That sounds like a plan. Just don't let them screw it up like you did with the Vatican ambassador."

Donatello changed the subject, saying, "Where are you? What are you doing?"

The words snapped Garrett into the present. He said, "I'm at the palace. What do you mean?"

"Nothing. My phone is showing you in the EUR. The Zello app is saying you're south of the city center. Must be a glitch."

Garrett felt his face flush at the mistake. He said, "Don't worry about my location. Worry about your own. Kill that son of a bitch. Tonight."

He hung up and returned to his vehicle to emplace the alarm, embarrassed at his own lack of operational security.

## CHAPTER 31

I waited on the screen to clear, hoping it was Bartholomew Creedwater on the other end and not George Wolffe. Creedwater—or Creed as he was known—was a Taskforce network engineer, which was a polite, politically correct way of saying "hacker," and we were using him to penetrate the terrorist bed-down site. But what we'd found wasn't very useful as of yet, because nobody at the Taskforce spoke Bosnian.

I'd ordered Creed to rectify that oversight. Working out of the Blaisdell Consulting office in Washington, DC—the name of the cover organization that cloaked Taskforce headquarters—he was supposed to come up and tell me what we'd found. I was afraid he'd also told Wolffe, which would lead to nothing but questions I couldn't answer.

Earlier, Shoshana had returned to our vehicle outside the KFC without issue, her quick reaction force of Brett and Aaron luckily not needed. She'd entered the car and said, "You were right. That location is not suitable for assault. I could feel the energy all around me. It's a red zone."

I chuckled, took the pentest device, and said,

"Did you get anything from the walk we could use? I mean besides the Wi-Fi exploitation?"

"Yeah. I took photos of every car on the street. May come in handy."

"Good work. Let's go see what we have here."

She continued, "And the stairwell leading up to the apartment has infrared surveillance cameras. One at the base, and one on the landing floor. It's good you decided not to assault. No way up there without being seen."

Incredulous, I said, "What? How would you know that?"

"What do you mean? I went up it."

And that set me off: "You did *what*? You were supposed to just walk down the street. You penetrated the complex?"

Miffed, she looked at Jennifer, then back at me, saying, "How was I supposed to get the Wi-Fi exploits from the street? We'd be trying to sort the devices from fifteen different apartments. What's your problem?"

I squeezed my eyes shut for a moment, praying for the ability to keep me from throttling her ass. I opened them and said, "So you're on camera now. Is that what you're telling me? You never, ever listen to me."

She leaned forward and, like a child exploring, she traced her finger around my face, saying, "If you had been there, you would have done the same thing, Nephilim. The mission is what matters. Why are you so upset?"

It was just one more bat-shit crazy thing with her. I glanced at Jennifer and saw her trying to hide a smirk. For the life of me, I couldn't get her to quit using my given name, which I despised. She thought it held some deep biblical meaning, and it should have aggravated me even more, but her use of it reminded me that she's about four beers short of a six-pack. And she was wickedly skilled.

I put the car in drive and said, "Look, *Carrie*, you pull that type of crap on the next mission and I'm going to go ape-shit on your ass. Just do what I ask. Nothing more, nothing less."

She'd leaned back into her seat and crossed her arms, looking like she wanted to rip out my entrails. She spat out, "I'll do what I must. Nothing more, nothing less."

I started to retort, but Jennifer laid her hand on my arm, gently shaking her head. I let it go.

We went back to our hotel, plugged in the device to our Taskforce laptop, dialed into the Taskforce VPN, and let Creed go to work. We'd sat around waiting for about an hour, bouncing lighthearted banter between us.

The team we had wasn't a real Taskforce construct, but we'd worked together enough that it might as well have been. Knuckles gave me shit about not taking the Bosnian at the gas station, and I'd turned it to Shoshana, chastising her in front of the group for penetrating the apartment complex and potentially compromising the mission, knowing I was going to get a rise out of her. Wanting the fireworks.

She surprised the hell out of me. For the first time, she didn't take the bait.

She smiled and said, "I never knew you were

such a pussy. Maybe that's why Jennifer likes me so much."

If there was such a thing as the entire room's mouth dropping open, that was it. In an earlier life, when I'd tried to kill her, I had been sure she was a lesbian. And she knew it, using it now as a jab at me because of her close relationship with Jennifer. There was a pregnant moment of silence, and then Knuckles started laughing, still not believing what she'd just said.

Everyone else joined in, and I raised a finger to my brow in a tiny salute, saying, "Touché, little Jedi, touché."

She beamed a smile at me, a little embarrassed that she'd caused the reaction, but enjoying it nonetheless. Aaron caught my eye and winked, happy that it had happened. Like me, he knew that Shoshana was a feral animal, and he was relentlessly trying to bring her out of that land, with Jennifer and I working toward that same goal. Tonight had been one more step.

The chuckles died down just as the computer had bleeped. I went to it with everyone coalescing around me. I'd clicked on and saw Creed sitting at the other end.

*Whew. No Wolffe.*

He said, "Good news and bad news. The good news is their security is shit. I had no trouble getting in. The bad news is there isn't a lot to exploit. No phones, no laptops, or anything of value that I can penetrate. Not a lot connected to Wi-Fi. They know that's bad."

Which was deflating.

I said, "So what's that mean? You can't do anything?"

And he smiled, which was his way of showing that he was smarter than everyone else. Every single time I leveraged him, he would draw out what he could do, like he was reading a play for the climax. It was trying, but because he was so good, I lived with it. Up to a point.

He said, "I didn't say that. The one thing I did find was an Xbox connected to the Wi-Fi."

"And? So what? Did they post their plan on a *Call of Duty* map or something?"

"No. But they're online with it."

At that point, I exploded. I leaned into the computer camera until I was sure he only saw eyeballs and said, "You'd better cut to the chase, or I'm flying home to rip your balls off."

I saw him recoil from the screen and Jennifer leaned into the camera, pushing me aside, saying, "Creed, ignore that. What do you have?" I tried to get back on the screen and she bumped my body away, glaring at me and saying, "Give it a rest, Neanderthal."

I stomped in a circle for a minute, and then acquiesced. Knuckles said, "Jesus Christ. You guys are a reality show in the making."

I said nothing, taking a seat. Creed stuttered, "The Xbox is connected to Wi-Fi. They use it for online games. And they use headsets."

Behind Jennifer, I said, "So?"

"So the headsets have microphones. They talk to people online. And because of it, I can hear everything in the room. They never turned off the box."

*Holy shit. The mother lode.*

I said, "And did you get something? Did you record it?"

He now returned to his smug look, saying, "I did. Unfortunately, they weren't speaking English in the room. But I got it."

I said, "Was it Arabic?"

"No. Definitely not Arabic. I don't know what it was, but I have it."

I said, "It's Bosnian. Get a Bosnian terp and get it translated ASAP. I mean within the next ten minutes. Something is going down soon here, and we need to know immediately."

## CHAPTER 32

That had been an hour ago, and now I was waiting on the results. The VPN finally connected, asking me if I wanted to use my camera, like I was a college student on a Zoom call. I clicked yes, waiting to see who was on the other end.

It was Creed yet again, not Wolffe. I internally had a little sigh of relief, but I knew sooner or later it would be my boss.

He said, "Hey, Pike."

I said, "So was it Bosnian?"

"No. It wasn't."

*What the hell?*

I immediately went to level eleven. "So we still don't know what was said in that room? Are you saying we can't figure out a language? We're the damn Taskforce. You're in DC. Go play it through a speaker on Embassy Row and ask someone to identify it."

He smiled his little infuriating smile and said, "We know the language. It was Croatian."

*Croatian? Why did the earlier messages say the guy was a Bosniak?*

I said, "You're sure about that? It's Croatian?"

He said, "Yeah, I'm sure. We have the transcript. There was a guy in the room talking to someone else. We don't know what any of it means, but here's the meat of it."

He messed with his keyboard and a paragraph appeared on my screen next to his face.

> The target is taking a small delegation out to dinner at 1900 tonight, at a restaurant called Rodeo Bahrain. Apparently, it's an American-themed restaurant, and his guests are foreign. The contact that gave us the itinerary said it was a little bit of a tradition since he took command. As for me, I already have my ticket out for tomorrow morning. I'll make sure it works, and then bug out.

I read it and knew we were now under the clock. The hit was tonight. I said, "Anything else? Did they give a name? Is there anyone we can alert?"

At that, Creed deflated, saying, "No. That's it, Pike."

I knew that wasn't fair, because he'd really come through with the penetration. I said, "Don't worry about it. Get me George Wolffe. Is he in the building? It's five P.M. here. It's like ten A.M. there, right? I've got two hours."

He said, "Let me check," and disappeared.

With the team around me looking at the screen, I said, "Okay, we know the location of the hit, and we know the time. But we still don't know the target."

Brett said, "Gotta be an American."

"Why? Why do you think that?"

"He's taking a foreign entourage to a place called 'Rodeo Bahrain'? A distinctly American restaurant. The only person who would do that would be an American."

I said, "Yeah, but the message says his guests are foreign, meaning he is not. If he was American, he'd be foreign as well."

Shoshana said, "They aren't going to target a Sunni Arab. The guy isn't talking about someone living here."

I said, "Maybe they are. Maybe this is the plan. Iran's now attacking the monarchy here. We don't know what the scope of this thing is. They've killed Israelis, Americans, and now maybe the Shiites are taking it to the Sunnis."

Shoshana said, "I don't believe this is Iran. It's someone else, and it's not about the Shia/Sunni divide."

"But you don't *know* that. We need to operate here with what we know."

Jennifer said, "There's that one line about this being a tradition since he 'took command.' That sounds like the Navy base. An American who took command on the Navy base and traditionally takes his foreign counterparts to dinner when they visit."

The computer bleeped and Creed came back on, looking flustered. He said, "Wolffe's not here. He's at the White House. Won't be back for hours."

*Shit.*

I looked at my watch, seeing we had a little less

than two hours to stop this thing. I said, "Okay, tell him I'm initiating an in-extremis Omega operation. It's not against my original target the Oversight Council gave me authority for. It's to stop this hit. If it goes bad, and we can get out, tell him we're flying out of here to Aviano Air Base in Italy. He'll have to bail us out from there."

Creed looked a little sick at the words. He said, "Pike, I think that's something you should tell him yourself."

"I don't have the time. Tell him I'm on the thread, but someone's going to die tonight if I sit on my hands. I gotta go. Thanks for the help."

He said, "Pike, I really—" and I disconnected.

I turned to Jennifer and Shoshana, saying, "I think you're right. It's an American, and we have about one hour to make a plan to prevent the killing."

## CHAPTER 33

Vice Admiral Gregory Stiles saw he wasn't going to have time to return home before his dinner tonight. He stuck his head out of his office door and said, "Megan, can you call my wife and tell her I'm not coming home first? Tell her I got caught up and am going to have to just leave from here."

His secretary nodded with a smile. Getting "caught up" was a regular occurrence. Admiral Stiles wore so many hats he could be a haberdashery salesman, and the job was so punishing, the commander from two years ago had committed suicide.

Known as the commander of the Fifth Fleet, the commander of NAVCENT, and the commander of combined maritime forces comprising three separate task forces for combatting piracy, counterterrorism, and Arabian Gulf security and cooperation, it was a wonder he could keep them all straight.

Tonight's dinner was with his foreign naval peers of CTF 151, the task force dedicated to counter-piracy. The ranking representatives of the naval forces working that mission from the

United Kingdom, France, Australia, and Denmark were paying a visit, and as had been his custom since taking command at the Naval Support Activity in Bahrain, Vice Admiral Stiles was treating them to dinner at Rodeo Bahrain, a fairly new restaurant that served steaks with an American country-and-western vibe.

It had become sort of an inside joke—no matter who showed up to visit, that was where they were going. It saved Admiral Stiles from having to spend any mental energy on the visiting delegation or worrying about cross-cultural issues—if you came to visit, you were getting an American steak. It was also within walking distance of the pedestrian gate outside of the naval base, saving them from trying to find parking in the congested downtown area of Manama.

And the walk allowed him to connect with his guests, breaking the ice on the way instead of doing so at a table.

The admiral's aide stuck his head in the door and said, "Sir, they're here."

Stiles grimaced and said, "Give me a minute. I'll be right out."

At 1830, I followed the hostess to a booth for two. The restaurant wasn't that big, with only a single room fronted by a bandstand, a country-and-western act from the Philippines tuning up their instruments. The décor looked like it had been stolen from a LongHorn Steakhouse franchise, with deer heads on the wall and rough-cut steel silhouettes of cowboys riding horses backlit by red lights, two wide-screen TVs behind the bar.

She showed us to a corner booth, which was perfect, and Knuckles sat across from me. He was wearing his usual, which is to say a ratty T-shirt with some obscure band's name on it, a puka bead necklace, and had his mass of black hair in a ponytail. If you didn't know any better, you'd think he was a granola-eating backpacker out traveling the world. Right up until you met his eyes.

He said, "Doesn't look that crowded. Not sure how they'll take him here."

I watched Brett and Aaron enter, getting their own table. They'd see where we were, and triangulate accordingly. I said, "If he's coming with an entourage, they'll want to separate the target. They don't want to take them all on."

I glanced around the place, seeing a smattering of Arabs, but mostly the tables were full of guys from the Navy base. I knew the killers were in here, though. They were watching. And waiting. Maybe back in the kitchen, maybe part of the waitstaff. I couldn't take anything for granted.

I saw a booth in the opposite corner with four locals, all wearing masks. Which was a little strange, because you had to have a mask to enter, but you could take it off after sitting down. Knuckles and I still had on our masks because we wanted to do what we could to shield ourselves from the surveillance cameras. Which made me think they were doing the same.

Knuckles said, "They won't take him in here. The choke point is the doorway. They'll wait until he's leaving, then attack."

I nodded and said, "I agree, but we need to pinpoint the target. We can't wait at the doorway for every guy who leaves. I think it's an American, but it might not be."

My earpiece chirped, Shoshana saying, "Pike, Pike, we're outside, and I have the Bosnian in sight. He's in a sedan right down the street, parked next to a dumpster."

I looked at Knuckles and saw he realized this was the endgame. I said, "What's he doing? Who's he with?"

"He's by himself, but in front of him is a panel van. Two people in it that I can see."

From the message, we knew they were going to attempt a capture, which is precisely why I'd taken such a lax approach by invading the space and biding our time. If I'd thought they were going to kill the target in some sort of gangland-type slaughter, I would have used different tactics. The panel van confirmed my thoughts. That was the exfil vehicle.

I said, "Okay, listen, when this goes down, I need you to close on the van. Ignore the Bosnian. They'll be using the van, and they'll separate. He's there for security and oversight, but the van is the key."

"The Bosnian is the *reason* for this whole thing. Who cares who they capture? He's the key. We should take his ass out right now."

I saw five older men enter the bar, all of them looking like they held rank, moving with a slight arrogance that told me they were men used to being in charge. I said, "Carrie, I get you want a little payback. Let's stop this killing and then get on him. One step at a time."

She said, "The van's on the move. It's headed your way. To the front of the restaurant."

That sent a jolt of electricity through me. I said, "Roger. All elements, all elements, the target just entered the restaurant. Group of five with sticks up their ass dressed in last decade's clothes. I don't know who's the actual, but it's one of them. Get ready."

I looked across the room at Brett and Aaron and got a slight nod. Knuckles said, "How are they going to get them out of the restaurant? This makes no sense. Why is the van moving now?"

I reached behind my back, getting my hand on

the butt of my weapon. I said, "Good question. I don't know. But they do."

At that moment, an explosion down the street rocked the room, the ceiling releasing dust like we were in Beirut. Everyone in the restaurant stopped, looking at each other. Another explosion happened, this one closer. From the sound of it, right next door at the hotel the restaurant was attached to. People began to stand up, some rushing to the door. The five-man group immediately turned around, one of them urging the others back out onto the street.

And I knew how they were going to get him.

Shoshana came on, shouting, "I've got explosions on the street. I say again, they're targeting the hotel next door."

The room was turning into pandemonium, with people either hiding under their tables or trying to run out. I leapt up, saying, "It's a diversion. It's a diversion. They're taking him now. Get on them."

I drew my pistol, saw Knuckles, Brett, and Aaron do the same, and we ran to the door, pushing through the cattle of the other panic-stricken people in the restaurant, only we weren't looking for a safe space. I saw the five-man crew walking at a fast pace, staring at the smoke rising fifty meters away. I sprinted toward them just as the van door slid open on the street, three men spilling out and racing across the grass to the front of the restaurant. They fired into the crowd, scattering everyone, then leapt on the leader of the group, piling him into the ground.

They hoisted him like a bag of wheat and

began running back to the van. I said, "Don't hit him! Don't hit him!" knowing my entire team was about to shoot. Knuckles took a knee, brought his pistol up, and let out a breath. He broke the trigger and the trail man shouted, dropping the body. The others tried to continue, now dragging the man, and I finally got in the fight, drawing a bead and hitting the lead man in the head.

He collapsed. The last one seemed unsure of what to do, which was enough time for Brett and Aaron to reach him. He attempted to hoist the man on his shoulders, but the target was now fighting like a wildcat. The last man saw Brett and Aaron with their weapons out and kicked the target to the ground, raising a pistol. Aaron split his head open.

The target leapt up and sprinted away, running like he was on fire. I let him go, racing to the front of the van. It began moving and I started shooting, puncturing the windshield. I couldn't see the driver, but I knew where to aim. I fired once, twice, three times, and the van veered off to the left, the accelerator floored. It smashed into a concrete wall, the engine still revving.

I saw a flash of headlights, a car about to run me down. I dove out of the way, then saw a Land Rover following close behind, Jennifer at the wheel. The vehicle went about fifty meters before the Rover hammered it in the right rear quarter panel, punching it into the wall of the alley, the Rover pinning it to the wall.

I started sprinting toward it, Knuckles right

behind me, saying, "Blood, Aaron, check out the van."

I saw a man exit the sedan with a pistol in his hands. Shoshana leapt out of the passenger side of the Rover and was on him, slapping the weapon high and tearing into his body with her elbows, knees, and fists. He screamed a keening wail, trying to fight back, and she circled his body, cinching his waist with her legs and wrapping her arms around his head, bringing him to the ground.

I shouted, "No!" and she leaned back, torquing his neck until it snapped. I reached her just as she was pushing him off herself with a leg, his body now lifeless, his eyes still open, a string of drool coming out of his mouth.

Jennifer came around the car with her pistol out, pulling security, looking for another threat. Shoshana stood up, breathing heavily.

I just shook my head. She said, "What?"

"Nothing. Check his body for anything you can find. Phones, documents, whatever."

I clicked on the net and said, "Blood, Aaron, you done?"

"Yeah. They had a little torture chamber in the back, complete with camera."

"Get the other Rover. We're leaving immediately."

Knuckles started searching the sedan and I said, "Leave it. There won't be anything in that. We need to go. Jennifer, get this thing back in motion."

She jumped behind the wheel and backed up

the Rover, showing me it could still function. Shoshana stood up and said, "I have a cell and a passport."

I said, "Good enough. Let's get the hell out of here."

## CHAPTER 35

George Wolffe followed Alexander Palmer down to the Situation Room, watching aides scramble up and down the hallway like the folders they were carrying were the cure for COVID. He said, "So it's gotten a little heated?"

"That's putting it mildly. When you try to blow up the commander of the Fifth Fleet, there's going to be a reaction."

"They didn't try to blow him up. That was a diversion."

Palmer chuckled and said, "Yeah, so I guess capturing him to torture him later is better. The Bahrain naval base is on lockdown and the monarchy is going nuts. They've invaded a Shia neighborhood called Sanabis and are cracking skulls. The bottom line is Keta'ib Hezbollah tried to kill him."

Wolffe said, "We don't know that for sure."

Palmer paused outside the door of the Situation Room, saying, "We don't? That's different from the report you sent."

"That didn't come out right. Yes, a militia under the sway of Iran tried to kill him. That's correct. What we don't know is if Iran had anything to do with it."

Palmer opened the door and said, "It might not matter. Look, we're hitting Keta'ib Hezbollah camps in Syria right now, and are leveraging the Iraqi government to put them on a leash inside Iraq. CTF 150 with the Eisenhower Carrier Strike Group is out, waiting on orders to hammer Iran. SOCOM is working up assault plans for decapitation strikes at the Natanz nuclear facility and inside Tehran."

Wolffe couldn't believe how fast things had progressed. He said, "What's Iran's position? What are they saying?"

"The usual bullshit. They have nothing to do with it, death to the Great Satan, any attempt at an attack will be the mother of all wars. Blah, blah, blah."

They entered the Situation Room, finding a scrum of people around a long table, each of them engaged in separate conversations, the smell of stale coffee heavy in the air. Wolffe saw President Hannister at the head of the table talking to the secretary of state, and he realized it was heated. Things really were ramping up. Fortunately, Hannister had been in a crisis like this before. It wasn't his first rodeo in the cauldron of a new Cuban Missile Crisis.

"Amanda, I get your position, but what the hell else can we sanction? Baby powder? We've already sanctioned every bit of their economy. More sanctions will just look like we're not able to do anything else, and it will have no deterrence on their behavior whatsoever. I might as well just get on TV and call them mean words."

She said, "I don't feel a preemptive strike at this stage is prudent."

Hannister said, "I don't, either, but we have to set the conditions in case it becomes prudent."

"Prudent for whom? The military?"

Wolffe saw Hannister's face sour and knew that wasn't a good choice of words. President Hannister said, "In case you haven't been listening, it's the *military* that's been urging restraint. It's the *military* demanding that we prove Iran is behind these killings."

She started to reply and Hannister finally noticed him. He waved Wolffe forward.

Wolffe reached him, Palmer right behind. To Amanda Croft he said, "Ma'am," then turned to the president. Hannister said, "I saw the report out of Bahrain. Anything you want to add? Anything new?"

"They were definitely Arabs, and they had a pretty good plan. It looks like they'd turned a panel van into a mobile torture studio. No fixed site to assault, no address for the authorities to track down. It was pretty smart. We think they intended to pull a William Buckley with the admiral, broadcasting his torture on the net. They had a fairly sophisticated setup in the back."

"Why didn't you capture the Bosnian?"

"It's a little complicated. They used explosive devices for a diversion in the hotel next door. Pike focused on preventing the killing of the target instead of capture of the man he was tracking, who was up the street. He could have taken him without a problem, but he went for the saving of the commander."

Hannister nodded, and Wolffe said, "By the way, how'd that work out? Is there any bleed from him about Pike's crew being there?"

"No, thank God. He has no idea what happened. He escaped and only saw a bunch of men wearing masks. Nobody knows what happened, only that someone tried to kill the head of the United States Fifth Fleet, and that someone is probably Iran. The investigation from the monarchy is ongoing."

Wolffe said, "*Might* be Iran. And they won't find anything from our end. Pike's already in the air."

"Tell him I'm happy he was there. He wasn't, and we'd be at war right now."

Wolffe just nodded. Hannister continued, "And the Bosnian? How does he fit in? Who's the paymaster for all this shit?"

"He's not Bosnian. He's Croatian. We don't know why the message said he was a Bosniak Muslim, but we believe it's because they were lying about being in the pay of Iran. It was a cover story. His passport says he's a Catholic."

Hannister rubbed his forehead and said, "What the hell. What is going on here? Who is he?"

"We're still running that down. He's not on any of our systems. I doubt he's ever been to the United States. He hasn't pinged, but he will eventually. He also had another identification which is going to be delicate."

"What?"

"He had a diplomatic passport for a group called the Sovereign Military Hospitaller Order of St. John of Jerusalem, of Rhodes, and of Malta. The name inside it was not the same name as his Croatian passport. It was Italian."

President Hannister rubbed his chin, looked at Amanda Croft, and said, "Isn't that the Knights of Malta? The ones with observer status at the United Nations? The group we give money to?"

She said, "It is, but they're a Catholic humanitarian organization. They help refugee camps and things like that. They can't have anything to do with this."

Wolffe said, "I'm not going to argue that, but I need additional authority, and this isn't the time for an Oversight Council meeting. It looks like you have your hands full here."

Hannister let slip a rueful smile and said, "Yes, it would appear so. On the plus side, Denmark, the United Kingdom, and Australia are backing us up. Apparently, they don't like their naval commanders being shot at any more than we do."

"That's a help?"

"No, it's not. It's just more pressure for me to act. We're reaching a point where it won't matter what we *want* to do. This is taking on a life of its own. If they have one more killing out in the wild—whoever it is—and they're successful in implicating an Iran proxy, we're taking it to Iran."

"What's Israel saying?"

"The usual crap. The hawks are screaming at us to neutralize the threat, like a kid brother hiding behind the older one. Behind the scenes, others are asking for calm. They still haven't publicly released the fact that their diplomats were killed the same way as ours, with the same proof of Iranian complicity. Sooner or later, that's going to leak, and that'll be it. Either Israel will be forced to strike—which could lead to a conflagration of epic proportions with every country in the Middle East—or they'll force us to try to cobble together some half-assed coalition to strike. It's coming to a head."

Wolffe said, "Sir, this could be for no reason. What if Iran's not doing this?"

"I know. What do you want to do?"

"The cell phone we found on the Croatian had an app called Zello, which works off data on the cell network, or straight off Wi-Fi. It has a geolocation function, and we have the location of the end station of its last call. It's in Rome, coincidentally the headquarters of the Knights of Malta. It didn't end in Iran or any other Iranian proxy location, like Lebanon or Syria. I want to go explore that."

"How long will that take?"

"Not long. Pike's already on the way. He'll be landing within the hour. I just need permission."

Hannister laughed and said, "Let me guess, still as an Israeli?"

"Well, yeah. Ten days of quarantine as an American wouldn't really help, but once on the ground we'll need some gates to be broken to get into the Knights of Malta for a few questions. He'll do that as an American consular officer."

Amanda said, "You can't go barging into their

headquarters and accuse them of trying to assassinate the head of the Fifth Fleet. That's not going to work."

"We won't. We'll just tell them we found out the Croatian was associated with the organization, and wanted to learn more about him. Right now, he was killed outside of the main assault, so we'll play it as just covering all the bases."

President Hannister looked at Amanda and said, "You've got whatever permission you need to turn this off. Give me something I can use with the Iranians. They're building up for the fight right now, and I need to turn it off—*if* it's not them."

Wolffe smiled and said, "Give Pike a chance before you set off World War Three. You're the commander in chief. What's happened has already happened. No need to rush to war. If you didn't rain down the bombs yesterday, no reason to do it tomorrow."

Hannister said, "If there's another hit planned that's pinned to the Iranians, and Pike can't find it in time, me being commander in chief won't matter. Iran will believe we think it's them. They'll strike first, and it will be against Israel."

Wolffe said nothing. Hannister finished the thought in Wolffe's head. "You and I both know what that means."

Garrett and the three remaining Turtles watched the BBC news feed out of Bahrain in silence. When it was over, Raphael said, "What happened to Donnie?"

Garrett said, "He's dead. Gone."

"How do you know?"

"Because I saw his body on the news."

"That may not have been him. It was a chaotic scene and the news cameras were bouncing around."

"It was him. He hasn't contacted me since right before the assault. He's dead, and we must continue on. The attack, even if it failed in its purpose, accomplished its objective. The world thinks Iran put those savages up to the mission, and the world is taking notice. Both Australia and the United Kingdom have condemned the attack. The United States has locked down the naval base and put a carrier strike group to sea. They just conducted air strikes into Syria against Keta'ib Hezbollah targets. We are on track. We must not lose our resolve."

The three remaining Turtles said nothing. He continued, "Donatello was a brave, brave

man. He did what he had to do. Don't let his
sacrifice be in vain."

Raphael said, "He had the contact in Beirut.
He was the one who was the expert on the Iranian
drones. The one who found the cache in Syria.
How can we duplicate that now?"

He said, "Leonardo was the paymaster. You
know how to contact him, right? You met him in
Beirut with Donatello, didn't you?"

Leonardo looked at the other two, then said,
"Yes, but it was just as Donnie's backup. I didn't
do any of the work. I was just a gun."

"But you can contact the man, yes? Donnie
wrote an after-action review of the meetings
precisely for this contingency. We planned ahead
for that, didn't we?"

He thought a minute, then said, "Yes, for
coordinating with the contact to get across the
border. But it doesn't help with the drones. Donnie was the one who knew how to operate them,
and the sole reason they think we're coming
is because we can increase their efficiency and
range. It's why they built the relationship. Donnie could talk that stuff. I cannot."

Garrett said, "Doesn't matter. You don't
need to talk about anything once you're on the
ground. Let them take you to the cache and then
kill them. You can at least launch the drones,
correct?"

"Yes. It's easy. Just input the coordinates, turn
on the motor, and let it go."

"Then we're good. Raphael, I want you to re-
place Donatello on this mission. It'll take two to
launch the drones."

"But I'm supposed to travel with you to Israel. What about that?"

"I can handle that mission alone. The Grand Master initially balked at two security personnel in the first place. I had to convince him. He'll be happy that it's only me now, and Michelangelo is already prepped for the mission in Jerusalem. He's the only one of us that looks remotely Palestinian. He's the only one that can use the ID cards we found in Syria."

Raphael said, "Sir, you make this seem easy, but it's not. We're not dealing with farm boys from Keta'ib Hezbollah out of Ramadi, Iraq. We're dealing with Lebanese Hezbollah. The king of terrorist organizations. Those guys don't fuck around. They have been training and fighting for years. They aren't a militia, and this is not going to be that easy."

Garrett said, "I know. But we have the Lord on our side. Trust in the prophecy."

Michelangelo muttered something. Garrett said, "Did you have something to say?"

"Yeah. I'm not sure the Lord is going to protect us from those nutcases under the sway of Allah."

"That's precisely why we're doing this. After this mission, there won't be any nutcases following Allah. It will cause the final crusade—and this time we'll win, bringing the second coming."

They heard a knock, causing them all to snap their eyes at the little basement door. The secretary cracked it open and said, "Garrett, the lieutenant would like to see you. If you have the time."

Garrett said, "Of course. I have all the time in the world for him."

The lieutenant of the Grand Master of the Knights of Malta was the second in charge of the entire organization. According to the constitution, as the religious superior and sovereign, he had taken a vow of chastity and set an example of living by Christian principles to all the members of the order. He was vested with supreme authorities.

In short, he was a powerful man who was one of the few who knew about Garrett's martial activities in Syria, and had been the deciding man for hiring Garrett's team. And yet, because of his vows, he was never comfortable with the decision.

The secretary nodded and left. Garrett said, "Start working the problem. I'll be leaving for Israel soon with the Grand Master. You guys have to figure out the Lebanon piece. We do this, and the Muslims will be eradicated. The third temple will be built, and we live in glory in the kingdom of the Lord."

Raphael looked at the other two, then nodded. "For Donnie."

Garrett said, "For the entire world," and left the room.

He went upstairs, and found the secretary at her ornate desk. So unlike what he had been given for office space, even as his job was much more important than hers. She stood and led him into the lieutenant's office, an ostentatious thing full of gilded drapes and ornate carvings. Marco Bianchi stood up, saying, "Garrett, thank you for taking the time." Wearing his full Knights cloak, the Malta cross emblazoned across the front, he looked vaguely like he would be more at home in the Vatican.

As soon as he saw him, Garrett knew something wasn't right. He'd met Marco multiple times, and he'd always worn a suit, albeit with Knights memorabilia pinned to his lapel. To have him meet with the regalia of his office was not a good sign.

Garrett said, "Of course, sir. How can I help you?"

Marco walked around the desk, took Garrett's arm, and led him to a chair, saying, "We have a problem. There was a man killed. He had a passport from the Hospitaller. A diplomatic passport. And he worked for you."

Garrett feigned shock, saying, "Who? Who was it? Donatello?"

Now Marco showed surprise, saying, "Yes, that's who it was. How did you know?"

"He's the only Turtle that isn't here. He took a vacation to Croatia. What happened? Was it a car wreck or something like that? I swear I've told them not to carry that passport when not on official business."

Marco returned to his desk, sitting down and saying, "No, it wasn't in Croatia. It was in Bahrain. Have you seen what's happened in Bahrain?"

"Yes, some sort of attack. But why does that involve Donatello?"

"He was killed in the attack. He's dead."

Garrett rubbed his head, like he was trying to

assimilate the information. He said, "Why was he in Bahrain? Did you send him there?"

Marco's eyes went wide. He said, "Us? No. That's my question. He works for you. Why was he there?"

Garrett said, "Sir, I have no idea. He asked for a little time to go home. His mother is not well. I told him he could, but only on his Croatian passport. What's going on?"

Marco surveyed him for a minute, then said, "I don't know, but I have a request from the United States of America for information on the man. They want to know why he was present at an assassination attempt on their naval commander, and I don't know what to tell them."

"Tell them what I just told you. We don't know. He was supposed to be in Croatia with his mother. Type it up and send it out, expressing shock and sadness. That'll be the end of it."

Marco glanced out the window of the Magisterial Palace and said, "Unfortunately, no, it won't. They don't want a message. I have a contingent flying here right now from the United States State Department." He looked at Garrett, and with mild sarcasm said, "Apparently, trying to kill the commander of one of their prestigious naval forces is a big deal. A message won't cut it. I'm meeting them here in four hours."

Garrett said, "Surely they don't think he was involved."

"No. They're just exploring all avenues, and he was found dead with the passport," Marco said. "So you don't know what he was doing? At all?"

"Sir, he was doing what you've hired us for. We believe in the mission. We *are* the mission. Donatello wasn't doing anything wrong. I don't know why he was there, or what to tell you."

Marco sat for a moment, then said, "You know, I was on board with hiring you before Syria. And I feel horrible about what happened to you. I feel responsible, which is why the Knights paid for all of your medical treatments. I'm sorry for what happened, but your existence in the Knights cannot become public. Please tell me this is not part of that."

Garrett heard the words and wanted to explode, ripping the man's throat out. *"Feel horrible about what happened to you"? You mean feel horrible that I was protecting your mission and had my balls cut off by the very savages you were trying to help? Is that it?*

He contained his fury, the only sign of stress an increase in his respiration rate. He said, "Sir, I appreciate everything you've done for me. And I still serve. I'm the lead for the protective detail of the Grand Master for his trip to Syria. I'm still a Knight."

Marco said, "Yes. Yes, you are. I'll see what the U.S. knows, and then come back to you. The Grand Master trusts you for his security, and this Israeli invitation is a new one for us. Keep that in mind."

Garrett stood and said, "Thank you, sir. I'm sorry about Donatello, but it has nothing to do with the Knights. I promise."

Marco stood up, shook his hand, and said, "I'll be in touch."

Garrett went back downstairs, finding the Turtles waiting anxiously on the results of his conversation. He said, "It's okay. They know about Donatello, but it's okay. I'm still the primary protective detail. I can still initiate."

Raphael said, "That won't matter if we don't get to the drones. Donnie was the man for that."

Garrett's laptop chirped on the desk. He picked it up, scrolled a bit, then closed the cover saying, "You guys need to figure that out. I have to go. I've got to check on something."

## CHAPTER 37

Inspector Lia Vairo pulled her car into a spot adjacent to a sprawling greenspace, seeing carabinieri personnel putting up crime scene tape and managing a small crowd. She exited her vehicle and walked to the side door of the apartment complex, flashing her badge at a man there.

Agitated, he said, "You guys can't start stringing up crime tape all over the place. It's in a single room. You can't make this entire building look like a murder scene."

And she realized he was with the apartment complex. She said, "Sorry, that's not my job. Not my jurisdiction. All I do is solve the crime."

She went up the stairs, down the hallway, and saw Jonathan the photographer. She said, "Another one?"

He said, "I'm not sure. I'll let Rio tell you about it."

She entered and found the same assistant from the other crime scene bent over a body. Only now, he was on her team. She said, "What do you have, Rio? Same thing?"

He looked up at her from the body and said, "Took you a while to get here."

She said, "Not all of us live near the EUR. Trastevere is a little longer drive."

"Trastevere? No kidding. You got a secret international student as a boyfriend?"

She smiled, saying, "No boyfriend, just a bad divorce that left me with the flat. My ex-husband rented it out before the separation. He got everything else, I got the flat."

He chuckled and said, "Lia Vairo from Trastevere. Never would have figured that."

She said, "I went to see the owner of this place first, before coming over. It's a VRBO rental, and the man who rented it is an American."

"You have him? You know who it is?"

"No. The identification is false. It's from an online resource that sells 'novelty identification' but really sells IDs that duplicate American ones, mainly for college students trying to buy drinks in bars. The owner had no way of telling what was real, and VRBO doesn't do any background checks to see."

Rio said, "So no help?"

"Maybe. Maybe not. Because of the company's liability for providing false identification instead of 'novelties,' they immediately respond to any law enforcement request, and I'm now waiting on the IP address of the guy who bought this ID. I'll bet it came from here, in Italy, but the killer is American. I promise."

Rio said, "We have the DNA from the kiss. If you can find him through the identification he used, all we need is a swab of his mouth."

Surprised, Lia said, "We got DNA from the kiss on the other body? When did that happen?"

Rio grinned and said, "Yeah, we did. I got the results right before this call, but I don't know if this is the same guy. It feels the same, but it's not."

"Why?"

"For one, this is not the woman's apartment. The killer rented the place instead of using the woman's own place like the other three. For another, he or she came to kill. The victim made it about five feet into the place before he wrapped her neck in a cord and squeezed the life out of her."

"So no sexual assault? Just a killing? That's like the other ones."

"Yeah, but this one was planned. It was calculated. You said yourself the others were crimes of passion. A lamp to bash someone's head, a knife found at the apartment to slit a throat. This time he brought the killing with him. And he murdered someone outside his usual targets. The woman is an immigrant from Africa. A black woman. All of the others were Caucasian and blond."

"So a copycat?"

Rio stood and said, "I'm not sure, honestly. It's not his MO. Not a streetwalker's house, and he's brought the weapon with him. I agree that the others were because something went wrong, but on this one he came in solely to kill. Maybe he's changing his MO. Maybe he's decided that just killing is better than anything else. I don't know."

Wearing gloves, he went to the open kitchen

window and held up a red cord of about a half-inch in diameter draped across the sill, most of it hanging outside, saying, "This is the killing weapon. And he left it here in the windowsill. Like he wanted us to find it."

She said, "It's bright red. What is it?"

Confused, Rio said, "It's a climbing rope. A kernmantle climbing rope. Nothing more."

"And he hung it outside the window? Why?"

"Who knows? He left it for a reason, though. He placed it."

She nodded, then repeated, "It's red."

"So? What's that mean?"

She turned a circle, then said, "In the Bible, there's a prostitute from Jericho who hid spies from the land of Israel. When the Israelites return to sack Jericho, she's told to protect herself by hanging a red cord outside of her window. The Israelites saw the cord and spared her life, even though she was a whore. Maybe I'm crazy, but I think it's the same killer and he used a red cord on purpose. It's something to do with her being a prostitute."

"But this cord didn't spare the woman's life. It's the method by which she died. Doesn't really fit into the biblical story."

"I know. But he placed the cord outside the window. Maybe he thought by killing her he was sparing her."

"That makes no sense."

Lia looked around the room and said, "This guy is crazy. Nothing he does makes sense. Get some DNA off of that rope, and let's match it."

A uniformed police officer came up the stairs and said, "Ma'am, we have a couple of United States officials who want to see you."

Rio stood up, saying, "What?"

The officer said, "I stopped them at the door, but they're pretty insistent. They want to talk to the officer in charge."

Lia looked at Rio and said, "More strangeness. What do you think?"

"Can't hurt to talk to them. But not up here."

"I agree." She turned to the officer and said, "Tell them I'll be down shortly."

In the park, Garrett heard the words through his tablet and felt like he'd been struck by the hand of God.

*She knows why I did it. She knows what this is about.*

She had recognized the significance of the rope, and it was a sign. Maybe she could end his agony. Maybe she was the one. Maybe she could break through the spell that had held him in pain since Syria.

He felt a stirring in his groin, a tingle that he hadn't felt since the torture in Syria. And became convinced. It was a sign.

She would have to die afterward, as originally planned, but that was already a given. He had no idea how she knew to track his fake identification. He had been sure all of his information was untraceable—but he hadn't considered the IP address when ordering. That would put him in Rome. Something that was too close to let go.

If she followed that thread, she might close in on him in a day—before he was to leave.

And how did they know he'd kissed the other one's cheek? It didn't really matter how they'd known, but they had his DNA now. They were much closer than he thought. All it would take was them showing up at the Knights of Malta with a swab kit and he was done.

No, she had to go. Tonight.

Through the cameras he'd installed, he knew her name was Vairo, and that she lived in Trastevere. That was enough to find her location. He would pay her a visit, but it wouldn't be just to kill her. He wanted to know how she'd figured out the rope. Maybe she deserved more than just a death. Maybe she deserved redemption. She was special, of that he was sure.

He saw a car enter the parking lot, circling around as if in confusion. It parked, and a man and woman exited. The man was tall, without an ounce of fat on him, with short brown hair like he cut it himself and a rough visage. He had ice blue eyes and a white slash of a scar that tracked down his cheek into the stubble of his beard. Garrett had met many men such as him in his career, and honestly considered himself to be in that fraternity. It was obvious by the way he carried himself, he was not someone to trifle with. But why was he here?

The woman was lithe, like a dancer, with a page-boy cut of black hair, but she moved like a leopard, searching the parking lot for threats. He recognized the danger in her immediately, like a dog sensing a threat at the door.

*Who were they? And did they have anything to do with him?*

He watched for them to enter his surveillance trap, but instead his video feed showed the inspector leaving the room. She appeared at the outside landing, but he now couldn't hear what was being said. He pulled out a small monocular, staring at the group.

Waiting.

## CHAPTER 38

I wound around the neighborhood known as the EUR, Shoshana giving me directions from her GPS for the last known contact from the Zello app in Bahrain. We found it, seeing it was a damn park. A large greenspace with kids running around and adults throwing balls for dogs. Which was bullshit. Why would the Croatian call a guy who was sitting in a park in Rome?

I said, "Okay, this is a bust. Let's get out of here and back to the hotel. Maybe Knuckles and Brett will come up with something from the Knights of Malta headquarters."

Shoshana said, "Not yet. Keep going. Circle around."

I said, "What, are you looking for someone else to kill?"

She snapped her head to me, giving me her death penetration stare, and said, "That man was going to harm me. Don't question my motives."

On the flight over to Rome, we'd had a little come to Jesus meeting, where I'd laid into her for killing the Croatian when he was clearly no threat. I was incensed by the death. The sole purpose of the mission was to capture his ass, and we'd been superseded by the potential for a catastrophic attack, and so I'd focused on the mission against the target instead of the Croatian. But by the time she'd killed him, we were in control.

The bottom line was she'd short-circuited any ability to find out what was going on solely for vengeance of the *Ramsad*'s death. And that wasn't something I could stomach.

I understood her loss at a visceral level, having lost my own family in a vicious murder years ago, along with friends killed and wounded in combat. If I could keep the mission in focus, so should she. But she wasn't like other people. She was extremely linear. You hurt me, and I'll exponentially hurt you, no matter the damage to the greater good. That's just the way she lived.

I put on the brakes and said, "You aren't even going to talk about this?"

She said, "Your Oversight Council gave us permission to explore here. Maybe you should listen to them."

I said, "Shoshana, they gave us permission because they're shitting their pants about going to war in the Middle East. Something we could have stopped if you hadn't snapped that guy's neck."

She said nothing, staring out the window.

I said, "Do you understand where I'm coming from here? This isn't like Lesotho. This isn't Poland. You can't run around killing people all the time. Sometimes we need the answers they have."

She turned to me and said, "Why did you invite me to the wedding?"

*What the hell?*

Incredulous, I said, "What does that have to do with anything? I'm just asking you not to kill everyone you meet."

She turned away and said, "You didn't want me at the wedding. You invited me because you felt it a debt you owed. Because I saved your life. Nothing more."

I ran my hands through my hair, pulling at the roots. I said, "What the hell are you talking about? Where is this coming from?"

She looked at me and said, "I can see it. I feel it. You didn't want me there."

I was really regretting my choice of teams. I'd decided that we should split up the Israelis so we could act American, if that was called for, or Israeli, if that was the better choice, leaving one or the other to do the talking. Aaron and Jennifer were getting our hotel rooms, and, since the interview with the Knights of Malta was a pure U.S. State Department affair, Knuckles and Brett were doing that. Which left me with Shoshana. The dark angel.

And this ridiculous discussion in the heart of Rome while I was trying to prevent more deaths. But I understood it. She had always been a stone-cold killer, but in her heart, she was also vulnerable.

I sighed and said, "Shoshana, you look at me and call me Nephilim. My given name. Why is that?"

She considered for a moment, then said, "Because it is what you are."

"So I'm some giant from the Old Testament saving the world."

"Not a giant. But saving the world, yes. You are pure."

I turned to her and said, "And so are you. You are *me*. Not having you at the wedding would be the same as not having Jennifer there."

She sat still for a moment, then said, "Do you mean that?"

I chuckled and said, "Look into my eyes. Do that weird thing. Figure it out for yourself."

She smiled and said, "I just don't know who to trust in this world. Aaron is my touchstone. And Jennifer. I'm just not sure about you."

I said, "Yeah, because I'm you in male flesh. You don't trust *yourself*. Let's get out of here."

I circled around the park, entered an apartment complex, and began a three-point turn to get back out. Shoshana said, "Stop."

I did, saying, "What now?"

She pointed to the end of the building, and I saw a bunch of crime scene tape. I said, "What?"

"Don't you think it's weird that the geolocation ended near here and there's now crime scene tape?"

I leaned back and said, "Yeah, maybe."

"Let's go see what's going on. It might be something that leads us to the Croatian's contact."

"Shoshana, come on. Why would this crime scene do that?"

She said, "It might be nothing, but then again, it might be something."

She exited the car and said, "It's time to be Americans. Get that State Department badge out. Let's go see."

I sighed again and exited the vehicle. I thought it was bullshit, but then again, with Shoshana, you never knew.

We reached the stairwell, and I showed a half-assed identification saying I was a consular officer for the United States. Of course, if they did any checking, we were done.

The officer wouldn't allow us up, but told us someone was coming down.

A woman of about forty appeared, with a fairly attractive face, a mole right above her lip, shoulder-length hair, and an air of being in charge. Immediately, when I saw her, I thought, *This should be Knuckles's job*, because her hard-ass appearance would melt when she saw him.

She said, "Yes? Can I see some identification?"

I flashed my counterfeit credentials, and she seemed to believe it. She said, "What do you want here? Do you have some interest in this killing?"

I said, "Killing? No. We're missing a man, and this was his last known location. We walked into this purely by coincidence. When I saw the tape, I thought it prudent to see what was going on, just in case."

Shoshana slipped past us and began climbing the stairs. The woman shouted, "Hey! This is a crime scene!"

Shoshana began running up the stairs and I thought, *Here we go. Crazy-ass shit yet again.*

The inspector sprinted behind her, and I followed, saying, "I'm sorry. She's really worried about her friend. Is it a man who was killed?"

The inspector didn't answer, instead shouting, "Stop! Stop going up!"

We reached the third landing and Shoshana exited, going to the door with two cops outside. She managed to get past them, and then was finally stopped in the foyer, two officers holding her in place.

She wasn't fighting them.

Which was a blessed relief, because if she had, they'd both be dead.

We entered behind her. The inspector said, "What the hell is going on? Why are you here?"

Shoshana looked at me and said, "This is it. He was here. The *Ramsad* killer was here."

## CHAPTER 39

I was prepared to haul Shoshana's ass out of the building just to prevent a catastrophic compromise of our cover, but when I heard her words, I paused. Shoshana had some ethereal ability to see past the mortal world. She could sense things that others could not. In the past, I had scoffed at it, but deep inside, where the primordial instinct lay, I believed. It wasn't something that could be explained, and I'd be the last person to ever admit it. But I believed it was real.

The inspector looked at her, then at me, saying, "What's she talking about?"

I said, "Nothing. She has a habit of going off the rails. Sorry to bother you."

I glared at Shoshana and said, "Time to go."

The inspector snatched my arm and said, "What's she talking about? What's a *Ramsad*? Is that like a prostitute?"

I said, "No. She's just crazy to find her friend. I'm sorry this happened."

Shoshana looked toward an open kitchen window, seeing a rope hanging half in and half out. She said, "That red cord is the weapon, isn't it?"

The inspector heard the words and squinted her eyes at me, wondering what Shoshana had seen. I'll be damned if she wasn't reading me the same way Shoshana did. She understood I didn't want to talk in front of the other uniformed personnel. She said, "Okay. Get the hell out of here. Right now."

I said, "Gladly. Just let my friend go."

They did, and we began walking down the stairs. I said, "What was that all about?"

Shoshana said, "The mastermind was here. The killer of the *Ramsad*. I felt it. I could smell it. I saw it. I could taste it. That body in there was his kill."

I knew she was trying to explain to a mere mortal what she saw, using the senses of an average human, but she hadn't "seen" or "smelled" or "tasted" anything. It was something else, and I wasn't sure if it was just her wanting to believe it true, or if it really *was* true.

We reached the landing and I heard footsteps above me. Like I thought would happen, the inspector appeared and said, "I don't know who you are, but I'm going to find out. And it won't be pretty if you have information for our investigation and are holding out."

Her Italian accent was adorable, making me wish yet again Knuckles was here.

I glanced at Shoshana and said, "Look, we have no idea what's happened here, but we might have information about it from another investigation. We came here because of that. We had no idea about any killings in Rome. We're looking for a guy who's working against U.S. interests, not a killer of whores. If you tell us what you know, we'll do the same. I think we're looking for the same man, but for different reasons."

"My name is Lia Vairo. I'm in charge of this investigation. I can pull you in by the authority vested in me."

I looked at Shoshana and said, "What do you think?"

Shoshana did her weird stare over the woman, then turned to me, saying, "Yes."

I saw Lia disconcerted with the stare, just like I felt when Shoshana did it to me. That thing wasn't pleasant.

Lia said, "What the hell was that?"

I said, "I know you can arrest me. I'd prefer it if you didn't. This is much bigger than a murder. I'll help you find the killer, and you'll help me prevent a lot more deaths than these whores here in Rome."

She bristled, saying, "They might be whores to you, but they're humans to me. Maybe I'll haul you in right now."

Shoshana took her arm and bored into her eyes. She said, "Don't do that. We want to help, but we can't do it in official channels. Please, trust us."

Lia pulled her arm away halfheartedly, saying nothing, just staring at Shoshana.

Shoshana touched her arm again, this time gently, saying, "Give us a place to meet. Outside of official channels."

I honestly thought Shoshana's next words would be "These are not the droids you are looking for," but that didn't happen.

Lia said, "Why the secrecy? Why should I do that?"

I said, "Because I'm asking. Nothing more. You want to solve this crime, and I want to solve mine. But I can't do it officially."

She said, "Are you CIA? Is that what this is? Is the killer some CIA asset you're trying to protect?"

I laughed and said, "No, we aren't CIA, and I have no idea who this killer is, but I think he's about to kill a lot more people than these women in Rome. And I'm sorry I called them whores. I understand they're human, and I meant no disparagement by that, but if you can help us find him, it'll help us both out."

"So why the unofficial location?"

"Let's just say it would be better if the government didn't know we were looking. Both the U.S. government and yours."

Her brow furrowed, and I could tell she didn't believe a word I was saying. "So you're not U.S. State Department?"

Shoshana produced a passport and said, "Actually, we're Israeli. Following a lead."

"*What?*"

I rolled my eyes, now realizing we were going to jail. I thought about calling Jennifer before they took my cell phone, and Shoshana spoke again.

"This guy is killing from the Old Testament. And he's going to keep killing until he reaches Revelation in the New Testament. We want to stop him."

I thought, *What the hell is she talking about? Old Testament?*

Lia said, "So the red cord he used to murder is real?"

Shoshana said, "Yes. It was."

Lia nodded, and I was beginning to believe they were both crazy. *What the hell does a red cord have to do with any of this?*

We heard Lia's name shouted from the stairwell, then the clomping of feet. Lia glanced back, then pulled a card from her pocket, saying, "This is my house. Meet me there tonight at seven. Don't tell anyone about the meeting. And I mean *no one*."

Shoshana took the card, dialed a number on it, and Lia's phone rang. She said, "That's my phone. Call it if something happens."

"What's that mean?"

Shoshana glanced at me, then said, "The killer doing this will attack anyone he perceives as a threat. *You* are that threat."

The clomping of feet ended, and a man appeared in the doorway. She said, "Rio, no problems. They were just leaving."

He gave me his hard cop stare, saying, "What did they want?"

She said, "Nothing. Just a mixed-up thing. Let's get back upstairs."

They left and we walked back to our car. I said, "What the hell was that about the Old Testament? I mean, I'm glad it worked out, but what was it? You mentioned it the first time you asked me to join you, then on the flight to Zurich. Why do you keep talking about that?"

She said, "I'm honestly not sure. I've felt from the beginning that the killer of our people and yours wasn't from Islam. It's biblical. The murderer of that woman didn't do it for joy. He has a greater scheme, and I don't know why, but it involves Israel."

"Then why is it biblical? Maybe it's earlier than that. You have your own crazies."

She saw where I was going and said, "The killer isn't Jewish. Of that I'm sure. There are no Jews in the Knights of Malta, and that woman was murdered using a red cord."

I said, "What on earth does a red cord have to do with any of this?"

She walked to our vehicle, saying, "You need to read your Bible more."

I let that pass, because she was probably right. We entered the car and I said, "Okay, I can believe some of your bullshit, but this is a bit much. How am I going to sell that crap to the Taskforce? More importantly, how are you going to sell it to the Mossad?"

She looked at me with pain and said, "I'm not making this up. I think the killer is trying to bring about the End of Days. And we need to stop it."

## CHAPTER 40

Garrett entered the Knights of Malta Magisterial Palace in a rush, wanting to use his computer to locate the residence of one Inspector Lia Vairo. He knew it wouldn't be that difficult, given what he'd gleaned. From what she'd said, she was the owner of the flat due to a divorce, and Trastevere was a touristy area full of students and expats renting apartments, so finding a local living there through a records search—given he now had a name—should be fairly easy. Especially with the database access he had.

He stalked past the secretary at her ornate desk, heading to the stairwell leading to his dungeon office, and she stopped him, saying, "The U.S. State Department are coming in twenty minutes. The lieutenant would like you to remain behind after they leave."

And he realized that the killings of the women weren't the only threat he faced.

He said, "Of course. I'll stay as long as I have to. I was just running down to my office and then back to my car. I'll be here when they leave."

He jogged down the hallway, went down the

stairs, and found Raphael and Michelangelo still there. He said, "Where's Leonardo?"

"Just went out for a bite to eat." He pointed at a clock showing the late afternoon and said, "We were going to do the same."

"Not right now. When is Leonardo returning?"

"Maybe an hour, but he did get in touch with the contact in Lebanon. The man's agreed to meet us without Donatello."

"Good. Very good. At least something is going right. When do you fly?"

"Tomorrow morning, if Leonardo can purchase the tickets."

"Okay. Good. Keep your Zello phones operational. In the meantime, you guys stay here. I might have a mission for you."

"What?"

"Two U.S. State Department investigators are coming here with questions about Donatello. Apparently, they found his Knights diplomatic passport and are wondering what he did here."

Raphael showed alarm, saying, "What are they looking for? What do they have?"

"I don't know. I have a meeting with the lieutenant right after they leave. I don't have time to explain right now." He looked at his watch and said, "I'll be back in less than ten minutes."

He jogged back upstairs and passed the secretary, saying, "Just got to run to my car. Are they here yet?"

"Not yet."

"Okay, I'll be right back."

He left the building, but didn't go to his car parked on the road near the Spanish Steps. Instead, he shadowed the wall down the courtyard and sat on a stone bench, keeping an eye on the security guard blocking the archway that led inside to the parking area.

A late-model Acura sedan appeared and the driver spoke to the guard for a moment before being allowed inside. They parked in a space ten feet away from where Garrett sat and two men exited, both wearing knit polo shirts and chinos, but neither looked like any State Department personnel he'd ever encountered. But they were definitely American. One was tall with shaggy black hair pulled into a ponytail in a shoddy attempt to make himself look presentable. The other was a short black man with a physique that made him look like a fireplug, his muscles straining the shirt he wore. The ponytail man glanced his way and Garrett recognized the same skill he'd seen with the man and the woman at the murder scene.

Garrett glanced away, pretending he hadn't noticed their arrival. He waited until they'd gone inside, thinking about his options. He'd expected them to be on foot, like most everyone else in the area due to the lack of parking—just as he was routinely forced to do before coming to work. He hadn't realized the order had given them parking privileges, but he should have assumed that would happen.

He went back in, saw the secretary, and said, "I'm back. Are they here?"

She said, "Yes. They just went in."

"Okay, I'll be downstairs until they're done. Just let me know."

He left without waiting for an answer, entered his little office, and saw Leonardo had returned. He said, "So we're good for Beirut?"

"Yes. Raph and I fly tomorrow. But you really have to be ready. We do this, and we might not come out alive. I don't want the trip to be for nothing. The contact is not someone to trifle with."

Garrett nodded and said, "Yes, yes, I understand. Trust me, I gave my manhood to finally understand. Don't question me."

The men in the room all heard the words and glanced away, not wanting to face Garrett's fury.

Garrett said, "But we have an immediate problem. There are two men upstairs who are from the United States asking about Donatello. I don't think they're U.S. State. I think they're something else. I need Raph and Mikey to track them to wherever they're going next. They came in a car, so you need to get your scooters. How far away are they?"

Raph said, "Just up the street, but why?"

"I don't know. I honestly don't know the damage done by Donatello. But it could be significant, and we need to tie it off, right now. Do you still have a limpet mine?"

Michelangelo said, "I have one left, but I have to get it."

"Do so. Get the bike, get the mine, and come back here. You have probably about an hour. Maybe less."

Raph said, "Are we going to kill them?"

"No. Not yet. I just want you to follow them. It may be nothing, and I don't want to draw attention. It could be just a simple inquiry. But if it's not, I want to be ready. And I need some explosives of my own."

Leonardo said, "Why?"

"I need an ISIS necktie for another problem. Don't ask."

The three Turtles looked at each other, each wanting to say something, but none did. Garrett said, "Let's go. Get on it."

They left the room in a rush and he rubbed his eyes, wondering if his entire plan was now falling apart. He went to his computer and began his research on the inspector, digging into every database with which he had access. It took him into a vortex of searches, with one after another coming closer, then failing. He slapped his computer keyboard in frustration, wishing he could leverage Leonardo's skill for the search, but that was impossible.

He continued.

Thirty seconds later, like a miracle, her address spilled out from a search engine. He stared at the screen, wondering if it was a trick. It was not. He had her location in Trastevere.

He clapped his hands and smiled, and heard a knock on his door.

He closed out his search results and said, "Yes?"

The secretary entered and said, "They're gone. The lieutenant would like to talk."

She didn't look like it would be a good conversation. He said, "I'll be right up. Thank you."

She left, and he went on Zello, to the Turtle channel they'd created, saying, "Do you have them? They've left."

Raph said, "Yeah, we have them, but they didn't take a car. They went on foot back to the square."

*What the hell? Why would they leave the car?* And it became clear—they were reporting to someone else close by and moving the car would be too much of an effort.

"Okay. Stay on them until they come back to the car. They're meeting someone."

"What do you want us to do?"

Aggravated, Garrett said, "Just follow them for now. Nothing more. Find out who they're meeting and get some pictures. I have to go."

He went upstairs to Marco's office, knocked, and entered. The man was still in his robes and didn't look happy. Without preamble, he said, "Donatello was literally killed during the assassination attempt. According to the U.S., he attempted to run over people trying to prevent it."

Garrett said, "That's impossible. You know Donatello. You know he wouldn't do that. Why would he try to kill a United States naval commander in Bahrain? That makes absolutely no sense. They're hiding something. Something else is going on."

Marco turned to gaze out a window, saying, "Perhaps. No doubt it is strange, and I've been around politics enough to realize that someone may be asking questions solely to prevent questions about their own conduct, but I've also seen enough corruption to realize that something else may be going on. What was Donatello doing in Bahrain?"

"Sir, I told you, I have no idea. I honestly don't know. What did they ask you?"

"What do you think? They wanted to know what he was doing in Bahrain. He had a damn diplomatic passport from our order, of all things."

Garrett heard the curse word of "damn" and knew the man was extremely upset. He said, "And how did you explain that?"

Marco turned from the window and said, "I told them he was a functionary. A good kid who helped out with our humanitarian mission. They asked how the name on our passport differed from the name on his Croatian passport and I used that to tell them he'd stolen it. But you and I know that's not true. I approved that passport with the different name. And now it's all coming home to roost."

Garrett said, "Nothing is 'coming home to roost,' sir. Donatello protected your activities in Syria, just as I did. I don't know what he was doing, and as a member of my team, it's ultimately my fault he traveled with one of your diplomatic passports, but it isn't the end of the world. What are their next steps?"

Marco said, "They believed me. I told them about his bent toward dispensationalism to throw them off. About how he believed in the End of Days and maybe that had something to do with him being in Bahrain, but it had nothing to do with their naval commander. I made it seem like he was a religious fanatic, searching for the truth. They seemed to buy the theory."

Garrett wanted to punch the man in the face

right there. He'd just given away the keys to the kingdom. But he did not. He said, "Sir, I think that was for the best. We're good. None of this will blow back on the order. I'm just as sorry as you about Donatello's death, but that's not something we could prevent. Every organization has bad seeds. I'm just sorry I brought this one to you."

Marco nodded and said, "If they reengage, we'll have to have another talk about how to cut your unit out of our existence. You understand that, right?"

"Of course, sir. I serve at the pleasure of the order."

Marco nodded, then turned back to the window, letting Garrett know the meeting was over. He stood for a moment, about to say something else, then thought better of it. He left the room and went back down to his office, seeing a satchel on his desk. He opened it and found about a quarter pound of Semtex explosives, blasting caps, motion sensors, and a remote trigger.

He started to build his device, then heard his tablet buzzing on his desk. He snatched it up, seeing an alert from Raph.

He opened the messaging app and a picture appeared. The two "State Department" personnel were meeting with a woman and a man in Piazza di Spagna, just up the road from the palace. The text said, "They walked up here and are meeting these two for dinner. What do you want us to do? Doesn't seem that threatening."

He zoomed in on the picture, ignoring the "State Department" hippie and black man who'd visited the palace, focusing on the other two. When the image resolved, he almost dropped his tablet. It was the same two who had shown up at the crime scene. The predators who had come to talk to the inspector.

He texted back, "Did you get the scooter and limpet mine?"

"Yes, we did. Why?"

"The men will come back to the car here, at the palace. When they do, trace them and kill them."

He could feel the alarm even as the return text didn't describe the emotion. Raph said, "Why? Why would we do that?"

Garrett couldn't very well say that the other two had been at a crime scene he'd created after killing four other women. As much as he'd have liked to, he could not.

He texted, "I just finished with the Lieutenant of the Grand Master of the Knights of Malta. There is a threat here to our mission. I need you to eliminate the threat. Those men are close to determining our status."

He waited, then Raph came back, texting, "The scooter is up the street. The limpet mine is in the saddle bag. We can do it, but are you sure? Maybe we should follow the other two. See who they are."

That wouldn't do. It would probably lead them to the police investigation resulting from his littering of bodies. It would be up to him to eliminate that threat, which is why he'd asked for the explosives.

He texted, "No. Kill these State Department guys and we cut it off. Just do it. You and Leo-

266 / BRAD TAYLOR

nardo are leaving tomorrow for Beirut, and Michelangelo and I are headed to Israel with the Grand Master. We'll all be clean. Make it one more Keta'ib Hezbollah hit. If we do it right, it'll be a benefit."

Knuckles exited the Magisterial Palace and waited for the doors to close before saying, "You believe any of that shit?"

Brett chuckled and said, "What part?"

"All of it. That fucker knows more than he's trying to sell us."

Knuckles's phone dinged and he read a text from Pike. He stopped walking to the car and said, "Pike's up the road at a bistro. Wants to talk."

They shifted course and went to the guard stationed at the entrance, saying, "We're going to leave our car here for about an hour. Is that okay?"

The guard, having been told they were important individuals and misunderstanding the question, stiffened and said, "Yes, yes. Nobody will do anything to the vehicle. I'll make sure of that."

Knuckles leaned in, looked left and right conspiratorially, then whispered, "It's a rental. Don't shoot anyone trying to break into it. I just want to make sure you don't tow it away."

The guard smiled, finally getting the joke.

He said, "Yes, sir. The car will be here when you return."

Knuckles laughed and said, "How much security do you guys have here? I mean, outside of you at the gate. It doesn't seem like this place is very secure."

Now friendly, the guard said, "It's just us out here on the gate during the day. At night, when the place is closed, there are security inside, but the true protection are the cameras all over the place." He pointed into the guard shack and said, "If we see something during the night, we call the police."

Knuckles smiled and said, "Good to know," then exited through the arch onto the street outside.

They began walking to Piazza di Spagna, Brett saying, "What was that all about?"

"Just checking. Those guys are a bunch of liars, and it's nice to know their security posture." He held up a thumb drive and said, "Same reason I asked to use the secretary's computer. We now have their network."

They entered the square next to the fountain, went left, and walked to an outdoor café, the area threaded with umbrellas and tourists walking about. Brett saw Shoshana and pointed. They took a seat and Pike said, "So did you get more than we did?"

Knuckles said, "That depends. What did you get?"

"Nothing. The geolocation ended up at an apartment complex with a crime scene."

"Crime scene? Like a terrorist attack?"

"No. Like a murder." Pike flicked his head to Shoshana and said, "Carrie here thinks it's the guy behind all the killings of our diplomats. Because she 'read the room.'"

She bristled at his disparagement, but Knuckles said, "Why? What did you see?"

It was the first time Knuckles had ever indicated he trusted her instincts. Surprised, she said, "I saw colors. It was red. I smelled the death outside the room. I mean I could sense . . . Wait, wait, that's not right. I can't explain it. I just—"

He chuckled, holding up his hands and cutting her off, saying, "I get it, I get it."

She smiled her little shark grin and sat back, saying nothing. Pike winked at her and said, "She might be right. We have a meeting with the inspector in a couple of hours. What did you find out?"

"Not a lot. They said the guy was a Croatian Catholic who they used for menial stuff. According to them, he came to the organization through their relief efforts in the Bosnian war. He was supposed to be visiting his sick mother in Croatia, and they have no idea what he was doing in Bahrain. According to them, he was a good kid, but had a bent towards something called dispensationalism. Which is apparently a biblical theory that has to do with the end of the world."

At that, Shoshana sat up, saying, "He told you the Croatian was a believer?"

Knuckles said, "Believer in what? He's a devout Christian, is that what you mean?"

"No, I mean dispensationalism."

Pike chuckled and said, "Shoshana has a theory

about the Bible's book of Revelation going on here. She thinks that these guys are trying to start the End of Days. You know, the seven seals and the horses of the apocalypse?"

Knuckles didn't join in the humor. He said, "Well, that's exactly what the person we met told us. This guy was a true believer in that stuff. I was raised Catholic, and that wasn't something we were taught. It's from somewhere else."

Brett said, "I'm a Mississippi Baptist, and we didn't run around with that, either, but I'll tell you, I knew some who did. They constantly thought every earthquake was a precursor to the End of Days. Everything was a prophecy."

Knuckles turned to him and said, "But these guys are Catholic. That's not what they think. It just isn't."

Brett said, "I'm not arguing here, I'm just saying I've seen it, and the people who believe it take it to their core. No offense, but it's usually a bunch of white folk like you guys. It's a real thing. You want to know why so many American evangelical Christians support Israel? It's because they need Israel to own the entirety of the promised land in order to fulfill the prophecies in the Bible. The End of Days and the second coming of Christ."

Surprised, Pike said, "I didn't know you were such a biblical scholar."

Brett smiled and said, "Not a scholar. I just had to go to Sunday school for close to eighteen years, or get my ass kicked by my mom. Kept me out of prison and into the Marine Corps, if you want to know the truth."

Pike laughed and said, "Why Israel?"

Shoshana said, "Because it's how the prophecy unfolds in the Bible. In order for the third temple to be built, bringing about the second coming of your Christ, the Israelites must own the totality of the promised land, and right now, according to some, we do not. We took Jerusalem in the Six-Day War, but we didn't take back the entirety of the land. And we didn't take back the soul of the realm—the Dome of the Rock, where the first two temples stood and where the third must be built to conform to the prophecies. We left that under the administrative control of Jordan, along with the Al Aqsa Mosque on the same grounds."

Pike said, "Why would you do that? Why not just retake it and build the damn temple? Let it go up and then defuse the whole situation when the earth doesn't split apart. Seems to me that location has been nothing but trouble since."

She smiled and said, "Because it's also the oldest religious building in Islam, created after the Muslim conquest of Jerusalem way, way back when. Like in the first century. The Dome was built long after the second temple fell, and according to Islam, it's covering the location where Muhammed ascended into heaven. It's the holiest site in all of Judaism, but it's also the third holiest site in Islam, after Mecca and Medina. If we had taken it following the Six-Day War, we would have engendered a six-year war, and against all of Islam instead of a few pathetic armies. The nation of Israel would not have survived, so the leaders during that time took a pragmatic approach, but some in my country want to take it back very badly. As do some in your country."

Pike shook his head and said, "What the hell does this have to do with Keta'ib Hezbollah and the killing of our diplomats? It makes no sense."

Knuckles said, "Well, it doesn't make a lot of sense to us, but it does to someone. Let's just talk about what we know. They're lying about the Croatian. We know that because we found his information from a sleazebag Syrian refugee in Switzerland tied into the killing of the *Ramsad*. We didn't stumble onto the Croatian's dead body after a wayward flight to see his ailing mother. We tracked it to Bahrain because he was bringing money to a terrorist cell. He's a bad dude, no matter why he was doing it, and those assholes in that palace lied to us."

Pike nodded slowly, then said, "So are we saying that a Catholic charitable organization that has been around since the Crusades is now killing Israeli and American diplomats? I just don't see it. What's the point?"

Shoshana said, "They want to bring about the second coming of Christ. And in so doing, destroy Israel. That's the point."

Knuckles said, "Hey, come on. Not everything is about destroying Israel."

Shoshana flashed her eyes at him and said, "I only tell you what I see. I'm not spouting conspiracy theories. *They* are."

Brett said, "But they're Catholic. Knuckles is right. That's not their thing. If it were an evangelical organization from the United States that danced with rattlesnakes and spoke in tongues,

I could believe it, but a chivalric order from the Crusades under the control of the Catholic Church, with a seat at the United Nations? With the pope as their ultimate leader? That dog just don't hunt."

Shoshana squinted her eyes, saying, "I don't know what you mean. These dogs *are* hunting."

That caused all of the men at the table to laugh. She leaned back in her chair and crossed her arms, not amused at being the butt of a joke.

Pike said, "Calm down, Carrie. We're not laughing *at* you. It's just an American saying, meaning you have a dog that's supposed to flush prey for you to capture, but it refuses to do so, leaving you without meat on the table. Meaning your theory has no meat. It's not correct."

She took that in, nodded, then said, "I'm right. I feel it. It might not be the organization itself, but something inside of it is rotten."

Pike said, "I can't argue with that. Something *is* rotten. You two head back to the hotel. Aaron and Jennifer have our reservations. We'll meet you there. We've got to make contact with the Taskforce in an hour, and then me and Shoshana have to go meet this inspector to see if she's got anything we can use."

Knuckles stood up and said, "You sure that's a good use of our time? Why would the murder of a prostitute have anything to do with this?"

Pike just looked at Shoshana, letting her answer. She said, "It's the *best* use of our time. Trust me. She's tied into the killer just like we are. That dog *will* hunt."

## CHAPTER 42

Knuckles and Brett reentered the small parking area for the Knights of Malta, getting a little salute from the guard on the way. They retrieved the Acura sedan and began to exit when Brett said, "Hang on a second. Don't leave the courtyard yet. The GPS needs to see the sky."

Knuckles put on the brakes, waved at the guard, and reversed back into the courtyard until he was in the open. Brett put the hotel into the navigation system, saying, "Westin Excelsior sounds a bit excessive for us, but I'm not complaining."

After a minute, the GPS gave them a route, and Knuckles began driving, saying, "That damn hotel is like a mile away as the crow flies. Look at that crazy route."

Brett chuckled and said, "I guess they're all one-way roads. Still only says six minutes."

Knuckles began threading down the narrow lanes, taking directions from the female voice on the GPS. He said, "What did you make of all that Shoshana crap?"

Brett considered for a moment, then said, "On the one hand, I'd say it was crazy. On the other, she's done a ton of crazy shit in the past that ended up being the right call. Hard to say, honestly."

Knuckles looked at him and said, "Yeah, I'm the same way, but this is sort of a different level. This isn't looking at someone and deciding that individual is bad. She's looking at an entire eco-system and declaring it all bad. Based on seeing a crime scene, which is a little nuts. I mean, I'm all about believing her in the heat of the moment, but I'm not sure about this. End of Days rants and the second coming of Christ is a bit much."

Brett said, "I agree, but Pike believes her."

Knuckles looked at him and said, "How do you know that?"

"Because I know. He just believes her. He plays a big game teasing her, but he's always believed her. His Bible knowledge is for shit, but he thinks she's real."

They took another turn and Knuckles left the conversation alone, instead cursing the byzantine route the GPS was dictating.

"This is stupid. There has to be a better route than what we're taking. Did you specify some-thing like 'only take small one-way roads'?"

Brett didn't answer, his eyes glued to the rear-view mirror. Knuckles said, "What's up?"

Still looking, he said, "Our route has been one turn after another, and that scooter behind us has been following since a block away from the palace."

Knuckles looked in the rearview mirror, see-ing a small motorcycle with two people riding, both wearing full-face helmets. Which, in and of itself, was a little strange. Every other scooter rider wore a little skullcap helmet, but these two acted like they were about to race at Laguna Seca—or were trying to hide their faces.

They finally broke out of the cloistered alleys and onto an actual two-way road, the route taking them to a dead end with a hard right next to the gardens of Villa Medici, the home of the French Academy in Rome. An expansive green-space, with acres of botanical gardens, it required Knuckles to basically conduct a U-turn, heading back in the direction he'd just traversed, but now on a different road called Via Sistina.

He watched behind him, seeing the motor-cycle making the same turn. That was a bit much. The motorcycle accelerated until it was just off his back bumper, waited for a car in the other lane to pass, then goosed the throttle.

It hovered for a moment right off the quarter panel of the sedan, then sped up, the two on the bike showing wide eyes as they left.

Knuckles said, "What was that all about?"

Brett snapped upright and said, "Which side is the gas tank fill?"

"What?"

"Which side is the gas tank fill!"

Knuckles looked at the display on his dash-board, saw the arrow, and said, "My side, my side. Why?"

Brett screamed, "Lock it up! Get out! Get out!"

Any other human on earth would have looked

at Brett like he was insane. Fortunately, Knuckles was not like any other human on earth.

He slammed on the brakes hard enough to cause a skid. They skittered across the oncoming lane, hammered a guardrail, skipped back into their lane, and slammed into a retaining wall, crumpling the trunk.

Both snapped out of their seat belts and dove out of the car, crawling away on hands and knees. There was a small *wump*, then a gigantic explosion, lifting the car off the ground, the shrapnel of sheet metal splattering everything around them.

The car slammed back onto the ground, burning furiously. Knuckles scrambled backward, away from the fire, screaming, "Brett! Brett!"

He saw Brett on the other side of the car running toward him and patting out a fire on his arm. Brett reached him and collapsed, saying, "You okay?"

Knuckles took over the fire watch of his clothes, patting out the flames and saying, "Better than you, I guess."

They both sagged into the concrete for a moment, hearing sirens in the distance. Brett rolled over and said, "This is going to be a shit storm."

Knuckles pulled out his phone and said, "Yeah, it is. We've got about five seconds to get the Taskforce to backstop our cover as State Department."

He dialed his phone, looking at Brett, amazed at how close they'd come to being eviscerated in the explosion. Brett went up on an elbow, checking for other damage to his body. He said, "Looks like Shoshana was right. Those fucks are out for blood."

Before the phone connected, his voice turned grim. "Out for blood? They haven't seen that yet. But they will, so help me God."

## CHAPTER 43

L ia Vairo went through the gate to her apartment complex, glad that it wasn't later in the night. While the flat was hers free and clear from the divorce, it left a lot to be desired as a place to live.

All too often she'd come home from a late-night crime scene and had been confronted by youthful revelers out to have a good time. Students at the nearby John Cabot University or the American University rented all of the flats on her block, and routinely became annoying after the sun went down, but she'd never felt a threat.

Well, almost never. There had been a time or two where she wasn't sure they were students, but instead castoffs preying on students and had seen her, deciding to prey on her.

She'd made short work of those youths and continued to enjoy her flat, free of any financial encumbrances. Tonight, she parked her car and entered the courtyard to her complex, thinking about the woman and man she'd met at the last crime scene.

The man called Pike was not from the United States State Department. Of that she was sure.

She could feel the violence coming off him like a waterfall. But he didn't hold her attention. The woman did.

She was something else entirely, like she could see the world through a different lens. Lia was intrigued, and wanted to hear what they had to say tonight.

She went past the guard shack, waving at the man inside. He waved back, completely useless. The complex was supposed to be "gated," but all it really encapsulated was welfare for the guards who sat inside and did nothing.

She went up the stairwell to her flat, seeing the usual students out on balconies giving her catcalls, which she ignored.

She reached the second floor and saw three men on the stoop, one smoking from a vape pipe, like he was trying to re-create the beatnik era of the sixties. There was no reason for them to be here, because the steps ended at her apartment only, which aggravated her to no end each time it happened.

They shuffled to let her go by and she entered her apartment, kicking off her heels and immediately freeing her breasts from a bra, tossing it to the side.

She poured a glass of wine and sagged back, checking the time.

She had about an hour before the two showed up. Unbidden, the investigation began running through her mind, an endless reel she just couldn't stop. An unwanted feature of her job.

The guy was a killer who'd been extremely careless in the first three murders, but in the last, he'd been very, very careful. Like it was a setup for something. If in fact the last murder was his.

She began to do the same circle of analysis she'd done since the first murder. *What if? What if? What if?* She couldn't be locked into a certain frame of thought, because if she did, she'd miss the killer. In point of fact, she couldn't assume the final one was connected, even if the Israeli said it was. Although that woman seemed to have some knowledge, Lia did not, which is why she'd agreed to meet them.

Garrett parked his car down the street from Lia's Trastevere apartment and surveyed the neighborhood. It looked like a bunch of students or other malcontents. It most definitely wasn't an area of wealthy people that would remember his presence.

He exited and walked a couple of blocks to the gate of the complex, seeing several youths on the curb and a guard in the shack. He approached and, taking a risk, he said, "I'm here for Lia Vairo. She's expecting me."

The guard made no attempt to check the validity of his claim, instead looking at a computer and saying, "Apartment 2 F."

He said, "Thanks," and entered the complex. He went up one flight of stairs and saw a group of young men lounging. They muttered under their breath about him, and one actually rose up, as if he was going to challenge his ability to continue.

He saw Garrett's eyes, and did not. Garrett started up, and then had a thought. These stairs ended at only one apartment. The inspector's. He returned to the men and said, "Hey, you guys want to make a little money tonight?"

The one who'd thought about challenging him said, "Like, how?"

"I'm seeing my ex-wife tonight, and her new boyfriend might show up. I don't want that to happen."

He pulled out a wad of euros and said, "You keep anyone from coming up these stairs for an hour, and this is yours."

The man said, "Give it to us now, and we'll do it."

Garrett peeled off some bills and said, "This is half. When I leave here, you get the other half."

The man took it and, like he was in charge, said, "Okay. Nobody up. Nobody down. You got an hour."

Garrett smiled and said, "If you fuck me, I'll kill you."

The man saw the evil in his eyes and realized he'd made a deal with the devil. He nodded and said, "I got it, I got it. We'll be here. I promise."

Garrett went up the final steps, the landing ending at a single apartment. He rang the bell and waited, a pistol hidden under his jacket.

The door opened and he saw Lia Vairo in her street clothes, but the shirt untucked and not wearing a bra, her nipples prominent in the button-up sheer blouse.

He showed his gun and said, "Inside. Inside."

She didn't show the fear he wanted, but she complied, backpedaling barefoot into her flat.

He sat her in a chair, the gun still on her. She said, "You're the one, aren't you?"

He waved the gun about and said, "Yes, I am. I'm the one you're looking for, but you and I are connected, in more ways than one."

He saw her confusion. She asked, "How?"

"You understood the red cord. You know what I'm trying to do."

She shook her head and said, "I have no idea what you're trying to do."

He chuckled, saying, "Initially, I was just going to kill you to throw off the investigation, but I realized you could help me. Even if you didn't want to."

He heard a buzzing on the counter and turned toward it. He saw a phone about to vibrate itself off the table. He caught it, looked, and said, "Who is this?"

She said, "I don't know. I'm a police officer. It could be anyone."

"Answer it and tell them to get lost."

She took the phone, saw the number, but showed no reaction. She said, "No, we can't meet at this hour. I have guests."

She listened, looking her killer in the eye, and said, "I told you to come at the end of the day. That's what I said. The end of day. It's too late now."

Still looking at Garrett, she said, "I understand. It's not like there are a lot of them. Only one."

CHAPTER 44

I waited for the connection to go through its myriad of security protocols, ensuring the video was encrypted, knowing this wasn't going to be a good conversation. I glanced behind me, seeing the rest of the team waiting. Well, the team we still had control of, anyway.

It hadn't been a good day. We'd come up with nothing from our leads, and then some assholes had attempted to eliminate Knuckles and Brett, using the same tactics the Israelis employed against the nuclear scientists in Iran, and now they were in a heavy police interrogation with a cover that was so skinny it was anorexic.

Which told me we were on the right thread— even if we didn't know what that was. But I knew the folks in DC wouldn't see it that way.

The screen cleared and I saw an incredibly agitated George Wolffe. Before I could even talk, he said, "Jesus Christ, Pike—you have two Task-force members under police control in Italy? After telling everyone they're State Department? This is not what I would call a covert operation."

I returned his fury, saying, "Are you shitting me? *That's* the concern? Somebody tried to kill them with a limpet mine slapped on their vehicle. And that someone is tied into the Knights of Malta. The damn attempt itself tells us we're on the right thread."

"Pike, their cover won't hold. Nobody in the U.S. mission in Italy has any idea about them. This is going to crack open, and we still have the threat out there."

Having thought about it, I said, "It'll hold if you get Amanda Croft on the case. She's the SECSTATE. Get them backstopping and this will all go away."

He said, "We're already doing that, but the fact that it was a car bomb is going to draw attention."

And I'd thought about this, too. I had a solution, even as it sickened me. I said, "Put out a press release saying that Keta'ib Hezbollah is responsible, just like happened with the other diplomat. Get the focus off the targets and on the perpetrators."

He looked at me like I was nuts, then said, "You want me to do their work for them? Claim it was an Iraqi militia under the sway of Iran who tried to kill diplomats in Rome? Have you lost your mind?"

I closed my eyes for a moment, wondering if I wasn't, in fact, nuts. I opened them and said, "Yes. Give them the credit. Get the press on that angle instead of who the two were. Right now, everyone's talking about the bombing like it's a possible mafia hit in a gang fight. The focus is on Brett and Knuckles. We need to short-circuit that."

"Pike, if I do that, we might go to war. The

pressure is becoming unbearable here. President Hannister can't take another attack like that without responding."

I rubbed my head and said, "I get it, sir, I really do, but a Taskforce compromise at this juncture will short-circuit everything we're trying to do, and they'll find it with a little bit of digging. Look, you don't have to say they claimed credit. Just say it's related and you're exploring. Get the United States involved. I need my men back. I need the State Department to engage. They can bloviate like they always do, babbling about how they take it seriously or are in discussions with other diplomats, I don't care, but I need Knuckles and Brett back. I can't have them sitting under police exposure because some Rome authority thinks it was a Cosa Nostra thing."

He said, "Well, maybe that's a better angle. Leave it as a case of mistaken identity from a gang fight. At the end of the day, it could have been anything."

I said, "Are you kidding me here? You pull that shit and we *will* go to war. It's coming, and we can stop it. Get them back. Use the State Department."

He sighed and said, "Pike, I don't think you get what's happening here. The Fifth Fleet is in the Hormuz Strait, and they're waiting on the word to attack. The 82nd Airborne is on the way to Kuwait, loaded for war. If I convince the National Command Authority to do what you say, I could be pulling the trigger."

I said, "Sir, just let the NCA know what you're

doing, because of Taskforce activities. I get they'll be under pressure when the fake story goes out, but if they know it's fake, then they'll keep the status quo. Screw all the talking heads on TV. For once."

I saw Wolffe rub his face like he was trying to scrape away everything I'd said. He sighed and said, "Can you at least tell me you're onto something? Besides telling me a chivalric order under the command of the Vatican is evil?"

I leaned back and said, "Yes, sir. We're onto something. The administration might not like it, because it's really rotten, but we're onto something, and I don't think it's Iran."

"Do you have any *proof* of that? Anything at all?"

"You mean besides the fact that someone tried to murder two of my team an hour after visiting the Knights of Malta?"

He said, "That's just another attack. It's no more proof than the death of Gabrielle Hernandez."

I bristled and said, "Sir, this attack was planned because they went inside that building. Because they were asking questions. There was no targeting here based on being a U.S. diplomat. How the hell would they target Taskforce personnel as State Department when *we* didn't even know we were going to be State Department when we landed? Come on now."

I saw him exhale, then heard, "Yeah, yeah, okay. I get it. That's more than just a coincidence, but it would be nice if you could give me something concrete. Is there anything you need? Anything we can do from here? Because if I pull this trigger, it's going to go critical mass very, very soon."

I said, "Give me tonight." I looked at my watch and said, "I'm meeting someone in thirty minutes who might help us, and I really have to go to be there in time. Just give me that."

I caught Shoshana waving her hand behind me. I turned and she said, "I'm calling now to let her know we're on the way."

I knew why she'd said it. She was trying to tell Wolffe that the plan was already in motion, and him trying to stop it could adversely affect the very thing he was trying to achieve. Which was actually pretty smart.

George said, "You're leaving now? Who's the contact?"

"Sir, if I told you that, you'd really think we were crazy. Just trust me on this, please."

He said, "Pike, I need more than that."

I saw Shoshana dialing and said, "Hang on, sir."

Shoshana put the phone on speaker, then waited on it to connect. When it did, she said, "Hello, Lia, this is Shoshana, the woman you met today. I just wanted to touch base and say we're on the way. Should be there in the next twenty minutes."

The speaker spat out, "No, we can't meet at this hour. I have guests."

Perplexed, Shoshana looked at Pike and said, "We had a meeting. What do you mean you can't now?"

END OF DAYS / 289

Shoshana held out the phone so we could all listen in, and the phone said, "I told you to come at the end of the day. That's what I said. The end of day. It's too late now."

Shoshana heard the words and I saw the dark angel inside of her start to blossom, but I didn't understand why. She looked at me while speaking into the phone. She said, "We're coming. Hold on. We'll be there within twenty minutes. And I'm bringing a wrecking crew."

The speaker said, "I understand. It's not like there are a lot of them. Only one."

The phone disconnected and I said, "What was that about? What wrecking crew?"

"You. You and everyone else in this room. Did you not hear what she said?"

On the couch, Jennifer said, "Holy crap. It just clicked. She said 'end of day' as in End of Days."

Shoshana stood up, her face a mask of death. She said, "Lia's under the control of the killer, and he's the only one there."

I heard someone calling my name and realized I was still on the virtual private network video with George Wolffe. He said again, "Pike! What's happening?"

I turned to the computer and said, "I need an immediate hit on a cell phone and the follow-on exploitation of the Wi-Fi network it's associated with."

I typed in the number, sent it, and he said, "What?"

"Sir, I don't have time to explain. Get Creed on the cell number. Tell him to ping it, then exploit it, finding the Wi-Fi node it's attached to. I have to go."

"Go where?"

I stood up and said, "Go save the inspector." I heard him yelling at me, but like everyone else, I was too busy putting on lethal kit to answer.

## CHAPTER 45

Lia disconnected the phone and handed it to the killer. He said, "What was that about? I'm not good with surprises."

She said, "Nothing. A woman who wanted to talk to me about a missing persons case. She's been flighty since she initially reported. The kid's a runaway. There's no reason for you to go after her as well."

He chuckled and said, "You think I'm some sort of monster, and I can see why, but you miss some things."

Lia tried to appear sympathetic, saying, "What? Let me help you. Let me keep you from making another mistake."

He said, "You *will* help me. Right now. Take a seat in that chair."

She did. He went behind her and pulled her arms together, saying, "Where are your hand-cuffs?"

She flicked her head to her purse, and he said, "Hold your hands there."

He found them, then returned, threading the cuffs through a spine of the chair, then cinching them to her wrists.

He returned to her front and said, "I'm not a bad man. I'm honestly not. I'm trying to cleanse the world of vermin just like you do in your job, but I'm going to do it with a single event instead of one at a time."

Lia realized he was crazy. Like, literally batshit crazy. He had a strange flicker in his eyes, both of them dancing around, as if he was on a different plane. She'd seen it before with addicts, but she knew he hadn't taken drugs. He was clinically insane.

She said, "Let me go now, and we can both do what's right. You do yours and I'll do mine."

He laughed and said, "It's too late for that. You've found my little brood of bodies, but I promise you, from the depths of my soul, I didn't want to kill them. I really didn't. Well, except for that last one. I set her up to find you, and you graciously took the bait."

She said, "You don't need to do this. It's not too late for redemption."

She saw his eyes open at the term. "Redemption? Yes, yes. That's what this is all about. The Rapture is coming soon. You're a good woman, so you'd be one of the chosen, but I'm going to have to send you earlier than the rest of humanity."

He went in front of her, judging her mouth's angle to his waist, and said, "Yes. This will work."

She let her false sympathy disappear, spitting out, "What the fuck do you want?"

He grabbed her hair and shook her skull, saying, "I want what was taken from me. I want pleasure. I want to eliminate the scourge of humanity in the world. You can help with the first, and by your death, you'll help with the second."

He released her hair, letting her head fall back against the chair. She said nothing. He went to the backpack he'd brought and said, "Have you ever heard of ISIS?"

She remained mute.

He said, "Of course you have. Savages. Evil incarnate. Spawn of that religion called Islam."

He pulled out what looked like a collar, only it had lumps in it, and a small digital display like a watch. He said, "They are the reason the world is so twisted. They represent all that is wrong on our earth, and it's been that way since the Crusades."

He approached her and she began to struggle. He slapped her face and said, "Be still. This thing isn't that precise. You move too much and you might set it off. It has a motion detector, but I'm not sure how sensitive it is."

She said, "What is it?"

He placed it around her neck and cinched it tight, using a Fastex buckle to complete the loop, just like a dog collar. He said, "It's called an ISIS necktie. Something they used to great amusement in Syria. They would put it on a man, then tell him if he could run outside the range of the signal, he'd live." He held up what looked like a key fob. "Of course, that never happened. His head was popped off his body by the explosives as he ran away."

Lia had thought she was dealing with a serial killer. She now knew it was much, much worse. This man was something else entirely. She began to pant, the adrenaline flooding through her body, her skin beginning to sweat.

He cupped her chin and said, "Don't worry. I won't use this to kill you. It's just a precaution to gain compliance."

Breathing through an open mouth, feeling the death coming, she said, "Compliance for what?"

He said, "I'm ashamed to show you. But I'm glad you took off your bra. It might help."

He reached forward and ripped open her shirt, her breasts spilling out. He said, "Oh, nice. Not as good as the other whores, but still pretty good."

He cupped one, looked in her eyes, and said, "You understood about the red cord. You can help me."

She slammed her eyes closed and he slapped her again, saying, "You *understand* me. Don't do that. Look me in the eye."

She did, seeing an abomination. She said, "I *don't* understand you. Why are you doing this?"

He said, "I didn't want to kill those women. I really didn't. I served the Church faithfully, doing humanitarian deeds all over the world. In Syria, I realized that what they were doing wasn't enough. It wasn't enough to put a Band-Aid on the pain and destruction. What was needed was to eliminate the pain and destruction."

Hesitantly, she said, "So what does that mean?"

He smiled and said, "It's the red cord. The walls of Jericho need to come down. The Israelites must take control of the promised land. I'm the spy for Jericho, only I'm going to do it worldwide."

She said nothing, not understanding what he was blathering about. He reached for his belt, releasing it. He dropped his pants to his knees, then pulled down his underwear.

She was revolted, her eyes going wide, her head rolling back, the entire insanity of the moment threatening to break her.

He grabbed her hair, jerked her forward, and said, "If you can finally give me pleasure, I might let you live. We're one, me and you. We understand what's needed."

She twisted her head away, ripping her hair out of his hands. He snatched her face and said, "Don't fight this. It's your chance at redemption."

She slammed her head to the left, toward her kitchen counter, and saw her Amazon Echo Ten rotate on its base, looking for a face to recognize. It reached her and stopped.

## CHAPTER 46

Outside the apartment complex, Aaron driving and Shoshana about to go nuts in the backseat, I said into my phone, "What's Creed got? We need to go in."

Jennifer said, "He's working it. He's got something called an Amazon Echo Ten. It's a thing you use for Zoom calls. Lia apparently has it because of the pandemic and being forced to work from home."

"How does that help us? We're running out of time here, and the building is four stories."

She came back a little curt, saying, "Well, if you'd wanted me to climb it, maybe I should be in the car, commando. You shouldn't have left me here watching a computer."

After I'd convinced George Wolffe to bring on Creed, we'd been at a little bit of a quandary. Brett and Knuckles were still dealing with the Rome authorities and absolutely no help. I was sure with Wolffe and Amanda Croft on the case they'd be released soon, but not in the time we needed. That left me with Jennifer, Shoshana, and Aaron. Since the entire assault was predicated on the inside information Creed could get us, that meant some Taskforce personnel had to stay behind to coordinate. And there was no way I was staying behind. That left Jennifer, and she was none too happy about it.

She wanted to get in the fight like no tomorrow, but I couldn't order Aaron or Shoshana to coordinate with the Taskforce. So I'd ordered her to stay behind. In truth, Creed had a crush on her from previous operations, and would probably work harder with her on the other end of the VPN.

She knew that and hated me for putting her on desk duty. But then again, sometimes we all have to sacrifice for the greater good. Not every mission required a monkey. Sometimes it required a bikini model. Too bad she was both . . .

I said, "We're about to exit the vehicle. Give me something."

And like magic Jennifer said, "We've got the Echo. Passing control to you now."

Creed had been able to access Lia's phone, and like all normal humans in today's society, she had her phone automatically tether itself to the home Wi-Fi. Because he had the number, he was able to springboard off the phone into the network itself. He'd scanned it and found that Lia owned a device from Amazon called an Echo Ten. A basic screen for virtual talks, which had become a mainstay after the pandemic had hit in Italy, but it had a twist. It would find your face and follow it if you moved around, rotating on its base.

The entire concept was creepy to me, not the least of which was that the thing answered to voice commands, but the worst of it was it could also act as a surveillance camera if the owner wanted, rotating around the room to see what you wanted it to see. Meaning we now could see inside the house.

I pulled out my tablet, hit a Taskforce app, and was looking at the inside of the room. I saw a window in what appeared to be a kitchen. I gave a command to the device and it started rotating, searching for a face. It found one, and when it focused, I almost dropped the tablet.

A man was standing in front of Lia with his pants down around his knees, his hand in her hair. She was in a chair with her hands behind it, cinched tight, and she had some sort of thick necklace around her throat.

And she was scared out of her mind, the fear from her eyes penetrating my soul.

I slammed the tablet to the floor, pulled out a small explosive charge from my backpack, press-checked my pistol, and said, "We go, right now. There's only a single threat. Aaron, find the back of this place. Prevent a squirter. Shoshana, on me."

Aaron said, "Wait, wait. Let's make a plan here."

I said, "No time. You guys can stay here if you want, but I'm going killing."

Shoshana saw the ferocious violence exploding from me, looked at the footwell where the tablet lay, and saw the live picture on the screen.

Something she was intimately familiar with when she'd been abused in the service of the Mossad. She hissed, a feral sound that penetrated the car.

Aaron leaned forward and saw the tablet himself. He looked at Shoshana and said, "No mercy," then exited.

Shoshana and I both left the vehicle at a trot, jogging to the stairwell of the apartment, seeing a bunch of twenty-somethings all out having a good time. We pushed through them, and then reached a guard shack. We walked past it, and the guard came out, saying something in Italian.

I turned to him and he instinctively read the violence leaking out. I said, "I don't speak Italian."

In English, he said, "What do you want?"

I said, "I want you to get back in the fucking shack."

He nodded and retreated. We began running up the stairs. We reached Lia's landing and faced three guys sitting on the steps like cats in the sun, one of them smoking a vape.

I tried to go past them and the vape guy stood up, also saying something in Italian. I don't know what he uttered, but it was really irrelevant, as I was sick of the roadblocks. I looked at the other two and said, "Shoshana, eliminate the threat."

She said, "Gladly."

The vape guy appeared confused, but that only lasted a moment, because the next thing he felt was pain. Shoshana ripped him off his feet, torquing his elbow until the joint shattered. He screamed and launched himself at Shoshana, his useless arm trailing him like a piece of toilet paper attached to his shoe. He tried to use his weight alone to subdue her, throwing himself on her body with his one good arm reaching for her neck. She grabbed the arm and rotated, using his momentum against him, flipping him off her back and tossing his ass off the stairwell to the ground below.

He continued screaming all the way down.

The other two leapt to their feet and I plowed into them, clocking the first with a straight right punch to the temple with all of my weight behind it, causing him to drop like a sack of wheat.

I grabbed the leg of the second man and jerked it up in the air, slamming him onto his back on the stairs. He flailed his arms and tried to get away from the pain, but I used the stairs as leverage. I twisted his ankle until I heard a satisfying pop. He shouted in pain, keening like a wounded rabbit, and I dropped the leg, bodily picked him up, and sent him to follow his leader two stories below.

Breathing heavily, Shoshana pointed and said, "What about him?"

I looked at the guy I'd knocked out and said, "Fuck him. Let's go."

We went upward, now with our weapons out, and reached the landing to the apartment. Shoshana said, "What do we do?"

And I realized she was good at killing, but had no skill on room clearing. I wished I'd sent her to the back and had Aaron with me.

I pulled out my small door charge and said, "Look, when I initiate this, there are only two things in that apartment. A threat, and Lia. Do you understand?"

She nodded, and I said, "If it's not Lia, kill it. I don't care if it's a dog. If it's something breathing, and it's not Lia, kill it."

CHAPTER 47

Lia heard the shouting outside and dared to hope. The killer heard it as well, whipping up his pants and saying, "What did you do, you bitch?"

Chained to her chair, half-naked, she said, "Nothing. It's the kids. They always do this. It's why I hate this place."

The killer turned from the noise, becoming calm again, like a light switch had been flipped. He said, "Then I guess it's just you and me now."

He advanced to her again and said, "If you take my manhood in your mouth, it might alter your fate. I really would like that."

Lia thought it almost seemed as if he was begging. Desperately trying to get someone to love him after his horrific torture.

And she almost considered it, to save her life. Almost.

She said, "Tell me what you want. Tell me what I can do."

There was a small scratch on the door, a little tick. Nothing that anyone of ordinary skills would recognize, but the killer did.

He looked at her and said, "You bitch! How do they know?"

He raised the key fob device and the lock on her door exploded, a piece of the cylinder flying out and hitting him in the fist. He screamed, clutched his wounded hand, and then started sprinting to the back of the house.

Two people came in, guns raised, clearing the immediate area. Lia was astounded at the turn of events. She jerked her head toward the back and screamed, "He's that way! That way!"

The man she knew as Pike ran to the back, talking into a radio. The woman came to her and said, "Are you okay?"

Panting, Lia said, "Get out! I'm wearing an explosive collar. He has the detonator. Get out!"

The woman floated a weird gaze on her, not unlike the killer. She said, "My name is Shoshana, and I'm not going anywhere. And you're not going to die."

Lia finally recognized her as the woman from the crime scene. Pike came back in and said, "I'm not sure about you Israelis. Aaron missed him out the back. He exited on the fire escape, but he never reached the ground. He's gone."

Shoshana gave him a laser stare, and Lia saw him subtly flinch. He said, "What do we have?"

"A woman with a dog collar of explosives, and a man with a detonator on the loose."

Pike said, "Not on the loose." He bent down and picked up what looked like a key fob and said, "He dropped this on the way out."

Pike finally looked at Lia, saw her condition,

and said, "What the hell, Carrie? Cover her up. You're going to leave her exposed?"

*Carrie? She said her name was Shoshana.* Lia saw the woman inwardly retreat at the words, just as Pike had earlier. Experienced at reading people as an inspector, she studied them both, trying to understand who had entered the room. They might be just as crazy as the man who'd left. They might even be working together with him.

Warily, her eyes went from one to the other. They'd just saved her life, so she was willing to give them the benefit of the doubt, but she wasn't convinced she was out of danger.

Pike averted his gaze from her exposed breasts, then left the room, going to the back again. Shoshana covered Lia, and while she did so, Lia said, "Why does he call you Carrie? That's not what you told me your name was. Is that your real name?"

She said, "No. It's a nickname he's given me. It's from some crazy person who has the ability to physically alter her world."

Shoshana bent down to use a key on the handcuffs and Lia said, "Like Carrie from Stephen King?"

"Yes."

"Why?"

Shoshana stood up and dropped the handcuffs in her lap, saying, "Because I have the ability to alter my world. But I'm not crazy."

She draped a blanket over Lia's shoulders and Pike came back in, saying, "He's gone, damn it. Aaron thought he had him, but he didn't."

A man appeared at the front door. Pike said, "Aaron, meet Lia. Lia, this is Aaron, the one who should have captured your tormentor." Pike looked at Aaron and said, "Where did he go?"

Aaron smiled and said, "Said from the guy who's left at least three bodies outside here. As for the target, I honestly don't know. I saw a shadow on the fire escape, backed up into an ambush position, and he never appeared. My bet is he's in an apartment below us, but unless you want to start clearing from top to bottom, we should just go."

Pike pointed at Lia and said, "She's got an explosive neck ring. I've got the denotator, and I'd go at it, but you have more experience."

The smile left Aaron's face. He went to her, studying the explosive collar like a botanist looking at a new bud. She said, "Do you know what you're doing?"

He gave her a reassuring smile, soothing and just. He said, "Yes. I think Shoshana told you I'm from Israel. Trust me, I've done this a few times before, and not only in training like your police."

He touched her cheek and said, "Please lean your head back slowly."

She began to calm down, doing as he asked. He took about ten seconds looking, then said, "Pike, all I need are a pair of scissors. This is not complex. It's a simple device."

Lia said, "Second drawer on the right." Pike went to the left in the kitchen and she said, "Right. Go to the right."

He found the scissors and returned. Aaron said, "If you two would go in the bedroom, I'd appreciate it."

Lia said, "Why? Why are you sending them away?"

"Because I'm not God. There's no reason for them to be in the blast radius."

She jerked upright and said, "Call the police. Call them right now. We have explosive ordnance personnel."

Pike said, "Relax. We're not leaving the room, and the reason is I trust him more than anyone you could bring to this fight."

Shoshana approached and said, "I told you I'm not leaving. And you're not going to die."

Lia started to cry, the tears coming unbidden. Aaron stroked her cheek, saying, "Shhhh. This isn't that bad. It's easy. Lean your head back."

She did so, and before she knew it, he'd snipped a wire, then reached around her neck and unfastened the buckle. He stood up, holding the necklace of explosives like the tail of a rat.

He said, "Well, that worked."

Incredulous, she said, "You didn't think it would?"

He smiled and said, "You never know."

I said, "Time to go. Her police will be here soon, and we have no sanction here."

Lia stood up, saying, "Wait, what? You're going to leave? I have to report this. I mean, we just met the killer. He's real. I have a face now. I can't let you just leave, even if you saved me. We need to find this guy, and I need what you know."

Pike said, "I understand that, and we're going to find him, but the 'we' part doesn't include you. I'm sorry."

Lia said, "Are you crazy? The killer just tried to murder an Italian inspector by placing an explosive device around her neck. And that person was me! You aren't going anywhere."

She looked at Shoshana, who in turn waited on Pike. He said, "I'm sorry, but we're leaving. And if you mention us saving you to anyone, we'll disappear like a bad dream. You knew we weren't State Department the minute you met us. And we aren't. We'll find that guy for you, but we can't do it in the open."

They started walking to the door. Incensed, Lia said, "I have your names. I'll contact the United States State Department. I'll find you."

They stopped at the door. Pike said, "You won't find us that way. I promise."

Shoshana turned to her and said, "You won't do that, because I wouldn't do that. You and I are the same. We saved your life, and you will protect ours."

Lia stood firm, but her stern visage began to falter.

Shoshana continued. "This man has killed more than streetwalkers. He's murdered friends of mine. I understand your quest for justice, and I promise he will get it. I'm going to rip him apart. Do you understand?"

Lia touched her throat, still feeling the collar, seeing the absolute conviction in Shoshana's eyes. She paused, then said, "I guess justice is justice. But at least let me know, even if it's for nothing more than closing this case."

I opened the door and said, "You'll know, I promise. I'm pretty sure we're going to have to come back to you to get him."

"Why?"

"Because you own the monopoly of violence in this country, and I intend to leverage it."

## CHAPTER 48

Garrett held his hand over the mouth of the young man, whispering at him to remain quiet. Wearing a T-shirt and boxers, he was college-age and had been reading a book and drinking beer when Garrett had entered through the window. Garrett put his hand to the kid's forehead and the blood from his wound dripped onto the student's face, causing him to moan. He tightened his hands, and the student became rigid, staring at him but no longer fighting.

Moments earlier in Lia's flat, he'd heard the small tick from the front door and instantly knew someone was outside. His primordial instinct, gleaned from years of conducting raids against terrorist safe houses, was the only thing that had saved his life. And his mission.

He'd thought he'd hear a knock next, but instead they'd explosively breached the door, sending the lock cylinder into his hand and knocking the detonator loose.

He'd raced to the back bedroom, threw open the window, and exited onto the fire escape. He'd glanced below and saw a man coming up the alley, and knew it was rear security.

He'd gone down one flight, then ripped open a window, spilling into the first apartment he could, finding the young man reading a book in his bed. Before he could react, Garrett was on him.

He said, "Shush. No noise."

The student nodded his head.

He waited, listening for someone coming up the fire escape. After a minute, he believed the man hadn't seen him, or was at least waiting on him to continue down the stairs.

He sat up, releasing the student. The student said, "What do you want?"

"Nothing. I just want to get away from here. Don't do anything crazy, and you'll be fine."

The student nodded, and he pulled out his phone. Garrett turned to him and said, "What's your Wi-Fi network?"

He told him, and Garrett connected, pulling up the Zello app. He called the Turtle channel and heard Raph answer. He glanced at the man, and then began speaking Croatian, saying, "I need some help. I need a car to come get me."

Raph said, "Where have you been? We did the hit today, and I've been trying to contact you for hours."

*Hit?* And the mission slammed home. Garrett realized his fixation on the inspector had caused him to lose focus on what the others were doing. On his orders.

"How did that go? Are they dead?"

"No. I'm sorry, sir, they escaped. We missed them."

"You missed them? How?"

"I don't know. We placed the mine and they

bailed out of the car like they knew what was about to happen. I mean they reacted like we would have. Like Special Forces. No hesitation or anything. They didn't act like civilians."

*I knew those fucks weren't State Department.*

He said, "So they're on the loose, right now?"

"No. There was an enormous police response, and they were taken into custody. They're out of play for a few days. Even better, for some reason, the U.S. is blaming Keta'ib Hezbollah for the attack, as if they claimed credit. At least that worked out."

Garrett ran that through his mind, then said, "Who claimed credit?"

"Nobody. The U.S. State Department put out a statement."

Garrett thought, *Something else is going on here.* He said, "You're on the way to the airport now?"

"Yes. Our flight leaves in four hours. Now, what's happening with you? What's wrong?"

"Too much to tell you right now. I'm in Trastevere, and I can't get to my car. It might be under surveillance. Can you come get me?"

"Trouble how? What's going on?"

"I don't have time to explain! Just trust me."

"Sir, we're on the way to the airport. We can't come get you. We're in an Uber. We're on the way to the mission."

"And Michelangelo? What's he doing?"

Garrett heard the exasperation leaking through the phone, Raphael having no idea of the predicament he was in.

Raph said, "I don't know. He's supposed to fly with you tomorrow. He's probably getting drunk right now before heading to Israel. You know how he is. We did the hit today and then packed up, taking the first flight out that we could find. We didn't want to hang around after the attack."

*Shit.* Garrett backed off, not wanting them to wonder about the mission. Not wanting Raph to wonder about *him*.

Raphael said, "Sir, we're about to meet some very bad people. Are you okay? Should we abort?"

Garrett said, "No, not at all. I'm fine. As you said, I'm flying tomorrow. Just contact me when you get there. Do you have the linkup information? After you meet the Knights people at the airport?"

"Yes, we do. We meet the Knights of Malta folks at the airport, stay in their place, and then meet the contact. What's going on with you?"

"Nothing. I'll find my own way home and leave my car." He looked at the man on the bed and said, "Everything is fine."

He hung up the phone and turned to the student, saying in Italian, "Do you have a car?"

"No. I have a bicycle."

He realized he couldn't leave the student alive after this. He was a weak link who could compromise the mission. He said, "Where's it parked? And is it locked?"

"It's in the rack on the side of the complex. A beachcomber with a Kryptonite U-lock on it. You want me to show you?"

He thought, *Smart man.* If Garrett let him leave the apartment, he would begin sprinting once he hit the street. He said, "No. Just give me the key."

The student leaned to a nightstand, rummaged through a drawer, and pulled out a key ring. He separated one and held it up, his hand trembling.

Garrett took it, then said, "One other thing. You don't have a red cord or sash here, do you?"

## CHAPTER 49

I'd now been running on about three hours of sleep over the last twenty-four, working to get Knuckles and Brett released after our operation in Trastevere, my head sagging down every few minutes as my brain demanded rest, only for me to jerk back awake. Everyone else was racked out, but I could not go to blissful sleep just yet, because I'd been told that George Wolffe wanted to see me via our VPN.

It was closing in on 4 A.M. in Italy, which meant it was about 10 P.M. in DC. That he wanted to talk this late was an ominous sign. Maybe he'd failed to get the State Department to engage for Brett and Knuckles.

We'd returned to the hotel after the hit in Trastevere, the adrenaline still coursing through me, and Jennifer—acting as my TOC commander—had told me that Wolffe wanted me to stand by for contact, and like a good soldier, that's exactly what I was doing, although it was starting to piss me off. If you wanted to talk to me, then give me a call. Don't make me wait like a teenager pining for a date-night phone to ring.

I heard a door open and saw Jennifer come out of our bedroom wearing Nike shorts and a T-shirt, saying, "Still no word?"

I said, "Nope. Not sure why, but it can't be good. Go back to bed. At least someone will be alert when we go to war."

She stood next to my chair and said, "What happened in that room? What happened with Lia? I saw the video feed from the Echo, but it cut right when the action started."

"Nothing, really. It was easy. Aaron missed the guy climbing out of the back, but there wasn't anything that would be what I'd call outside the ballfield. No gunfire. No real contact."

She looked at me for a moment, then said, "Okay. If you say so. It just seemed you guys had touched the beast. Shoshana was on fire when she came back."

I chuckled and said, "Well, that part is true. The guy we're chasing is in fact a beast. I think the man we're hunting wants to start World War Three to cause a biblical apocalypse, and he's also apparently a damn serial killer. I mean a real, honest-to-God serial killer. He *is* the beast. Shoshana wants him in a bad way, but nothing happened during the assault."

She rubbed my back and smiled, and I felt the connection. Ever since we'd met, she'd protected me from my worst instincts, and she was attempting to do it now. She leaned in and kissed my head, saying, "Don't let that bad man get to you. I saw the video."

Meaning she'd seen what that asshole was doing right before we entered, and because of it, she was afraid of my talent. She knew my history and was leery I'd fall back into the abyss because of his craziness.

Truthfully, I had a skill few on earth possessed, and she was afraid I'd use it indiscriminately. It wasn't anything that could be leveraged for money, power, or fame, but it was potent. Maybe ten or twelve people on planet earth had my talent, and when the worst happened, when the bad man came, I was the person you wanted to show up to help. Jennifer understood my power, and she didn't want that unleashed in the wrong way. And she wasn't wrong.

The truth is that at one point in time I had been just like the guy I was chasing, my moral compass broken. But I was way beyond that now. I was on a different plane, not the least because of Jennifer.

I turned and brushed her cheek with my lips, saying, "All I'm worried about right now is rolling this guy up so I can get married. Something none of these DC assholes seem to remember."

She chuckled, then said, "I'm serious, Pike. Don't get wrapped around this guy. I saw you when you found out he was killing women. Don't do it. Let's find him and eliminate the threat, but don't turn into Shoshana."

I leaned back and said, "Hey, that's not fair. Not fair to her. She doesn't kill out of anger." Which was something I'd done in an earlier life. To the point that I was almost a serial killer in my own right.

She ran her hand through my hair and said, "I know, but since I've been with you, I've seen the beast on my own. I've killed for vengeance, and I've regretted it ever since. I still have dreams."

Not for the first time, I wondered about the world I'd pulled her into. I'd done many, many things I'd regretted, and I really didn't want my wife to feel the same. It wasn't exactly a good foundation for a long-term relationship.

She said, "Shoshana is like you on this one. The *Ramsad* was her touchstone. She'll kill now just to relieve the pain, even if it's not right. Just like she did in Bahrain."

I pulled my head away from her hand and said, "You know *you're* the one who created that monster. She wants to be *you* not me."

She laughed and said, "Monster? Come on. She's not that. She is what she is, but she's a little off on this one because of the *Ramsad*."

"Yeah, well, her instincts are still pretty damn good. I don't know how she does it, but she's like a cadaver dog sniffing the ground. When she finds something, it's usually right, and she was right on this one."

She lowered herself to my level in the chair and said, "I get that. I really do. She's my brides-maid for a reason. Just don't let her do anything that will make me regret she's my bridesmaid."

She locked on to my eyes and I saw the earnest-ness of her plea. She didn't want Shoshana to do something evil, even if it meant a greater good. I nodded and said, "I hear you. I understand."

She stood up and said, "That didn't come out right. Don't ever let her do anything that makes *her* regret being my bridesmaid. She loves me and I love her. We are the same, even if we're different. Keep her from doing something in the heat of the moment she'll regret. I don't want another Bahrain killing."

I said, "Her, or me? Are we really talking about her?"

She flashed me a little grin and said, "Very good, young Jedi. You're learning."

And then the VPN finally opened up. After hours of waiting, I heard it beep and saw George Wolffe behind the camera.

He said, "Creed tells me you've been an active little operator tonight. Tell me you have something."

"Sir, I do, but it's not what you think is going on, and you're not going to like it. I didn't find a rabid Iranian Qods Force operative. I found a serial killer."

"What?"

"I know it's crazy. It's why I didn't tell you before. There's a serial killer running around Rome, and he's also tied into the killing of our diplomats."

"Pike, how does that have anything to do with the murders of Israelis and Americans? What the hell am I supposed to do with that? Take the Oversight Council an Italian criminal case? I need closure. Things are getting to the breaking point, not the least because of your idea to blame Keta'ib Hezbollah about the attempted murder of Knuckles and Brett. I *need* something here."

I said, "Hey, sir, you've been here before. Only you used to be me, on the ground. I understand the pressure, but give me some time here. It'll close."

"Pike, we don't have time. The Iranians are starting to react. We may not be able to control this. I need *proof* it isn't them, or they may give us the proof with a war. They're ramping up everything in the Hormuz Strait. They're becoming convinced we're going to attack them because of the assassinations, and they have very little time to preempt that."

"Then talk to them. Can't anyone talk to them? Do we have no contacts at all?"

"We have no diplomatic relations with them."

"I understand that, sir, but we have contacts. Don't we?"

The question hung in the air, and he got quiet. I said, "Sir, don't we have someone? Anyone?"

I thought, *How on earth could we not have at least one back channel with Iran? Even if it's secret? We're going to go to war because we can't talk?*

And I realized *I* had a contact. How I was the sole human on the face of the American defense establishment that did was beyond me.

I said, "Sir, I have someone in Lebanon. Do you want me to reach out?"

"Who?"

"A Druze. He's the guy who helped me capture the Ghost years ago. A good dude. But he's also tied into Hezbollah. The real ones, not that Iraqi militia. He can get us through to someone."

"Pike, a Druze in Lebanon isn't going to stop this thing. He's not even Muslim."

"I get that, but he *is* connected. He stopped that asshole Lucas Kane from killing the peace envoy. Remember? I didn't tell you guys then, but he did it with Hezbollah's help."

I saw his eyes grow, him saying, "Are you telling me you used a sanctioned terrorist organization to complete a mission?"

I leaned back in my chair in frustration, then just started rattling off facts: "Yes, sir, I did. And it worked. You didn't seem to mind then. The facts are what they are: A Croatian guy tried to kill our commander of the Fifth Fleet, which we found through a Syrian refugee in Switzerland. That's not an anomaly. That's a fact. The Croatian is employed by this weird-ass order known as the Knights of Malta here in Rome, and he made a Zello call from Bahrain with a geolocation to the site of a crime scene in the EUR neighborhood of Rome related to a serial killer. The inspector of that crime scene was assaulted tonight by the killer. He was not Iranian. We interdicted him with the help of Creed as he was about to kill the inspector. I'll leave out the gross-ass sex stuff, but that guy is involved in all of it. He's nuts, and he's also very, very smart."

I leaned back and said, "This is not about Iran. It's about the End of Days in the Bible."

He said, "What on earth does that mean?"

I looked at Jennifer and said, "I'm honestly not sure. It's something Shoshana believes, and the inspector has evidence pointing the same way. There's some crazy cult stuff going on, and it's tied into the Knights of Malta. They're trying to cause an apocalyptic war to cause what they think will be the second coming of Christ."

Wolffe rubbed his eyes and said, "And you

want me to take that to the president of the United States? Seriously? You want me to go tell him a chivalric organization that's been around since the Crusades, known worldwide for helping refugees in war-torn countries regardless of religion, backed by the Catholic Church, is trying to start a war with Iran so they can 'cleanse' the earth?"

I slapped the table and said, "No, damn it. I'm not saying *they* want to do it. I'm saying people *in* it do."

I heard a knock on the door and said, "Hang on. Someone's here."

Wolffe said, "Hopefully your wayward minions."

Jennifer opened it, and sure enough, it was Knuckles and Brett, both smiling. They came in and I said, "Hey, so you're not going to jail for the next twenty years?"

"Nope. My little booty call paid off. Amanda Croft brought some leverage and we were given dip creds. They let us go."

"Dip creds" were diplomatic credentials. I said, "Well, considering you were the target, I'm not really shocked. It's not like you tried to blow *yourself* up."

Brett laughed and said, "So what's going on here?"

I pointed at the screen and said, "Wolffe wants some proof that you weren't targeted by Iran, or he's going to launch some missiles."

Wolffe said, "Pike, cut that shit out. Knuckles, what happened?"

I stood up and he took my seat saying, "State

took over. Gave us cover, and we were released. They think it's one more attack in a string of them. They were glad to get rid of us and pass the case to their intelligence agencies. We're free and clear, but the embassy here sure is confused about us."

Wolffe laughed and said, "Well, they can be confused all day long. President Hannister has your back. Do you have anything I can take him to prove it wasn't some militia from Iraq under the sway of Iran?"

"No, sir. They had full-face motorcycle helmets on, but it wasn't a militia. They tracked us from the Knights of Malta headquarters. They knew we were there, and watched us leave."

"What about the guy who Pike found tonight? Was he involved?"

Knuckles said, "I have no idea. We've been in a closed interrogation for the last ten hours."

Jennifer pulled up a screenshot from the inspector's Echo Ten camera on her tablet and showed Brett. He said, "Hey, Knuckles, isn't this the guy from our visit to the Knights? He was sitting outside on a bench."

Jennifer brought him the tablet. He took one look at it and said, "Yeah, that's the guy that eyeballed me on the way in."

I leaned into the screen and said, "I told you. You still think this is the Iranians?"

"Who is he?"

"I have no idea, but I will tomorrow. I'm going to kick that door down first thing."

Wolffe said, "Send me the information. I agree the circumstantial evidence is breaking away from the Iranians but hold what you've got until I get some clearance. I can't authorize you to invade a Catholic order controlled by the Vatican, claiming they're killing foreign diplomats, without some overhead cover."

I said, "Don't worry about that part of it, sir. I'm not going to do it as an American."

"What's that mean?"

"He's a no-shit serial killer, and I know an Italian police inspector who's a little pissed at him."

## CHAPTER 50

Raphael and Leonardo exited the aircraft along with everyone else, some struggling from the sleep deprivation from flying all night, and others, like them, only mildly affected from a four-hour flight to Rafic Hariri International Airport in Beirut. They threaded through the tunnels reaching the immigration and customs area, and saw the lines for immigration. A sign said "Flight Crew and Diplomatic Personnel" and they went that way.

The Knights of Malta had reciprocal diplomatic relationships with multiple countries around the world, and Lebanon was one. Unlike what had happened with Donatello, Raph was sure that this time they'd be passed through like every other arriving diplomat, to include their bags being treated as sacrosanct.

And they were.

After showing their diplomatic passports, they were escorted to the baggage claim area, picked up their bags, and were then escorted by an officer right out the door, nobody ever once acting like they wanted to check the luggage for contraband. Which was good, because they most definitely had contraband in the form of weapons.

Outside of the customs area, Raph found a line of people all waiting on arrivals, then saw his name written on a single piece of paper, held by a local man wearing a threadbare coat and tie.

He went to him and said, "I'm Raphael."

The man smiled and said, "A pleasure to meet you. Come, come. Can I help you with your bags?"

"No. This is it. One bag apiece."

Obsequious to a fault, the man said, "My name is Omar, and I'm the designated liaison from the order's diplomatic mission here. My car is right outside. Come, come."

They followed him out of the airport to a lot outside, loaded their bags, and were on their way.

"We have a nice place for you to stay. We don't get many visitors here anymore since peace has broken out."

He looked embarrassed and said, "I don't mean I want war. Most of our work now is with children's hospitals."

Raphael chuckled and said, "I know what you mean. We do what we can for the Lord. I was here in 2006, back when Israel invaded."

"With the Knights?"

"No. It was before my time with the Knights. I was here for other reasons."

Omar had no answer to that, and was afraid to ask. They drove in silence out of the airfield to the south of the city, then slowly entered the dense concrete of Beirut, new buildings springing forth through the rubble of the latest fight. Omar took lefts and rights, then said, "You see the damage here? That was from the giant port explosion last year. It was like a nuclear bomb. People say it was intentional. What do you think?"

Raphael said, "I don't think anything. That isn't our concern. Protecting the Grand Master is all I'm concerned about. As you were told."

Omar took that in and continued threading through the city center in silence. Eventually, he said, "This ceremony in Israel is a big deal, isn't it?"

"It is. It's why we're here. We're security for the Grand Master."

"Why did you come to Lebanon?"

"We're like the U.S. president's Secret Service. We travel where we might be of assistance. If anything happens in Israel, we're here to provide support. It probably won't matter, but you never know. If we're here, it might make the difference between life and death."

Omar looked at him and said, "Who would want to kill the Grand Master? He's not the president of the United States."

Raphael said, "Nobody that I know of."

Leonardo chuckled from the backseat.

They traveled the rest of the way in silence, threading through the city until they reached a four-story building. Omar said, "This is us. I'm sorry I couldn't get you closer, but I'll come get you tomorrow morning to take you to the Knights' consular building."

Raphael and Leonardo exited the vehicle,

Raphael saying, "That won't be necessary. Our mission must remain low visibility. We won't be going to the consular section."

Omar nodded, confused. He said, "I was told to extend you all courtesy. Is this the extent of that?"

Raphael smiled and said, "Yes. Keep our visit to yourself. It's not exactly secret, but our job is made harder when people know we're around. It's easier to protect the Grand Master from behind a hidden veil. I'm sure you know what I mean, living here."

Omar's eyes widened. He said, "You fear the Party of God? Is that it?"

Leonardo pulled his bag out of the car and said, "We don't fear them. We just don't want to let them know we're here. You understand?"

Omar nodded, held out a key, and said, "It's 310, on the third floor." Leonardo took the key and Omar held out a card, saying, "If you need anything, this is our number. Should I expect to take you back to the airport after the Grand Master's visit?"

Raphael shouldered a rucksack and said, "Maybe. We'll let you know. Thank you for the assistance."

They left Omar on the street and walked into a utilitarian lobby with a single elevator. They took it up to the third floor, found the apartment, and entered, seeing a two-bedroom space that looked like it had been furnished by Ikea, with spartan chairs, twin beds, and an anemic kitchen devoid of any food.

After exploring the area, Raphael took a seat

in the den and said, "Might as well get this over with. Give the contact a call."

Leonardo smiled and said, "You mean the Party of God?"

Raphael said, "Yeah. The real Hezbollah."

## CHAPTER 51

I parked the car outside the Trastevere apartment complex and said, "Okay, we go in quietly. If she wants to play ball, we're good. If not, we'll do it another way."

Jennifer said, "You actually think she spent the night here after last night?"

And that was a good question. I said, "Well, we won't know until we try, but she probably spent the last six hours with her police compatriots, and then collapsed."

I looked at Knuckles and said, "You have your script, right? Know what you're doing?"

He said, "Yeah, I got it. You're pimping me like you always do. Let's go."

I'd brought Jennifer, Aaron, Shoshana, and Knuckles with me, leaving Brett in our TOC to respond to anything the Taskforce might throw out. Shoshana, Aaron, and I were just a familiar face to gain entrance. Jennifer and Knuckles were the ones I wanted to use to convince her to do my bidding without contacting her higher headquarters. In essence, I wanted her badge and authority to allow me to take the bad guy down, but when that happened, he wasn't going into the Italian judicial system.

We began walking past the guard shack, now in daylight, and a new guard appeared, saying something in Italian. I thought, *Here we go again . . .*

Knuckles said, "Do you speak English?"

He nodded and said, "Can I ask your business?"

Knuckles said, "Just going to visit a friend."

"What's the name? I'll call up."

That most definitely wouldn't do. I said, "Did you have a police presence here last night?"

"Yes. Is that about your visit?"

"Yes, it is."

"In that case, I really can't let you pass. Let me call the police."

Knuckles turned to him, his face as hard as stone, saying, "You asked my business. If you don't get back in that shack and let us go, you're going to see what that means."

The guard looked startled at the change in his demeanor. He saw the violence in Knuckles's eyes and quit. Just like that. He stuttered something, then retreated to the guard shack.

I grabbed Knuckles's elbow and said, "Hey, man, we don't want to make a scene here. Stop that shit."

He said, "Fuck that guy. They could have prevented the assault last night. They did nothing. They'll do nothing now."

And I knew he was right. Well, maybe.

I said, "Aaron, watch him. No phone calls."

Aaron nodded and went into the shack with the guard, scaring the shit out of him.

We went up to the third floor, and I knocked on the door, waiting to see if anyone would answer.

Nobody did. The damage we'd done to the lock was still in place, the door handle and lock cylinder gone, a jagged hole in its place with duct tape over it. I said, "Maybe she didn't stay here because she no longer had an ability to secure the door."

I knocked again, and the door cracked open. I saw Lia through the crack, an internal chain holding the door closed, her eyes bloodshot, mascara smearing until it looked like someone had beat her. She'd clearly not had any sleep.

I said, "Hey, you remember me?" I pulled Shoshana forward and said, "And her?"

"Yes. What do you want?"

"I think I've found your killer, and I want your help to get him."

She said nothing, just holding the crack of the door. I said, "We really need to talk, and I've brought some people in to do that. Can we come in?"

She closed the door, worked the chain locks, and opened it back up. She was wearing a T-shirt, shorts, and a silk robe, the front cinched tight. She looked at me and said, "I can't do this. I'm not doing this. Not today."

Knuckles stepped in and said, "Hey, we only want to talk. You don't have to do anything at all. We both want the same thing."

He gave her his hippie look of concern and empathy and I instinctively knew what was about to happen. For some reason, anyone of the female persuasion fell for that guy. It was ridiculous, but also the reason I'd brought him.

She said, "Who are you? And why are you here?"

"I'm with Pike. You and I are trying to do the same thing. My name is Knuckles, and I wish I'd been here last night, but I was in your police headquarters because someone put a bomb on my car. That someone is the man you're chasing. He tried to kill me, and now I want to kill him. Can we come in?"

She opened the door.

We entered, and she said, "So what's going on? Who are you with? CIA? FBI? Should I call my headquarters?"

Jennifer recognized she was not right. Not right at all. She said, "Hey, I saw what happened last night. I get it."

Lia flashed her eyes, letting Jennifer know she had no idea of what she'd been through. She collapsed in a chair, giving a brittle laugh. She said, "Get what? You ever been told to take a dick in your mouth or you'll die?"

Lia was going for shock value, but she didn't understand who she was talking to. Which is why I'd brought her. Jennifer squatted down in front of her, locked eyes, and said, "Yes. I have. And I was rescued by the men in this room. When I say I understand, I *mean* it."

Lia said nothing, her mouth parting at the words.

Jennifer pulled up a chair and sat down across from her. She said, "I know the fear you felt. I know the sense of helplessness. I have literally been there. Pike is the one who prevented it, just like here. Since then, I've followed him to do the same. I was the one on the other end of the computer who gave him the intelligence to save you."

From the chair, Lia looked at me and said, "Who is this?"

I smiled and said, "My protégé. Trust her. We penetrated your house last night through some things I can't discuss, but it's the reason you're alive. Talk to her."

She flicked her head to Knuckles and said, "Who's he?"

"He's with me."

She took a deep breath, let it out, then said, "I can't do this right now. I'm still . . . a little screwed up."

Knuckles took a knee in front of her, grasped her hand, and said, "I understand, but sometimes you don't get the chance to quit. Sometimes you just have to keep going. For the others. For the other women."

And I saw he was connecting. Jennifer looked at me, and I shook my head, telling her to let Knuckles work his magic. He had some weird ability with the opposite sex, and I wasn't going to question it. He was always hooking up with women, but unlike a simplistic bar hound, he was *always* sincere in his efforts. He had no ulterior motives other than a connection. While he might have used his charms in another situation that would end up with the woman in bed, in here, it was completely different, more like a priest.

Lia nodded, then said, "So what do you want?"

Knuckles asked for a tablet, Jennifer gave it to him, and he went through what had happened to him the day prior. He showed her the picture of the killer with his pants down, and she inhaled, the shock of the night coming back home.

He said, "This man was at the Knights' headquarters right before a bomb was placed on my car. I think he was the trigger for the attempt. We can't do anything because we aren't law enforcement. But we thought you might."

She took the tablet and said, "You're sure this man was there? At the headquarters for the Knights of Malta?"

"Yes. Right before my car exploded."

I said, "Is that enough?"

She stood up and said, "Yes. That's most definitely enough. You'll have to testify to his presence, and we'll have to get the crime report from the explosion, but that's enough for me to arrest him. Let me contact my department and we can go. I'll have a carabinieri team meet us at the palace."

She saw the change in the room and said, "What? Do you want my help or not?"

I said, "We want your help, but you can't contact the police and he's not going to the Italian justice system. He's ours."

"Who are you?"

I said, "Well, we aren't CIA or FBI." I pointed at Shoshana and said, "Some aren't even American. But we're most definitely on your side here."

She said, "Are you really Israeli?"

Shoshana said, "Yes. I am. Will you help us?"

She said, "Let me get myself together."

She went back in the bedroom and we sat around looking at each other, wondering if she was on a phone calling a SWAT team to come get us.

Shoshana began pacing, rubbing her hands together. She said, "This is going to be good."

I said, "Not yet. It might be good, but not yet. Don't force this."

She looked at me with a little bit of venom, then said, "He's there, and he's mine."

I said, "Shoshana, if you screw this up, you're not in the wedding. I mean it."

Jennifer glared at me, and honestly, I couldn't believe that had slipped out of my mouth. It was cruel, but it was the only thing I had. Threatening her with an ass-beating would have only been a challenge. Jennifer was right about her. She wanted to be a bridesmaid, and so I said it.

Shoshana looked at Jennifer, then at me. Jennifer said, "He doesn't mean that."

Shoshana said, "Okay, Pike. I'll follow your lead right up until that lead doesn't work. Agreed?"

I smiled and said, "Carrie, if my lead doesn't work, you can kill whoever you want."

She squinted her eyes at my sarcasm, and Lia finally exited, wearing jeans and a simple blouse, her face now cleaned up, looking as attractive as she did when we first met. I saw Knuckles take notice and thought, *Oh, boy.*

I said, "You ready?"

"What's your plan?"

"Basically, it's this: You're going to be the face of the operation. We're going to be the muscle.

You get us into the palace, then locate the guy with your Italian and your badge, and we'll take him down. We'll exit the building with him, and then it's over. When it's done, they need to think it's an Italian operation all the way through."

"But what are you going to do with him once we have him? He's a serial killer here in Italy, and he deserves justice."

I smiled and said, "Honestly, that's two steps ahead. I haven't thought that far yet, but we're going to find out about his killing spree all over the world and why he was doing that. Once we're done, you can have him. If he's still alive."

She didn't like the sound of that and paused. Shoshana said, "He's getting justice. That's all that matters."

She nodded and picked up her purse. I said, "We're good?"

She looked at the screenshot on the table, seeing him holding his penis in his hands, her eyes wide open in fear. She said, "Yes. We're good."

## CHAPTER 52

We exited the building and went down to our cars. Lia tried to enter Knuckles's car and I said, "He's not coming with us. You need to get in ours."

She said, "You've got four people already in that car. Why cram into one?"

"He's already been there under a different name. It's just us going in because they'll know he's not Italian police. He'll be nearby for backup."

She glanced at him and he said, "Hey, you get this done and I'll take you to dinner. Paid for by the U.S. government. You pick the most expensive restaurant here in Rome, and I'll pay the bill."

For the first time, I saw a smile that was genuine. And thought, *What is it with that asshole?*

We left, Lia giving directions, and within twelve minutes were outside the Magisterial Palace of the Knights of Malta. We rolled up to the gate, and the guard blocked our advance. She showed her badge, then said, "Let us in."

He did so.

We parked and I left Jennifer behind the

wheel, telling her to coordinate with Knuckles and Brett for support because we might be coming out in a run.

Shoshana, Lia, Aaron, and I entered the complex, getting stopped immediately by a secretary behind an ornate desk that looked like it had been used by Christopher Columbus. I realized we were dealing with an organization that was older than our entire country. And that this was going to be very delicate.

The secretary said something in Italian, and Lia flashed her badge, then showed her a close-up of the killer's face, without the penis or Lia in the picture. She rattled off a bunch of Italian, and the two had a conversation, the rest of us just standing there like we understood what the hell was going on.

Eventually, I saw Lia hold up a hand, waving it back and forth as if the conversation was over, like she was telling the woman she was sorry for the intrusion. She flicked her head to the door and began walking, confusing the hell out of us. We followed her outside and back in the car.

I said, "What happened?"

"His name is Garrett and he's some sort of protection detail for the Knights. He's known as the leader of a group of Croatians called the Ninja Turtles. Basically, he's the internal security for the Grand Master and other order activities. He's an American"—she looked at Shoshana— "as you suspected. But he's not here."

Shoshana said, "Where is he?"

"He left this morning. Apparently, there's a big ceremony happening in Israel in two days, and the Grand Master of the Knights of Malta is representing the Catholic contingent. The Vatican didn't think it prudent to send an official delegation, so they sent him. He is, after all, considered a head of state."

Aaron perked up and said, "Israel? He's going to Israel?"

Lia nodded and said, "Yes. The prime minister is giving some speech at an archeological dig in Israel, and he's invited a slew of Christian organizations to attend. Most are from the United States, probably because he's trying to curry favor, but the Knights of Malta are going from Italy on behalf of the Roman Catholic Church."

I slapped the dash and said, "So he now knows we're looking for him? What if she calls him? He'll be in the wind."

She said, "No, I told her that he was not a suspect for anything. I said the picture was a surveillance camera footage from a robbery at a jewelry store across the street and we were talking to anyone who might have been nearby. She doesn't think we were hunting him for a crime. It's why I ended the interview. I didn't want her to alert him."

I said, "Good. Good. When is he coming back?"

"Four days. We can return in four days and just take him quietly, without upsetting the applecart of the Vatican and Italy."

Shoshana said, "Where in Israel is this event happening?"

"Megiddo. It's apparently an ancient archeological site. They've found something there that

Israel wants to celebrate. Something from the Bible, to give a reason for Christians and Israelis to bond."

Shoshana sucked in a breath, then said, "Pike, we can't wait for him to return. This is it. We need to figure out what he's doing, right now."

"What do you mean 'this is it'? Why can't we wait?"

"Megiddo is an ancient city, one of the oldest in the world. Lia's right. It's in the Bible over and over, right up until the end."

I didn't know why she was getting so upset. "The end of what?"

"The end of the Bible. Revelation. The End of Days. It speaks about a climactic battle between the forces of good and evil right there in that city."

I still didn't get it. *Megiddo? Who the hell cares about that?*

She said, "Don't you see? It's what he's been trying to do all along."

Frustrated, I said, "No, I *don't* see. Just because he's crazy doesn't mean I can see the crazy."

She said, "He's not coming back. This is his End of Days. In the Bible, Megiddo is known as Armageddon."

And *that* I could understand.

## CHAPTER 53

Sitting in the rear of a private charter jet, Garrett finally achieved deep sleep. He was safe, flying away from the investigation that was building into a crescendo. His dreams coalesced around a young woman dead on the floor, her robe open, and in the dream, her neck encircled by a red sash. He stood up from her body, for some reason wearing no pants, and heard a thumping at the door. He turned to jump out the window and faced Inspector Lia coming through it, holding a pair of pruning shears.

He jerked awake, disoriented, sweat popping on his brow like small beads of mercury. Across from him, Michelangelo said, "Hey, you okay, boss?"

"Yeah. I'm fine. Just haven't had a lot of sleep the last few days."

Michelangelo nodded, believing Garrett was talking about the toll the planning of their mission was having, and Garrett certainly wasn't going to disabuse him of the notion.

After he'd killed the hapless university student, he'd fled down a back stairwell, found the student's bike, and rode the four miles to his own place across the Tiber River, waiting on the police to pull him over with every stroke of his pedals. He'd ditched the bike on the street, knowing someone would steal it and possibly help with a misdirection if it was ever recovered, and packed his bags for the trip to Israel. He had enough time for about three hours of rest before Michelangelo arrived to take him to the airport.

Now halfway through the three-hour flight to Ben Gurion Airport near Tel Aviv, Garrett was feeling the effects from the lack of sleep, the dream he'd just had startlingly vivid in his mind's eye.

Michelangelo said, "What did the Grand Master say to you when we boarded? He didn't seem like he was pleased to see me."

The Grand Master's entourage had taken the front half of the Learjet, leaving the back for Garrett and Michelangelo, both in the last two seats next to the baggage compartment, which was fine by Garrett. He didn't want to sit with those prima donnas anyway.

Garrett said, "He wanted to know why you were here because I'd told the lieutenant that I would be the only security on the trip. I told the Grand Master that you would remain behind in Tel Aviv purely as support."

"But I'm not going to be in Tel Aviv. I'm going to be in Jerusalem."

"He doesn't need to know that. Tell me you have the charges made."

In his previous life in the Croatian Special Operations Battalion, Michelangelo had been an explosives expert. He'd designed the limpet mines used and his background was the reason he had been chosen for the Jerusalem mission—that, and with his swarthy skin and black hair, he could pass for a Palestinian.

In the end, Garrett knew they would have to accomplish this one by themselves, because there was no way Keta'ib Hezbollah—or any Muslim group—would agree to attack what they were targeting.

"Yes, I have them. Four shaped charges daisy-chained together. They'll get the job done. If they're not confiscated when we land."

"They won't be. We're representing the Vatican and are almost a sovereign nation in our own right. They'll treat the entire group as diplomats."

"Any contact with Leonardo and Raphael?"

"They told me they'd landed, and that's it. They'll be fine."

"How are you going to give them the trigger from Israel? You can't count on a cell network for Zello out in the middle of the Syrian desert."

"Sat phone. We both have one."

"Those can be tracked. It's how most of the terrorists were found that we helped kill."

"Only if someone is looking for a suspicious number. This isn't that. We'll be good. We're not talking on them daily. Just to trigger. By then it'll be too late."

Garrett saw Lieutenant Marco Bianchi coming down the aisle and quit talking. He reached them and said, "The Grand Master would like a word."

Garrett stood up, saying, "Of course."

He followed Bianchi to the front of the aircraft, seeing the Grand Master, Geoffrey Chaucer, seated in a beige leather captain's chair and, like Lieutenant Bianchi, wearing the Knights' military uniform instead of the more formal robes.

A simple black jacket with epaulets, each man wore two rows of ribbons above the left breast pocket and a red patch with the Maltese cross on the left shoulder, the only distinction between the Grand Master and the lieutenant being a large Maltese cross pin below the Grand Master's right breast pocket.

Looking to be about seventy years old, Chaucer was British, as was the Grand Master he'd replaced—a man sacked by the pontiff from an internal dispute over the distribution of condoms in the developing world, a power struggle that had created schisms within the order unlike any that had been seen since the seventeenth century, pitting allies and enemies inside the Vatican against each other.

Once again, the order learned the lesson they'd seen with the Knights Templar. It didn't pay to become too powerful, and picking a fight with the leader of the Holy Roman Church was not a good way to succeed.

After his election, unlike the previous Grand Master, Chaucer didn't wear the ostentatious uniforms prescribed by the order. Garrett always thought they were ridiculous—something from the Napoleonic era, the jacket bright red and festooned with sashes, ribbons, brush epaulets, and medals all over the place. Garrett always thought they looked like something a dictator in a third-world country would wear.

When Geoffrey had been ordained as the Grand Master, his first order had been to tone down the pageantry and to return to its roots of charity and chivalry. In other words, bend the knee to the Holy Roman Catholic Church.

It was something Garrett saw through completely, but he knew Geoffrey Chaucer had little humility. He might attempt to show it through a minimalist uniform, but he was as egotistical as the man he'd replaced.

Chaucer said, "Garrett, please, take a seat," pointing to the one across from him.

Garrett did, saying, "How can I help you, sir?"

Chaucer fiddled with a pen in his hands, then said, "Garrett, I knew we needed your skills in Syria, and I appreciate you coming with us here in Israel for the same reason, but this is a very delicate visit."

Unsure of where the conversation was headed, Garrett said, "Yes, sir. Of course. My only reason for being here is the same reason I was in Syria. To protect members of the order. You know that the majority of my protection in Syria involved negotiating between factions, right? I didn't fire a shot in anger unless one was fired against someone from the order."

Chaucer said, "Yes, yes. I know. And I've heard about the death of the one everyone seems to call a 'turtle' in Bahrain. That has caused significant repercussions with the United States, and now you've brought another 'turtle' with you here. I was told it would be only you."

"Sir, he is not coming to Megiddo with you. That will be only me. He's remaining behind in Tel Aviv purely for support. Protection requires more than the five feet around you. He's going to coordinate with level three trauma centers, find evacuation routes, everything I used to do when I did emergency evacuation site surveys for United States embassies. It's just prudent."

"And so that's why you've leveraged the diplomatic passports to also travel to Lebanon?"

And now Garrett knew why this was happening. Someone in the Lebanese Knights of Malta consular office had reported.

He said, "Precisely, sir. Since Megiddo is so far north, I've taken the liberty of moving two 'turtles' as you call them to our consulate in Lebanon. All I'm doing is covering our bases. Protecting the order."

Chaucer leaned forward and said, "This visit is very important. It's much more than listening to a speech from the Israeli prime minister. We have diplomatic relationships with countries all over the world, but not here, in the land of our birth. This trip could do that for us."

Garrett said, "I understand, sir."

"We don't need to jeopardize this with any overt security protocols, as if we're afraid that the entire Israeli security system cannot protect us."

"Sir, it'll be just me, I promise. The rest will be invisible. *I'll* be invisible. I'll just be in the background, coordinating with the Israeli security services. That's it."

Chaucer leaned back and said, "The prime minister of Israel will be the man speaking.

END OF DAYS / 347

There will be delegations from multiple evangelical churches in the United States, not to mention a representative from the United States State Department. I highly doubt you alone will be able to contribute. It's going to be blanketed with security. Nothing is going to jeopardize this."

Garrett thought, *How naïve.*

## CHAPTER 54

Raphael and Leonardo clomped down the stairwell a little after ten in the morning, heading to a café for the linkup and hoping to get a little breakfast along the way. They exited onto the street warily, as if they expected a suicide bomber to come running up at any minute.

That didn't happen. What they saw was a cloistered street not unlike Rome, but a little filthier, with bits of trash caught by the breeze floating around. People were walking about normally, not acting as if they feared for their lives or scuttling for cover like Raphael had seen before. He expected some shock from people seeing them exit the building, two Caucasian strangers on the street, but everyone completely ignored them.

Leonardo had never been to Beirut, and Raphael had told him how bad it could be, with bombs flying through the air and shooting all over the place—but Raphael had only been here for a brief stint, during the 2006 war with Israel.

After a moment, he laughed and said, "Looks like things have changed since I was here."

Leonardo shook his head and said, "It's like

you described our childhood during the Bosnian war, and then we entered Croatia today. What the hell, man? I thought it was going to be a mess here."

Raphael said, "*You* were the one who was here with Donatello. *You* should have known."

"That was Tripoli, and honestly, that place looks a lot like this one. I thought you had some secret knowledge of Beirut."

They gained confidence, shouldering their backpacks and walking up the street, following the directions they'd been given. Eventually, they found the shop, a little street corner café serving espresso and scones.

They took a seat at an outdoor table, as instructed, and ordered from an attractive Lebanese waitress with a flawless understanding of English.

She left and Leonardo said, "I could come back here, afterward. Just for the vacation."

Raph said, "Me, too."

A car pulled up across the street and a man exited. He stood for a moment, looked both ways, and the car drove away. Raph studied him. He had what Raph would call a "Taliban beard," with it shaved into a spike, and was dressed in rough pants, a button-up shirt, and a jacket. He had no skullcap or Kaffiya, his head bare.

He approached the café as if he wanted to enter it, then at the last minute veered to their table, taking the one remaining seat. He said, "My name is Tariq Bazzi, and I understand you need some help."

Startled at his brazen approach, Raph slid his chair back, putting a hand on his backpack, all of his fears coming true.

Tariq said, "Don't touch that bag. I'm not the only one here. You won't live to open it."

Raph released the zipper but kept his hand on the top, saying, "We won't go quietly."

Leonardo put his hand on Raph's wrist and said, "This is our contact."

Tariq said, "Leonardo, correct? I remember you from before. The moneyman, right? Tripoli?"

Leonardo nodded and Tariq said, "I'm sorry about Donatello. He was a good man. I hope he died in a good fight."

Raph said, "He did. Now, what do we do from here?"

"It's a long trip to where you want to go, with multiple checkpoints and rough terrain. I can get you there, but it's going to be expensive."

"It's a four-hour drive from here."

"It's a four-hour drive on a highway in Italy or the United States. It's a twelve-hour drive for you two. Do you think we're going through official border crossings? We're going to have to traverse the Bekaa Valley, go through the mountains, and then enter Syria through checkpoints that we control."

"Twelve hours?"

"Yes. As I said, expensive. You're paying me for my skill, and I'm the one that's going to get you to your contacts on the other side. I have no idea what they want you for, or your area of expertise, and I don't want to know, but it's going to cost money."

Raph bristled and said, "We have the money, if you are who you say you are. I'm not paying just to get rolled up by Hezbollah thugs in the valley, or Assad regime forces in Syria."

Tariq laughed and said, "Then you've come to the right man, because I deal with all of them. Smuggling is what I do. On this side of the border, I'm Hezbollah. On that side, I'm regime. Nobody touches me because I'm too important to all of them."

Raph said, "We have whatever money you require."

"Then let's get that out of the way first. You guys have Venmo? That's kind of a thing now for the Assad regime."

Leonardo said, "No. We have prepaid debit cards."

"That'll work. Half now."

Leonardo reached into a thigh pocket and pulled out four cards, handing them over. Tariq took them, then said, "Is this your gear?"

"Yes."

"I'll have to inspect it before we leave. No offense."

Raph said, "That's not going to happen. Just assume we have weapons. We have no explosives, but we do have weapons."

"No inspection will cost more."

"Why?"

"Because I'm bringing security with me if you won't let me check the bags. Check them, and it's me and one other guy. Don't check them, and it's an entire car following with my men. I don't like surprises."

Raph shook his head, then kicked his bag over, a large frameless backpack. Tariq opened the top compartment and saw a pistol and what looked like a shortened bolt-action rifle with a large cylinder underneath it. He said, "What's this?"

"An air gun. A silent weapon."

Tariq laughed, continuing to search. He said, "You ever hear of silencers for your pistol? We even have them here, and I can get you one."

"I'll live with what I packed."

Tariq went to the lower compartment, finding clothes, Clif bars, and a Thuraya satellite phone. He said, "Thuraya. Should have gone with Inmarsat like I have. Thuraya is compromised by the intelligence agencies."

Raph said, "Only if someone is hunting you. Nobody is hunting us."

"Maybe. Maybe not. What you're doing is secretive, and who you're meeting is important to my business. You will not turn that phone on while we're together. Agreed?"

Raph nodded. Satisfied, Tariq zipped it up. He looked at Leonardo and said, "Yours?"

Leonardo slid it over. Five minutes later, Tariq was finished. He said, "The pistols are fine, but they stay in the bags until we reach our destination. The sat phone is not, but if it stays in the bag during the trip, you can keep it. The air gun is just stupid, but you can keep it as well."

He pulled out an ordinary cell phone and made a call. While waiting on it to connect, he said, "Two it is, but you leave with the bags here. No stories about having to go back to your hotel for something you forgot. Agreed?"

Raph nodded and a white Toyota Land Cruiser with a snorkel snaking across the hood came around the corner, its paint scarred and dirty from trips far away from Beirut. A burly man with dark skin was behind the wheel wearing sunglasses above a thick beard. Tariq said, "Load up. Let's go."

Surprised, Raph said, "Now? Just like that?"

"Yes. Just like that."

Leonardo said, "We have to pay the bill."

"You're already paying the bill. Everyone in that place, from the waitress you want to bed to the man making the espressos, works for me."

They hesitated and Tariq said, "I'm not going to put a hood on your head. Quit being such babies. You're the ones paying for this."

They grabbed their bags and loaded the Cruiser. In short order, they were out of the city, driving south past the airport on Highway 51, the four-lane road that traversed the entire country along the Mediterranean coast. Eventually, the driver took a left on another major road and began heading east, into the Lebanon Mountains chain.

The road dropped down to two lanes, and then began winding back and forth following the contours of the ridges and switchbacks, getting higher and higher. Eventually, they crested the top of the range and began dropping down the other side. They entered a town called Jezzine, the Bekaa Valley spilling out below them. The driver pulled the SUV into a small gas station and stopped. Tariq turned around with a SIG Sauer P229 pistol in his hands. Startled, Raphael raised his hands and said, "What's going on?"

The driver brandished his own pistol.

Tariq said, "I'm sorry about this."

Tariq tossed two black hoods into their laps. "Don't worry, this isn't a kidnapping. You're going to have to trust me. I can't have you knowing where the start of my smuggling route begins."

And Raphael realized why he'd made them leave their own guns in their bags. He said, "We're not putting those on, and you've put your life in jeopardy by suggesting it. We've paid you well."

Tariq laughed and said, "Don't be so dramatic. I'm not going to shoot you if you don't, and you've only paid me half. I'll just take the rest of those prepaid debit cards and leave you here. I won't force you to put them on. Once again, this isn't a kidnapping, but just as you have your secrets, I must have mine."

Leonardo said, "Let's do it."

Raphael said, "Fuck that. Why?"

"Donatello and I had to do the same thing once before. In Tripoli. It worked out."

Raphael reluctantly shoved his head into the bag, glaring at Tariq as he did so. He felt the vehicle leave the gas station, then leave the paved road, bouncing for the next hour down the slope and into the valley, the roads coarse and rustic, the shocks on the vehicle groaning in defiance as the frame of the vehicle traversed the pitted trail.

Eventually, the vehicle stopped and Tariq said, "You may remove the hoods."

They did so, seeing a small compound around them, cinder-block buildings without siding, sheet metal roofs, and naked power lines going from building to building.

Tariq said, "We can eat here while we wait."

"Wait for what?"

"We can't attempt to cross the next mountain range until dusk, reaching the top in the darkness, then crossing the other side right before dawn. To do otherwise is dangerous."

Tariq opened the door and said, "Come on. I have fruit and cheese for you. I'm like a Lebanese tour guide. No matter how much you pay, I promise a grand dinner but give you only snacks."

He laughed at his joke, and Raphael heard gunfire no more than a hundred meters away. A lot of gunfire. He reached inside for his backpack, saying, "Enough of this shit."

The driver stopped him with a hand, shaking his head. Tariq said, "You're safe here in my care."

"What the hell is the gunfire? Rebel troops fighting the government or something?"

Tariq's eyes widened in surprise, then he began laughing, saying, "No, no, no. That's not fighting. That's training."

"Who the hell is training out here in the middle of nowhere?"

"The same people you're going to meet on the other side of this mountain chain in Syria. Hezbollah. The Party of God."

## CHAPTER 55

Walking toward the Oval Office, Alexander Palmer whispered, "Can I ask why there's a priest with you?"

George Wolffe said, "Just in case I need last rites."

They reached a couch about twenty feet away from the door and Wolffe turned, saying, "Father, if you could sit out here until I call you, I'd appreciate it."

The priest nodded, taking a seat, and, like everyone else in the modern world, pulled out his phone and began scrolling.

Wolffe and Palmer kept walking, and Palmer said, "Seriously, why's he here?"

Wolffe said, "Because I'm about to tell a story involving the belief in the end of the world, a Catholic organization from the Crusades, and a serial killer. He's here for backup for questions I can't answer."

They entered the Oval Office and Palmer grabbed his arm, saying, "What?"

Before Wolffe could respond, President Hannister said, "George, come on in. We have little time."

Wolffe pulled away from Palmer and said, "Yes, sir, that's correct, because I've got Pike primed for an operation tonight that could help solve this whole riddle, but he's going to need Omega authority to penetrate what's basically the embassy of a sovereign country."

All eyes in the room snapped to him at the words.

Wolffe advanced to a table between the two couches holding the principals to his left and right, facing the president behind the Resolute Desk.

He said, "It's not Iran. I'm positive about that. It's a cell of nutjobs with the power of the Catholic Church using an organization that's been around since the Crusades to bring about the End of Days. They want to start a war against Iran, which will bring control of the Temple Mount under the Jewish state of Israel, and bring about the second coming of Christ."

He waited for the incredulous looks or for someone to tell him he was borderline insane. Instead, the other principals looked at Kerry Bostwick, the director of the CIA, and he said, "I told you. It isn't just me spouting crazy shit."

Wolffe said, "What's that mean? What did you hear?"

Bostwick said, "There are people inside Mossad who believe the same thing. They've tracked it from another direction, and they have multiple reasons to believe this is not an Iranian attack."

The secretary of defense said, "But that doesn't alter what the Iranians *are* doing. They just blew up a refinery in Saudi Arabia using drones flown from Yemen by the Houthis. Drones built by Iran. They're trying to show us their reach and the global implications to keep us out of a fight, but in so doing, they're about to cause a fight."

Wolffe said, "Where do we stand with the Fifth Fleet?"

"They're out, and getting buzzed by Iranian fast attack boats every day, each time coming closer. We know it's not to provoke us to attack, because that would be catastrophic to them, but they're filming each time they come by. They're gaining intelligence. My fear is that when they feel like they have enough, one of the strikes won't veer away. They'll have conditioned our sailors to view it as just another zip-on-by and then slam into our ships."

Amanda Croft, the secretary of state, said, "Not to mention the launching of rockets into Israel from Gaza. Iran is flexing right now, showing us what will happen if we retaliate against them for the killings. And now they have hard-liners who are literally claiming credit for the assassinations, opportunist assholes looking to upset the moderates there, claiming it's in response to Soleimani and the killings of the Iranian scientists."

Wolffe said, "So this report is too late? You guys want to go to war? Is that it? You realize this is playing right into the nutjobs' hands, right? Iran has moderates who don't want to go to war. They also have nutjobs who do, just like the U.S. and Israel. You're listening to the nutjobs. And if you go to war, you're going to make every Arab nation take a stand. I get they don't like Iran right now, but don't forget the Arabic proverb, 'I against my cousin, I and my cousin against the world.' You do this, and it's not going to stop in the Middle East."

President Hannister said, "No, of course we don't want to go to war, but we need something to prove it isn't the Iranians. As Amanda said, the hard-liners are literally bragging about it. This ship is about to crash ashore unless we can do something."

"Sir, use the Swiss to contact them. Use someone to get to the moderates and tell them we don't think it's Iran."

"A: we've tried that and been rebuffed. Nobody wants to talk to us through diplomatic channels for fear of retribution. They're on war footing, and the hard-liners have the edge. B: I'm not sure it *isn't* them. I've got their own people bragging about it."

Wolffe stared at the wall for a moment, then muttered, "Israel will wipe out Hezbollah in Lebanon. Eliminate them completely the minute a war starts."

President Hannister said, "What was that? What about Hezbollah?"

Wolffe focused back to the room and said, "Sir, I can get you your back channel to the Iranian theocracy, but you're not going to like it. I can get through to them through Hezbollah. Those guys are now a political party in Lebanon, and like all political parties, they want survival. They will not want to go to war without reason, because they'll be destroyed."

Kerry Bostwick said, "How can you do that?

We have no contacts with them. All of our Hezbollah contacts are through the Israelis."

"Pike knows a guy who knows some guys. That's all I can say, but in order for this to work, I need to let Pike penetrate the Knights of Malta Magisterial Palace in Rome. He's standing by right now for the word. And that building is literally a sovereign state."

There was a multitude of cross talk, everyone asking questions or arguing with the person to the left or right, until President Hannister raised his hand and said, "Okay, okay. Enough chatter. Why don't you finally give us your crazy theory?"

Wolffe nodded, then took a deep breath. He let it out and said, "Okay, here it is: There's a serial killer in Rome who's working for the Knights of Malta. He has a team around him known as the 'Ninja Turtles' who are all from Croatia. These men have been doing the killings."

Wolffe then described every bit of intelligence they had, to include the Zello geolocation against the crime scene, the attempted assassination of Knuckles and Brett, and the rescue of the inspector. He ended by saying, "What we know, from the second in command of the Knights of Malta himself, is that the man killed in Bahrain was fascinated with dispensationalism. With the End of Days."

President Hannister said, "I go to church every Sunday. I'm not waiting on the End of Days. What do you mean?"

Wolffe said, "I hear you, sir. I have a guy outside who can explain it. He's a priest who's written books on it. It's sort of a fascination of his, and you'd be amazed at how it's altered our own history through the years."

"Bring him in."

Wolffe left and returned with a man in a priest's collar, saying, "This is Father Obrien. He is not cleared for anything other than the discussion we're about to have."

Father Obrien looked hesitant, then said, "Mr. Wolffe said you'd have some questions about dispensationalism?"

President Hannister said, "Yeah, like, what is it?"

"Basically, it's the belief in the prophecies in the Bible, specifically in the books Daniel and Ezekiel in the Old Testament, and the book of Revelation in the New Testament. It's not a firm thing, like everyone believes in it one hundred percent, but a majority of Christians do believe in it to a greater or lesser degree, and some believe in it absolutely."

"Such as?"

"Well, such as the Branch Davidians in Waco. That was a dispensationalism sect that went bad, with David Koresh saying he was bringing about the apocalypse. And he did."

"So it's a cult thing? Dispensationalism?"

"No, sir, not at all. Some Christian denominations definitely take it to the extremes, but all of them touch it at one point or another— even Catholics—and it's not just Christians. The Jewish faith has some of the same beliefs, and it all revolves around the third temple built on

362 / BRAD TAYLOR

the grounds of the original temple erected by King Solomon on what's called in the Christian world the Temple Mount, but is known as the Noble Sanctuary to the Arabs. The area holds the Al Aqsa Mosque and the Dome of the Rock, both very important to the world's three great religions, all of them with their own prophecies, and all of them in conflict. To be sure, dispensationalism isn't unique to Christians, and it isn't written in stone, like you'd say you were a Catholic or a Methodist. It's just a thought process that some take to a greater degree than others."

President Hannister said, "Okay, so this third temple is the basis of the predictions? That's what everyone wants, and what the Arabs will fight against?"

"No, it's bigger than just a temple, if you really follow the prophecies, with tendrils that extend out in myriad ways. The biggest one is that the biblical land of Israel must be controlled completely by the Jews, to include Jerusalem. After the Six-Day War, that seemed to be fulfilled, but the Temple Mount was not taken, and that caused consternation both with the Jews and the Christians."

He saw the president of the United States look left and right, attempting to see if anyone else was understanding what he said, and realized he was losing him.

Father Obrien shifted tack and said, "There are a multitude of different things that must happen to bring about the prophecies, depending on who's doing the readings, and a multitude of people who are willing to bring it about, both warlike and not. For instance, one of the prophecies is that there must be a red heifer born to be sacrificed at the new temple, one that is red through and through, without a speck of another color. Red eyes, red snout, and red hair. Without that, the temple cannot be consecrated. It's in the Bible. So a cattle rancher from Mississippi set about breeding red heifers, trying to get one that fit. He traveled to Israel as a guest of one of the Jewish groups that believed in the prophecies, and began breeding cattle in Israel. The bottom line is it's a real thing, and not just a bunch of crazy nuts like the Branch Davidians. Ordinary people believe in it, and it's strong."

President Hannister shook his head and said, "I'm Presbyterian, and I've never even heard about this stuff. Does the Catholic Church buy into this? Are there organizations in the Church who believe the same?"

"No, not really. There are some who might read into the prophecies more than others, but for the most part, the Church doesn't proscribe prophecies in literal detail, such as the need for a red heifer, from the words of the Bible. The Church is much more ephemeral about such things. While we most certainly believe there will be a second coming, the literal reading of the prophecies are mainly from evangelical Protestant churches."

President Hannister glanced around the room, and Wolffe knew where he was going next. He wanted to stand up to prevent it, but was too late.

"What about the Knights of Malta? Do they believe in this dispensationalism?"

Taken aback, Father Obrien said, "You mean the order of the Knights of Malta, Jerusalem, and Rhodes?"

"Yeah. Do they believe in dispensationalism?"

Confused, the father said, "No, not to my knowledge. They're a lay organization that does humanitarian work around the world. They don't proselytize or anything of that nature. All of the members take a vow of chastity just like I did, and they don't have a path that's separate from the Church."

President Hannister said, "Okay, thank you very much. Would you please return outside?"

Father Obrien looked at Wolffe, then said, "Yes, sir, but before I do, what do the Knights of Malta have to do with this discussion?"

Wolffe stood up, flashing a glare at President Hannister. He said, "Nothing at all. We're just trying to learn about domestic threats here in the United States. Like Timothy McVeigh, or David Koresh. As I told you when I asked you here, it's a growing threat. It has nothing to do with chivalric organizations in your orbit."

Wolffe took his arm, leading him out of the room, saying, "Thank you for coming."

Five minutes later, he returned, saying, "No disrespect, sir, but when I bring someone in here for background, you really shouldn't press them on an ongoing operation."

President Hannister's face soured, and Wolffe held up a hand, saying, "You want to fire me, sir, then do so, but I have a team that can stop this whole thing, and they need to penetrate the con- sulate of some weird-ass pseudo-state inside the sovereign state of Italy. I can't wait anymore. It's midnight there, and he needs to get the information to his contact in Lebanon."

President Hannister looked around the room, then said, "The vote is for penetration of the building for evidence disproving Iranian involvement of assassinations against Israeli and American diplomats."

Wolffe said, "Sir . . . just getting the information won't solve the problem."

President Hannister glared at him and said, "One vote at a time."

Wolffe nodded, and five seconds later he was leaving the room on a secure cell phone, saying, "Tell Pike he's a go." He exited the West Wing of the complex, glanced left and right, then said, "And tell him to contact his buddy in Lebanon. We're going to need him."

## CHAPTER 56

I saw the text message from the Taskforce and said, "Okay, looks like we're a go. No killing."

Inside our minivan, Shoshana grinned, saying, "This is going to be fun."

I said, "You heard me. No killing. In fact, no violence at all."

She said, "That'll depend on spider monkey here, won't it?"

We were just down the street from the Magisterial Palace for the Knights of Malta, and we were waiting on the word to go inside and find out what those assholes were up to. We'd been stationary for damn near three hours, with Brett back at the hotel talking to Creed about hacking into the camera system they employed. We didn't need Creed to control the system, just freeze it for the entire time we were inside. If someone looked, they might grow curious why the roaming guards didn't appear on-screen, but more than likely, they'd just assume they'd missed them. That act alone was outside of my mandate, but I was betting I'd get the go-ahead, and it was closing in on one in the morning, and

I didn't have the time to begin the race from a cold start.

Creed had penetrated the network through the help of Knuckles. Yesterday, while he and Brett were acting like State Department members and waiting to see the officials inside the building, he'd asked to send an email, and had used a thumb drive to do so, sending an innocuous message that contained all the malware we could want straight into their system. I would have chastised him for being so brazen, but now it was paying off.

I contacted Brett and said, "We're a go. Does Creed have the cameras?"

"Stand by."

I looked at Jennifer and said, "Get ready to climb."

She was wearing yoga pants, Vibram Five-Fingers shoes, and a Lycra top, her hair in a ponytail. Her preferred method for breaking into something. She said, "I'm ready. You guys are the weak link."

I laughed and said, "We'll be there, just drop the rope."

I looked at Shoshana and said, "You go up first, I'll follow. Get inside and wait. No crazy stuff."

She finally got aggravated and said, "If you think I'm such a risk, then take someone else up there. Aaron is here. And so is Knuckles. You don't want me to go in with you, just say so."

And she was right. If I could take either one of them, I would have done so in a heartbeat, but she had something they did not. I'd left Brett back at the hotel to coordinate with the Taskforce, and I needed Jennifer to climb the wall, but honestly, we were looking for a needle in a haystack here. We only had the information from Lia, and all she knew from the secretary she'd talked to was that Garrett had an office in the basement.

I didn't want to give Shoshana too much credit, but I wanted her ability to see things. Not that I'd ever tell her I believed in that crap. But I did. And so I'd left Aaron and Knuckles on the outside as a reserve to get us out of trouble if things went bad.

Knuckles thought it was crazy, telling me that he should go in, and in any other situation I would have agreed. This time I didn't, and Aaron, knowing Shoshana's capabilities, understood why.

I said, "Hey, Carrie, I need your mental skill here, not your physical. Don't let me down."

She looked at me in surprise, saying, "Seriously? You finally believe?"

She looked at me with her wolf eyes and smiled, knowing I was lying. Not wanting to give her too much credit, I said, "No, I don't. But I might after tonight. Just don't kill anyone."

Brett came on, saying, "Creed's got the cameras. It's all you guys now."

"Can he see us even as he freezes the feeds to the guard shack?"

"Yeah, we can see it all."

I said, "Okay, we're on the way. Tell us when we spike on the feeds."

The palace itself took up damn near a complete block, with the ground floor housing multiple retail outlets. We needed to get inside and get down to the basement to search for anything involving the "Ninja Turtles." The easiest way would be through the courtyard, which, of course, would mean taking out the front guards. While I would have loved to do that, we needed to accomplish the entire thing covertly, which is why I'd decided to use my own personal spider monkey.

Our biggest problem was the retail stores on the ground floor. They were very expensive outlets, Jimmy Choo and Hermès and others, all literally built into the outside walls of the palace. They would have their own surveillance and alarm systems above and beyond the palace, so we had to defeat that. I went with the old-school way: just get above it and in.

We exited the van, then raced down an alley until we were underneath a small outside balcony with French doors three floors up, the balcony itself looking like a place someone would only use to step out and start singing. I crouched below it, waiting on an alert from a nosy neighbor. The light from the street was muted, but still bright enough to highlight us if someone in the building next door happened to glance out the window.

I took a knee underneath it, handed Jennifer a roll of knotted rope, and said, "Koko, get going. The longer we wait here, the more the opportunity for compromise."

She slung it over her shoulder, tested a piece of stone from the building, and then began climbing the old structure like she was scrambling up a climbing wall at a gym. Shoshana watched her go up and said, "That never fails to amaze me."

I chuckled and said, "Me, either."

In short order, she was on the balcony, and the rope slapped down to us. I said, "Up you go."

Shoshana looked at me and said, "I promise I won't kill anyone."

She was dead serious, like she thought I didn't trust her. She still didn't get sarcasm. I didn't have the time now to correct her. I said, "Okay, thanks. Get your ass up the rope."

She said, "I want you to trust me. Like you do Jennifer."

Exasperated, I hissed, "I trust you, damn it. I trust you. Get up the rope!"

She started climbing, and I waited until Jennifer said, "Secure."

I scrambled up after her, pulled up the rope, and we all sat on the balcony, listening for any alert. We knew there were guards inside from Knuckles's earlier reconnaissance but had no idea how many.

I heard nothing and clicked into the net, saying, "Blood, Blood, we're about to penetrate."

He came back, saying, "I have you. West balcony. You're good."

I looked around and said, "How? I don't see a camera."

He said, "I don't know, but we're looking at you right now."

Which told me these guys had more than just

overt systems. If he could see me, they'd invested in covert systems. Not a good sign.

I said, "Can you see guards inside? Is there anyone moving around?"

I was now worried that they'd just seeded the building with motion detectors and heat sensors. If that was the case, we were headed back down.

"Not in the basement where you're going, but we've seen them moving about on the other levels."

If they could move about, so could we. I said, "Anyone inside of our breach point?"

"Not that I can see."

"Okay, Knuckles. Knuckles, we're breaching."

I heard, "Roger that."

And I flicked my head to Jennifer. She spent about forty-five seconds on the lock, then swung it open. We entered one at a time, dropping like cats into the room. I whispered, "Find a stairwell. Need to get to the bottom."

## CHAPTER 57

We moved through an ostentatious office, entered a hallway, and found a stairwell leading down. We went down it like a pack of panthers, moving slowly, waiting for any sign that someone was ahead of us. We passed one floor, then saw a flashlight. We crouched down, and it went beyond us, not taking the stairs. We kept going and then reached the bottom floor, the stairwell spilling out and widening like it was trying to impress anyone who saw it.

I grabbed Jennifer's shoulder, telling her to wait for a moment. She did, and when I thought it was safe, I whispered, "Find the secretary's desk. Lia said the basement was behind that."

She nodded and we began wandering about. We went one way, bumping into offices and rooms full of archives, then went the other. My earpiece came alive with Knuckles saying, "I'm watching you. You're in the lobby. Keep going left."

Other than vague illumination, I couldn't see shit-all of what he was talking about, but I said, "Roger."

We reached an ornate desk with a small hallway behind it and Knuckles said, "That's it. You're there."

I flicked my head at Shoshana and she began walking down it, reaching a utilitarian door, something that looked like it was hiding a storage space. She opened it, and we saw a staircase leading down, black as sackcloth. I said, "Get inside and I'll close the door. Don't turn on the lights until I do so."

Both of them nodded and entered the black hole of the stairwell. When they were in, I followed, gently closed the door, then turned on my headlamp, saying, "Light it up."

They did the same and we raced down to the bottom, finding a closet-like space with the ceiling so close you wanted to duck.

There was a lone desk with a computer on top, the rest of the room full of cleaning supplies and other detritus. I looked at Shoshana and said, "Is this it?"

She glanced around the room, closed her eyes, then said, "Yes. This is it."

I grinned and moved to the computer, saying on the net, "Blood, Blood, I have a computer. I need to crack it."

He said, "Stand by."

I said, "Start searching this room. See what you can find."

They began looking and I flipped over the keyboard for the computer, seeing a yellow sticky note that read, "Jennys#."

I couldn't believe it. *This asshole is using the same damn password as the guy in Zurich? What a dumb-ass.*

I booted up the computer, got a password screen, and typed in what I'd found. And received a bad password alert. Confused, I did it again, with the same result. There was no way this was a coincidence. This was the same password we'd used in Zurich given to us by the Mossad, and this was the same asshole that had dictated its use there. I typed it in again, getting the same results.

I called Brett, saying, "Blood, Blood, I can't get in. Can Creed?"

He said, "No. That computer is not on the net."

"Can I put it on the net?"

"Well, yeah, if you can get into it and connect it to Wi-Fi."

*Great.*

Jennifer came to me, saying, "There's nothing here. Just cleaning supplies. I'm not sure this is the lair of the bad man."

Shoshana came up and said, "It is. I promise it is."

I said, "But there's nothing here but this old computer. Are you sure?"

She turned her face to me, blinding my eyes, and I held my hands up, saying, "Turn off the damn headlamp."

She did, then said, "Pike, this is it."

I said, "Yeah, I think so, too, only because I found a password underneath this computer that's exactly the same as the one that the Mossad gave us in Zurich. No way is that a coincidence, but it doesn't work here."

Jennifer said, "What is it?"

I showed it to her and said, "It's the Jenny's number thing. With the hashtag that worked in Zurich."

She said, "Jenny's number?"

"Yeah. Just like before. Jenny and a hashtag."

She said, "Move over."

And she typed 8675309, then hit the enter button. And the screen cleared.

I said, "What in the world?"

She grinned and said, "That's Jenny's number."

I couldn't believe it. The idiot in Zurich had literally used the password sent, when they were sending him a clue of what the password should have been.

I said, "You are a literal genius." I clicked on the net and said, "We're in. Putting in the dragonball now."

I connected an extraction device that looked like a blob of different cables, all designed to use a different port, then connected to the Wi-Fi of the palace. I hit the power button on the ball, and Brett said, "Creed sees it. He's got it. Stand by."

Three minutes later, he said, "We have a mirror of the drive. Free to go."

I said, "Thank the Lord. Knuckles, Knuckles, we're coming out same way we came in."

He said, "Roger that. Good job. Standing by."

I turned to my partners in crime and said, "Going out the same way. Slow and steady."

We went up the stairs, waited at the door, listening. I clicked on the net and said, "Any activity?"

"None that we can see, but there's no camera at the basement door."

I said, "Roger that," swung the door open, and hit a security guard right in the ass.

If I'd have thrown it open with my weight behind it, I probably would have slammed him into a wall, knocking him off balance for a strike. Instead, it basically tapped him in the butt, pushing him out of the way and causing him to freak out.

He shouted, flipped his light on me, and I reacted instantly, knocking the light to the side and ripping his legs out from underneath him, flattening him on the ground, but it was too late.

His scream had alerted others.

I cradled his head in a rear-naked choke as he thrashed around, fighting me, hearing the slapping of shoes. I hissed, "No killing, damn it! No killing."

Shoshana's headlamp went down the narrow hallway and I saw two more guards coming our way. I finished the choke, cutting off the blood flow to the guard's brain, but it required me to remain steady, which left Shoshana on the loose.

I saw the fight in strobe light, the headlamps and the guards' flashlights bobbing up and down. I squeezed hard, felt the guy beneath me go limp, and leapt up, racing down the hallway. I saw one man slam into the wall, then the other get wrapped up by Jennifer, the two of them fighting for control. She torqued his wrist, rotated his arm, and forced him onto his belly. I hammered him in the head with a straight punch, knocking him out, then turned to the one still out of control. Shoshana leapt on him, swinging around his back just like she'd done in Bahrain, bringing him to a sitting position on the floor, her arms around his neck.

I screamed, "Don't do it!"

And she put his ass to sleep just like I'd done seconds ago. She pushed his body off of her and stood up, saying, "You have no trust in me."

I exhaled and said, "You have to admit, it's not just me. There's a guy in Bahrain who might beg to differ."

She huffed something in Hebrew and Jennifer scrambled to us, saying, "Can we argue about this later?"

I said, "Good idea. Let's go. Same way. If I were to guess, we've taken out the entire force."

We started running up the stairs and Brett came on, saying, "There's nothing on the cameras that we can see, but the guard shack outside is going batshit. Don't know if they had radios or what, but they're reacting."

"What's our time?"

"Seconds. One of them is on the way right now."

Shoshana said, "They'll never reach us."

Sprinting up the stairs, I said, "You can't beat the speed of light. With a radio, we're in trouble."

We reached the second floor and I clicked on the net, saying, "Knuckles, Knuckles, we're on the way down, but there could be a response on the street. Reposition to the alternate."

He said, "Understand you don't want help, correct?"

I opened the French doors and said, "Yes. Correct. The response is going to come from the police. Don't interdict. We'll get out on foot. Meet you at secondary RV."

He said, "Roger that," just as Jennifer flicked the rope over the balcony. I looked at Shoshana and said, "Go."

She grabbed the rope, swung over, and began clambering down. I turned to Jennifer and said, "Don't wait for me to get to the bottom. Give me about ten feet, release that thing, and come down."

Her eyes wide, panting through an open mouth, she nodded. I grabbed the rope and began going down it as fast as possible, hand-over-hand on the knots. Twenty feet above the ground, Jennifer cut the slipknot and I went weightless.

*Oh shit.*

I hit the ground hard, rolling over with the rope landing on top of me. Shoshana ran to me and said, "Are you all right? Did the rope break?"

I groaned just as Jennifer landed next to me, leaping off the wall like a lizard escaping a cat. I stood up and said, "Ten feet. *Ten feet!*"

She looked chagrined and said, "I can't judge the damn distance in the dark. Anyway, you're still walking."

I shook my head, hearing sirens closing in. I said, "Let's get the hell out of here."

## CHAPTER 58

Raphael twirled his cup on the table and said, "So how long do we wait? It's been four hours and the sun is now going down."

Tariq said, "Not much longer. Trust me, I know the time."

Leonardo said, "It's not like we're pushing, but clearly we aren't wanted here."

Unlike Beirut, the people here did indeed stare at the two Caucasians drinking tea, wondering why they had arrived. No one said anything, assuming they were in some way connected to Hezbollah, but it made Leonardo nervous all the same.

Tariq said, "Here's the deal: We're going to go just north of Mount Hermon, through some of the roughest terrain in Lebanon or Syria. Mount Hermon has the highest United Nations outpost in the world. They call it 'Hotel Hermon.' It's the last checkpoint for the United Nations buffer zone between Syria and Israel along the Golan Heights. Because of it, we can't just blaze our way through."

Raph said, "And you're the smuggler? Why on earth would you choose this route?"

"This is the way to your contacts. If you wanted to go to Damascus, it would have been much easier. You wanted to go to Daraa, which, as you Christians say, is a whole 'nother kettle of fish."

He assumed a southern United States accent for the last piece, causing Raph to finally smile.

Raph said, "So we're not going to have any issues with some border patrol from the United Nations?"

Tariq said, "No. Not at all. The road we use is not even a road, and they'll be to our south, on the tip of the mountain, but very close. I use it specifically because it creates a seam. Nobody in the civil war in Syria wants to cause a problem with the UN mission along the Golan Heights, because it will finally cause someone in this godforsaken world to actually take a stand. It's a narrow bit of no-man's-land that I use to get through."

Raph said, "I'm fine with that. And I'm fine with taking a stand."

Tariq smiled, looked at his watch, and said, "Then let's load up. No hoods this time."

Leonardo moved to enter the vehicle and Raphael said, "Before we go, are you sure you're getting us to the men we need to meet?"

Tariq said, "Yes. I am Hezbollah as far as you're concerned. Trust me on this. If you want to talk to the devil, I'm the man who will lead the way."

Raphael went to the Land Cruiser and said, "Okay, but understand, I'm keeping my pistol out for the rest of the trip."

They began driving out of the Bekaa Valley, crossing a half hour of flat terrain, and then began climbing the hills, using a dirt road that barely existed. The engine groaned each time the vehicle slammed over a piece of rock, but it kept moving forward. Leonardo looked at Raphael, amazed they were taking such a path.

Raphael caught the glance and, in Croatian, said, "He's getting us there."

Leonardo replied, "Right until we fall off a cliff."

The road wound around the ridges like a snake, a rough trail better suited to mountain goats, climbing ever higher, but the Land Cruiser seemed to eat it up, having no trouble. Eventually, the sun set and they were cloaked in darkness, scaring the hell out of both Raphael and Leonardo.

Looking over a sheer cliff to his left, Raphael said, "We should wait until tomorrow to continue. It's getting too dark."

Tariq laughed, pulling out a pair of PVS-5 night vision goggles, something that the United States military hadn't used since the 1980s. The driver pulled his own out, putting them on. Tariq said, "We do this every day. Trust us."

The sun dropped behind the mountains, and they began driving in the dark, the only light coming from the dashboard and the feeble glow from the parking lights.

Raphael looked to his left, saw a drop-off of about a hundred meters in the starlight, and said, "You're not going to try to traverse this range without lights, are you? Those goggles you have weren't even good when the U.S. went into Grenada."

Tariq said, "The driver knows this terrain, just as a horse does. He could do it without these shitty goggles."

They kept climbing higher and higher, winding around one switchback after another, the road growing more and more rough until it became impossible to see it against the mountain itself, becoming something only animals would use. Looking at the cliff to his left in the dim moonlight, Raphael finally said he'd had enough.

He said, "Stop. Stop right now. This is insane. This isn't even a road."

The driver stopped and Tariq said, "The top is about a hundred meters ahead. From there, it's all downhill, but just as dangerous. You want to quit now?"

Raphael considered for a moment, then said, "A hundred meters ahead?"

"Yes. You paid me for a reason. I'll get you to Syria without anyone knowing you arrived, but I told you it wouldn't be easy."

Raphael looked at Leonardo, who nodded. He said, "Okay, let's go."

They reached the top of the mountain pass, Mount Hermon rising to the right of them, and the driver stopped. Raphael said, "What's happening?"

"There is a checkpoint ahead."

"A checkpoint here? On top of the ridge?"

"Yes. It's never happened before."

"They've seen us?"

"I don't know if they've seen us, but they've

heard us coming for thirty minutes. What do you want to do?"

Raphael considered, then said, "Keep going. Put the lights on. Let's see if we can get past them."

The driver did so, illuminating the small goat track and amazing Raphael that anyone would actually dare to drive on it. They went forward, the lights illuminating a checkpoint with a small pickup truck blocking the road, the truck itself painted in United Nations colors.

Two men appeared out of the darkness, and both were wearing United Nations uniforms. Raphael said, "What the hell is this? I thought you said they were to the south?"

Tariq pulled out his pistol and said, "They are. These are not United Nations."

The driver pulled up next to them and Raphael saw both men were armed with AK-47s and both were wearing the blue beret of the United Nations. The driver talked to them in Arabic, the conversation going back and forth. Eventually, he rolled up the window and conducted a three-point turn, then headed back the way they'd come.

Raphael said, "What are we doing?"

Tariq said, "Going back to the valley. We can't continue here. Our path is blocked."

"What does that mean?"

"It means your mission is done. We can't continue on. I'm sorry, but those men are not with me. I can't pay them off, and I can't call someone to let us through."

Raphael said, "Stop the car."

"What?"

"Stop the car. Now. We're out of view of the checkpoint."

The driver did, and Raphael said, "We need to be in Syria tomorrow. Can you do that now, from a different crossing?"

"Tomorrow? No way."

Raphael said, "Then we go tonight."

"How do you propose we do that?"

He reached for his backpack, pulling it forward, saying, "Are you sure those guys aren't United Nations personnel?"

"Yes. This location is run by the battalion from Nepal. They even make a joke about being the ones that have to work here because they're from the land of Everest. The people we talked to at that checkpoint spoke Arabic. Nobody in Nepal speaks Arabic. They're fake, and I don't know who they are, but I'm not going to cross them until I talk to my bosses."

Meaning Hezbollah.

Raphael said, "We're going through."

Tariq said, "You can't shoot those guys. The real UN post is right up the hill, on top of the peak. They'll react before we can get away."

Raphael said, "Unless I use my worthless air gun."

Leonardo helped him unpack the weapon, which wasn't an "air gun" at all, but an Umarex AirSaber arrow rifle. With a folding stock and a cylinder below that held the compressed air, it could fire an arrow faster than any compound bow, and just as silently.

Tariq said, "What are you going to do?"

"Get back up there and eliminate the threat. Those guys are working for someone else, and if it's not the UN, and not Hezbollah, it's not our problem, right?"

Tariq nodded, and Raphael pulled out a quiver of four small carbon fiber arrows with wickedly sharp broad heads. He said, "I'll be right back."

He went out on foot, circling around the dirt track they'd used, seeing the high ground illuminated by the stars. He crept up the crest of the ridge, then saw the truck to his front. He advanced slowly, identifying the two men by the light of the cigarettes in their mouths. He took a knee and loaded an arrow.

The best part about the AirSaber was its lack of signature when used. It was as quiet as a person exhaling, making it much more silent than any suppressed weapon. The worst part was he had to reload it like an old-fashioned muzzle-loader from the Civil War, cramming in a new arrow for the next shot. Meaning it wasn't quick. Because of that, he was forced to wait until the two were separated, giving him the ability to take them down individually.

He kept the scope of the rifle centered on the chest of the first man, waiting. After seven minutes, the second man turned away, walking to the tailgate of the truck and dropping his pants to urinate.

Raphael didn't hesitate. He broke the trigger, hearing nothing but a *woof* of air. The small arrow hit the man in the throat. He looked confused for a moment, grabbed the fletching protruding from his neck, then fell over.

Raphael didn't even wait to see the results, bending over and loading another arrow. If his shot didn't work, it was irrelevant. Either they both died, or he'd be on the run.

He raised back up, saw the urinating man zip up his pants, then circle back around the truck, confused about the disappearance of his partner. He said something in Arabic, looking left and right, and Raphael squeezed the trigger again.

And missed.

The arrow clipped his neck at the jugular, causing him to spin, but didn't bring him down. He screamed and Raphael jumped up, racing toward him.

The man had a hand to his throat, shocked at what was happening, but was willing to fight. He saw Raphael and let go of his throat, releasing a torrent of blood as he snatched a knife from his belt.

He snarled and raised it in a saber grip. Raphael blocked the arm, tackling him and pinning the hand with the weapon to the ground. The man thrashed below him, but Raphael knew the massive amount of blood spraying from the wound would be the difference between victory and death. He made no attempt at further damage, just holding the man on the ground.

Eventually, the loss of blood took its toll, and the man quit struggling, a slow-motion affair where his instincts wanted to continue the fight for survival, but his brain gave up.

Raphael waited for a moment, then stood up. He went to the truck, found the keys, and backed it out of the way, then returned to the Land Cruiser down the slope.

He surprised Tariq and the driver outside the vehicle, causing Tariq to literally jump when he appeared. He said, "Let's go. It's open."

The driver got behind the wheel of the SUV, and the headlights illuminated Raphael's body. Tariq saw the blood coating his arms and took a step back. Raphael said, "What? It's open. Let's go."

Tariq slid into the passenger seat, saying, "Okay, okay. We'll go."

Raphael got in the backseat, seeing Leonardo grinning. He said, "Just like old times, huh?"

Raphael opened a pack of wet wipes and began cleaning off the blood, saying, "Almost. I never got this much blood on me."

Tariq said, "Are you sure we can pass?"

Raphael held up a wet wipe, coated in red. He said, "Yes. Let's go."

## CHAPTER 59

Inside our hotel room TOC, I watched George Wolffe pace about through my screen. He should have been sitting in front of the camera, but he was not.

He advanced to his computer and said, "That's all you got? You penetrated an embassy for a sovereign state and that's *all* you got?"

I said, "Hey, sir, let's be honest here. They're just pretending. They aren't a *real* sovereign state. It's like someone saying they're a member of special operations and then you find out the guy is just an interpreter."

My joke went over like a lead balloon. His eyes bulged and he said, "You took out three men. *Three men!* And this is all you got out of it? How am I supposed to take this back to the president?"

"Sir, this is enough to find a thread. We know two of the Turtles went to Lebanon, and we have a name. We also know the serial killer in charge of them is in Israel for an important speech from Israel's prime minister at Megiddo—otherwise known as Armageddon, as in the final battle between good and evil in the Bible—and he's got some crazy theory about starting the End of Days. That's enough to start the hunt."

"What do you propose? What do you think you can do with this?"

"Well, first of all, I have two Israeli assassins with me who are being paid by the Mossad. Israel isn't going to be an issue, because that Megiddo speech isn't for a couple of days. Plenty of time. Secondly, I have the name of a Hezbollah smuggler—a guy called Tariq—and a man who can find him. I contacted Samir al-Atrash, the man I told you about earlier. He's willing to help, and is doing research on the name as we speak."

He shook his head and said, "I don't have authorization for the Hezbollah contact just yet. You can't use him."

I balled my fists and said, "Can you guys pull your head out of your ass at least once? The guy isn't Hezbollah. He's Druze. I mean, really, I have a television here. I see the attacks coming from the Houthis in Yemen into Saudi Arabia and the rockets from the Gaza Strip. Iran is flexing its muscle, and it's only a matter of time until Hezbollah is ordered to do the same from Lebanon. When that happens, we won't be able to turn this off."

Wolffe glowered on the screen, saying, "We work within a world of walls, a land of give-and-take. We get our authority from the duly constituted officials under the United States Constitution, and those walls have served our nation well. I need authority before continuing."

I said, "Sir, the entire Taskforce is already outside our own constitution. What are you talking about? Why are you waiting for permission?"

He said, "I get that, which is precisely why I'm not breaking through more walls without authority. Do you understand?"

He thought I was going to completely ignore anything the Oversight Council told me, and because of it, he was warning me off. Which, honestly, was pretty smart, because that's what I was going to do.

I said, "Sir, I got it. You want me to stand down and I will, then I'll fly back home on the Rock Star bird and get married. I'd ask you to attend the wedding, but I'm pretty sure you'll be sucked into defending America from Hezbollah hit teams blowing up our oil refineries as Israel launches nukes at Iran."

He leaned back and said, "What do you want to do?"

"I want to fly to Lebanon and talk to Samir. Find out what this Hezbollah smuggler was doing with two Croatian Special Forces guys. When I find a fix, I'm going to launch Knuckles and Brett against that target for the finish. Meanwhile, I'm taking the rest of the wrecking crew to Israel to take out the serial killer. *That's* what I want to do."

Wolffe thought a moment, then nodded, saying, "I think I can roll that up into the Omega we were given for the Knights of Malta headquarters. It's a stretch, but I can sell it after the fact."

I couldn't believe what came out of his mouth.

Incredulous, I said, "Are you really authorizing me to cross international borders, talk to a guy in Beirut tied to Hezbollah, turn a team loose there, and then take the remainder of my team to Israel all on that initial Omega authority?"

Wolffe grinned and said, "You know the charter. Omega is for the threat, not the geographic boundaries. It's exactly why the Taskforce was created. No gaps between competing authorities and individual fiefdoms."

I chuckled, knowing the jeopardy he'd just put himself in, and said, "Didn't take long to ditch that 'walls' speech you just gave. Yeah, I get it, but this is pushing that authority to the limit. But I get it. I'm not the one who's going to explain the fallout after I get this done. We'll fly tomorrow."

"I understand Israel. I have no questions about rolling up that guy inside the country, but what about Lebanon? You think you can find the guys loose there now?"

"Honestly, sir, I don't know. We have a name, and I have a contact. If this guy is as big a deal inside Hezbollah as he bragged about in the emails we found, my buddy will know him. If not, we're out of luck. But I'm thinking he will. These 'Ninja Turtles' have a plan, and the contact is facilitating it for money. If I were to guess, they're going to launch another strike from inside Lebanon using Iranian weapon systems to inflame the war, outside of Hezbollah control, and Hezbollah isn't going to like that. We'll find them."

Wolffe closed his eyes for a moment, and I

realized he was as tired as I was. He returned to the screen, saying, "You need to stop them. I mean, really stop them. I'm not going back for additional authorities on this. When you find them, kill them. A hit like that, from Lebanese territory, will be the final nail. We'll be at war."

I was a little taken aback at the statement. We didn't *ever* kill on command. Unless the target was designated DOA. Now growing serious, I said, "Are you telling me the Oversight Council has designated this target as DOA?"

He looked away, thinking about his next words. He came back to the screen and said, "I don't have time to go back to the council on this. I'm telling you that they are designated DOA. Me alone."

I nodded and said, "Good enough for me, sir. We'll get it done. I have to brief the team and get prepped for movement. Anything else?"

"Yeah. What about that back channel to Iran? Is that real?"

I was startled by the question. I was about to spread my team over two different countries, killing people wholesale while trying to keep myself out of jail, and he was asking me to conduct geopolitical diplomacy?

I spread my hands and said, "Hey, sir, that's national command authority shit. I can't do both. If you want me to find the guys in Lebanon, I can't also start negotiating with Hezbollah."

He said, "You just told me that Hezbollah wouldn't like what's going on. You *can* do both."

I shook my head and said, "I'm going into a very, very dangerous situation just to find these

guys. I might end up on a Hezbollah video trying
to accomplish the first mission."

Wolffe leaned forward and said, "This is important, and it's also not part of my authority,
but I think it matters. We're about to be at war,
and I don't mean that in a small-war sense, like
Afghanistan, where America has forgotten we're
even there. I mean a full-on war, drawing in
every damn Arab country there is, with suicide
bombers detonating on U.S. playgrounds. Iran is
serious. They think their back is to the wall, and
if you're right, they don't even know why."

I shook my head, thinking, *Why am I in this
position? I'm the hammer looking for a nail.* I could
do what he wanted against the men attempting
to light the fire, but I wasn't the man who did
diplomacy. That was someone else's job.

I sighed and said, "Sir, I might be able to do
that. If you want it, I can try, but I can't do it
on my own. I need some no-shit, real national
command authority statements. I can try to get
the message passed, but I'm not going to be the
diplomat here. If President Hannister wants to
talk to the theocracy, I think I can do it, but I'm
not going to be the one debating with some Hezbollah terrorist."

Wolffe nodded and said, "That's the first mission. The primary one. We need to turn down
the rhetoric on this."

"So Hannister is going to pass me a message?
That he wants passed to Iran?"

Wolffe rubbed his face and said, "No. Not yet.
But he will."

## CHAPTER 60

Raphael watched the cliffs to his right, the growing light of dawn finally giving him the ability to see how crazy the traverse had been. He white-knuckled the handle above the door, his foot reflexively hitting a brake pedal that didn't exist in the back of the vehicle.

Eventually, they descended low enough into the Syrian desert plain that they picked up an actual, honest-to-God road. Raphael breathed a sigh of relief, and sagged back into his seat, the hills still around him, but no longer posing a threat.

Tariq directed the vehicle to a village that looked like a cross between a Mad Max movie and a Disney set. The view around the village was spectacular, with the houses built into the side of the mountains like Swiss chalets, only the structures were of a dismal cinder-block construction, with leftover debris and broken cars littered about.

Tariq said, "This is Jandal. You're now in Syria. This is where we're going to meet your contacts."

Raphael nodded, and they entered the town

END OF DAYS / 395

on a small two-lane rutted asphalt road, thread-ing through the concrete buildings. Eventually, they stopped at an outdoor service station that doubled as a coffee shop. Tariq said, "Go get a table on the patio. We're going to fill up."

Raphael looked at Leonardo, then exited the vehicle, taking a seat in a rusted iron chair, Leo-nardo sitting across from him. Leonardo said, "This is much harder than I thought it would be."

Raphael said, "Tell me about it. You didn't do the killing last night."

Leonardo said, "Who do you think those men were?"

"I don't know, but they weren't good men. They were trying to smuggle just like this asshole, and they paid the price."

Leonardo nodded and said, "I'm not sure we can complete this mission. We're living one lie after another."

Raphael saw he was scared and said, "This is no different than the last time we were here. The only difference is we were official then. These men aren't any more dangerous."

Leonardo gave a halfhearted laugh and said, "Yeah, the last time we were here, they cut our boss's balls off. Looking forward to it."

Raphael said, "Hang on for a day. You have the skill. You're just disoriented by the language and the culture. You remember what you told me before? About the Bosnian war?"

Leonardo looked at him, then slowly nodded.

Raphael said, "You wished you were old enough to make a difference. And now you are. Those savages then did more than just cut off balls. They raped our women and tortured our fathers for sport. These men are the same, just like the ones you wanted to fight. No different."

Two men approached the table asking in English if they could take a seat. Raphael said, "There are other tables here."

The first, dressed in a track suit and a two-day stubble of beard, said, "We think we'd like to sit at this table." He didn't say it as if he was asking permission.

Raphael looked toward Tariq filling up the tank of the Land Cruiser, and the second man, wearing camouflaged pants, boots, and a loose-fitting combat blouse, said, "Tariq knows us. And now we want to know you."

Raphael pushed a chair out with his foot and said, "Go ahead."

They sat down, track suit guy saying, "So you believe in the Prophet?"

"I don't know what you mean."

He leaned forward and said, "Where are you from, you pasty monkeys?"

Raphael said, "Bosnia."

"Did you fight there? Against the Crusaders?"

"No. It was before my time. I was too young, but I saw the damage. It's why I'm here now."

Track suit studied him, then said, "Because of the Ummah? Because of what was done to the faithful?"

Raphael locked eyes with him and said, "Yes. It's why I'm sitting in front of you. I told myself it would never happen again, and the only way to accomplish that is to fight."

Satisfied, track suit said, "So you know about drones, is that correct?"

Raphael said, "Yes. I wouldn't say I could build one, but I know how to make them work."

"Good, because we have some that have been in storage, so to speak, and we're getting asked to prepare them for use, but don't know how to get them in the air. They're big."

"The cache in Daraa? Is that the one?"

Surprised, the camouflaged man said, "How do you know about the cache?"

Raphael said, "We work in the same circles. I was in Daraa once before, during the war against the rebels. I saw them then."

Daraa was a city in southern Syria, on the edge of the borders of the Golan Heights, Israel, and Jordan, and was the wellspring of the current civil war inside the country. In 2011, it was the first city to rise up against the Syrian regime as the Arab Spring was sweeping the Middle East, with students protesting peacefully against the government. As had happened all over the Middle East, that peace lasted only as long as the regime held patience.

Daraa was where the first slaughter occurred, and where the civil war began, the city itself now reduced to rubble, but the fight against the regime continued. In 2018, Russia engendered a cease-fire in the province, the crux of it being that Assad's men wouldn't come in, but the rebels had to leave.

The Russians literally bussed the rebel fighters out of the city to other areas in the country, only to have them continue the fight. In the vacuum that was created, Hezbollah, a stalwart defender of Assad, took control. The land now belonged to Iran, even if it wasn't overtly said out loud. The Americans and the Russians just wanted the shooting to stop, and if that meant Hezbollah seizing terrain, then so be it. The immediate fighting inside the Daraa province was done. The future fight against Israel didn't factor into the equation.

Until now.

Track suit said, "Did you fight then?"

"Yes, I did. I killed many, many infidels, and I'm here to kill more. My guide Tariq can speak to that."

Track suit waved his hand and said, "Originally, you were supposed to just train us on the drones. Things have changed. We have orders to prepare to strike the heart of the Little Satan, and we don't know how to get them in the air."

Surprised, Leonardo said, "Israel? Why? What's going on there?"

Track suit said, "Haven't you seen the news? Israel and America are preparing for war against Iran. They've created a precondition to destroy the country, and we'll retaliate from here."

Leonardo looked at Raphael, who said, "What precondition?"

"They're blaming our sister militia in Iraq of killing people. Diplomats and others affiliated with the Great Satan. We've talked to the men in charge, and they say it's all a lie. Basically, America and Israel have tried to eliminate the Islamic

Republic of Iran for decades, and haven't been able to do so, so they're creating conditions to attack through force. We'll respond from here."

Raphael heard the words and thought, *This is going to work.*

## CHAPTER 61

We landed in Beirut, a place where being Israeli wasn't an asset. Lebanon gave a rat's ass about the virus, but took a dim view of anyone with an Israeli passport. They weren't the best-loved members of the neighborhood, COVID be damned. We taxied to the FBO hard stand and I said, "Okay, sorry about this, but you're going to be flight crew here. Staying with the plane."

Shoshana said, "Pike, I know what you said on the flight over, but you want me there. You *need* me there."

I looked at Aaron, who understood where I was coming from. He said, "Shoshana, let it go. Soon we'll be back in Israel, and it will be Pike asking to continue."

Which wasn't what I wanted to hear, but he was speaking the truth. My being in charge of our little team had always been based on consensus, and that had been bent at every moment. Aaron and Shoshana followed me out of deference, not command. Israel, which is where we were going next, would break it. No way would I be able to claim team leader when we hit the

END OF DAYS / 401

ground in Israel, where the Mossad was paying for the hunt. I wasn't sure what to do about that yet, since I also answered to the Taskforce.

One bridge at a time. Right now, I had to become the undercover diplomat for the United States of America, having received a back-channel message from the president of the United States. It was short and sweet, basically saying, "We don't think it's you. Don't cause a war." And now I was supposed to pass that along.

The pilot opened the door, letting the stairs down, and I leaned forward, pecking Shoshana on the cheek. I said, "If I could take you, I would. Because I trust you."

Her eyes went wide at the gesture. Aaron smiled and she looked up at me in a new light, saying, "Okay, Nephilim. I trust *you*. We'll see you soon."

Jennifer grinned at the exchange, and Shoshana flicked her head to Knuckles, saying, "So you'll take him instead?"

I started walking to the front of the aircraft, saying, "Yeah, might be meeting a female. You never know."

Jennifer, Brett, Knuckles, and I exited the aircraft, went through customs and immigration, and were let loose in the city. I gave instructions for the team to get some rental cars and dialed my phone, waiting with a little trepidation.

Samir al-Atrash was a member of the Druze sect in Lebanon. I'd trained him and his men a long, long time ago as a member of the Lebanese Defense Force's special operations component. Since then, he'd drifted a little bit, becoming bitter after the 2006 war with Israel, to the point that he'd become disillusioned with the LAF and had left the service.

A few years ago, I'd contacted him for some help tracking down a terrorist threat, and he'd helped out—but not before I'd been captured by Hezbollah and had one of my fingers cut off.

Jennifer had saved me from a much worse fate, using him and his men, and when I'd seen him, I was sure he'd set me up. I'd almost killed him then in a blind rage. At that moment in time, I wanted to beat him to death, but Jennifer had convinced me that it wasn't a betrayal from Samir. I'd spared his life, but it hadn't been pleasant. And now I was going to ask for his help.

The phone rang through and I heard his voice. I said, "Samir? It's Pike Logan."

He said, "The last time I heard from you, we almost had a civil war here in Lebanon. And now, it looks like we're headed for the same thing, only this time it's war with Israel."

I chuckled and said, "The last time I was here, I prevented a civil war. I'm trying to do the same now. Did you get the information I asked for?"

"I did, but it's not as easy as you think."

"All I need to know is where that guy is. He's got some killers with him who are about to turn your world upside down."

"That's what I mean. The man you're after is one that the Hezbollah hierarchy cares about. He's very valuable. They don't want to turn him over to the Americans, even if it means what you say."

I segued to my primary mission, one that he

didn't know about yet. "Do you have someone within the hierarchy with you? Because I have a message I want to pass."

"A message from whom?"

"From the top of the United States. Look, Samir, this shit going on isn't what it seems. We're trying to unfold it, but right now we need to let Iran know that we know it isn't them. We need them to back down."

Knuckles came to me holding a couple of key fobs, saying, "We've got vehicles. Waiting on you."

I nodded, then heard Samir say, "You want to talk to Iran?"

Off the phone, I said, "Bring them here. We're leaving now."

On the phone, I said, "Yes, that's what I want. Do you have someone who can do that?"

I heard nothing for a moment, then, "I do, Pike, but this is very dangerous, both for me and for you."

I said, "Yeah, I get that. The last time I saw you I lost my pinky finger to some pruning shears. We're outside the airport. Where do we go?"

He gave me an address, and I said, "You're shitting me. You want to meet there?"

He said, "I thought it appropriate."

I turned to my group, saying, "Jennifer and I are going in. Brett and Knuckles separate short of the location. Anything goes wrong, kill all of them. I mean every single one."

## CHAPTER 62

Raphael and Leonardo loaded back into the Land Cruiser, now following a Toyota HiLux pickup truck out of the village. They reached a real two-lane highway and picked up speed, driving south.

Tariq said, "So I assume everything went well?"

Raphael said, "Yes, as far as I can tell."

"You know all of this land is now owned by Hezbollah, right?"

"That's what he said. Why?"

"Just that you're now in a different world. This isn't Lebanon. Or Rome. You cross these people, and you're going to die."

Raphael smiled and said, "I've been here before. Trust me, I get it."

Tariq caught his eye in the rearview mirror, but said nothing else. After passing through several small villages, they reached the bombed-out outskirts of Daraa, Leonardo saying, "This looks like Sarajevo after the war."

Tariq said, "The regime just pounds it with artillery. Like it's target practice. Nobody wants to be anywhere near the city now."

They continued south, leaving behind the devastation. After another forty minutes of driving, the HiLux left the paved road and headed out into the desert. Tariq followed. Raphael saw a small compound in the distance, nothing around except for the rocks and small scrub trees. No orchards or other agriculture. The buildings were clearly here for something other than farming.

The pickup truck circled the compound, then pulled up short next to an overhang built of tin. Underneath were four Samad 3 UAVs.

Built in Iran, and used to great effect in Yemen against Saudi Arabia, they were basically suicide drones. With a wingspan of nearly fifteen feet and a payload of forty pounds of explosives and ball bearings, it was like a small airplane. Not controlled by an operator using a tablet or other device, it was fire and forget, with a range of more than 1,500 kilometers. All that was needed was to load the coordinates to the attack point, release it, and it was on its way, like a slow-motion bullet fired from a gun. Developed and perfected in Iran, it was named after a leader of the Houthis, Saleh al-Sammad, who was assassinated by the United Arab Emirates in 2018.

It was used almost daily by the rebel movement in Yemen, the most famous being an attack on a Saudi refinery in 2019 that caused reverberations throughout the oil industry, and by extension, the world. It was a crude cruise missile that Raphael intended to use not as a signal of deterrence against a target with little meaning, like Hezbollah wanted, but as a spark against a lake of gasoline.

Tariq saw the HiLux doors open, and the two men exit. He said, "Okay, this is your show now."

Raphael slowly nodded, and left the vehicle.

He went to the two men and said, "So you've got the Samad Three. Good drone."

"Yes, but our problem is we can't launch it from here. We don't know how. It's too big to simply toss in the air, and its push motor doesn't work on the ground. You see four of them here, but there used to be six. We wrecked them trying to get them in the air."

Raphael said, "I know. It requires a rack to launch from. Did you not get any instructions with them?"

Embarrassed, track suit said, "No. They just gave them to us. It's why you're here. We know how to put in the coordinates and the weapon payload, but don't know how to get it off the ground."

Raphael laughed and said, "I understand. It has to have speed to gain altitude, but once it does, it'll fly. That's the easy part." He glanced around the stall, seeing several steel latticework frames against the wall, lined up one after the other. He counted six, then said, "Did those come with the drones?"

"Yes. It was the scaffolding surrounding the frames for protection."

Raphael couldn't believe what he was hearing. These men were as dumb as a box of rocks. He said, "That's not for protection of the drone. That's the launch platform. You mount it in the bed of a truck, fire up the engine, then begin

END OF DAYS / 407

driving. Once you've built speed over the wings, you launch it in the air."

Inside the vehicle, Tariq said to Leonardo, "We've done our duty. Pay us the rest of the money and we'll be on our way. I don't want to know what's going on here."

Leonardo said, "You're not going anywhere."

Tariq pulled out his sat phone, raised the antennae, and dialed a number, saying, "Yes, I am. I got you here, and that was the deal. I'll need the rest of the cards now."

Leonardo said, "We're going to need help getting back to Beirut."

"That wasn't the agreement. I get you here, and I'm done."

"Well, it's the agreement now. If you want those other debit cards, you'll wait."

Tariq gave a sour look, and the phone connected. He said, "Package is delivered. I'm coming home."

The man on the other end of the line said something, and Leonardo saw Tariq's eyes squint. He said, "What do you mean?"

The man on the other end of the line said something else, and Tariq said, "I'll be coming back soon."

Leonardo waited for him to hang up, then said, "We can't get out of here by ourselves. The agreement was here and back."

Tariq laid the sat phone on the dash, the antennae still out and connected. He said, "That is *not* what we agreed to. I have other endeavors in the works. I don't have time to wait for you to play with these guys. You do what you want to do, but we're leaving."

Leonardo pulled up his pistol and said, "You'll wait. At least for a little bit."

The driver saw the pistol and reacted violently, turning around and attempting to grab it out of Leonardo's hands. Leonardo broke the trigger, splattering the driver's brain matter against the windshield.

The two men near the HiLux ducked, looking at the Land Cruiser. Tariq slammed his back against the door, holding his hands out, shouting, "No, no, no!"

Track suit whipped out a pistol, aiming it at Raphael's head. "What was that?"

Raphael spread his hands wide, showing he had no weapon. He said, "I don't know."

Track suit said, "Tariq is valuable to us. He is a friend. You are not. Raise your hands."

Raphael did so, saying, "I'm only here to help with the drones."

Camouflage guy came to him, searching up and down his body. He pulled out a Glock 19, tossed it in the dirt, then nodded to track suit, who said, "Tell your partner to come out without a weapon. And to release Tariq."

Raphael shouted at the SUV and Tariq exited, his hands in the air.

Track suit said, "What's going on?"

Tariq said, "Nothing. Everything is fine."

Track suit said, "Where is your driver?"

Panting, Tariq said, "In the car. In the car."

Track suit looked at Raphael, pointed his pistol, and said, "Get your other man out here, or I'll kill you where you stand."

The words were still hanging in the air when his head exploded like a watermelon thrown off a roof. Camouflage man whirled, and he met the same fate, his head absorbing two rounds from a Glock 19. He dropped, and Leonardo appeared from the other side of the Land Cruiser.

Raphael sagged a bit, then said, "Good shooting."

Tariq said, "What have you done? They're Hezbollah. We're all dead now."

Raphael went back to the Land Cruiser saying, "You were dead the minute you got in the vehicle with me."

He dug around the backseat, came back out, and tossed the hood he'd been forced to wear earlier. He said, "Put that on. Don't worry, I'm not kidnapping you."

## CHAPTER 63

Garrett heard the alarm go off and rolled over, the jet lag still kicking him in the butt. He sat up, put his feet on the floor, then thought about just getting back in bed. Today was nothing more than an orientation day, with the Knights' members meeting the other church groups who had gathered for the trip to Megiddo. The day was beginning with breakfast, and then would include scripted tourist events designed to inculcate in the group of visitors an undying support for the state of Israel.

He showered, dressed, then took his Thuraya sat phone and went to the window to let it find a satellite. It connected, but he had no messages. He was beginning to worry about the mission in Syria. The last he'd heard, they had landed in Lebanon, but that had been over twenty-four hours ago. If they had failed, the only thing left was Michelangelo, and Garrett wasn't sure his attack would be enough. It was a failsafe, last-chance attempt. He thought about calling them, but understood the risks involved.

Satellite phones in Syria were routinely moni-tored by a plethora of intelligence agencies, both from the West and the East, not to mention the Assad regime itself. He decided to leave the phone on the windowsill and see if he had a message when he returned.

He went downstairs to the breakfast event, meeting the Grand Master and the other men of the Knights of Malta entourage, then met the other organizations who had traveled for the event, most evangelical megachurches based in the United States, all incredibly happy to be invited.

He did his best to keep up appearances, and honestly didn't have much trouble doing so, as the true anointed Knights of his group were the ones people wanted to meet, not some nobody on the edges.

He heard plenty of people talking about the prophecies of the Bible, but none who would actually bring it about. And felt a calm by the words.

Toward the end of the breakfast, the Grand Master pulled him aside and said, "Spend today doing whatever security preparations you must, because tomorrow, I don't want you to be a single blip on anyone's radar."

"Okay, sir. That's my mission for today. And thank you for keeping me out of the mess of politics of this trip. You guys can enjoy the trip to Jerusalem. I'll prepare the protection."

Grand Master Chaucer said, "I can't afford you to interrupt anything tomorrow. If it's not settled today, it's not getting settled. I'll trust the Israelis for my protection."

Garrett smiled and said, "It will be fine, sir. As we both know, the Lord will protect us."

He left the breakfast and went to find Michelangelo. Going to his room, he pounded on the door. Michelangelo opened it, clearly hungover from the night before. Garrett barged in and said, "Can you not spend one night focused on the mission?"

Michelangelo rubbed his eyes and said, "What the hell, what time is it?"

Garrett said, "Close to ten in the morning. Is that too early for you?"

Now aggravated, Michelangelo said, "I *am* focused on the mission. But it's not for two days."

Garrett opened the drapes to his hotel room, the light spilling in and causing Michelangelo to wince. He said, "The tour today goes to the Old City of Jerusalem. You're going to be on it. I need you to find out how you can get into the Dome of the Rock. There are apparently specific entrance requirements, and you need to find out how to get your backpack inside."

He said, "I'm going as a Muslim. Not a Christian."

"Reconnaissance is reconnaissance. Pack your shit. Leave the explosives here, but take the backpack. Find out the security limits. And stay away from the cameras. When you go back, I don't want them to make a connection with this visit."

Michelangelo bobbed his head up and down, moving to the bathroom to clean up. He said, "What are you going to do?"

"Find out what the hell happened to Raphael and Leonardo."

Garrett turned to leave the room, saying, "You're good, right? You know what you have to do?"

Michelangelo said, "I'm good. I got it. I know what I need to do."

Garrett nodded, and exited. He used the stairs to get back to his own room, checked the phone, and saw no messages. He held the phone in his hand, knowing he shouldn't call, but also knew the rest of the mission was a waste of time if they were dead.

He dialed, waiting on the satellites to pick up the signal and transfer it back to earth.

It connected, and he heard, "Is this it?"

"No. Not yet."

He heard exasperation. "Why the fuck are you calling? Every time this phone touches a satellite, it's a potential compromise."

Garrett exhaled a sigh of relief and said, "I know, but I had to *know*. You're good to go? You got what you needed?"

"We are. We have the drones and means to launch them. It's going to take about forty minutes for the birds to get to you, so we're going to need a little advance warning."

"I got it. Don't worry about that. I'll give you the trigger. Just keep this phone operational."

"There's one other thing. We've killed some of Hezbollah's men here. It's no big deal right now, but it will be in a day or two. Somebody's going to come looking, and we have no security to defend ourselves."

Garrett said, "Can you hold on for a day? Until tomorrow?"

"I think so, but it might be close."

"Do so. Tomorrow is the attack, and it's going to be early. Wait for my call. When it comes, launch them all."

## CHAPTER 64

We took the rentals to the town of Sidon, about forty minutes outside of Beirut, to a café that was the same place I'd been captured years before. Jennifer saw the location and said, "I don't think we should go in there."

I said, "Well, we don't have a lot of choices here."

I clicked on the net and said, "Knuckles, Blood, you staged?"

Knuckles came back and said, "Yeah, we're staged. But if I were you, I wouldn't enter that damn place. Bad Ju Ju."

I said, "Yeah, maybe."

Sidon was a coastal city full of backpackers and foreign tourists, the promenade next to the water dotted with restaurants and nightclubs, and this café was a place that anyone would feel safe. Unless a bomb had gone off inside it years before, and you were captured by a bunch of terrorists.

The sun beginning to set, it was becoming crowded on the promenade next to the café, making it hard to see a threat. Walking to the door, I felt a little post-traumatic stress, but suppressed the feeling, holding Jennifer's hand. Before, she'd been on the outside. Now I had her with me. I wasn't sure if that was good or bad.

I walked into the interior, surveyed the room, and saw Samir in the back, sitting with an older guy dressed like a local, wearing a tweed jacket and a white skullcap. Samir waved, and I waved back, telling the hostess I was with him.

I went to the table, glancing around me as I did. I saw two men to my left at a table, and two men to my front against the wall. They were all young, mid-twenties, and were dressed in a more Western style, with two of them wearing ball caps, but they had a hard air about them.

Security. At least that's what I hoped. If they were simply protection, I had no issue with it. If they were trying to roll me up like had happened the last time I was here, they would all die.

Samir stood up and hugged me, and I returned the embrace. He turned to Jennifer and did the same, truly seeming to mean it. He held her shoulders and said, "It's good to see you, Koko. Climbed any walls recently?"

She smiled and said, "More than I care to admit."

He said, "Sit, both of you, sit. It's really good to see you."

We did, and I said, "Who's your friend?"

The man was glowering at me like he wanted to set my balls on fire. Not exactly a good start to negotiations.

The man said, "You can call me Muhammed."

I laughed and said, "Sort of like John Smith, is that it?"

He didn't get the joke, looking at Samir. I said, "Sorry, I'm not trying to cause a fight here."

Muhammed said, "What do you want? Why did you come here?"

I said, "I need the phone number for one of your men. He's with some people who are trying to start a war. I want to stop them."

He said, "It is *you* people who are starting a war. You people who are looking for a pretext to cause a fight."

I looked at Samir and said, "Is this the guy? Can he talk to the leadership?"

Samir glanced at Muhammed and said, "He can talk to the leadership of Hezbollah. I can't promise they'll do the same with Iran."

I turned to Muhammed and said, "We're about to be at war. If we do that, it'll be the end of your existence. It'll be total. Iran will be gone, and so will Hezbollah. You understand that, right?"

"I understand that you will pay a heavy price for such a thing. Afghanistan and Iraq rolled up times ten."

I said, "Exactly. We don't want that. We really, really don't, no matter what you guys think. We *do not* want a war. You think we're making up the killings around the world to give us an excuse, but the killings are real."

He hissed, "The killings are from someone else. You're just using them as a punching bag. We have nothing to do with them."

I leaned back and said, "Yes. We know that. You are not responsible for them. Someone else is causing it, and they're blaming you to cause us to go to war. You people are playing into their hands. Every strike you do, every show of force is backing us up against a wall. We need you to stop."

He looked at Samir, then said, "How do I know this is true? How do I know you aren't just trying to gain an edge on the fight?"

I said, "Honestly, you don't. But do you have a smartphone?"

He looked confused for a moment, then said, "Yes."

"Is it an iPhone?"

"Yes."

"I'm going to AirDrop you a message from the president of the United States. It's a message from my commander in chief. It's real."

Surprised, he said, "I can't trust that."

I said, "I know. There's no way to prove it's a true message, except for one thing: I traveled here, to Lebanon, to give it to you."

I pointed at his two security teams and said, "At great personal risk, I might add. My national command authority wants to head off a war, and they asked me to do this."

I kept my eyes on him, and an attractive woman approached our table. About twenty-five years old, she had that sultry look that seemed to be inherent in Lebanese women. I glanced at her, did a double take at her beauty, and saw Jennifer smile at my reaction.

I waited on her to say something, but she went

to Samir and hugged him. I looked at Jennifer and she said, "Don't tell me you thought she was coming over here for you."

I blustered something and she said, "You don't recognize her?"

And I finally did. She was Samir's niece, someone who'd been kidnapped on the same mission where I'd lost a finger. I'd slaughtered quite a few people to save her. She was older now, and it showed in all the right ways.

Samir returned her embrace and said, "We have some business to conduct, if you don't mind."

She ignored him, coming over to Jennifer and giving her a hug. She then looked at me and with a bubbly smile said, "I still owe you."

Like she'd lost a game of beer pong instead of being captured and almost killed. Her resilience was the essence of the entire country. I said, "Yes, if I remember, it was a beer."

She laughed and said, "One day I'll pay."

She kissed me on the forehead and left. Muhammed watched the entire exchange, finally saying, "What was that?"

I said, "Nothing. Past times. Your phone?"

I could tell the encounter had worked in our favor. I wasn't the infidel from the Great Satan. I was something different. Muhammed pulled out his cell. I opened my AirDrop application, seeing "Dora the Explorer" as the only available destination.

I said, "I don't see your phone."

He said, "Look for Dora."

I looked up from my iPhone and said, "You're shitting me."

He smiled for the first time and said, "I have a daughter. She named my phone."

I laughed and said, "I have my own daughter, adopted from Syria. I get it. It's on the way," and we finally bonded. He relaxed in the chair, retrieved the message, and said, "I will take this to my command. I can't promise anything."

I said, "That's all I ask. Just do what we both want here. Nobody wants a war. Well, almost nobody." I looked at Samir and said, "Which is why I need that number for the smuggler."

Muhammed said, "You don't need to worry about that number. We've talked to him, and he's okay. We'll be taking care of him."

"No offense, but I don't think he will be. He's in danger, if he's not already dead. Do you know where he is here in Lebanon? Can you get to him?"

Muhammed glanced at Samir, and Samir nodded, encouraging him to talk. He came back to me and said, "He's not in Lebanon. He's in Syria."

"Syria? What the hell for? How did he get there?"

"He's helping us with some things."

I said, "Muhammed, give me the number. He may have thought he was helping, but he's with the men who are trying to get us into a fight. They want us at each other's throats. Give me the number, and if he's fine, he's fine. If not, I'll handle the problem."

"We can deal with this."

I rolled my eyes and said, "Okay, then *do* it. In the meantime, give me the number. It's just a sat phone. It's not like I can use it to break apart your security systems here in Lebanon. Just give it to me."

"What will you do with it?"

"Stop a damn war."

## CHAPTER 65

The Rock Star bird took off, circled the coast of Lebanon, and then began crossing back into the country, the city of Beirut lit up in the nighttime sky. We'd left so quickly I hadn't had time to tell anyone what was going on, just instructing Knuckles and Brett to show back up at the aircraft for immediate exfiltration. They'd turned in our rental vehicles and had met us planeside. Jennifer and I had run up the stairs behind them, closing the door with me still on the phone. Five minutes later, we were airborne.

After we broke the ten-thousand-foot mark, Shoshana came forward and asked, "What are we doing? Why are we leaving?"

Still on the phone with George Wolffe, I held up my hand, waving her off. Truthfully, I was glad I had an excuse not to answer, because I wasn't really sure what the hell we were going to do, but I knew that staying in Lebanon wasn't the answer. Muhammed had finally given me the number, and I'd had Jennifer inject it into our system through the Taskforce after leaving the meeting. It was a long process, because Project Prometheus requests had to be washed of fingerprints before entering the intelligence community, but it was what I had to deal with. The NSA could find that phone if it had contacted a satellite, and because of the way sat phones worked, it would have a geolocation assigned to it. The problem was that the tail of getting that information back to me could take hours.

We'd left the café in one piece, with Samir satisfied that I hadn't done anything to put him in danger. Honestly, I would have liked to spend a few days on the coast with him and his niece, just drinking beer, but that wasn't going to happen anytime soon.

Muhammed had actually become almost human. I knew he was a Hezbollah killer, but we were working for the same solution on this problem set, so I would respect his position. Someday I might be hunting his ass, but not today.

In the rush to get the number in the system and the team into the aircraft, I hadn't had the time to tell anyone what we were doing, spending it all talking to George Wolffe on my secure phone. I'd kept arguing with Wolffe all the way through takeoff, the sticking point being that we were now going into Syria. Lebanon was okay, and Israel was even better, given we had Aaron and Shoshana, but Syria was an entirely different basket of shit.

He didn't want to do anything there without consulting the Oversight Council, but I told him we didn't have the time for a debate, using his own words against him about the original Omega authority. We'd thought it would be in Lebanon, but that didn't alter the facts of the matter: terrorists don't care about state boundaries, and that's why we existed. Syria was no different than Lebanon as far as the Taskforce charter was concerned.

Well, except that it was a hell of a lot more dangerous.

I hung up the phone, Shoshana started to say something else, and I held up a hand, saying, "Jennifer, any geolocation?"

"Not yet."

I said, "Brett and Knuckles, we need to talk."

They came forward and I said, "Remember when I said I was going to target you against the so-called Turtles in Lebanon?"

Wary, Knuckles said, "Yeah?"

"Well, I'm still going to target you against them, but it's going to be in Syria."

Brett said, "Syria? How are we going to get in there? You think you can just land in Damascus and have us rent some vehicles like we did in Beirut?"

"No. I don't think that will work."

Knuckles looked at Brett, then at me. He said, "Soo . . . what are we doing?"

"We're waiting on the geolocation of the bad guys. When we get it, you're going to go find them."

Brett said, "And how are we going to do that?"

Knuckles was the first one to realize what I was saying. "You're shitting me. You want us to jump? Into an unknown drop zone inside a combat zone? Into Syria?"

Jennifer came forward in a rush, saying, "I have

the geolocation. It's right outside of Daraa, Syria. Out in the middle of the desert."

I took the tablet, looked at the location, then told her to take it to the pilots. I said, "Yeah, that's what I'm saying. We're thirty minutes out right now. Get ready."

Brett said, "You're shitting me."

I said, "I shit you not. You remember in Brazil, when you told me this bird was equipped for in-extremis free-fall operations? And I was the one who had to exit the bird? Now it's your turn."

He shook his head and said, "This is border-line crazy. You want me and Knuckles to free fall into Syria based on a grid from the NSA?"

I said, "I do. The smuggler was taking them to meet Hezbollah members for some sort of attack in Israel. I thought it would be in Lebanon, but it's not. The Croatian guys are going to use whatever they find with the Hezbollah men to start a war. If they're Katyusha rockets targeted at an Israeli city, it'll be a bridge too far. I'm pretty sure they've already killed the Hezbollah contacts. We don't know the target, but we do know where they're being launched from. Stop them."

Brett said, "You're going to really owe me for this."

I slapped his shoulder and he went to the back of the plane. He unscrewed two panels in the wall of the aircraft and started pulling out the free-fall rigs from their hiding place, Javelin parachutes that were extremely precise under canopy.

Knuckles said, "So we can get in, but what about exfiltration? How are we getting out?"

I said, "I honestly don't know, but I'll figure it out."

He grinned and said, "You damn well better."

I said, "There's a lot of special mission unit activity in Syria now. Old friends. I'll leverage them. You get this done, and I'll get you a linkup to exfiltrate to Jordan. Just get in, kill them, and start your escape and evasion."

He went back to the rear of the aircraft saying, "This is seriously seat-of-the-pants shit here."

Unlike every other SEAL I knew, where a half of a plan was better than wasting time developing a whole one, Knuckles always preferred an operation to be wired tight before execution. This was probably driving him nuts, but I knew he was better than just about anyone in a fluid situation.

Jennifer came back and said, "Twenty minutes out."

The time was speeding up, like it always did before a mission, with the seconds seeming to fly by faster and faster. Aaron and Shoshana helped the two with their parachute containers and rucksacks, Knuckles and Brett cramming in anything they could think of for the mission.

Knuckles loaded a GPS with the coordinates from the NSA phone track, then did the same for Brett's GPS, both of them mounted on a board affixed to their waists. Knuckles said, "How high are we?"

I said, "Seventeen thousand feet. We can't go

any lower because of air defenses. Do you want O2?"

He said, "No. No time for that. If we get out quickly, it won't be a problem. People go up Everest without oxygen, so I guess we can fall without it for a few seconds."

At eight minutes out, acting as a jumpmaster, I helped them put on the harnesses, then cinched their SIG MCX weapons to their sides, finally clipping the small rucksacks between each of their legs.

I said, "Did you remember any food?"

Knuckles looked at Brett, and he shook his head. Knuckles said, "We're going hungry if you don't get us out."

Jennifer ripped open an overhead bin, grabbed a bunch of PowerBars, and shoved them into their blouses, first Knuckles, then Brett, saying, "In case you have to eat on the run."

I heard the pilot shout up front and glanced that way. He had on an oxygen mask, telling me he was going to depressurize the aircraft. I gave him a thumbs-up, felt my ears pop, and tapped Brett on the shoulder. He bent down and cranked a small handle at the back of the aircraft, retracting a plate on the floor, the wind racing through the cabin like a banshee and starting to buffet inside the plane.

The aircraft itself wasn't built for free-fall operations, and only had a hatch for use in extreme conditions, which this qualified as. Instead of leaping out in a grand exit like a regular airplane, the jumper had to inch himself into the hole, then fall forward into space. It wasn't elegant, as the jumper would basically squeeze himself into the hatch and then drop like he was doing a cannonball at a community swimming pool, but once in the wind, it would be like any other exit.

I knew, because I'd done it once.

I sent Jennifer to the cockpit for the count-down, then positioned Knuckles in the hole, the wind whipping into the aircraft, the land a far, far distance away. At seventeen thousand feet, we couldn't do this for very long because of the lack of oxygen, but we could do it long enough.

Knuckles clamped a pair of night vision goggles to his helmet, and I heard Jennifer shout. I slapped his shoulder. He gave me a thumbs-up, then shouted at Brett, saying, "Ten thousand. Open at ten."

Brett nodded, and Knuckles disappeared like he'd been flushed down a toilet, disappearing into the blackness of the night. Brett snapped on his own NVGs and then struggled to follow him, every second giving distance between the two of them. He flopped into the hole, wrapped his arms around his chest, and dropped out of the plane.

I began cranking the hatch closed, screaming, "Jumpers away, jumpers away! Pressure, pressure, pressure!"

The air stilled in the plane and I took a seat, exhaling. Shoshana sat next to me and said, "When we get to Israel, can we just land?"

## CHAPTER 66

Knuckles hit the aircraft's slipstream and began to tumble, the wind pulling him behind the plane as he fell. It wasn't a surprise. He expected the turbulence, knowing it was going to happen, and rode it out until he was in clean air, the aircraft disappearing in the distance. On his back falling to earth, he threw out his arms and legs, then twisted until he was flat and stable, facing the ground.

It didn't feel like falling. There was no sense of gravity, like he'd jumped off a high diving board or a cliff. Honestly, it felt more like standing up in the bed of a pickup truck speeding down the road, the wind trying to knock him over.

He gained control of his body, his hands and legs now acting like little stabilizers, each flick of his palm working unconsciously, just knowing what to do, like a person riding a bike, the shifting of weight without conscious thought coming naturally from many previous rides.

He glanced at his altimeter, saw he was passing through fifteen thousand feet, and rotated, doing a circle in the air looking for Brett. He saw nothing in the darkness, but that also wasn't unexpected. He glanced at his altimeter again, saw he was passing through ten thousand feet, and reached for the ball at the base of his parachute container. He pulled it out, felt the satisfying, lifesaving blossom of his canopy, and he was suddenly in a quiet place, the wind gone, the adrenaline retreating.

He pulled down the handles to his risers, took a look at the GPS on his waist, and turned the canopy, aiming toward the location it highlighted.

In that moment, Knuckles felt free. Floating to earth, high above the land, he was doing what he loved. He lowered his night vision goggles over his eyes and scanned the horizon for Brett, knowing he could be up to a mile away. He saw a blip in the distance, a blinking on and off. He raised his NVGs, and the blip of light was gone, telling him it was infrared.

He pulled the NVGs down again, and definitely saw the light. It was Brett, but he was a long way off. He didn't think that would be a problem, simply happy his teammate was under canopy. Brett would do the same thing he was—flying to the grid on the GPS. They'd eventually link up, either in the air or on the ground.

He passed through five thousand feet, still steering the parachute toward the grid on his waist, and felt the speed of his parachute pick up. The Javelin wasn't something he'd typically want on an infiltration of this type because it was built for sport jumping, with an aspect ratio that required skill to land, something made more complicated in a night landing.

The parachute itself had a forward thrust of nearly thirty miles an hour in zero wind. Meaning if he did nothing at all, he'd hit the ground as fast as if he'd jumped out of a car doing that same speed.

Flying with the wind would exponentially increase his velocity. If he wasn't careful, he'd slam into the earth at sixty miles an hour. He could, of course, control that speed right before he touched down, and if he did it right, facing the wind to counteract the forward thrust and stalling the chute, he'd touch down like a feather. The problem was he had no idea how the winds were flowing at ground level, and didn't even know what the ground looked like.

Controlled correctly, the parachute could land on a dime, but at night, flying blind, with no idea which way the wind was blowing, it was decidedly dangerous. The Javelin worked well in daylight, when one was landing on a football field full of cheering fans, but at night, with uneven terrain, it was dangerous as hell. The only good thing was that the aspect ratio of the parachute was one of the best in the world. For every foot he went down, he would go three feet forward, getting closer to the target.

He reached four thousand feet, the usual opening altitude for a HALO jump, and could dimly see the ground below him in his NVGs. He continued forward, letting the canopy fly, wanting to get as close as possible to the grid on the GPS.

He reached two thousand feet and began searching the ground for a landing spot. There were no lights at all, the earth completely dark. He passed one thousand, still letting the canopy do its work. At five hundred feet, he slowed the canopy down, trying to judge the wind.

He felt nothing. He continued to fly, still holding at half speed, and abruptly saw the ground directly beneath him, a hill rising up out of nowhere.

He had a split-second decision of lifting his legs and trying to clear the hilltop at speed, or jerking his risers down and stalling the parachute.

He opted for the latter, having no idea what was beyond the rise of earth. He slammed his handles down, tucked his legs for a landing fall, and met the hill. The parachute slowed, but not nearly enough for a championship landing on a football field. He slammed into the earth, his body pounding into the side of the hill.

He flipped over, landing on his back with the parachute settling behind him. He sat up, took stock of his body, and saw he was okay. The parachute caught the wind, billowing out behind him and trying to jerk him backward. He pulled his cutaway pillow, releasing it to blow away down the hill.

He stood up, checked the grid to the location of the sat phone, and saw it was about ten kilometers away.

He thought, *Great spot on that one, Pike.*

He pulled off the parachute harness, released his MCX rifle, and shouldered his pack, starting to move to the GPS location, his night vision goggles still over his eyes.

He crested the hill and kept walking, moving slowly, looking left and right for any threat that might appear. He had no idea about any Russian, regime, or Hezbollah patrols, and didn't want to be surprised. He went down and up one draw after another, resting at the top of each one to see if anyone was close. An hour later, he crested another hill, seeing the land flatten out ahead of him. And also saw movement.

He crouched down, brought up his weapon, and waited. The person was walking across from him, following the small ridgeline of the wadi, and if he continued to do so, he would pass right in front of Knuckles. Through his NVGs, Knuckles drew a bead on the body, seeing a rifle in the man's hands. And knew who it was.

He let the body come closer and then said, "Flash."

The man dropped to the ground, rotating his weapon toward the noise, but did not fire. He said, "Thunder."

Knuckles stood up and said, "That was the most fucked-up parachute insertion I've ever been on. Did you see our spot? We're miles away."

Brett came up to him and said, "I'm going to kick Pike's ass for this. How do you let us jump out of a plane with no drop zone, and no way to get out after the mission?"

Knuckles chuckled and said, "He'll get us out. If there's anything Pike believes in, it's his family. And that's us."

Brett said, "So what now?"

Knuckles looked at his GPS and said, "Looks like seven klicks that way, but we're closing in on dawn. We need to get there before first light."

Brett looked at the terrain around them and said, "That's going to be hard to do."

## CHAPTER 67

The rising sun began cresting the mountains to the east, the long shadows finally disappearing from the Syrian desert plain. Raphael struggled with the nose of the first drone while Leonardo lifted the tail section into the back of the pickup truck.

They'd positioned the launch platform in the bed of the truck before the sun hit them, then had taken a break, eating breakfast. In the small building adjacent to the drone storage area, Raphael had pulled the hood off Tariq's head, saying, "Time to eat."

Tariq was understandably scared, but he ate what Raphael cooked on a hot plate, scarfing down the food. He said, "What are you going to do?"

"The same thing Hezbollah wanted. Afterward, I'm going to need you to guide us out of the valley and back into Lebanon."

"When will that be?"

Raphael looked at his watch and said, "About three hours from now."

"What are you going to do? What crazy thing do you have planned?"

Leonardo said, "Not your concern."

Raphael wiped his mouth with a napkin and said, "Put the hood back on."

Tariq did so, and Raphael cinched his ankles and wrists with zip ties, saying, "We have to go to work; if you try to escape, you'll die. Understand?"

Tariq had nodded, the hood jerking up and down.

Raphael had backed the truck up to the drone shed, then he and Leonardo had manhandled one of the drones onto the rack in the bed. Once it was settled in place, Raphael said, "Put in the grid to the building here. All we want to see is if they work."

"We'll be wasting one of the drones."

"We have four. Two will be plenty, and if we don't know they work, we can't be sure they'll accomplish the mission."

Leonardo jogged to the front door of the building they'd slept in, retrieved a grid from his GPS, then scrambled back into the bed, loading the grid reference into the computer of the drone, including a single waypoint to the east. If the machine worked, it would fly to the waypoint, then turn around and fly home.

Leonardo said, "It's loaded. Should I start the motor now?"

The Samad 3 drone had a push-piston engine, with the propeller located at the back of the tail, and Leonardo wasn't sure when to engage it. Raphael said, "Let me get the truck going, then fire it up."

Leonardo nodded and sat in the back, scrunched by the rack next to the tail, the wings extending out over the bed of the pickup, the nose above the cab. Raphael got behind the wheel, started the truck up, and drove out of the compound. He leaned out the window and said, "I'm going to get it to thirty miles an hour. Start the engine as soon as I gain some speed. I'll stick my hand out when to release."

Leonardo nodded and said, "What if this doesn't work?"

"We load another one until we figure it out. It can't be that hard. Those savages in Yemen are blowing up Saudi Arabian oil refineries with these things."

He pulled his head back inside the cab and bounced along the rock-strewn terrain, then entered the rutted road. He glanced back at Leonardo, got a thumbs-up, and goosed the engine. Leonardo pressed the ignition for the drone and the two-foot wooden propeller began spinning, barely clearing the bed of the pickup in the rack and threatening to chop off Leonardo's arm. The vehicle gained speed, the air beginning to rush over the wings, providing lift for the aircraft in the back of the truck.

Leonardo grabbed the release rope beneath the rack and waited, squinting his eyes against the dust and avoiding the propeller. He saw Raphael stick his hand out the window and jerked the cord, releasing the drone. It raced off the rack, floating above the cab of the truck, and began climbing higher and higher, the propeller pushing it forward with greater and greater speed. Raphael stopped the truck and soon enough, the drone was lost from sight.

They sat, the engine of the truck ticking. Leonardo said, "The waypoint is like two minutes out. It should be back in four minutes."

They waited, hoping it would work. At three minutes, Leonardo pointed and said, "There it is."

The drone came screaming back at them, now at full speed of one hundred and twenty miles an hour, coming lower and lower until it went over the top of the vehicle. They both ducked, watching it slam into the front of the building, right on target, shattering the walls from the impact.

Leonardo said, "Looks like it works. Hope it didn't kill Tariq."

Raphael laughed and said, "Let's get the next one loaded, only this time with the explosive payload. Garrett should be calling soon."

Driving the up-armored SUV, Garrett heard the Grand Master from the rear say, "Garrett, if you don't mind, can you pull into a convenience store for a spot of coffee?"

Garrett looked in the rearview mirror and said, "Yes, sir, as soon as one appears, but this road doesn't look very conducive to finding one."

Garrett had found out the night before that the grand speech by the Israeli prime minister was going to happen at nine in the morning, which had required them to wake up before the sun had even risen. It was only a little more than an hour's drive to Megiddo from Tel Aviv, but with the security protocols in place, they would have to arrive at least two hours early.

Garrett had assumed that the various organizations who had traveled here would all convoy together, but that wasn't the case. The U.S. State Department was coming from the new embassy in Jerusalem, and the other church groups were all staying near the Old City, wanting to get in a bit of biblical tourism while they were here. That left the Knights of Malta entourage on its own, with nothing more than a location and a time to arrive. The Grand Master had been a little miffed at the arrangements, having expected an escort or other official trappings.

Having not done any driving in Israel, and not wanting to be late, Garrett had insisted they be on the road by 0530—much earlier than needed, but if anything happened en route, it gave him plenty of time to flex his mission.

He'd called Raphael before getting on the road, telling him the schedule for the event, then had gone to Michelangelo's room, banging on the door until he woke up.

Bleary eyed, Garrett saw that he'd been out again last night. He'd said, "The Jerusalem trip? How did that go?"

"Okay. There are eleven gates to get to the Temple Mount, but only one for infidels like us."

"And the other gates? Will that Palestinian ID card work to get you through them?"

While operating in Syria, they'd come across multiple Palestinian refugees who'd given up their dismal life in the camps of Lebanon, Gaza, or the West Bank and had picked up a gun for the pay from various militias. The men had no pass-port to travel anywhere in the civilized world, but there wasn't any immigration control for the militias in Syria. The only thing they owned was identification issued by the Palestinian Authority and Israel. Several of them had crossed Garrett and the Turtles, seeking to harm the Knights' work in Syria. After they'd died, Garrett had saved the cards. He'd then manipulated one for Michelangelo, the only man they had who could pass as a Palestinian.

"Yes. All I need is proof that I'm a Muslim, and I can use it, but believe it or not, there are multiple different types of Palestinian identifica-tion cards. We lucked out. I had to get a certif-icate to enter, proving I was a Muslim, and the identification worked fine, but only because the man we killed was from Jerusalem. If we'd have used a different one, from someone in the West Bank or Gaza, I would have been questioned about how I was even on Israeli terrain."

Garrett nodded, once again realizing how many single points of failure there were in this mission. In the past, his motto had been, "Two is one, one is none," and this near miss was exactly why. He said, "You have the certificate now?"

"Yeah, they all went to the Wailing Wall to shove a note in, and I went to get my certificate. I'm set for tomorrow. I'm going through the Gate of the Tribes inside the Muslim quarter."

"And the security?"

"It's tight. I mean really tight. Metal detectors and X-ray machines at every entrance, security guards wandering around. They don't want any trouble."

"So how will you do this?"

"The guards are there to prevent a clash from the Muslim people praying and the Jewish and Christian visitors. People like us aren't allowed to pray. We're only allowed to visit. In fact, we can't even get into the Al Aqsa Mosque or the Dome of the Rock. But the certificate beats that because they'll think I'm a Muslim."

"And the metal detectors and X-ray machines? How will you get in the charges?"

"They're built into soda cans. It looks like a six-pack of soda. Muslims are allowed to bring all sorts of things into the compound, and they have picnics there all the time. I've packed my bag to look like a picnic. Six-pack of soda, sandwiches, blanket, chips. It'll work. I promise. The only thing that will stop me is that sometimes the Israeli security perimeter only lets in men above a certain age. Guys that won't start throwing rocks. I don't know the cutoff, but think it's forty-five years old or so. If that's the case, I'm done."

"We can only do what we can do. I have to meet the Grand Master downstairs in a few minutes. We're heading to Megiddo."

"What about Raphael and Leonardo?"

"They're set. They have the weapons. It's coming soon. You don't need to do anything unless I call. Get to Jerusalem in the next hour, and keep your Zello app open. I'll either tell you to attack, or tell you to fly back to Rome to get out of the blast radius of the war. If it's to attack, do so, then meet me here, back in Tel Aviv. Either way, we're flying out of here today."

After that, Garrett had gone down to the lobby, met the Knights' leadership, and then retrieved their SUV. Finding an armored vehicle for rent had been a chore, but not nearly as hard as it would have been in the United States. It was exorbitantly expensive, but gave the Grand Master the flair he always strived to achieve, since he was missing his Israeli pageantry of an escort.

Now driving to Megiddo, he was being asked to stop for a cappuccino in the heart of the Israeli desert on a two-lane road that was much like a highway in Arizona—which is to say, there wasn't going to be a gas station anytime soon.

At seven forty-five in the morning, I heard my computer ding, the Taskforce Inmarsat phone hooked to it, and raced over, seeing a message from Knuckles. *In position. Two men so far, but can't judge total force.*

I typed, *Call me now.*

The Inmarsat buzzed, and I routed it through the computer, Jennifer strolling out of the bathroom wearing a robe, her head in a towel. She said, "What's going on?"

"They found the possible target."

I clicked the "accept" button and said, "This is Pike. Go ahead."

"We've got two men at a compound loading what looks like a drone on the back of a pickup truck, and I don't think it's the first one. Either they're mentally deficient at operating them, or the drones aren't working, because the front of the building is caved in and I can see the wreckage of another drone."

"What kind of drone? Like a quadcopter?"

"No, like a mini-predator. Looks to be about twenty feet long with a wingspan of about fifteen.

They're mounting it in the back of a pickup truck."

"Send me a picture."

"Stand by."

The computer dinged and I pulled it up, seeing what looked like a miniature airplane with a push propeller in the back, but it was not anything I recognized. I said, "Got it." I glanced at Jennifer, saying, "Sending it to the Taskforce now."

She slid behind the computer in her robe and began typing a message.

I said, "So what are we looking at? Is this them?"

"Pike, I don't honestly know. The grid from the NSA intercept is here, but I don't see any Hezbollah-looking dudes. Just these two, and interdicting them is going to be very hard. We're in an overwatch position about three hundred meters away, and getting to them without being seen is asking for an ass kicking. We're in the hills, but they're in flat terrain with zero cover. I can wait until they're done and they return to the compound, but attacking them out in the open here isn't ideal."

"Do you think they're the Turtles?"

"Could be. They're not Arab, if that's what you mean, but they could also be Chechens working for Hezbollah. I don't know. What did you get from Shoshana and Aaron?"

Both of our Israelis had left at the crack of dawn to go meet their Mossad contact somewhere. We weren't read on to the meeting, and I had no idea when they'd return. I said, "Nothing yet. They're doing their top-secret meeting, but haven't come back. I don't know what they're going to find out."

Jennifer waved at me and I said, "Hang on."

I looked at the screen, reading off a Taskforce report. I said, "The UAV is a Samad Three, built in Iran and used primarily by the Houthis to attack Saudi Arabia, but it's also been passed to Hezbollah. It's basically a suicide drone. A slow-flying cruise missile. You're definitely looking at Iranian armament, and if those guys are loading it up, it means they're going to use it for an attack."

"What do you want me to do?"

"I don't want you to endanger yourself, but don't let them launch."

He laughed and said, "Wow. So endanger myself, or let them launch?"

I didn't say anything for a second, and he came back, saying, "Brett thinks he's found a way. They're loading it on the back of that truck for a reason, which means they're going to drive it for a launch platform. There's only one road going in and out of this place. We can position for an ambush along the road about a hundred meters from the compound. We won't have to do a frontal assault."

I said, "Perfect."

He said, "Maybe. Maybe not. If we're wrong, the drone is on the way."

I heard a knock on my door, Jennifer opened it, and I saw our Israelis. I said, "Execute that plan. Carrie just came back. Let me see what I can find out and I'll call you back if something changes."

Knuckles said, "Roger that. Any word on exfil?"

I looked at Aaron and pointed at a chair, saying into the Inmarsat, "Yes, Wolffe has the message. He's working it."

He said, "Small comforts. We do a shoot-out here, and we're going to be on the run."

"I know. Worst case, head to the UN buffer group along the Golan Heights."

He laughed and said, "That would *definitely* be the worst case. Call me when you figure something out. I'd rather sneak out of here because the Israelis have solved the problem than run out of here like Butch Cassidy and the Sundance Kid with the entire Bolivian army on my ass."

I said, "You got it. Hang in there."

I disconnected and said, "Well, what did you guys figure out?"

"They're here, and the serial killer is with them. We matched all the pictures from immigration and his name is Garrett. He's acting as their head of security. We have identification for most of the diplomatic group, except for one guy. Garrett and the rest are driving to Megiddo—they left early this morning—but one named Michelangelo is not. He arrived with them, but isn't listed as attending the speech. We don't know where he is."

"Okay, so they're calling off the speech?"

"Unfortunately, no." She saw the look on my face and held up her hands, saying, "We have elections coming up, and the prime minister isn't going to miss this opportunity. There are delegations from four countries, to include the United States. Do you think he's going to call off this event in our own country? In effect, say he can't protect them in our own land? He'll look like a coward."

Incredulous, I said, "You guys realize the best case is he just ends up dead. Worst case he gets his entire country in a war with Iran."

Shoshana said, "Pike, trust me, I get it, but it's out of our hands. The prime minister is surrounded by Shin Bet. This Garrett guy can't do anything to harm him. He's one man."

## CHAPTER 69

G arrett finally saw the turnoff for the Megiddo national monument, having stopped some twenty minutes before at a coffee shop just off the Iron Interchange, a spaghetti-like mess of roads where four highways converged. He left Highway 6, joined Highway 65 to the east, and saw a truck stop advertising a coffee shop. He pulled into the parking lot, reminding the men they were on a time schedule.

The Knights' entourage took another twenty minutes at the stop milling about, deciding on what to purchase and talking to the locals gathered there. He knew the Grand Master enjoyed such settings, but felt the press of time.

Eventually, they'd returned to the highway, and twenty minutes later, Garrett found the turn for the monument. It was another ten minutes down a small blacktop before he saw the parking area.

Pulling into the tourist compound, he saw a security checkpoint and a modern building at the back, the Megiddo hill and excavation rising behind it.

He stopped at the checkpoint, noticing that

the entire car park had been closed to the public. He rolled down the window, and passed across the diplomatic passports of the Knights in the vehicle. The names were checked off a list and he was waved forward, a police officer showing him where to park. He did so, then exited, saying, "I'm the head of security for this group. Is there a way I can take a look at the setup before we begin?"

The uniformed Israeli passed him off to a man wearing a suit, who said, "I'm with the security team for the prime minister"—meaning Shin Bet—"what can I help you with?"

"I just want to see the setup. I'm the security man for this group."

He sized up Garrett for a moment, then said, "That's not necessary. We control the entire venue."

Garrett smiled and said, "I'm sure you're correct, but I *do* get paid for this. All I want is a walk-through."

The agent considered for a moment, then said, "Tell your group to head into the visitors' center for their security passes."

Garrett leaned into the vehicle and relayed the instructions, then stood up. The agent said, "Do you have any weapons?"

Garrett raised his arms and said, "No firearms, but I do have a knife. Other than that, just an iPhone, a Thuraya sat phone, and a GPS."

He said, "Leave the knife in the vehicle."

Garrett did so, placing a folding blade on the driver's seat, then turned back around. The man said, "Raise your arms, please."

Garrett did so, and the agent gave him a pat-down, then said, "Follow me."

He led Garrett past the visitors' center to the hill that housed the remnants of Megiddo.

An ancient city built on a hill that protected the Aruna pass through the Carmel Mountains, it had been inhabited thousands of years before Christ was born, with more than twenty-six civilizations having been uncovered—the earliest from 7000 BC. The hill had become a layer cake of archeological digging, with one conquest after another taking the city and then leaving their mark on the earth. It was reputed to house the stables of King Solomon, and was said to be the most fought-over piece of terrain in the history of human conflict—but Garrett only cared about the final one prophesied by the Bible. The one he planned to engender today.

They climbed the steps to the archeological digs, past the museum and visitors' center, until Garrett saw a shaded overhang with a podium, in front of it several stands of temporary metal stadium seating, also shaded. He said, "Is that where the speech will be given?"

"Yes."

"May I go look?"

Aggravated, the agent said, "All of this has been cleared before we even arrived. After that, it was cleared again personally by my detail."

"Please, humor me. I have to report back to a boss just like you."

The man grimaced, but said, "Follow me."

They went to the stands and Garrett pretended to look at the structures, as if he were searching for potential threats. He went to the podium and pretended to examine underneath it, but in reality pinpointed the actual grid in his GPS.

He stood up, looked around in a 360-degree circle, and said, "I guess there won't be any snipers. This is the highest point around."

The agent scoffed and said, "You Americans. Always with the conspiracy theories. Do you think this is the first speech the prime minister has given? We protect him each time."

"What about a rocket attack? This is sort of open ground, and it's an easy location to find even if you're just using Google Earth."

"We have the Iron Dome. It's ninety percent effective against missiles from Gaza or Lebanon— and those missiles aren't even accurate enough to hit this place. More than likely, if they tried, and the Iron Dome didn't kill the missiles outright, they'd land ten kilometers away."

They started walking back down the stairs, Garrett saying, "But all it would take is one lucky shot."

"Yes, if either Hamas or Hezbollah were dumb enough to try. If that happened, they would be wiped from the earth."

Garrett thought, *One can hope.*

Reaching the visitors' center, Garrett shook the agent's hand, saying, "Thank you for your patience."

The agent said, "Enjoy the show," then walked away.

Garrett chuckled, realizing he had no idea how true his words would be.

He went back to the SUV and called Raphael on the sat phone. When he answered, Garrett said, "I have the grid. Prepare to copy."

He relayed it, then said, "We're within the hour. Are you ready?"

"Yes. We've done one test. We're ready."

"Okay. Stand by. I'll call when the audience enters the stands. Is the weapon set with a proximity fuse?"

"Yes. It'll close in to about twenty meters of the grid then explode, throwing out ball bearings as it continues forward. The death radius should be thirty meters or greater."

"Perfect. I'll need to contact you before he takes the stage because of the flight time. I have no idea how long his speech is going to be. Stand by."

He disconnected and saw a caravan of cars enter the parking lot, the middle one flying the flags of Israel on the bumpers. He knew who it was, and felt his adrenaline rise.

They parked, the security men spilling out, searching for a threat, and then the primary phalanx of men entered the museum/visitors' center. He followed behind, entering the building to find a buffet of food and all present enraptured by the presence of the prime minister of Israel.

He sought out the Grand Master and said, "I've checked the area, and it's secure. I'm going to hang back at the SUV, letting the Shin Bet handle the security."

Chaucer said, "Thank you. I think that would be best. Now if you'll excuse me, I would like to talk to the prime minister."

Garrett went back to the SUV, hoping the

grin and grip wouldn't take too long. He opened the door, sat behind the wheel, and turned on the ignition, engaging the air-conditioning, waiting. Eventually, he saw the mass of people exit the visitors' center and head up the same stairs he had earlier. He waited until they were at the top, lost from view, and pulled out the Thuraya, dialing Raphael.

The phone connected, and he said, "Forty-minute flight? Is that right?"

"Yes. From our calculations, that's how long it's going to take to reach your location. We had to program some waypoints in to fly around the Golan Heights. It'll be coming in from the West Bank."

"Launch it now. Call me as soon as it's in the air."

He hung up, then played with the radio, trying to find a station that actually spoke English, but failed. He waited seven minutes, growing more concerned with each passing second. He looked at his phone, willing it to ring. He didn't want to initiate a call and possibly interrupt the launch. Maybe they just had a small problem and were working to resolve it. He knew from his past Special Forces experience that a headquarters interrupting a mission because of a simple lack of contact was the last thing he should do.

*Trust the man on the ground.*

He waited another five minutes, and couldn't contain himself. He dialed the phone. He heard, "Hello?"

"Raphael? What's the holdup? Is it on the way?"

"This isn't Raphael. He can't talk right now because he took a bullet through the head. Who's this?"

Garrett disconnected the phone, incredulous. He sat for eight minutes, contemplating his options, somewhat in shock. The voice on the phone was distinctly American. Somehow, the United States had managed to locate his men *inside Syria*. It was unfathomable. He'd conducted plenty of counterterrorist operations in U.S. Special Forces, and they were lucky to find the man they were looking for one out of ten times, with the entire intelligence apparatus of the United States on their side. And these men had found his like a laser beam.

*How? How had they done that?*

Breathing heavily, his anger building, he glanced out the window to a car approaching the security checkpoint. It prevented the vehicle from entering, and a man leaned out, clearly arguing with the uniformed officer. The passenger door opened and a woman stood on the footwell, shouting over the cab of the vehicle.

And he recognized who they were. The predators from Rome. They'd found him here, in Israel.

He snarled, put the SUV in gear, and began racing across the parking lot.

## CHAPTER 70

Knuckles slithered through the folds of the earth, scraping across the rocks and following behind Brett in a low crawl, his head in the earth, his weapon dragging behind him. He saw Brett stop moving and waited. Brett turned and pointed to the top of a hillock, then inched his way up. He reached the crest, glanced over, then pushed himself back down.

He whispered, "This is the best spot. The road comes in at an angle, then veers away at this point. The shot will be less than seventy meters."

"Can they see us? Do we have defilade?"

"Not really, but the scrub growth up top will give us concealment. They won't see us until we start shooting."

"Did you get eyes on them?"

"Yeah. They're loaded and ready to go."

Knuckles crawled up the side of the hill himself, slowly moved to the crest between the scrub brush, and used the scope on his weapon to survey. He saw a truck about two hundred meters away, a man in the cab, waiting. Another man was in the bed of the pickup, crammed in between the steel of the truck and the rack holding the UAV.

In his hand was a rope. Knuckles surveyed the road and saw Brett was correct, this was the best place to engage.

He glanced back down to Brett and whispered, "Come on up. Get ready."

Brett slithered up next to him and pulled his rifle forward. Knuckles dialed the scope to its highest magnification of six-power and scanned the road to their location. He said, "I'll take the cab. You take the man in the back. Roger?"

Already in the prone, building a firing position, Brett said, "Roger."

Knuckles saw the man in the cab talking on a satellite phone, then holler at the man in the back. The man in the bed pulled out a GPS, loaded something in it, then connected the GPS to the UAV.

Knuckles said, "They're prepping. Get ready."

Brett said, "I'm on it."

"Wait until you can call your shot. We don't take them out quickly, and they'll be by us and gone."

The truck started moving down the road, coming closer and closer. It gained speed until it was doing nearly thirty miles an hour. The man in the cab held his hand out the window, and Knuckles shouted, "That's it! Start shooting."

He broke the trigger, the first round penetrating the windshield, followed by three more. The truck veered off the road, and he knew he'd struck the driver. He went to the bed, saw the man hit by Brett's rounds, but he was still moving. He fired as well, and the man jerked upright, then tumbled out of the bed, the rope wrapped around his arm.

The drone released, launching into the air. They watched it fly over their heads and disappear. The truck kept going, slamming into the hill they were on, coming up the slope before the angle became too much. It tumbled back down, flipping over and over, finally stopping on its side.

Knuckles said, "On the truck. Let's go."

They raced down the side of the hill, slipping in the loose gravel, their weapons at the ready. They reached the truck and Knuckles said, "Check the guy who fell out."

Brett ran to the body, his weapon leading the way. Knuckles circled the cab, aiming through the spiderwebbed windshield. He saw a body in the cab, eyes open, the skull with a split in it creating a trench through the forehead. He heard a ringing on the floorboard and saw a Thuraya satellite phone. He reached through the broken glass and pulled it out. He glanced back to Brett and saw him running back to the truck with a GPS in his hand.

He answered the phone and heard, "Raphael? What's the holdup? Is it on the way?"

Brett reached him and he held up a finger, saying, "This isn't Raphael. He can't talk right now because he took a bullet through the head. Who's this?"

The phone disconnected. Knuckles said, "Guess he didn't want to talk. What do you have?"

"I've got the GPS with the grid to the terminal point for the UAV."

Knuckles pulled out his Inmarsat phone, dialing it and saying, "What is it?"

"I don't know the exact location by reference.

Only by the grid numbers. This GPS's map isn't that good, but it's in Israel, and the closest thing on this graphic is the Megiddo National Forest."

The phone connected and Knuckles said, "We took out the targets, but they managed to get the UAV in the air. It's on the way, and it's headed to Megiddo."

Pike said, "Shit. That's not good. We're driving there right now, about ten minutes out. How much time do we have?"

"Just a guess, but I'd say thirty or forty minutes. I go with thirty."

"Send me the grid to be sure, and the exact time of launch."

"Will do. I've also got a Thuraya number from someone who called asking about the status of the drone."

"Someone called the men there?"

"Yep. I answered, and he didn't want to talk to me."

"Send that as well. What's your status right now?"

"There are two other UAVs in the shed and a Toyota Land Cruiser. I figured I'd blow them up, then start hauling ass in the Toyota. I don't suppose you have a direction we should go yet?"

"Not yet. Sorry. I'm going to have my hands full for a little bit. Besides that flying bomb, we have one other Turtle on the loose and no idea what he's trying to do."

"Yeah. I figured that's what I would hear."

"I gotta go, sorry. I need this phone."

Knuckles said, "See you at the wedding. Maybe."

He lowered the phone and Brett said, "Let me guess—we're on our own."

"At least for a little while. Let's check out that building."

They approached at an angle, using whatever cover they could find, entering through the wreckage the drone had caused. It was a simple three-room structure, the main room destroyed by the UAV.

They silently went forward to the room on the right, clearing it rapidly and finding three dead men, all apparently killed somewhere else and dragged here, judging by the scuff marks and blood trails.

Brett whispered, "My bet is we found our Hezbollah dudes."

Knuckles nodded and went to the next door, waiting on Brett to get his muzzle on it. Knuckles swung it open, Brett entered, and Knuckles flowed in behind him, Brett taking the right side, Knuckles the left.

He saw another body on the ground, this one with a hood on. He went to it and checked for a pulse. As soon as he touched the neck, the body began thrashing about and screaming. Knuckles saw he was hog-tied and said, "Calm down. Calm down."

The man did and Knuckles pulled off the hood, seeing an older Arabic gentleman. He said, "Who might you be?"

"I've been kidnapped. Two men kidnapped me from Lebanon and brought me here."

"You're from Lebanon?"

"Yes. They killed my driver."

"Your name?"

"Tariq."

Knuckles laughed and said, "As in Tariq the smuggler for Hezbollah? That Tariq?"

The man cowered back, wondering if he had gone from the frying pan into the fire. Knuckles said, "You came from Lebanon to here? In that Land Cruiser? And can get back to Lebanon the same way?"

He slowly nodded. Knuckles bent down and cut the binds on his wrists and ankles, saying, "Well, Tariq, we might just want to hire you for your services."

## CHAPTER 71

I hung up the phone, turned to Shoshana, and said, "You've got to get those people out of the speech. I get it's important for the government, but they weren't able to stop the drone."

"How do they know it's headed here?"

"They have a rough location. It's coming somewhere around here."

She didn't look convinced. I turned on my sarcastic voice and said, "Now, it could be headed to the city twelve miles away, or it could be going to blow up some hikers in the national forest, but we both know that's not the plan. It's coming *here* and we have less than thirty minutes to stop it. Get on the phone to your top-secret Mossad contact and get this event canceled."

She picked up the phone, saying, "I'll try, but I don't have contacts with Shin Bet. All I can do is call my contact in the Mossad, and I'm just a contractor. It's not like I have a direct line to the prime minister."

I said, "You'd better get something moving, because in twenty minutes there's going to be a freight train full of explosives and ball bearings hitting this place."

She dialed, got a beep, and said, "No cell service."

I pointed to the Inmarsat on the seat and said, "Use the sat phone. Get someone."

She picked it up and while she dialed, I thought through the problem set, saying, "What about the Iron Dome you guys always brag about? When it crosses into Israeli territory, it'll get shot down, right?"

"No. That system is made for high-altitude rockets, not UAVs flying close to the earth."

"But you guys have something to pick up incursions, right? I mean, surely you've seen the Houthi success in Saudi Arabia with these things and thought about it here, right?"

"Truthfully, no we don't. Not an automated system like the Iron Dome. We're still trying to figure that out, but if it crosses the Golan Heights, there will be an alert, and someone will scramble. If it's programmed to fly around the Golan, that will be a problem. If they were smart, they'd cross to the south, through Jordanian airspace, then enter through the West Bank. We don't have nearly the air defense architecture there. It'll be inside Israel and coming from south to north instead of from a threat country. But we do have alert aircraft."

I said, "You guys are worse than we are at this shit. You need to get those alert birds in the air."

She held up a finger and started talking: "Sir, this is Shoshana. Garrett, the guy we talked about at our meeting, is no longer the individual threat.

He's managed to infiltrate some of his people into Syria and has launched a Hezbollah Samad Three drone. I don't think he ever intended to conduct an overt operation on his own. He's just terminal guidance for the weapon system. He's no longer the threat, and Shin Bet can't protect the prime minister simply by keeping an eye on him. We need to tell them about the danger, and we need to stop the UAV."

She listened for a second, then said, "How do *I* know? I know because I know!"

The phone spat out an argument that even I heard, something about regretting hiring her and how she was causing problems. I saw her face darken, and she said, "Listen to me, you shit, there is a missile headed to Megiddo, and it's going to evade our systems. When it hits, it's going to kill members of the Vatican, thirteen different evangelical churches from the United States, the U.S. State Department delegation, and our own prime minister! Get off your ass and find that thing, or we're going into a war that will wipe out our country."

Shocked at her vehemence, I almost missed the exit to the Megiddo national monument. I swerved at the last minute, taking the road and looking at her. She listened for a little more and said, "Sir, I apologize. Just find the UAV. It's small, but a lot bigger than what we usually see. It'll probably be coming from the West Bank." The other end said something, and she said, "We're there now. I'll get the Shin Bet to evacuate."

She hung up, then looked at me, saying, "I don't think I'm going to get hired by them again."

464 / BRAD TAYLOR

I said, "What happened?"

"They don't believe me, but they believe enough to not be the ones holding the bag if they're wrong. They're launching alert fighters from multiple bases. They'll find the drone, but I don't know if they'll kill it."

"Why?"

"Too many layers. Too many people in the chain of command. I mean, if the CIA called an air base in the United States to find a threat, you'd get a response, but you wouldn't get cooperation. You'd have a bunch of people launching fighters in the air to protect their asses on the ground. The pilots wouldn't know why they were in the air, but the men on the ground would be protected because they issued the order."

"Great. You *are* as dysfunctional as we are."

She smiled and said, "We aren't dysfunctional. You and me. It's why we're here, right now."

And I realized she was right. The dysfunction she was talking about was the reason the Task-force was created. It was the reason Knuckles and Brett had eliminated the threat in Syria, and the result of that mission was why she'd made the call.

"So what now?"

"We get to tell the Shin Bet to call off the speech." She grimaced, hating her role. She wanted to be the killer, not the diplomat, and I understood that. She said, "This should be great fun."

I turned to the road leading to the Megiddo

monument and looked at the time, saying, "If it was a straight line, we're too late. It's going to hit in seconds."

We entered the small road to the parking area, and I saw a security checkpoint. I said, "What do we do with that?"

"Just go forward."


Avril Sharon buckled the oxygen mask to his helmet, closed the canopy to his F-16 Fighting Falcon, gave a thumbs-up to the ground crew, and taxied to the runway. He received clearance for takeoff and thundered into the sky, believing it was just one more chase against phantom ghosts stalking Israel.

He attained cruising altitude and saw his wingman appear to his left. He said, "Here we go again. Probably chasing a damn balloon."

His wingman laughed through the radio and said, "Yeah, if these guys keep this up, they'll win by bankrupting us with a million alerts."

They circled around, heading toward the Golan Heights, Avril saying, "Never chased a phantom out of the West Bank, though. What do you suppose that's about?"

"No idea. Let's just clean our sector and go home."

They crossed into the West Bank, came within spitting distance of the border with Jordan, and banked away, not wanting to cause an international incident. Avril scanned the area and said, "I see nothing. You?"

His wingman didn't respond. He called again, "Do you see anything?"

"Nine o'clock low. Nine o'clock low. Looks like an aircraft flying low and slow."

Avril banked, focused on the area, and saw the target. It *did* look like an aircraft, but it had no canopy. He understood that distance was its own enemy—and that he could be thinking the plane was much farther away simply because of its size. He flew forward, the aircraft eating up the ground, got above it, and said, "That's not an aircraft. It's a UAV."

He called back to his headquarters even as the UAV broke the border between the West Bank and Israel, now twenty miles away from Megiddo. He couldn't be faulted for that. He had no clear idea why he was even up here, and didn't want to be a laughingstock by blowing out of the sky an Israeli UAV surveying the West Bank.

"Got a bogey UAV headed north, just broke the border. Is that my target?"

The man on the other end of the radio was just as mystified as he was, the orders that had filtered through their respective commands simply telling them to search and report. He said, "Stand by. Stand by."

Avril tracked the drone, seeing the distinctive white excavations of Megiddo against the green of the hills in the distance. It jerked to the right and lowered altitude, moving into what he recognized as an attack run. He called back, "UAV is lowering altitude. I say again UAV is lowering altitude. Headed to Megiddo hill. Right at Megiddo hill. Is it ours? Is it our UAV?"

The man on the other end said, "Waiting on an answer. Stand by," and Avril thought, *Why on earth would anyone strike an archeological site? That thing has to be Israeli.*

But the UAV *was* lowering into a strike run. Avril called his wingman and said, "You seeing what I'm seeing?"

"I see it, I see it. What's your call?"

Avril said nothing. The UAV was twenty seconds from Megiddo at an altitude of one hundred feet when he flicked the arming switch on his Sidewinder missiles. It reached ten seconds out, flying at more than a hundred miles an hour, and he achieved lock-on, pulling the trigger and whispering, "Please don't be Israeli . . ."

## CHAPTER 72

I rolled into the checkpoint, lowered my window, and the uniformed Israeli said something in Hebrew. I said, "English?"

He said, "How can I help you?"

I said, "This is going to sound crazy, but there's a threat against this place right now. We need you to alert the Shin Bet and get everyone off that hill."

He bristled, and I knew why, but the time was so close I couldn't think of any way to soften the blow. Trying to get past the checkpoint with some social engineering wouldn't stop the drone.

He said, "What do you mean? What threat?"

"There's an unmanned aerial vehicle flying here right now from Syria. It's got a warhead that's going to kill everyone on that hill. You need to evacuate them immediately."

His face went slack in shock. He put his hand on his pistol, like I was the drone, and said, "Sir, what are you talking about? Please step out of the car."

Shoshana opened the passenger door, stood up, and began yelling in Hebrew across the top of the cab. He backed up, drew his weapon, and I said, "Shoshana, that's not helping anything."

She said, "It'll get someone here besides this monkey in a uniform."

I turned to him, and saw his eyes focused on the parking lot, his gun out, now pointed away from me.

I turned and saw an SUV racing straight toward us, like it was going to ram us head-on. I slammed our vehicle in reverse, hit the gas, and spun into the grass on the side of the road, Shoshana barely hanging on. The SUV kept coming. The guard jumped aside and it hammered the wooden drop bar, shattering it, and screamed away. I got a quick glimpse at the driver as he sped by and couldn't believe it.

I looked at Shoshana, wanting to make sure I wasn't projecting. I said, "Did you see the man behind the wheel?"

I had my answer in her expression before she even spoke. She said, "It's the *Ramsad*'s killer."

I put the car in drive and went back to the gate, finding the guard completely confused, shouting in the radio and waving his pistol at me. I saw a platoon of men rushing to us and said, "This isn't going to end well."

Shoshana said, "Let me handle this."

I said, "Do you have some secret Israeli code word for badass to stop the beat-down we're about to get? Because I've been trying to get one for the United States, and have failed to do so."

She smiled, and the men coalesced around our vehicle, with her shouting in Hebrew. They shouted back, and she pointed to the direction the SUV had gone, screaming at them. At that moment, I knew we were done. They didn't believe her, and had no inclination to stop the event on the top of the hill, thinking the threat had just left.

I slapped my hands on the wheel in front of me and the man outside my window waved his pistol about, which did nothing but aggravate the hell out of me.

I said, "Do you hear what she's saying?" I had no idea what Shoshana was shouting, but was pretty sure it was along the lines of, "Get everyone out, or they're going to get killed."

He brought his pistol up, pointing it at my head, and I raised my hands, saying, "We're all about to be dead, you dumb fuck."

At that moment, an enormous explosion split the sky to the south, at the edge of the mountain, loud enough to shake the vehicle. Everyone turned to the noise, seeing a fireball in the air, bits and parts of machinery falling to the ground, and an Israeli F-16 screaming straight up over the top of Mount Megiddo.

I looked at Shoshana and said, "Points given here. You aren't that dysfunctional."

She smiled and said, "Let's go get Garrett. There's still one more on the loose."

I nodded, turned to the man with the weapon at my head, and said, "We no longer want to enter. Sorry for being pushy."

I put the SUV in reverse, and he shouted something. I hit the gas, flying backward at a high rate of speed. I did a J-turn, the front of the vehicle whipping around, and was headed back down the road away from the checkpoint, seeing a lot of men waving their arms in the air behind me.

We reached the main highway and I said, "Which way? North or south?"

Garrett headed north on Highway 4, wanting to put distance between him and the predators, wondering how on earth they'd managed to track him and his team, not only here in Israel, but also in Syria. There had to be something connecting them together, and his eyes fell on the Thuraya phone next to him, the antennae still out and transmitting.

He snarled, pulled over to the side of the road, and threw it in the footwell, crushing it with his boot. Breathing heavily, he went back onto the highway, planning his escape. There was no way he could travel back to Tel Aviv or any other port of entry. He needed to get to Lebanon, and the closest border crossing was at the tip of Israel. There was the Rosh Hanikra crossing, but it was reserved for UN members and official Israeli personnel. He couldn't use that, sure he'd be arrested if he tried, but he knew another way. An old railroad built through a tunnel that once connected the land of Israel with Lebanon, right under that crossing point.

It was now a tourist site, closed to all traffic but visitors, but it was the border. If he could get there, he could get under the wall. If he could cross into Lebanon, he could escape, leaving behind the predators chasing him.

And then he remembered the secondary mission with Michelangelo. Maybe all wasn't lost. Maybe they could still create the final crusade. He pulled out his cell phone, held it up, and saw he had no service. He glanced at the shell of his sat phone and beat the wheel in frustration.

My Inmarsat phone connected with Taskforce headquarters, and I heard the usual statement about Blaisdell Consulting, along with who I'd like to talk with. When using the VPN, I had a direct encrypted video chat to the heart of the Taskforce, but when using the Inmarsat telephone, I did not. It was unencrypted, and prey to a multitude of different penetrations. And so I had to dance around the issue.

I said, "George Wolffe, please."

I heard, "Sir, there's no George Wolffe that works here. You might have the wrong number." The voice was from the same woman who'd worked the cover of the Taskforce since it was created. A sweet old lady named Margaret, she'd given my daughter birthday cards year after year.

Sitting on the side of the road, Shoshana looking at me like I was crazy, I said, "Marge, it's Pike Logan. I understand what you're doing, but I'm in a little bit of an emergency. Please, put him on the line. Skip the subterfuge on this one. Anyone listening will not be worse than the threat I'm trying to stop."

"Sir, I'm sorry, but no one here works by that name."

I thought, *Okay, pull the trigger.* I said, "I have a Prairie Fire emergency. I say again, Prairie Fire."

Prairie Fire was the code name for a team about to be overrun and in dire need of help. It could be called on any channel available—VPN, email, chat, telephone, smoke signals, whatever— and when it came in, the Taskforce stopped everything to refocus.

I knew I was pulling a card I shouldn't, because nobody was in dire trouble—well, I hadn't heard from Knuckles yet—but I figured it was better than nothing.

Margaret said, "Please stand by."

And put me on hold like I was trying to get a cable service outage resolved.

Shoshana said, "He's getting away. Let's just pick a direction."

I said, "Hold on. Five minutes here could save us fifteen if we're wrong."

Wolffe came on the line, saying, "Can you go encrypted?"

"No, sir, I can't, and I need a geolocation of a Thuraya handset right fucking now."

He heard, "Jesus, Pike, don't say that crap on an open line. Can you go secure? You're in the one country that sucks up more data than the old Soviet Union."

"I can't, sir. I'm on a time crunch here, and I don't have cell coverage for the Taskforce phone. I only have this satellite phone, and I also don't have patience for the bullshit. If it comes out in a leak, at least it'll be because we *can* still leak shit.

We just stopped the UAV suicide attack from the Hezbollah drone here, but there's one more Turtle on the loose, and we don't know where he is."

I heard nothing for a second, then, "You stopped the attack?"

"Yeah, I did. Well, with the help of the IDF Air Force. But there's another guy on the loose, and we don't know what he's got planned. It could be a culmination point."

Wolffe said, "Maybe, maybe not. Your contact worked out. We now have a back channel with Iran. They're willing to listen, and they've stopped the rocket fire from Gaza and the Houthi attacks from Yemen. With your stopping the attack from Syria, we have some breathing room."

I took that in and silently patted myself on the back, but knew it wasn't enough. I said, "That's great, sir, but there's a third player to this party and it's Israel. I have no idea what that other Turtle is doing, but it's not going to be good. We've tamped down the bonfire, but the logs are still burning. He's going to try to start it up again. I've left Jennifer and Aaron in Tel Aviv to find that guy, and they're chomping at the bit to prevent this war, and Garrett's sat phone number is the key. Give me his location."

I heard a sigh, then, "What's the number?"

I read it off to him, heard him pass it to someone else, and while we waited, he said, "What's Knuckles's status?"

And I was ashamed to realize I didn't even know. He was my second in command, and the commander of our entire unit was asking.

I said, "Sir, honestly, I have no situational awareness of his status. I've been so wrapped in this firestorm in Israel, I haven't had time to contact him. He did his DOA action in Syria less than an hour ago, and he's now on the run. What can you give him?"

Wolffe heard the concern in my voice and said, "Don't beat yourself up. I get the pressure. I've got a line to a combat search and rescue package from Jordan, on standby from your old SMU, but I need to know where to send them."

I gave him Knuckles's Inmarsat number and said, "That's good news. Have them make direct contact. I'm sure he's more than willing to accept the call."

He said, "It won't be that easy. I still have to get the counter-ISIS guys to agree to launch. The CSAR package is on standby for those troops, and right now they're asking who the hell I am. They don't want to launch only to be unavailable if some of their guys get in trouble."

I said, "Tell them he's a SEAL, and he's going to write a book if he has to escape and evade by himself. That should get those SOCOM guys moving."

He chuckled and said, "Okay, Pike, we're on it." He paused a second, talked to someone else away from the handset, then said, "And I've got your grid. The phone is no longer on the network, but the last location was on Highway Four, outside of Acre, Israel. Does that help?"

I looked at Shoshana, saying, "I have no idea."

She said, "He's north. He's headed to the border."

## CHAPTER 73

Garrett continued driving faster than was necessary on the highway, looking above him every few minutes for a strike from a circling drone—a fear only someone who had engendered such death would wonder about. Eventually, he realized he was traveling faster than the speed limit, and slowed down. The last thing he needed was to be pulled over by some roving police patrol.

He kept checking his iPhone for a signal, and was routinely rebuffed, making him curse the fact that he had destroyed his satellite phone. Sooner or later he would reach a town or city, as the highway was the main north-south road. He was sure that Israeli phones worked throughout the country, and regretted not spending the money on a local one. His cell was from Rome, and apparently, his service didn't transfer, which had the potential to cause the death of the entire mission.

One more single point of failure he should have seen. He'd avoided them one time after another, from the killings of the women to the

Palestinian identification for Michelangelo, but now they were so close to success. So close.

He began praying, begging God to help him on his quest, just like Abraham had when he'd traveled to sacrifice his son. Just like Moses when he'd spent the time in the wilderness. Just like he'd done in Syria when they'd mutilated him, and he'd come out pure. He *was* pure, and he knew it. *Felt it.*

He saw a signal on his phone, his prayers answered. He pulled the vehicle to the side of the road, not wanting to lose it. He checked the connection, saw he had enough for Zello, and initiated the application, saying, "Mikey, you there?"

Michelangelo answered immediately, saying, "Yes, I'm here. What's happening?"

"You need to initiate the attack. Do it now."

There was a pause, then, "What happened to Raph and Leo?"

"They're gone. Execute the attack and I'll meet you back in Tel Aviv for the flight out."

He heard a pause, then, "What happened?"

"I don't know, but they were stopped. It's just you and me now. We're the only ones standing."

"Okay, okay, I'm on the way."

The manner in which he said it gave Garrett concern. He said, "What do you mean, you're on the way? You mean you're on the way to the Temple Mount? Is that it?"

"No, I mean I'm on the way to Jerusalem. I'm still at the hotel."

Garrett wanted to throw the phone through

the windshield. He said, "Are you still in Tel Aviv? I told you to go to Jerusalem this morning."

Hearing the accusation in Garrett's voice, Michelangelo said, "Yeah, that was before the damn sun had risen. I had to shower, eat, and get packed. I'm going, I'm going. I didn't know this was time sensitive."

Through gritted teeth, Garrett said, "Get your ass there, plant the explosives, and get out. There are people hunting us. You need to go—now!"

He heard a scrambling of feet, then, "Okay, sir, I'm on it. I'm on the way."

Garrett pulled back onto the highway, knowing he was going to leave Michelangelo to his fate. He would not be meeting him in Tel Aviv. His only solution was to get to Lebanon, and he knew where to do that.

At the very tip of this highway was a place called the Rosh Hanikra Grottoes, a tourist site where people could go underground to see the sea wash inside. It also held an old railway system that connected Lebanon to Israel through the tunnels carved by the ocean and the original British Mandate, built before Israel existed as a country. He'd visited it once and seen how the tunnels worked, even walking down the railway of one tunnel through the splashing water until he was told to turn back by the tour guide.

The connection between the two countries had been closed decades ago, but it existed. He didn't know how he would penetrate it, but it was the closest escape. The crossing to Lebanon on the above-ground section of Rosh Hanikra was a nonstarter, as it was heavily fortified by the IDF, but the tunnels underneath weren't patrolled. If it didn't pan out, he'd reassess, maybe trying to go south, to the Eilat crossing point and into Egypt.

He checked his watch, wanting to do a reconnaissance before he tried to penetrate in the night.

I hit the gas on our vehicle, pulling out onto the highway at a rate of speed that was most definitely not allowed.

I said, "Call Jennifer and Aaron. Tell them to get ready. I don't know where the lost Turtle is going, but the guy we're chasing does."

She nodded, staring at me intently. I said, "What?"

She glanced away, embarrassed. She dialed the phone and said, "You believe. You think he's bringing about Armageddon, like I said all along. That's all."

I said, "I think he's a lunatic killer that almost started a war, and he's still on the loose. And he's got some other nutjob out there. Is that good enough?"

She patted my arm and said, "Yes, Nephilim. That's good enough. You don't know what you see, but you see it, just like I do."

I turned to her, ready to shut down the crazy conversation, and she held up a finger, telling me to shut up, her phone to her ear. It was the second time she'd done it, and it aggravated me.

I bit my tongue and excised my annoyance by increasing my speed. She looked at me and said, "Don't kill us before we can kill him."

I said, "Don't hold your damn finger in my face."

I saw her eyes open wide and she said, "Is that not something I should do with Aaron?"

I couldn't believe it. Even in the heat of this thing, she was still trying to learn how to be a human in a relationship. And I realized she had meant nothing by it. I laughed and said, "Carrie, you really need to spend more time with Jennifer."

She held her finger up again, then started talking on the phone, saying, "We're on the trail of Garrett. When we find him, we'll find the final Turtle. Pike wants you guys ready to go. Wherever that may be."

She listened, then looked at me, saying, "Nephilim will tell you when to launch. I'll tell you when Garrett's dead."

She hung the phone up and I said, "What does that mean?"

"It means this man is mine. I will get my vengeance."

I started to say something, and she gave me a look of pure venom, saying, "Don't tell me to stop, Pike. I'll wait until we find out his plan, but when we do, I'm going to extract all the pain he gave my *Ramsad*."

I was taken aback at her rage. I'd seen it before, but not in such a controlled state, sitting right next to me. I said, "Okay, Carrie. We solve this problem, and he's all yours."

She nodded and we continued racing down the road, going twice as fast as the law allowed.

Like magic, ahead of us, I saw an SUV. I said, "Is that him?"

She said, "I never got a license plate. I don't know."

The SUV was driving the speed limit, lazily heading down the road. I increased my own speed, came up behind it, and then attempted to pass, just to see.

I came abreast, and from the passenger seat, Shoshana said, "That's him."

I sagged back into our lane behind him and said, "Disable the vehicle. Right now."

She reached behind the seat, pulled out an MCX rifle, and lowered the window, taking aim at the left rear tire. She pulled the trigger three times, and nothing happened.

I said, "Are you even aiming?"

She glared at me and said, "I hit the tire."

The SUV sped up, racing ahead of us. I said, "I'm going to bring you up next to him. Put that fucker down."

I floored the pedal, jumping into the next lane and getting abreast of the SUV. Shoshana leaned out of the window, the rifle stabbing out. I saw Garrett flinch, and she began firing, the bullets creating nothing more than small divots in the glass, like she'd hit a regular window with a pebble.

And it hit home. *It's armored. That's why the tires didn't go. He's driving with run-flats.*

At that moment, he swerved into us, and his vehicle was much, much heavier than ours. It was like having an M1 Abrams tank pushing a golf cart at speed. He hit my rear quarter panel, punched his engine, and we spun off the road, colliding with the ditch on the far side hard enough to cause both of us to slam about like a couple of marbles tossed into a dryer.

I shook my head, looked at Shoshana, and said, "You okay?"

She nodded and said, "He's going to get away. I can't let him get away."

I said, "He's not going to get away. Sooner or later, he's leaving that vehicle. And when he does, he'll be a turtle without a shell."

## CHAPTER 74

Garrett swerved back onto the road, seeing the car behind him spin out into the ditch. Breathing heavily, he wiped the sweat from his brow and continued on. He was committed now. Highway 4 was a one-way road to the end of Israel. He thought about circling back around and driving to Tel Aviv just to hide for a day, but then realized that if Michelangelo actually accomplished his mission, he'd never get out. The entire country would be locked down because of the coming war.

He drove as fast as he could push the heavily armored vehicle and eventually began passing settlements. He looked at his phone, saw he had a strong signal, and initiated the Zello app, saying into the speaker, "Mikey, what's your status?"

"I'm halfway to Jerusalem. I'll be inside the Old City in about thirty minutes. What about you?"

"I'm driving back to Tel Aviv. I should be there in an hour."

"And the Grand Master? Is he with you?"

"No, you idiot. Do you think I'd be calling if he was in my car? He wanted to stay behind to talk to the prime minister. The Israeli security detail will bring him home, but we're going to be gone by then."

"Okay. Hey, look, I can't set these charges off inside by myself. I'm going to have to do it remotely. Is that okay?"

"What do you mean?"

"I mean I'm not a suicide bomber. I'm not going to get blown up doing this. I'm going to emplace them, and then leave, setting them off by cell phone."

Confused, Garrett said, "I'm fine with that. Why are you asking?"

"Because I can't guarantee initiation. It's just a link I thought you should be aware of."

Garrett thought a moment, then said, "That won't work. We've had several single points of failure on this mission, one that Raph and Leo ran into. One that caught Donatello. I need you to execute."

"You're saying you want me to blow myself up?"

"No. I'm saying you need to ensure the explosives go off. I don't care how you do it, but when you leave the charges, they need to be counting down. I don't care if it's a Wile E. Coyote thing, with a burning fuse taped to a black ball, we can't afford another point of failure."

He heard nothing but breathing. He said, "You can do that, right?"

"Yes, sir. I can do that. I'm on the way right now. You're coming back to Tel Aviv?"

Garrett saw the end of the highway, the Rosh Hanikra Grotto lookout ahead of him. He said,

"Yes. I'm about forty minutes out. I'll call when I arrive."

He parked the SUV in the lot, looked at the ticket counter for the cable cars going down, and thought about his options. Which was to say, he had very few. After the attempted vehicle interdiction, he was sure he was on every intelligence radar on the planet, not the least with one of the most effective on earth—the Mossad—and if he used his credit card to buy a ticket on the cable car, it would register. He might get his reconnaissance, but the police would coalesce on this location.

And he couldn't execute his plan without a reconnaissance. He wasn't sure it would even work, and if it was a dead end, he'd need to be able to escape.

He leaned his head back, closed his eyes, and prayed to the God who wanted this to occur, searching for an answer as to what he should do. He saw the dead women he'd killed, taunting him, and he snapped his eyes open. Was God talking to him?

And God spoke.

A child pounded on his door, her mother behind her. He rolled down the window and said, "Yes?"

She heard his accent and said, "You're an American?"

"Yes. Yes, I am."

Clearly rehearsed for this eventuality, having seen many American tourists, she said, "I'm like the Girl Scouts here in Israel, and I'm selling

486 / BRAD TAYLOR

cookies. If you buy six boxes, you get a free ticket for the cable car to the grotto."

He smiled and said, "I'll take twelve boxes, and only one ticket."

I continued up Highway 4, saying, "What are we doing now? We're chasing a ghost. He could be anywhere in this country."

Getting antsy in the passenger seat, Shoshana said, "I should have done this with Aaron. He'd find the man."

Which sort of hurt. I said, "We talked about this before we left. With a split team, we needed an Israeli on each one. It's why you're with me and Jennifer is with Aaron. And if you want to push it, I wish Jennifer was with me right now."

She glared at me and I said, "Hey, I didn't start this. You did."

She said, "He's trying to cross the border. He's going to Lebanon, where his men would have been if we hadn't killed them."

I said, "If he was trying to get out of the country, he'd have traveled to Jordan, or Eilat for crossing into Egypt. Going to Lebanon makes no sense."

She said, "Lebanon has diplomatic relations with the Knights of Malta. He's going to use that."

I said, "So do Egypt and Jordan. For that matter, Israel doesn't, but there's a Knights consulate in the West Bank that gives them the same rights as any other diplomat. He could be going to any of them."

Miffed at my logic, she said, "He's going to Lebanon. The grid we received was outside of Acre, on the road to the north. If he was going to Jordan, he'd have headed east, and he could have done that when he left Megiddo. Same for the West Bank. Megiddo is right next to it, but it has too many security checkpoints, and if he was trying to cross into Egypt, he'd have gone south, not north."

I couldn't really argue with that logic. I said, "So we'll just chase him down on this road? It ends at the border?"

"Yes, but we need to get Aaron moving. We won't have time to stop what he has planned."

"I agree, but where?"

"Jerusalem. They're going to target Jerusalem."

Continuing down the road at a high rate of speed, I said, "You know something I don't?"

"Yes. Well, no, but yes."

"What the hell does that mean?"

"The *Ramsad*'s killer is trying to start the End of Days. With the miss on Megiddo, he's got one arrow left in his quiver, and he's going to use it carefully. He has no more drones or missiles. He has one last man, and Jerusalem is where I'd send him if it were me. To the Temple Mount."

"Why would Israel care if he hit that place? You already told me that Israel hadn't taken control of it. An attack there wouldn't get Israel to do anything. It would just cause everyone to get mad at Iran, both Arabs and Israelis."

She said, "True, an attack by supposed Iranian militia members wouldn't cause the fight, but one that was pinned on Israel would."

## CHAPTER 75

Jennifer hung up the phone and said, "We need to go to Jerusalem."

Aaron said, "Why? Did they find the lost Turtle?"

"No. Not yet, but Shoshana says we need to go there."

Aaron went to the window, thinking. He turned back around, saying, "They've got nothing?"

"They're on the track of Garrett, but they don't have a location for him. Shoshana thinks we need to go there."

"Why?"

Jennifer shrugged, not having an answer. Aaron said, "Never mind. Pack a bag, and make sure it has a weapon. If she said go there, she's probably right."

Jennifer started shoving things into a backpack, saying, "Can't you guys call your Mossad badasses and do this?"

Packing his own bag, Aaron laughed, saying, "I can barely get them to do anything even when I *have* concrete proof. There's only one person I could have called to get support, and he died in Switzerland. Trust me, the current leadership isn't going to listen to the ravings of a woman they tried to kill."

Jennifer stopped her work and said, "What's that mean?"

Aaron continued packing. He shoved in a magazine of ammunition and paused. "Let's just say that Shoshana's ability to see things didn't work out well for the Mossad. They fear her, but don't trust her."

"And that's how she ended up with you?"

He started packing again, saying, "Yes, because the *Ramsad* who was killed could see deeper than these people. Because I don't fear her, but I *do* trust her."

Michelangelo entered the outskirts of the concrete jungle of modern-day West Jerusalem and followed the signs to the Old City. Driving through the city, following the route of the bus he'd taken a day before, he noticed an increased police presence, with cars and uniformed personnel on every corner, a different environment from even his visit yesterday.

He wondered if they were looking for him. He ensured he followed all traffic laws, inching forward to the Old City.

He knew there was a parking deck next to the Jaffa Gate, and sought it out, his head on a swivel from the increased police presence. Eventually, he found it, taking a ticket and pulling into an open space, the juxtaposition of the modern-day parking machine stark against the ancient walls he was about to penetrate.

He exited the vehicle, putting on his backpack. He walked up the stairs from the parking garage and went toward the Jaffa Gate, seeing a Jewish community celebration, a crowd of people all chanting songs and walking toward the gate waving flags, around them uniformed police now wearing helmets. He fell in behind them and entered, then threaded his way through the Christian quarter and into the Jewish quarter. He checked his map, took a left, and began walking through the cloistered cobblestones to the Muslim quarter, ducking his head every time a patrol of riot police passed him.

Garrett paid for his cookies and took the free ticket, telling the girl she was doing God's work. She smiled and nodded, not understanding that she'd just given him a way into the grotto that couldn't be tracked by the intelligence agencies of her own state.

He walked to the cable car station and saw multiple people milling about, a tour bus belching exhaust adjacent to the building. He mingled in with them, walking to the platform like any other tourist. He passed his ticket to the person manning the entrance and they boarded, the cable car beginning its descent at an incredibly sharp angle. It wasn't a long trip, but it was disconcerting, almost like they were sliding straight down. The tourists in the car busied themselves with pictures and chatter. Garrett simply waited on the car to dock.

Once it reached the bottom, he exited, ignoring

the tour guide taking the rest of the patrons to see the crashing of the sea inside the tunnels. He wanted something else—the old railroad.

He split from them and went down a tunnel on his own, the walls carved out decades ago. He reached a narrow-gauge railroad track with a sign next to it explaining the history. He glanced behind him, saw no one, and began walking down the tracks, leaving behind the overhead lights of the tourist space.

He continued until he couldn't see anymore, the blackness reminding him of the hood he'd been forced to wear in Syria. Of the hole he'd been held in. The memory hit him like a sledge-hammer, and he paused in the tunnel, not wanting to continue. Not wanting to find out what was down the path.

He shook his head, clearing the fear. He pulled out a small penlight and continued on, hearing the echoes of the tourists grow fainter behind him. Eventually, the only sound was the crunching of his boots in the gravel. Ten minutes later, he reached the end, his penlight illuminating a brick wall that spanned the entire width of the tunnel, the tracks continuing underneath. He slapped his hand against it, feeling it solid. He looked for a door, sure they wouldn't have simply blocked the entire tunnel, but found nothing, and realized he'd had more hope than fact with his plan.

*Of course they wouldn't leave open an infiltration route from Lebanon. What the hell were you thinking?*

He felt a little stupid, rushing here to escape from a tunnel that he himself, as a Special Forces commander, would have ordered blocked. He took a seat on a rock, just resting in the darkness. He pulled out his phone and was surprised to see a signal.

He initiated the Zello app, pulled up the location for Michelangelo, and saw the icon in Jerusalem, just inside the Old City. He smiled and initiated a call. Mikey answered, and Garrett said, "How's it going?"

"I'm here, but there are police all over the place. I can't get into the Temple Mount."

"Why not?"

"Apparently, there's going to be some sort of Palestinian protest, and the Israelis have blocked the gates."

Garrett almost took the Lord's name in vain at the news. He said, "So how long is this supposed to go on?"

"The guard said they'll open the gates in an hour or so if no protests materialize. Are you back in Tel Aviv?"

"Not yet, but I will be soon."

"Do you want me to stay here? Or roll over a day?"

"Stay there. If it opens back up, do the hit. If not, we'll roll over."

He hung up, shaking his head at how hard this was becoming. It was almost as if God was thwarting his plans. Placing trials in front of him to see if he was worthy. And then he remembered Abraham's story. That's exactly what this was. He needed to prove he was worthy.

The thought gave him confidence. He stood up, moving quickly back down the tunnel. He'd leave here and travel to Eilat, coordinating with Michelangelo along the way. Mikey would be like the son of Abraham, sacrificed for the glory of God.

He entered the primary cave, seeing the railing with tourists taking pictures of the sea spray crashing into the grotto. He went behind them, heading to the exit, and saw another crowd of tourists enter the grotto. Inside the group were two people he recognized. Two people who struck the same unbridled fear in him that he'd felt in the tunnel.

## CHAPTER 76

Highway 4 began winding up into the cliffs on the northern border of Israel, and then abruptly dead-ended, turning into a parking lot for an overlook, the place jam-packed with tour buses and other vehicles, the view out over the Mediterranean Sea incredible.

I pulled into the lot, not caring about the scenery. I said, "So this is it? What do we do now?"

Shoshana hissed, and pointed. The up-armored SUV was in the parking lot, the distinctive gouges in the driver's window easy to see. And it was empty. She said, "He's here. He's trying to get to Lebanon."

"How? How on earth would he do that here?" I pointed to a walkway along the shoreline leading to a cable car station, saying, "Is he going to take that into Lebanon? The crossing site above this is like Checkpoint Charlie in West Berlin. He'd have better luck sneaking out of a prison than trying to cross here."

She said, "This grotto has an old railway from the British Mandate, before we even had a country. It connected Lebanon to Israel before the 1948 war of independence."

I rolled my eyes and said, "So you guys never closed that down? How come Hezbollah hasn't used it to flood Israel with weapons and men?"

"Pike, I don't have that answer. What I know is he's here, and I'm going to kill him."

I said, "Hang on there, gunslinger, we need to—" Before I could finish my sentence, a young girl knocked on our window. I lowered it and said, "Yes?"

She said, "You're American, too?"

I looked at Shoshana and said, "Yes, have you seen another American here?"

She pointed to Garrett's SUV and said, "Yes. That man is also American. Are you together?"

I said, "We are, but we're late. Where did he go?"

She became coy and said, "I'll tell you the same thing I told him—if you buy six boxes of cookies, you get a free ticket on the cable car."

"Is that where he went?"

She just looked at me. I would have made an evil joke about the Jewish propensity for a profit, but Shoshana cut that short, handing over a wad of shekels and saying something in Hebrew. The girl took the money, nodded, and said something back, then handed Shoshana twelve boxes of cookies and a couple of tickets.

The girl went back to her mother, and Shoshana said, "He's in the grotto right now. Let's go find him."

I said, "Weapons? What's the security posture?"

"Leave them here. I can't remember the security, but we can't take a chance on getting stopped."

I didn't like hearing that, but pulled out my Glock from its belly holster and shoved it under the seat. She did the same.

We went down the wooden walkway to the cable car station, joined the small queue behind a family of four, and waited our turn. They boarded and began their descent. The next car arrived, and with nobody behind us, we had it all to ourselves.

I waited until we'd cleared the station, then said, "So much for security."

She said, "Better safe than sorry."

"You have any idea what we're about to find here? Given your incredible memory of the security posture?"

She shot me a look and said, "Yes, I *have* been here before. It's a grotto."

I gave her an expression of amazement and said, "Really? I wondered why it was called a grotto. So it's *really* a grotto?"

She scowled and said, "There's only one way in and out, but once inside, there are tunnels that spread out all over the place, like an underground maze. The old train tracks will be to the left when we exit. Is that better?"

I chuckled and said, "Yes, Carrie, that's better. Just remember when we find him, we need his answers before you go ape-shit on his ass."

Truthfully, I was hoping to stop her rage.

I knew what killing for vengeance did, and it was just as hard on the killer as it was on the one killed.

The car docked and she said, "I know," but I could tell she wasn't listening.

We exited the cable car, following the path to the entrance of a cave. We entered, the darkness of the space dramatically different from the daylight just outside, forcing our eyes to adjust to the gloom.

I saw a cave that looked like something from the ending of *Planet of the Apes*, with lit walkways leading in multiple directions and the sound of the ocean crashing about, the briny smell of the sea heavy in the air.

Shoshana pulled my arm and we went to the left, searching for the old railway line, dodging tourists who only wanted to see the ocean crash into the walls. We cleared a main group, saw a lit tunnel, and then the serial killer.

He locked eyes with me, I saw the recognition, and then he took off running, straight down the tunnel. Shoshana grunted like an animal, sprinting right behind him. I shouted, "Wait, wait! Don't follow him into a trap."

She ignored me. I started racing behind them and we hit the railway tracks, the tunnel getting narrower, the light starting to fade as we went beyond the tourist area.

I leapt over a chain telling visitors not to continue, and the light disappeared, leaving me running blindly in the dark, following the sound of the footsteps in front of me like a bat in the night.

I heard a noise that wasn't footsteps, sounding like something heavy sliding in the gravel, then a scream. I ran forward, holding one hand out to prevent me from bashing into a wall, then was tripped up by a body on the ground.

I rolled over, raising my fists to fight, saying, "Shoshana?"

I heard a thrashing in the gravel and realized it was *two* bodies on the ground. Like every teenager on earth, I whipped out my cell phone and turned on the flashlight, seeing Shoshana enveloped around Garrett's body, just like she'd done in Bahrain, her behind him, his head cradled in her arms, her legs cinched around his waist, one of his arms stuck straight up in the air, trapped from when she'd wrapped him up.

I saw her snarl and leapt up, saying, "Don't do it!"

Garrett felt the death wrap around him as surely as if he was in the coils of an anaconda. He quit struggling. Shoshana had lost all semblance of reason, hissing into his ear, "The man you killed in Switzerland saved my life. And now I'll take yours."

I said, "Shoshana, don't. He's defenseless. Let's get him out of here and to your people. Let's solve the problem."

She seemed for the first time to realize I was there. She slowly shook her head and I said, "Killing him won't bring back the *Ramsad*. It'll only corrupt you. Don't do it. I'm not ordering. I'm asking."

Garrett said, "It won't matter what you do to

me. I've been chosen by God for a mission, and killing me won't stop that."

Disgusted, I said, "You sound like every terrorist I've ever heard."

With a weird light in his eyes, he said, "You'll never hear it again, because I'm going to stop every future terrorist of the Islamic faith. I'm going to wipe out Islam as a religion."

Keeping my light on him, knowing he couldn't see past the beam, I said, "What you're going to do is tell me where your last Turtle went."

He said, "Fuck you."

Shoshana glared up at me and said, "Let me kill him. Please."

I squatted down, getting right in his face and saying, "I *will* let her do that if you don't answer."

He said, "God has a plan for me, just as he did for Abraham. And God will protect me."

He slid his free hand into his front pocket, pulled out a folding blade, flicked it open, and stabbed behind him, hitting Shoshana in the shoulder, causing her to release her hold. She screamed, and I leapt forward, trapping his hand with the blade still in her. The force of my move caused her to scream again. I dropped the phone, needing both hands, but I was more than willing to fight in the dark. I didn't need to see to destroy him. As this asshole was about to find out.

I jerked his arm backward, pulling out the blade. I rotated against the joint in a tight, violent circle and heard it snap, eliciting a guttural shout. The knife bounced somewhere in the darkness and I rolled backward, bringing him with me, him on top and me on my back. I wrapped my legs around his waist, cinched my arms around his neck, then pulled his face into mine. I couldn't see it in the darkness, but I could smell the sweat of his fear.

I hissed, "I would have let you live if you hadn't tried to kill her. Reap what you sow, asshole."

Huffing above me, trying to get out of my guard mount, I ignored his thrashing, keeping him in place. Calmly I said, "Shoshana, do you hear my voice?"

In the darkness I heard, "Yes."

"Can you still fight?"

"Yes."

"Come to the sound of my voice. His neck is right there."

And I heard Garrett scream, the noise abruptly cut off by the sound of something breaking, as if Shoshana had cracked a stick in two. His body collapsed on top of me and I pushed it off, rolling over and finding my phone, the flashlight still on and shining in the darkness.

I sat Shoshana down and said, "Let me take a look."

She did so, saying, "I thought we weren't going to kill him until we had answers."

I put the light on her wound, saying, "That was before he tried to murder a member of my family."

She whipped her head to me and saw I was serious. She smiled and said, "I always knew you were sweet on me."

I chuckled and said, "Hold still."

The wound was a puncture, and it was deep,

but it was all muscle and tendons. Nothing vital had been pierced. I ripped the shirt on Garrett's body, making some bandages. I patched her up as best I could, saying, "You'll need some stitches, but you'll be okay."

She said, "What about the mission?"

I turned my phone to the body, aiming the light. I dug around his pockets and found a cell phone. I opened the Zello app the same way I'd done from the phone we'd found in Bahrain, and saw a history of voice chats, all talking about the Temple Mount. I pulled up the geolocation function for the person on that chat, and saw it was inside the Old City.

I shook my head. She said, "What?"

"I'll never question your visions again. That fucker is in Jerusalem, just outside the Al Aqsa compound."

## CHAPTER 77

Racing down Highway 1, Aaron behind the wheel, Jennifer saw the interchange approach for the turn south to Jerusalem, along with a healthy blanket of police vehicles on the side of the road, like they were waiting on something.

She said, "A lot more police on the road today. What's going on? Any idea?"

Aaron said, "Nope, but it's not good. The only time they do this is because of an indistinct threat. If it was something they've penetrated, the focus would be on that specific location."

He took the interchange to Highway 60, the road leading straight into Jerusalem, and she heard her Taskforce phone ring.

She answered it, Aaron glancing her way. She said, "Stand by," and initiated an encryption feature on the cell phone. She returned, saying, "I'm secure, do you have me?"

She heard Pike say, "I've got you, I've got you, listen, the final Turtle is outside the Temple Mount. We have no idea what he's planning, but it's not going to be good."

"He's there now?"

"Yes."

"Pike, we're still at least ten minutes out. If he's doing something soon, we can't stop him."

"He can't do anything right now. I've got the Zello chat logs. Apparently, the place is blanketed with Israeli security and they've closed the gates to the mosque compound. He's not in yet."

"We're seeing that here on the road as well. Police are everywhere. Why? What's going on?"

"I have no idea, but you need to get inside and find that guy before he's allowed to enter."

"What do you want us to do?"

"Take him off the board. I don't care how you do it, but don't let him enter the compound."

She looked at Aaron and said, "Can't Israel do this? If he's a known threat?"

"Fine by me, like I said, I don't care how you do it, but they're not going to find him by his name. From the chat logs in Garrett's Zello app, he's operating as a Palestinian. He's not going to surface at any entry point as a Knights of Malta guy."

She thought through the ramifications, then said, "Which means he can get in through any gate to the Temple Mount. Muslims can go through them all. We can only enter through one, the Moors Gate. How am I going to find him?"

"I'm sending the grid to his last known location. If he moves, I'll let you know. I have Garrett's phone, and it's tracking him like Apple's Find My Friends. The phones are tied together. When he moves, I see it. Right now, he's in the Muslim quarter outside of the Temple Mount, next to the Tribes Gate."

504 / BRAD TAYLOR

She said, "Send me the grid location, and send his passport information from immigration. I need a face."

Pike said, "Coming your way. Look, I'm at the Lebanese border, and Shoshana's been wounded. We're leaving here, and when we do, I'm going to lose cell coverage. Get inside the Old City and get it done."

Shocked, she said, "Wait, what? Shoshana's wounded?"

She saw Aaron's head snap to her at her words. Pike said, "She's okay. Tell Aaron she's okay. She just needs some stitches. She'll be fine."

"What happened?"

"Garrett tried to fight, and she eliminated him."

"Pike . . . we were supposed to bring him back to Lia. Have him stand trial in Rome. You told me you wouldn't let her do this. You promised you'd not let that happen. It's going to hurt her. It's going to bleed in her soul."

She heard nothing for a moment, then, "She didn't kill him out of vengeance. She wanted to, but she stopped when I asked. I killed him."

"You?"

Pike said, "It was pure, Jennifer, I promise. He stabbed her, trying to murder her after we'd told him to surrender. Shoshana wanted to kill him before, but she didn't. If she had, she wouldn't have a stab wound right now. When he attacked her, I got him off her and onto me. And yes, I had Shoshana kill him, but it was my call. She was just the tool. Now get your ass to the Temple Mount. Pictures and grids are on the way."

He hung up before she could say anything else.

Aaron said, "What was that about Shoshana?"

"Garrett stabbed her, but it's a clean wound. She's going to be fine. Pike is with her now."

He nodded, saying, "And Garrett?"

"He's dead."

She saw the smile trickle out and said, "Pike says he fought back. Shoshana didn't execute him."

Aaron turned to her and said, "I don't care how he died, as long as he's dead."

And Jennifer realized he was just like Shoshana. A man who took the biblical saying "an eye for an eye" to heart. She felt a chill, glad she wasn't on the bad side of either one of them.

She changed the subject, saying, "The final Turtle is outside the Al Aqsa Mosque. Pike couldn't get any information about his mission, but we need to stop him."

They entered the outskirts of Jerusalem, and he said, "We won't arrive to the Old City for at least five minutes, and it'll be a twenty-minute race on foot once we get there."

"Pike said from the chats that the Temple Mount is closed right now. They won't let anyone in to pray because of some potential protests. We should have that time."

She snapped her fingers and said, "That's it! Can you call your Mossad contacts and have them simply keep the place closed until we can locate him? Just don't let him in."

He grimaced, and she said, "I know you said getting overt action from them was impossible, but can't they just delay the opening? Keep it closed for another hour?"

They reached the outskirts of the Old City. He pulled off of the main road, into a parking garage outside the Jaffa Gate. He said, "I can try, but it's going to be nearly impossible. There are too many layers to wade through. The Mossad doesn't control the Islamic Waqf or the Israeli security of the Temple Mount."

He dialed his phone, spoke into it in Hebrew, then became aggravated, shouting. He hung up and said, "There was a possible violent protest by the Palestinians. It didn't happen, and now the Palestinians are starting to protest about the gate closures. Not a coordinated thing. Spontaneous."

"And? What does that mean?"

"We went to war in Gaza last year because of our strong-arming of the worshipers in the Al Aqsa Mosque. Hamas rockets hit just about every city in Israel. They aren't willing to take that risk again. They're letting the Muslims inside in ten minutes, and there's nothing I can do about it. We won't start launching tear gas and rubber bullets again to stop them."

She said, "Did you tell them that there's a terrorist posing as a Palestinian who's about to set off a bomb?"

He put the SUV in park, turned off the ignition, and said, "I did. They don't believe the scope of the threat. In their mind, there is a greater problem set here, and it's all politics. Honestly, I'm not sure if some don't want the attack to occur."

Jennifer said, "Surely your government doesn't want an attack at the Al Aqsa Mosque to be blamed on the Jewish faith?"

He said, "No, we don't, but I also know that they don't see what's happening. They don't know how close we are to total war. Some in my government want it, just as some in yours do."

He looked at her and said, "Politics have always been the death of people. We can stop that now. We have no help, and I can't ask you to do it, but we can prevent a war. I know America won't feel the missiles, and I know that Pike would say to leave, but will you help me?"

She couldn't believe he'd even asked. She said, "Aaron, just tell me what to do. This is your land. Your terrain. And if Pike were here, he wouldn't be running away, he'd be asking for the kill zone."

He realized he'd insulted her. He said, "Shoshana is rubbing off on you."

Still aggravated at his words, she said, "Maybe I'm rubbing off on her; now what the hell are we doing?"

He nodded and said, "We're going to roll that guy up before he gets inside the compound, but when we do, we're going to get attacked by the other Palestinians. There is no way to take him down without them seeing. They'll think we're doing something heinous. We're liable to get killed by the protestors, but we'll prevent him from completing his mission. Are you ready for that?"

She took a deep breath and said, "I'm ready. Let's go."

They exited the vehicle at a run, threading

their way through groups of police and tourists showing trepidation at the show of force. They reached the Muslim quarter, heading down Via Dolorosa, the path of Christ's final walk. Midstride, Aaron turned around, saying, "Look familiar?"

Jennifer said, "Yes. But I don't want to repeat that episode."

He smiled and kept jogging. They penetrated the Muslim quarter, going to the Tribes Gate, one of the eleven the Muslims could use, and the last known location for the final Turtle.

Except for a phalanx of police in riot gear, the entrance was empty.

## CHAPTER 78

Michelangelo almost didn't believe it when the gate opened, the security forces bending back to the pressure. There had been no organized protest, but there *had* been a groundswell of people coming out, aggravated at their inability to pray at the Al Aqsa Mosque. Most of the protestors were older, with a significant number of women. They'd begun chanting, pressing forward, and the Israeli security pushed them back. Eventually, a news camera had shown up, focusing on the women.

Ten minutes later, the Israeli forces faded away, leaving the security to the Islamic Waqf, the ones chartered for the sanctity of the compound.

He went forward in a group, his rucksack on his back, wearing a *taqiyah* skullcap, blending in because of his swarthy skin and dark hair. He reached the gate and showed the Islamic Waqf member his certificate, and was allowed to continue, bypassing all security, the chaos of the protest letting him slip through even a rudimentary search.

He went inside, not sure where to go next.

He'd been on the Temple Mount the day before, but hadn't been allowed to visit any of the Muslim areas. Because yesterday he'd been an infidel. But not today.

He saw the Dome of the Chain, a smaller structure that was adjacent to the golden Dome of the Rock, and thought about just placing his explosives there. But he knew that wouldn't work. They needed a fight. Needed the Muslim Ummah to rise up, and they were clearly primed to do just that thing. In order to ensure success, he needed something bigger. He stared at the golden dome ahead of him. The location of the Rock of Ascension—the place where the Islamic faith believed Muhammed ascended into heaven.

Jennifer followed Aaron through the city, finally ending at the Gate of the Tribes, one of eleven that Muslims could use to enter to pray on the Temple Mount, known in the Islamic faith as the Noble Sanctuary.

They scanned the crowd and didn't see their target. Aaron said, "He's already inside. We're done."

Jennifer said, "How are we done? This is your country. Can't you talk to the people here?"

She pointed to a bunch of young men and women wearing riot gear, saying, "Tell them he's on the loose."

"Tell them what? That I think there's a guy with a bomb? And I don't know what he's calling himself, but he's about to kill people? Look at them. They're all barely twenty years old. It'll take forty minutes to get anyone to penetrate the compound, especially after the fiasco we had here last year."

He slapped the wall next to the gate and said, "Nobody wants to trigger the next Intifada. They don't want a fight, and because of it, we're going to get a much bigger one." He looked at Jennifer and said, "We're about to lose."

She said, "Those people in uniform can get in. We cannot. We're not Muslim, but they can get in. Go talk to them. Get them to help."

He heard the words and said nothing, his eyes unfocused, thinking. He returned to her, now all business. He said, "Yes. Yes, they can. Are you ready to commit? I mean *really* commit?"

Jennifer saw the zeal in his eyes and hesitantly said, "Yes? What's that mean?"

He flicked his eyes to the left and said, "Those two riot police looked at you when we entered the gate area. They're like every other soldier. They want you to want them. Go get them to follow you."

"Follow me how?"

"I don't really care, but get them into that alley behind us. The small one."

She narrowed her eyes and said, "Why?"

"Because you're right. They can get in, and we need their uniforms."

Michelangelo surveyed the area, knowing the entire compound had religious significance for all the great faiths, but he knew this had to be big. An explosion of rage.

And that was the Dome of the Rock. Feeling the sweat on his back, the fear flooding through him, he knew what he needed to do, because it was the original plan: attack the Rock of Ascension. If he blew that apart, the third most holy site in all of Islam, it would cause a war, the Muslim world not caring who had done it. They would release their rage against the West on all fronts. Israel would be buried in fire, and the United States would come to their defense. And it would be the End of Days. Islam would lose. When the smoke cleared, Israel would control the Temple Mount, and would build the third temple, leading to the second coming of Christ.

He saw the entrance to the Dome, surrounded by Israeli security in riot gear, wearing helmets, elbow shields, and holding batons. They were antsy, but not looking for a fight. He went toward it, unsure if he was supposed to prove he was a Muslim.

He reached the entrance, tucked his head, and showed his certificate. The man at the gate waved him on, and he entered, finding a circular space full of people praying and taking pictures. But no rock.

He saw a stairwell to the left, strands of people vanishing down it, and went that way.

He descended the stairwell, entering a small, cavelike structure, people praying at an altar, others taking selfies inside. He tapped a man on the shoulder and said, "Where is the Rock of Ascension?"

"Above us. It's above us. We pray here, right underneath it."

He nodded and dropped his pack, going to his knees. He knew enough about the Muslim faith to fake a prayer, having seen the actions happen in a multitude of countries, starting with Bosnia. Bowing forward with the three next to him, he thought about what he should do. There was no rock he could use his shape charges against, nothing to destroy. But that might not matter. The attack all along had been psychological, and this place appeared to be sacrosanct, underneath the oldest Islamic prayer structure on earth. He could do it here and accomplish the mission.

He glanced about the room, saw nobody paying any particular attention to him, and unzipped his small rucksack. He went through the camouflage of bread and cheese, finding his six-pack of shaped charges. He daisy-chained them together, snapping wires into the blasting caps, and then tied them to a disposable flip phone, just like had been done against him in Syria. He set the built-in timer for three minutes, wanting to be far away when it went off.

He knew Garrett wanted a fail-safe Wile E. Coyote explosion, but he had no way to do that. This would work. He'd checked the cell signal throughout his walk in the Old City. It was strong. It wasn't Wile E. Coyote strong, but he'd be damned if he was going to blow himself up. When he called the phone, it would start the timer, and he intended to be off the compound when that happened.

He surreptitiously surveyed the room, saw nobody focused on him, and slid the bag over the edge of the prayer area, setting it underneath a nook. He pressed a button on the phone, then stood to go.

Jennifer walked to the two Israeli police officers who Aaron had identified and said, "Can you guys help me? There's a guy following me and he's starting to scare me."

The two twenty-something cops took one look at her and stood up, saying, "Yes. Was he Palestinian?"

"He might have been. I honestly don't know about that. I'm from the United States. But I know where he is. Can you do something about him? He keeps following me, and I'm scared."

They nodded, and Jennifer felt guilty about how easy this was going to be. She smiled and said, "This is my one chance to see the promised land, and I get followed by a weirdo. I really appreciate it."

One of them pulled out his baton and said, "Just show us where he is."

She said, "Follow me, he went this way."

She led them to the small tunnel that Aaron had identified, past trash bins and back doors to shops, both of them anxious to please her. She heard a shout behind her and turned, seeing one man on the ground, Aaron circling him in a rear-naked choke. The other man jumped back, holding his arms up, his baton out, yelling at her to stand back, thinking this was the bad man.

They didn't realize she was also the bad man.

The police officer on his feet smashed his baton into Aaron's shoulder, and she ran toward him as if she was escaping the tunnel. He turned and shouted, "Get back! Get back!"

She darted behind him as he raised the baton again. She grabbed his helmet and used it to lever him onto the ground, like she was twisting a steer by the horns. He forgot about Aaron and started to fight her. She torqued his head, using the chin strap of his helmet to cut off the blood flow to his brain, saying, "I'm sorry. I'm really sorry."

His flailing grew feeble, and he passed out. She lowered him to the ground, feeling dirty. Aaron stood up from his own victim, saying, "Strip them of the riot gear. Put it on. We're running out of time."

## CHAPTER 79

Racing back to Tel Aviv, I looked at Shoshana and said, "Are you okay?"

She grimaced, holding her hand against her shoulder, and said, "Yes, Nephilim. I'm good. I'm with family."

I glanced at her to see if she was making a joke, and saw she was not. I smiled and said, "That's why you're the bridesmaid."

She grinned at the accolade and said, "What now? They're going to find his body soon, and then the police will start hunting us. I'm sure we're on security cameras and they have our license plate."

I said, "Can't you get the Mossad to stifle that?"

"They're not going to overtly shut down a murder investigation. They might help us once we're in jail."

I said, "I'm not going to jail." I looked at my cell phone and saw I was out of coverage again. I said, "Get the Inmarsat and dial it for me."

She picked it up, saying, "I don't know the number you want."

I said, "Hit redial."

She did, then passed it to me. The phone signal went through its travel to the satellite, back to earth, then through the cell network in the United States. I heard the receptionist say, "Blaisdell Consulting. How can I help you?"

I said, "I need to speak to George Wolffe."

She said, "I'm sorry, sir, but nobody by that name works here."

I said, "Marge, it's Pike Logan. Please don't make me pull an alert again."

And she completely broke her role, saying, "Pike, this is not kosher. Do what you're supposed to do and quit calling an open line."

I laughed and said, "Marge, if I could do that, I would. And I'm with kosher people. Please get him for me."

Wolffe came on the line and said, "Pike, really, can you not get to a Wi-Fi node for the VPN?"

"Sorry, sir, but not right now. I'm headed back to Tel Aviv. Garrett is dead, but he's still got a Turtle on the loose."

He ignored my question, saying, "Garrett's dead? You killed a U.S. citizen?"

"Yeah, I did, but only because he pulled out a knife and tried to kill Shoshana. I left the body in a tunnel. I'm about to have some Israeli police on my ass, and I need some backup from the National Command authority to complete this thing. Can you give me that?"

"Get on the Rock Star bird and get out of there. We can protect your team much easier from the United States."

And that made me think about the team. I said, "What's Knuckles's status? Did you extract him?"

He said, "We did, but he'd actually found his own way out, which would have worked if he hadn't decided to destroy the other UAVs. He had that Hezbollah smuggler with him and was going for the border, but before they left, they blew up the final UAVs with some charges, and that caused some Hezbollah men to investigate."

"So he's okay?"

"Yeah, he's in Jordan after some high adventure. I'm trying to get him out right now, but we're getting a thousand questions from SOCOM about who they are."

I breathed a sigh of relief and said, "He's with my old Special Mission Unit?"

"Yes."

"They won't poke much. They understand the value of keeping your mouth shut."

Wolffe chuckled and said, "I know. Now you can get the rest of the team out of Israel and join him."

"Sir, we're headed to Tel Aviv right now, but that final Turtle is on the loose in Jerusalem. I have a location, and have Jennifer and Aaron on it, but there's something going on there right now, with police all over the place. I need to know what's happening."

I heard him exhale, then, "We're seeing the same thing here. Hamas is rumbling about causing another Intifada and Israel is reacting. Honestly, at first I thought it was because of your activities."

"It's not me. Not yet anyway."

"Then it's Hamas. They're saying they're going to cause an uprising in Jerusalem because of perceived injustices, but there's no clear indication it's even real. It could be just to spook everyone. Aren't you with the Israelis? Can't they answer that question?"

I said, "No. That's why I'm calling you. Why would Hamas do this? I thought we had the back channel going?"

"We do, but Iran only has so much control. Hamas is Sunni. Iran is Shia. Iran paid for the weapons they use, but apparently that wasn't enough for total fealty. Hamas sees an opening and wants to exploit it."

"What opening?"

"Israel is saying they're about to assume control of a block of East Jerusalem. Buildings occupied by Palestinians that were once owned by Jewish people."

"Now? They're going to do that *now*? Right in the middle of this shit?"

"Nobody but us knows what's going on outside the ropes. The police are going to force them out, and Hamas is putting out messages saying if they do, it'll be war."

"What. The. Fuck. There *is* going to be a war because that Turtle is going to light the fuse. Tell Hannister to turn it off. Tell him to tell Israel to wait a week. Getting the Palestinians riled up right now is absolutely the wrong thing."

"Pike, he can't order Israel to do anything."

"Well, you'd better get somebody's ass on this, because there's about to be a war that will wipe

Israel off the map, and I don't mean from some second-rate terrorist organization in the Gaza Strip. I mean from the entire Muslim world."

"What's going on?"

"The strike against the prime minister was the primary. We prevented that, but Garrett had a backup. He's got that final Turtle doing something on the Temple Mount. I don't know what it is, but it's going to be the fuse for a catalyst. He infiltrated as a Palestinian. Garrett wanted the End of Days, and everyone's playing right into his hands."

I finally heard some urgency in Wolffe's voice: "Okay, okay, I got it, but we don't do diplomacy here. You know that. I'll pass the message, but it's not going to be fast."

I said, "Did you just say we don't do diplomacy? After you had me do that very thing, passing a message from the president of the United States to Iran?"

He said, "I know, I know, but it's not like I'm the president's national security advisor. I'll do what I can, but in the meantime, can you interdict?"

"Do I have authority to interdict?"

He chuckled and said, "Have you ever cared about that in the past?"

I said, "I do now, because this thing has the potential to get messy, and I need to know you've got my back. I've got Jennifer and Aaron on it right now, but I can't make any promises about how this will go. Shoshana is wounded, and we're about an hour away from executing anything on our own."

"Wounded? Is she okay?"

I looked at her, saying, "She's a little dinged up, but she'll be fine. Just a stitch or two."

She nodded at me and I smiled, saying, "We're still in the fight, but it's coming to a close today. Right before he died, Garrett told me that he was a messenger from God, bringing about the End of Days. Whatever he's planned, it's in motion, and with the Hamas thing going on, it's going to be exponentially worse."

"Pike, I'm giving you the authority to execute. Stop the attack. I'm headed to the White House right now."

"And you'll have my team's back if we get rolled up?"

"Yes, I promise. Get it done no matter what it takes."

If I had any idea of the crazy antics Jennifer and Aaron were conducting, I'd have told him we'd entered into the "no matter what" territory already.

## CHAPTER 80

Jennifer put on the policeman's helmet and said, "None of this fits me. There's no way they'll let us pass."

Dressed in his own riot gear, Aaron said, "Yes, they will. Plenty of females serve here, and sometimes they have to make do with the wrong-sized equipment."

She turned to him, her helmet tilted to the side, saying, "This is like a bad Halloween costume."

Aaron said, "It's good enough to pass through the gate. Let's go."

She said, "I can't speak Hebrew."

"Follow behind me. I'll do the talking."

They exited the tunnel and Jennifer said, "Okay, Han, I'm with you."

He exited the alley, giving her a quizzical look. "What's that mean? Who's Han?"

"Come on. We're literally reenacting *Star Wars*."

He said, "What do you mean?"

"You know, when Luke and Han dress up like storm troopers and infiltrate the Death Star? That's what we're doing."

They approached the Tribes Gate and he said, "I have no idea what you're talking about."

She said, "Seriously? You've never seen *Star Wars*?"

"No."

She shook her head and said, "Let's just pray they shoot as bad as the storm troopers in the movie."

Aaron walked directly to the gate, Jennifer following behind. He was halfway inside the stone archway when he was stopped by another uniformed Israeli. They had a short conversation in Hebrew, Aaron raised his voice, and the man fell away. Aaron picked up speed and Jennifer raced to keep up. They exited into a courtyard of the Al Aqsa compound, right behind the Dome of the Rock.

He said, "We're in, but we won't last long. That officer who tried to stop us said they're looking for a fight up here."

Jennifer nodded, then said, "This place is much bigger than I thought it would be. He could be anywhere."

They circled around the Dome of the Rock, catching the stares of Muslims who'd come to pray. A group began to coalesce around them, shouting in Arabic. Aaron raised his hands, speaking Arabic in a calm voice. The crowd wasn't overtly hostile, but Jennifer could sense the anger just underneath the surface.

They reached the entrance to the Dome of the Rock, the small crowd following behind them, and Jennifer grabbed Aaron's arm, whispering, "That's the Turtle."

A man was exiting, dressed like a local with a skullcap on his head, looking at a cell phone.

Aaron raised his own phone and pulled out the picture they'd been given from immigration control. He glanced at it, then the man, then back to the picture. He said, "You're right. It's him."

The man saw their uniforms and began retreating to the Gate of the Tribes. Aaron said, "Stop right there!"

The Turtle began running, and Aaron chased him down, tackling him, and it was the spark that ignited the fire in the mob. Wrestling the man on the ground, Aaron began fending off people attempting to kick him, the crowd shouting around him. Jennifer fought through them, putting herself between the men on the ground and the mob, pushing people back, shouting, "This man isn't Muslim! He's pretending to be Palestinian!"

The mob either didn't listen, didn't speak English, or didn't care, closing in on them. Aaron continued to fight, rolling over on top of him, blocking his arms from striking, but the Turtle made no effort to cause harm, desperately working the cell in his hand. He pressed the call button and tossed it away, into the crowd. A young man picked it up, holding it in the air, and Jennifer sprinted to him, sliding her legs behind him and pushing forward, slamming him to the ground.

She grabbed the phone and was hammered from behind by a teenager jumping on her back, knocking her to the ground. She rolled over, kicking the man off her, and saw Aaron slam the Turtle's head into the stone, then leap up.

She crab-walked backward as the crowd began beating her with anything they had, the ordinary people bending to the collective insanity that all mobs become. Canes, umbrellas, fists, and feet all rained down. She curled up in a ball and Aaron exploded into the scrum like a grizzly bear, flipping people through the air until he reached her.

He jerked her to her feet and she handed him the phone, saying, "He dialed it. It connected. By the time I got it in my hands, it had connected."

He said, "But it didn't go off. It's on a timer. He initiated the timer."

A rock hit him in the shoulder, the crowd growing more and more angry. He whirled, seeing more people picking up stones. He said, "It's got to be inside the Dome. He just came out of there." He turned to the mob, his back to her, drew his baton, and shouted, "Go, go!"

She raced to the entrance, hearing the mob begin screaming at her "desecrating" the sacred space in an Israeli uniform. She entered the rotunda, the people inside shocked at her appearance. Some cowered, expecting tear gas and rubber bullets, like had happened across the compound in the Al Aqsa Mosque last year. Others with more courage began shouting at her. She looked left and right, the desperation beginning to grow. She had no idea how long the timer would run, and no idea where the Turtle had left the destructive device.

She ran around the rotunda, circling the Rock of Ascension, and the crowd began to follow her, now shouting at her in Arabic. She reached a stairwell leading down into darkness and took it, skipping down the steps three at a time, the people above following her.

She reached a small cavern with a family inside, the father holding a backpack in his hands, a ringing coming from it, the mother seeing her appear and wrapping her arms around her children.

Jennifer ran to the man and said, "Is that your backpack?"

Startled, he said, "No. It just began ringing. It was hidden below the rocks."

She snatched it out of his hands, placed it on the ground, and ripped open the zipper just as the mob from above gathered the courage to storm down the stairs. The woman leading the procession saw her and began screaming, pointing her finger at the abomination of an Israeli policewoman inside the sacred area.

Jennifer ignored her, tossing out crackers, bottles of water, and sandwiches, exposing the six-pack of soda cans at the bottom, four daisy-chained together with a flip phone in the center. She gently opened the phone and saw a timer passing through one minute.

*Holy shit.*

The mob began to advance on her and she turned, shouting, "It's a bomb! Get out of here! It's a bomb!"

Her words split apart the rage of the crowd as if she'd dumped a barrel of water on a match, the anger turning to fear. The crowd panicked, storming back up the stairs, trampling over each other to get away. The mother and father were left in the cavern, the children cowering in terror.

Jennifer looked at the device, trying to determine how to disarm it. She didn't have the expertise to know if it had a fail-safe, and saw the clock ticking through thirty seconds. The children began crying and Jennifer looked at the mother, saying, "Don't worry. It's coming with me. You stay here."

She stood up, the backpack in her hand, and raced up the stairs. She broke through the entrance to the Dome and saw that the Israeli police had stormed into the compound, all of them holding the crowd back, the smell of CS gas in the air, Aaron at the rear.

She ran to him and said, "I can't disarm it, and it's about to go off!"

He took the backpack, laid it on the ground, opened the zipper, and saw the clock counting down through ten seconds. His eyes snapped open and he said, "No time, no time, no time."

He snatched up the backpack and began running through the crowd, smashing into people like a fullback going for the end zone, bashing them aside. He raced to the western edge of the compound overlooking the Wailing Wall and launched the backpack into the air, the ground two stories below full of Jewish worshippers.

It reached the apex of his throw and exploded, a nova of light and sound, the four shape charges going off harmlessly in the air, the explosion scattering the crowd below.

Aaron put his hands on his knees and began

breathing heavily. Right behind him, Jennifer stopped running and did the same thing, gasping for air next to him. She bumped him with her hip and said, "Hell, I could have done that."

He laughed and said, "It was a secret technique I learned in the Samson teams."

They were both slammed to the ground by the Israeli police, the lieutenant of the force livid at his actions. The sergeant of the guard said, "I don't know who these two are, but I have two of my men in their underwear downstairs saying they were assaulted."

## CHAPTER 81

Amena raised her glass of water and said, "Is it time for my toast? Is that what I'm supposed to do?"

She was jumping the gun a little bit, but it was only because she was about to split at the seams, overjoyed we were home. I said, "Not yet, honey. Not yet. Let's order our food first."

We were seated around a long table in a private room at Halls Chophouse, having dinner after the wedding ceremony. Halls was the best steakhouse in the city—actually the best steakhouse I'd ever eaten in—and the cost of paying for everyone here would verge on driving me to bankruptcy, but it was the least I could do since everyone had shown up once again for the wedding.

Luckily, the ceremony itself had gone off without a hitch. Jennifer hadn't had to throw any hand grenades and I hadn't made any embarrassing mistakes. We were now officially man and wife, even with her having a black eye that made the minister wonder if I was a wife beater.

She'd said she'd been hit by a door, which was about as lame a thing as possible, but it was better than saying she'd had her ass kicked by Israeli security after stopping a terrorist attack in Jerusalem as part of a top-secret U.S. counterterrorism Special Access Program. She was genuinely happy, which made me happy, and was all the more astounding considering the work it had required to get her and Aaron out of an Israeli jail on terrorism charges.

They'd been roughed up a little bit and had their phones confiscated, making it very hard for Shoshana and me to track them down. Luckily, Shoshana's Mossad contact had finally come through, saying they'd been arrested as terrorists attempting to blow up the Dome of the Rock. Shoshana had lost her mind at hearing that, telling the Mossad in no uncertain terms what would happen if they weren't released.

Aaron and Jennifer had simply taken their lumps, not saying a word, not wanting to compromise any ongoing activities. Their situation had been made worse—and better—when Jennifer was found with both an Israeli and United States passport. Worse because they'd assumed she was some sort of international terrorist, but better because the passport had been issued by the Mossad. When that came to light, the Mossad had interceded, not freeing them, but looking for a way out of the mess.

And that had come from me. I'd called George Wolffe, pulling my get-out-of-jail card. He was stymied about how to free them without making it look like Israel was releasing terrorists or compromising the unit, and I'd come up with the solution.

I'd called the detective Lia Vairo in Rome, and George Wolffe had worked through Amanda Croft, the secretary of state, coordinating an "extradition" to Italy to "face questioning" about an ongoing murder investigation. It let Israel off the hook, and allowed Aaron and Jennifer to go free.

Lia, of course, really did have a multitude of questions, and was pleased to learn that Garrett was dead, but upset she couldn't put him on trial in Italy. And she'd had a few questions about Knuckles as well.

Jennifer took Amena's hand and said, "Good to see you stayed out of trouble while we were gone, doodlebug."

My little refugee had a habit of getting in trouble whenever we were gone. I saw her glance at Veep and Kylie, and knew something had happened. I said, "What did you do?"

"Nothing! I didn't do anything wrong."

Kylie glared at me and said, "She was fine. Everything was fine."

I knew she was hiding something, but now wasn't the time to find out. I simply shook my head, letting it go. I turned to George Wolffe sitting next to me and changed the subject, saying, "What's up with the Knights of Malta? Did they admit to anything?"

"No. Well, they admitted it was a mistake to hire Garrett and didn't try to hide anything he'd done, giving the United States and Israeli intelligence access to all of their computers. But we've agreed to let sleeping dogs lie. The attacks on the Israeli diplomats were never acknowledged as having been by Keta'ib Hezbollah, and our attacks were met with tit-for-tat air strikes. The Vatican itself became involved, weighing in with both the United States and Israel. We agreed to just let it go because doing otherwise could simply inflame more tensions with Iran if the news came out that a Catholic organization was killing people."

"The final Turtle? The one who tried to blow up the Dome of the Rock?"

"He disappeared in the crowd. He escaped, but the Knights gave us his real name. He'll be found soon."

I nodded, not liking the answer as I looked at Jennifer's black eye. I said, "And Iran?"

Wolffe chuckled and said, "That back channel is still working. The CIA now has a dedicated case officer in Beirut talking to him. Iran can read the news and knows they escaped total destruction. They *could* crow about the attacks, pointing a finger at someone else from the West for short-term international political points, but they aren't. They're smart about this, taking the long game and using the back channel. Nobody wants a war."

The waiter came over and he quit talking about Iran, saying, "I didn't even look at the menu. What should I get?"

Jennifer said, "Bone-in filet. Extra rare."

He said, "I don't want extra rare."

She said, "Me neither, but that's what Pike gets every single time."

Amena said, "And me."

Jennifer shook her head and said, "He's training

her to be a savage. I can't get her to eat anything that he doesn't."

Wolffe laughed and gave his order, letting the waiter travel around the table. Knuckles pulled his head up from the menu and said, "Pike, you sure about this? Get whatever I want?"

I said, "Yeah. It's on me. You've earned it."

He said, "I'll take the seafood tower," and my mouth dropped open. That thing was damn near a hundred bucks in and of itself. Greedy bastard.

The waiter went to Brett, who smiled and said, "I'll have the same thing. And I don't even like seafood."

He gave me an evil grin and said, "You *do* owe me."

The waiter left us alone and I said, "Owe you for what? Saving your ass in Syria? If it hadn't been for me, you'd be tied up in a Hezbollah torture chamber."

Knuckles scoffed and said, "I'd already figured our way out. If I hadn't decided to do the right thing for Israel and the United States, that is."

"What happened?"

He got into story-telling mode, which is a talent unique to military people. Meaning, I was about to hear some exaggerations about standing knee-deep in grenade pins while he fought the horde of killers all by himself.

He said, "We found that Tariq guy and he was all about helping us, but said we had to wait until nightfall. Since we were sitting in a house full of dead Hezbollah guys, I told him that wouldn't work, and we needed to jump TOC somewhere else."

He looked at Brett, who said, "I'm the one who said we should just leave and not worry about the other UAVs. I mean, there were two of them, which means there are probably two hundred throughout the country. Getting rid of them is like trying to stop the rain by blocking a few drops."

Knuckles chuckled and said, "And he was right, in the end. I blew those fuckers up with their own charges, and we loaded the vehicle, Tariq losing his mind because he knew something we didn't. The place was crawling with Hezbollah."

Brett took over, as always happened in a military story between two people, saying, "We hit the road and were no more than five miles out of that place when I saw a trail of dust behind us. A damn caravan of guys coming our way. Tariq started screaming and I stood up through the sun roof."

Knuckles talked over him, saying, "Oh, bullshit. You looked at me and said, 'What the hell is that?' *Tariq* said it was Hezbollah and we were dead."

Brett said, "Okay, okay, but I did get out of the sun roof, and when they closed in, we were in fact dead. It was three pickup trucks full of fighters, one technical, and they wanted our scalps."

Knuckles said, "One of the trucks had a Dishka mounted in the back, and that damn thing started shooting. I mean, it was like an old west movie where we were driving the stagecoach and the bandits were trying to catch us.

I only had Brett on shotgun. Tariq was absolutely worthless."

Even I was surprised at the story. I expected to hear how they'd hid out for a day or so, but this was something else. A "Dishka" as he called it was a Soviet anti-aircraft machine gun called a DShK that Hezbollah—and others, like ISIS—mounted in the bed of pickups. Having had one fire on me once before, I could feel the adrenaline coming out of the conversation.

Brett said, "I killed the driver of the first vehicle, but the Dishka kept coming, and luckily he couldn't shoot on the move. Bullets were ripping all over the place, so much I was forced back in the SUV."

Knuckles laughed and said, "He actually told me to stop the vehicle."

Brett took umbrage and said, "We had a better chance of firing and maneuvering on foot than running around in a giant target. If we could have separated them from the machine gun, we stood a chance."

Knuckles held up his hand and said, "Honestly, he might have been right. I was racing down the trail, considering his call, the Dishka starting to ring the steel on our vehicle when two DAPS came out of nowhere, and they were letting it all loose."

I said, "DAPS?" I looked at George and said, "I thought you said it was a CSAR package."

He smiled and said, "It was, but it was from the SOAR. They don't do CSAR without protection."

SOAR was the 160th Special Operations Aviation Regiment, and a DAP was a Direct Action Penetrator—basically a Black Hawk helicopter that had been turned into a flying death machine.

Knuckles said, "The pilots let loose with the chain guns and shredded all of the vehicles, then circled around killing anyone who escaped. It was the best thing I've ever seen."

"So how did you get out? Did you cross back into Lebanon?"

"Hell no. I pulled over and helped with the fight. Another Pave Hawk came in, and we boarded it, flying back to Jordan. I don't know what Hezbollah makes of that mess, but they lost a lot of guys."

Wolffe said, "The sticky part was when they landed. Nobody knew who they were, but knew they were American."

I said, "Man, I can't believe that. Makes our story in the grotto look tame."

Knuckles looked at Shoshana, her arm in a sling, and said, "I didn't get dinged up, though."

She smiled and said, "I did what I had to do. And from hearing the story, I know I was right in insisting on the passports."

Knuckles chuckled and said, "Next time, you can keep them."

Everyone began laughing, the tension from the story broken. I said, "You came back to the wedding alone. What happened to Willow?"

He fiddled with a napkin and said, "She had business commitments. She blocked out the week, but we went beyond that."

"So I guess it'll be a boys' day tomorrow. Jennifer and Shoshana have some shopping planned, but the rest of us can hit the town."

He dropped the napkin and said, "I can't. I'm sorry, Pike, but I have my own commitments."

I said, "What the hell are you talking about? It's the wedding."

"I have a flight out of here at the crack of dawn."

"Where?"

"Uhh . . . back to DC. I have things I need to take care of."

I saw his face, and having served with him for years, he was still horrible at lying. I said, "Bullshit. What would be more important than this?"

I wondered about whatever trouble would cause him to leave us, his family. His ex-wife causing pain? A kid he'd just found out he'd fathered?

Neither was beyond the realm of the possible, but I wasn't going to push him. I said, "Okay, man, let's just enjoy the night."

He smiled, grateful for the reprieve, and Shoshana opened her big mouth.

She said, "He's not leaving for a problem. He's going to create a new one."

Knuckles whipped his head to hers and said, "What are you talking about?"

And it dawned on me what he was doing. "You're not going to DC, are you? There's a reason Willow isn't here, and it's not because she's busy."

He fiddled with his napkin again, glared at Shoshana's ability to read him, and said, "No. There's a lieutenant in Rome who has some questions of me."

I said, "You little man-whore. Lia?"

"Yes. Sorry, Pike, but I promised her a dinner."

# ACKNOWLEDGMENTS

Typically, I thank a plethora of people for the help they've given me on the journey of writing a book, but this last year has been decidedly unique. We, like many other families across the world, had a difficult and unprecedented year. Every trip I planned was canceled because the country in question didn't want infected Americans traveling there or, if I could get there, the United States might not let me come home.

I have an ability to write wherever I am—hotel bars, airplanes, the barracks of a security contract, you name it—and all of that was killed by COVID. I used to brag that I didn't have a writing desk, and now I was stuck in a house without any space at all dedicated to writing. But it wasn't like I had a lot of options. The libraries were closed, the parks shut down, the flights no longer flying, the security contracts all canceled because of COVID. I was on my own to write this book, and it was a little trying. There is only so much pacing around the house gets you for inspiration. Luckily, I had traveled the world during my military career and for various other research trips, and a lot of that travel didn't make it into any specific book. So, my first thank-you is to Apple Photos for saving all of that for me.

The germ of an idea for this book had been brewing for a few years. My wife, the Deputy Commander of Everything, had planned our research trip to Spain, Gibraltar, and Morocco for my book *Ring of Fire*, and also planned a two-day stopover in Rome on our way home. During that time, we took a Segway tour as Great American Tourists because we had walked miles the previous twelve days. Our guide led us to all the major sites in Rome, and during our tour we were almost overrun by a car with diplomatic plates near the Spanish Steps. That's where I first learned about the Sovereign Military Hospitaller Order of St. John of Jerusalem, of Rhodes, and of Malta—colloquially known as the Knights of Malta. Intrigued, I had our guide take us to the Magisterial Palace and got a quick class on the order. It didn't factor into *Ring of Fire*, but I knew then that I would eventually use it in a book. Two years later, while doing research for *Daughter of War* in Zurich, I asked our eighty-five-year-old guide (who was smoking me into the ground with her pace) if she knew anything about the Knights of Malta. She was the wife of a retired ambassador who had traveled all over the world. She held up her hand, showing me a ring with the Maltese cross, and said, "We don't talk about that in mixed company. Sorry."

That piqued my interest even more, but the order would have to wait yet again until I could work it into a plot. But now, stuck in my house, I could finally use it, because Amazon could deliver me four books about its history and modern-day status. All I had to do was figure out that tiny issue of a plot.

I'm not great at spitting out a story out of whole cloth if I'm describing a different culture or country, especially if I haven't visited. I need to feel the terrain, which is why I like doing the research trips to get the sights, sounds, and smells of the "battlefield." Luckily, only about 10 percent of my research actually makes it into a book, and so I went back to my other trips, pulling up memories and pictures that I hadn't used before, now praising my past lack of imagination that had caused those scenes to be neglected.

I wanted to use the grottoes just south of Lebanon in *Operator Down* because it's a very interesting place, but I just couldn't make it work. Luckily, I was able to use it in *End of Days*. By the same token, I traveled all over Switzerland for *Daughter of War*, with only some of that research making the page. Fortunately, I was able to use that detail to kill the *Ramsad* in this book. Full disclosure . . . it was actually the DCOE who had done the research, paragliding in Interlaken with her friend Betsy, the wife of a unit friend of mine. I relied heavily on her for the opening scenes: how the vans worked to take riders up to the hill, what the instructors were like, the process of prepping to fly, and the touchdown location.

For Bahrain, I had to rely on my memory from military deployments. I researched online to see how much it had changed and found that it hadn't changed much at all. "American Alley" was stuck in a time warp, looking the same as it had years ago. After talking with some friends, I learned the politics of Bahrain hadn't changed a bit, to include the Sunni/Shia divide.

Charleston, of course, was easy to research since I live here. I've included Halls Chophouse in one other book, but it really is the finest steakhouse around, and I've been to a few of them. Tommy, Billy, Justin, and the rest of the Halls family deserve Pike Logan to show up at their table every once in a while. In the same vein, Saltwater Cowboys really is the best place to watch the dolphins swim on Shem Creek.

Finally, a special thanks to my daughter, Savannah. Years ago, when she was still a small child, she asked me if Pike and Jennifer were going to get married. I said I had no idea (I was literally on book two at that point). She said, "Well, when they do, I know how to do it," and she began to describe this incredible scene where Jennifer rips off her dress and starts throwing grenades and slaying terrorists. I said, "I'll take that under advisement if they ever get married." She's now in college, but better late than never. Pike's daydream at the beginning of the book is all hers.

Enough about my writing trials. The actual people I need to acknowledge are my team at Morrow. For the first time in my writing life, I was late on a deadline, and David Highfill, my editor, let it go. Trying to work during COVID was a mess, and he and the rest of the Morrow team were gracious to understand that. Thanks also to John Talbot, my agent, who stood by me patiently while I'm sure they were all wringing their hands, wondering if I would ever finish. At the same time, the DCOE was patiently asking, "Isn't your deadline looming?"

It's been a weird couple of years, but I just re-read the book, and I've reached step twelve in what the DCOE has coined "The Twelve Steps of Brad's Writing Process." Meaning I said, "Hey, this thing is pretty good . . ."

# A Q&A WITH BRAD TAYLOR

1. **Tell us about Pike Logan and how you came up with the idea to write the first book featuring him.** Pike Logan is an amalgamation of men I served with, but he wasn't the inspiration for writing my first novel. I simply wanted to write about redemption because I like the "Rocky," come-from-behind story. But the conventional wisdom is "write what you know," so Pike Logan became a counterterrorist commando. I didn't set out to write a military thriller, but given my background, that's what it became.

2. **Did you know you were starting a series?** Not in the least. I didn't even know I would have one book published, much less over a dozen. I wrote my first novel because I wanted to, not because I thought I would get published.

3. **You use a George Orwell quote on your website: "People sleep peacefully in their beds at night only because rough men**

stand ready to visit violence on those who would do them harm." What does this quote mean to you? It actually hung above the bar in a unit I once belonged to. It was there because the people in that unit believed in it. Lived it. A simple sentence, it evoked the ethos of who we were—I should say "are." Pike Logan believes in the quote as well, but he's simply showcasing what I have seen in real life. Pike Logan is a fictional character, but he is real. He exists in greater numbers than the public is aware. Not as many as we need, but probably more than people believe.

4. You have a master of science in defense analysis from the Naval Postgraduate School, with a concentration in irregular warfare. Can you help us civilians understand what irregular warfare is and how that relates to defense analysis? It's not really that mysterious. Defense analysis is just the study of war. At NPS that was centered around the study of sea power. I was part of a fellowship sponsored by the assistant secretary of defense for special operations and low intensity conflict, and we studied warfare by asymmetric means, such as terrorism and insurgency, which is captured under the umbrella term of irregular warfare. A symmetrical threat is where both sides are doing the same thing—Top Gun dogfights, tank-on-tank battles, etc. An example of irregular warfare would be a suicide bomber

blowing up the pilots on the ground or IEDs attacking the supply convoys for the tanks.

5. **I'm sure you get asked how your military experience informs your writing, and we'll get to that, but I understand you travel quite a bit. How do your travels influence what you write?** It's impossible to know what a culture or country is like without visiting it. In the military we have a saying about learning the sights, sounds, and smells of the battlefield prior to going on patrol, and this is sort of the same thing. You can look at Google Maps all day long but getting immersed in the terrain and population is the only way you'll understand it. Because of that, if I can visit the places where a book is set, I will. Of course, I'm not crazy— I didn't fly to Syria or North Korea—but if I can travel there, I do so. I've been fortunate enough to have traveled to more than twenty-five countries in the last nine years for research, and I think it shows on the page.

6. **You and Pike Logan have some things in common. What are three traits that you and Pike share—and why did you choose them? And what is the main difference between you and Pike?** Tough questions. I honestly didn't choose any traits of mine to be included in Pike. If any did cross over, it was organic and not a deliberate decision. I'd say Pike's sense of humor is a direct reflection

of me, because I'm a little bit of a smart ass. Other than that, it would probably be that we are both type A personalities with a healthy ability to think on our feet. The main difference is Pike's innate, natural talent at combat. It's very, very hard to get to the level I achieved in SOF (special operations forces), but even then, there's a cut line. For civilians I liken it to the PGA tour. There is probably less than 1 percent on earth who have the skill to play on the tour, and yet nobody's ever heard of the name that's the hundredth on the money list—but everyone's heard of Tiger Woods. Both Pike and I played on the tour, but I'm one hundredth on the money list. Pike Logan is Tiger Woods.

7. **You often address current events within the defense world on your blog, shining a light on issues in the news and their repercussions. What do you most want to tell readers about the "real world" and how do you decide what topics to explore?** What I would most want to convey is that there are no "bumper sticker" solutions to national security problems. The world is a messy place, with a myriad of competing interests, and yet too often I hear talking head after talking head on TV espousing some simplistic solution to a complex problem— and that is exactly how I choose topics to explore. Generally, I'll get aggravated hearing "expert" after "expert" spout something— usually with a political agenda—and when it

reaches a certain point, I want to write about the stakes and complexity in play.

8. **Tell us about Pike's partner, Jennifer Cahill. Was it hard to get into the mindset of a woman when you started writing? Did you always think of the books featuring both characters? Or did you create Cahill to give the books something they might not have without her?** When I began to write my first book, I was looking to create a story of redemption, and Jennifer was a part of that from the very beginning. Everyone calls the books "Pike Logan thrillers," but it's always been Pike *and* Jennifer to me. I remember getting a review for my third book, *Enemy of Mine*, and the reviewer said that I had created Jennifer to gather female readers, which made me laugh. One, I never thought I'd have a single book published—much less three at that time—and two, the thought that I could be smart enough to even consider a readership split into segments with characters specifically created to draw in that segment was ludicrous. As for getting into her mindset, yes, that was very hard initially. Luckily, I have some strong real-life females as early readers who keep me on track. Although it is painful . . .

9. **The Pike Logan novels have been praised for their authenticity and realism. Do you ever find yourself researching weapons or tactics that have changed since you've**

**retired?** All the time. The world continues to turn, with new weapons, tactics, techniques, and procedures. Some things about combat never change, of course, but others march relentlessly forward, and I spend an inordinate amount of time staying on top of those developments—from tactical problem sets, like the latest developments in cyber vulnerabilities or the Army's newest rifle, to the strategic debates about hybrid warfare. It's a constant fight to stay on top of the evolution.

10. **Since you've retired, what's the most shocking or surprising development that you've seen in our military's defense complex?** Honestly, I've been surprised at some national security *decisions* made, but nothing in our military defense complex has shocked me. It's all an evolution, really, and, as I said above, I try to stay on top of that evolution. Something that was just a pie-in-the-sky thought eight years ago is now a functional defense capability, but no development simply springs on the scene out of nowhere.